JAN BURKE

FLIGHT

a novel of suspense

simon & schuster

new york london toronto sydney singapore

SIMON & SCHUSTER
Rockefeller Center
1230 Avenue of the Americas
New York, NY 10020

SIMON & SCHUSTER and colophon are registered trademarks of Simon & Schuster, Inc.
Designed by Karolina Harris
Manufactured in the United States of America

10   9   8   7   6   5   4   3   2   1

Library of Congress Cataloging-in-Publication Data
Burke, Jan

  Flight : a novel of suspense / Jan Burke.
    p. cm.
   1. Kelly, Irene (Fictitious character)—Fiction. 2. Police—California—Fiction. 3. Women journalists—Fiction. 4. Married people—Fiction. 5. California—Fiction. I. Title

PS3552.U72326   F58 2001
813'.54—dc21   00-052629

ISBN 0-684-85552-6

This one is for Peter O'Donnell,
who inspired me to spread my wings,
with admiration and thanks for a better view

ONE

Ten Years Ago

1

Blissfully unaware that the moment everything would change was near, they were bickering.

"You should have to do the kitchen, Seth," Mandy said, drying a tumbler. "I shouldn't have to do it just because I'm a female."

"Female," Seth scoffed, securing the latch on a compartment beneath a berth. "Not like anyone could tell you are. You're still an 'it.'"

"An it!" Mandy snapped the towel at the seat of his pants. She hit her mark, then squealed in dismay as he turned and easily grabbed her weapon away from her.

He grinned as he saw the belated realization dawn on her face—it had been a mistake to attack him within the confines of the yacht. She cowered, waiting for his retribution. He laughed and tossed the towel in her face. "Half the other girls in ninth grade have bigger boobs than you do, Pancake."

She shoved at him, and as he fell back in mock surrender, he knocked over a set of cookware she had not yet put away. In the silence after the crash and clatter, they each covered their mouths and repressed laughter.

"Quit the horseplay down there!" their father's voice called.

Seth glanced at the companionway, but their dad was too busy with his own work above to continue scolding. Seth looked at his watch. They probably wouldn't be at their dad's house until almost one o'clock in the morning—they had a lot to do before they could even take their dad's new boat back to number 414, its own slip.

Seth knew that some boat owners would have taken their yachts into the slip at any hour and cleaned up there, but his father never showed such disregard for others. Whenever he got into the marina after nine or ten o'clock at night, Trent Randolph, in consideration of the live-aboards whose boats occupied the slips nearest his own, always docked here first, next to a bait shop at an isolated point on the far end of the marina. "You wouldn't turn on bright lights and wash and vacuum a car at midnight on your driveway at home," he would tell friends who asked about this habit. "People live even closer together here."

They hadn't taken friends with them this time. This weekend's sailing trip to Catalina Island had been fun—especially, Seth thought, because it had just been the three of them. Trent Randolph had finally dumped Tessa, his lowlife girlfriend, not long ago. Seth hated her. She was the one who had split his folks up two years earlier, but that wasn't the only reason he didn't like her. She bitched about Seth and Amanda constantly, and Seth was almost positive she was playing his dad. He had no proof, but once or twice when his dad wasn't around, Seth had overheard her talking on her cell phone in kind of a lovey-dovey voice, all sexy and everything. And he knew she hadn't been talking to his dad. So maybe his dad had caught her at it, too—or just finally wised up.

He knew his dad wouldn't get back together with his mom. He knew they weren't happy together. And he wished he could stop wishing they would get back together anyway.

Better to think of good times. Like this weekend. Seth, Mandy, and their dad even spent a night camping on the island, something they had not done since the divorce. "It was like he could be a dad again," Mandy confided to Seth when they left Avalon. He had rolled his eyes, not willing to agree openly with her. One reason he liked the new boat was that he figured his dad had used it to get rid of Tessa—Seth recalled that she had been just about as pissed as his sister had been pleased with the yacht's name—*Amanda*.

"I still say you should help with the kitchen," Mandy whispered now as they picked up the fallen pots and pans.

"It's a *galley*, not a kitchen," Seth corrected. "You always say it wrong."

"Whatever. You should have to do it."

"Quit whining or I'll make you clean the head."

"The bathroom?"

He nodded.

"Why call it 'the head' and not, you know, something like 'the ass'?"

"Don't be a trash-mouth, Mandy," he said, turning away so she wouldn't see him laugh.

"It's not trashy. Even donkeys are called asses."

He wouldn't take the bait, and so they worked quietly for a few minutes. They heard their father's footsteps as he moved overhead, heard the thumps and thuds and other sounds of gear and life vests being stowed, rigging secured, decks hosed and scrubbed. Seth carried two duffel bags filled with camping gear toward the hatch, setting them near the companionway to be carried up later.

He was athletic; broad-shouldered and tall for sixteen. Dark-haired and green-eyed and a little shy. Mandy could make him blush furiously by using one of her nicknames for him: Mr. Babe-Magnet. "Every girl who becomes my friend develops a major crush on you," she once complained to him, "unless she already had one on you and became my friend just so she could get next to you."

"No, they like you for yourself."

She shook her head and said, "Right. Try to catch the next flight back to planet Earth."

He still thought she was wrong. At fourteen, she was slender but gawky, more bookish than he. The only reason he had started lifting weights was because he worried that without his father in the house, the duty of fighting off her unworthy would-be boyfriends would fall to him. He expected them to arrive by the busload once his redheaded little sister filled out a little. The only after-school fight he had ever been in—the one their mother chalked up to "Seth adjusting to the divorce"—had actually started when the other kid made a "see what develops" crack about Mandy. Seth had pummeled him.

"Where does this go?" Mandy asked, startling him out of his reverie. She was biting on her lower lip as she held up an oven mitt. Fretting over exactly where everything belonged. He didn't blame her. No use shoving things any-old-where they would fit. Their dad was a neat freak. Seth showed her the compartment where such things were stored and went back to work cleaning the head.

"Mom's probably called Dad's house," she said as Seth started polishing the mirror. When he didn't respond, she added, "She's going to be mad."

"Mom's always mad," he said, not pausing in his work. "He'll take us to school on time tomorrow, don't worry. She doesn't need to know we're up this late on a school night—right?"

"Right," Mandy agreed. "But if she calls—"

"Even if she finds out, she'll still have to let Dad take us every other weekend."

Mandy gave a little sigh of relief, a sound not lost on her brother.

A noisy boat pulled up nearby. They could hear the loud thrumming of its engines. A little later, above them, mixed in with the engine noise, they heard voices. Male voices. Their father and another man.

"Who could that be?" Mandy asked, moving toward the companionway.

Seth shrugged. "The guy from the other boat, probably."

The voices grew louder. They heard snatches of conversation, their father's voice as he strode angrily past the hatch: ". . . trouble . . . get up . . . not what police should . . . you think I'm going to . . . then . . ."

"I'm going to see who it is!" Mandy whispered.

"Some politico," he said, using a term they applied to most of their father's newest associates. "Can't you tell? Dad's making a speech to him."

"At midnight?"

"They bug him at all hours. Stay put."

They both listened, but the men seemed to have stopped talking.

"I'm going to go see," she said. She was up the companionway before he could stop her. The men were still quiet, so he thought Mandy was too late anyway—the other man had probably left. He squirted some toilet bowl cleaner into the bowl and began to scrub—let Mandy get in trouble for not working.

He heard a loud thud and wondered if his dumb sister had tripped. He listened and could hear quick footsteps—too heavy to be Amanda's. His dad running? He thought he heard her yelp. He stepped out of the head, listened. Hell, maybe she did fall.

He started toward the companionway just as she came stumbling down the ladder. Her face was white, and she was clutching her throat. A bright red wash of blood covered her hands, her arms, the entire front of her body.

"Mandy!"

Her eyes were wide and terrified, pleading with him. Her mouth formed some unspoken word just before she collapsed in a heap at the foot of the ladder. As she fell, her hand came away from her throat, and he was sprayed with her warm blood.

"Mandy!" he screamed.

There was a cut on her neck—blood continued to spray from it in smaller and smaller spurts.

"Dad!" he yelled. "Dad! Help!"

He heard hurried steps and looked up, expecting to see his father.

A pirate stood at the top of the ladder.

The man who looked down at him was wearing a black eye patch over his left eye and carried a glinting piece of steel—though it was a small knife, not a cutlass—and the man's dark clothes were modern.

Seth turned and ran in blind panic toward the bow. But there was no escape except through the hatch, and no shelter—except the small head. He dodged into it, turning to close the door on his attacker just as the knife came slashing. He raised his hands in defense, and the knife cut across his fingers. Screaming in pain, he whirled and threw his back against the door, catching the attacker's arm. The attacker shoved hard, moving one step in. Seth ground his heel into the man's foot. The man gave a grunt of pain and pulled the foot back even as he slashed with the knife, cutting across the front of Seth's neck. Only as he reached up with bloodied hands to cover the wound did Seth catch his own reflection in the mirror. Realizing that this was how the man had aimed the blow, Seth jammed his shoulder against the man's arm, pinning it to the wall, then hit the light switch. He felt dizzy, but forced himself to stay on his feet. With a fumbling grasp, he used his less injured left hand to pick up the open plastic bottle of toilet bowl cleaner on the sink counter. He put it up to where the man's good eye was peering in—and squeezed the plastic bottle between the wall and his palm.

He didn't think any of the chemical had hit the man—who must have seen it coming, because he jerked back, cutting Seth's shoulder as he pulled the knife arm from beneath him. Free of this obstruction, the door slammed shut and Seth's weight held it closed. Seth dropped the cleaner even as he struggled with the lock, his fingers slippery and barely functioning. He managed to grab a towel, to hold it against his neck, but soon he could not stand. The pain was intense, and he felt himself weakening, his own blood warm and sticky and dampening his shirt. He wedged himself between the hull and the door, even as the attacker began slamming against it.

The door shook beneath the blows. It would give, Seth thought. He tried to yell, but found he couldn't make a sound.

The pounding stopped. The small room swam before him. Seth bent forward, trying to fight the feeling of faintness. No sooner had he moved than the wood where he had rested his head splintered inward with a bang—split by a small ax. The attacker must have taken it from their camping gear. The man yanked the ax from the wood. Seth tried to drag himself away from the door before the second blow came, but found he could not. He brought his hands back to the towel at his throat, wondering if the ax's third blow would slice into his back.

Suddenly, he heard music—not music, really, but a short series of tones, a repetitive, insistent, three-note call—the sound of a pager or of an alarm on an electronic watch.

Do-re-mi-do-re-mi-do-re—

Seth heard the sound cut off. He waited, every muscle tense, for the ax to strike again—but the third blow never came.

Over the next few minutes, Seth drifted in and out of awareness, but a low rumbling made him open his eyes. The other boat was leaving.

He began to feel cold and sleepy. He must get up and help Mandy now, he thought, but in his pain and light-headed confusion, he could not locate the door latch. Still holding the towel against his neck, he groped along the wall with one hand and managed to turn on the light. He found the latch just as he lost consciousness.

2

Wearing rubber gloves, the Looking Glass Man checked all the blinds. On a less eventful evening, this last night of using this apartment would have filled him with a sense of regret. It was so perfectly suited to his needs—at the back of the building, over the carport, where no one would notice his footsteps across the floor late in the evening. The woman in the only adjoining apartment worked the graveyard shift. Still, he moved quietly.

The old television set was off; he had never watched it. The stove was clean but cold; he had never cooked on it. The meager, outdated furnishings in the apartment bore the marks of previous owners and tenants. The next tenant would not see any sign of his use of it. There was nothing he was so careful of as where he left signs of his presence.

He evenly sprayed disinfectant over the surface of the gray Formica tabletop, then wiped it with a white paper towel, moving his gloved hand in controlled, overlapping circles. He placed the towel in a white plastic bag.

When he was certain the surface of the table was dry, he took out a notebook with a stiff, cardboard cover. It was the sort of notebook one could find in any college bookstore, a black-and-white-marbled cover binding graph paper, used by science students to record experiments.

Inside, on the first page, he had written a quotation:

"God is in the details."

The quotation was from a famous architect—Ludwig Mies van der Rohe, who had designed the Seagram Building in New York. The Looking

Glass Man considered himself to be a kind of architect, too. When he had started the first of these notebooks, at the age of sixteen, the entries had been so benign—nothing more than recorded observations of little social experiments, his attempts to monitor the reactions of others to certain stimuli. But even then, perhaps intuitively, he had placed the quotation on the first page of the notebook. He now had many of these notebooks and had written this same quotation at the front of all of them. His faith in the importance of details was unshakable.

He turned to a blank page, and using a mechanical pencil, began to record data in block letters. Each letter took up one square of the graph paper's grid, the tip of the pencil lead never crossing a blue line. He wrote a heading, ANTI-INTERFERENCE, then noted the date and time for a series of events, from the time he boarded the fishing vessel *Cygnet* until the time he left it. It was difficult not to rush ahead to the most exciting minutes, those few spent on the yacht, the *Amanda*. He forced himself to work in a precise manner, recounting every one of the God-laden details in chronological order.

He left a row of empty squares beneath the last of these, then wrote:

TIME ELAPSED IN CRITICAL MODE: 18 M 51 S
FATALITIES: 3
RATING: 4
AREAS FOR IMPROVEMENT: TOO SLOW W/ THIRD VIC; NEARLY SUSTAINED
INJURY FROM CORROSIVE, WHICH WOULD HAVE REQUIRED MEDICAL
TREATMENT. SUCH TREATMENT MIGHT HAVE BEEN REMARKED ON BY
PHYSICIANS AND LATER CONNECTED TO CRIME SCENE. TOO EMOTIONAL.
SLOPPY!

He paused, then lifted the pencil, turning it upside down so that he could see the tip, and gently turned the pencil barrel so that the lead was at the proper length. He then continued to write.

COMMENTS: DID NOT LIKE WORKING WITH CHILDREN. NEVER WILL FOR-
GIVE RANDOLPH FOR FORCING THIS SOLUTION. HOWEVER, MUST NOT
THINK OF THIS. MUST CONSIDER THE NUMBER OF CHILDREN SAVED BY
THE DEATHS OF THESE TWO ADOLESCENTS. SHOULD BE ABLE TO CON-
TINUE NOW. SMALL SACRIFICE, ALL CONSIDERED.

He reread what he had written, checking for errors. He found none. Accurate records were so important. If one were to truly evaluate the effectiveness of his activities, one could not rely on memory. He knew the discovery of any of the more recent notebooks by others would greatly increase his chances of being prosecuted for certain of the activities recounted in them. It was a risk he had to take, though, in order to proceed in an orderly manner.

His hands began to perspire beneath the gloves. He disliked the sensation it caused.

He retracted the pencil lead, closed the notebook, and put it and the pencil into a briefcase. He went into the bathroom, fought off a sudden nausea, then quickly went back to work. He emptied the remaining disinfectant into the toilet and flushed it twice. He put the empty bottle into the white plastic bag.

He caught his own reflection in the mirror over the sink and paused for a moment, studying himself. He stared hard into his own eyes, looking for observable changes. It was a habit of his, staring at himself in the mirror. His sister used to chide him, calling him the Looking Glass Man. But while he admitted a fascination with faces, especially his own, it was with detached interest and not any real admiration that he studied his reflection.

Who was that, looking back at him from that silver surface?

The Looking Glass Man.

He switched off the bathroom light.

He gathered the bag and the briefcase, stepped out onto the landing, and locked the apartment door. Over the next few days, the apartment would be painted, the carpets cleaned. The new tenants would move in by the tenth.

He should not allow such trifles to disturb him, he decided. He had greater problems to consider. Crime and punishment. He thought of the photograph in his wallet, but he did not take it out. Thinking of the photograph always made him think of the judge—Judge Lewis Kerr. Kerr must be watched.

He allowed himself a small, soft sigh, then walked downstairs to the large metal trash bin. At last able to remove the annoying gloves, he added them and the roll of paper towels to the white bag, which he placed in the bin. The bin was quite full.

Trash day, he thought. Just another trash day.

3

"Maybe your snitch was wrong," Elena Rosario said.

Philip Lefebvre did not reply. He continued to watch a yacht moored to a dock near a bait shop.

"Lefebvre?"

He turned, then followed her gaze toward her partner, Bob Hitchcock, who was walking toward them. The narcotics detective's hands were in his pockets as he approached them, his head down. Hitch was a big man who was beginning to go soft around the belly and beneath his chin—and Lefebvre thought he was going soft on the job as well, coasting whenever he could. Any extra effort would have put Hitch in a shitty mood, and the fact that this surveillance call hadn't panned out had ticked him off.

Rosario, Hitch's partner, was easier to work with but harder to read, more reserved. And unlike Hitch, she wasn't a burnout case. When Hitch had argued against coming down here, she had said, "You want to tell the captain why we didn't follow up on a lead concerning Whitey Dane?"

Hitch had caved—they all knew this was exactly why he was being forced to work with Lefebvre in the first place. As much as Hitch resented having someone from Homicide assigned to the task force on Dane, there was nothing he could do about it.

Whitey Dane, long suspected of being behind a number of local criminal activities, including drug dealing, had proven slippery—although the police department had occasionally crippled his operations in the city, their efforts to bring charges against him were futile.

Every attempt to make progress in investigating his activities had met with a reversal. Informants were murdered or disappeared, undercover officers were unable to get anywhere near Dane himself. Rosario had told Lefebvre that most of her two years as a narcotics detective had been spent on a team that had tried to gather enough evidence against Dane to put him out of business. Instead, over that time, he had branched out from drug dealing and vice into other types of crime—and increased his influence on local politics and businesses.

Following a recent outbreak of violence in an area controlled by Dane, the task force was expanded—Lefebvre, a veteran homicide detective, had been assigned to work with it.

"So they've given us the golden boy," Hitch had said. "You sure you can stop giving interviews long enough to work with us?"

"He's already more aware of Dane's little oddball habits than you are," Rosario had said. "And you're just jealous because you think he's getting into that reporter's pants."

"Irene Kelly is a good-looking broad. So tell me, Lefebvre, what's she like in bed?"

Lefebvre had regarded him coldly but said nothing, and after a moment of uncomfortable silence, Rosario had said, "You were asking who makes the silk vests Dane likes to wear . . ." and had gone on to discuss Dane's affected way of dressing.

As she watched Hitch coming toward them now, she sighed. "Tonight had seemed so promising."

Lefebvre thought of the call that had brought them here. Just before midnight he had received a tip from an informant, an electronically disguised voice saying that Whitey Dane would be paying for a hit tonight aboard his fishing boat, the *Cygnet*. Whitey and the shooter were due back to the marina at any moment. The informant seemed to know what he was talking about—he knew Whitey's slip number, 305.

Lefebvre had paged Rosario and Hitch, who already knew exactly where Whitey kept his boat, and the three of them hurried to that section of the marina. Sure enough, the slip was empty. And so, for the past two hours, they had awaited the *Cygnet*'s return.

The slip had stayed empty.

"We're at the wrong marina," Hitch said now, addressing Rosario and avoiding eye contact with Lefebvre. "The whole time, the damned boat's been in the other marina."

"The Downtown Marina?" Lefebvre asked.

"Yep."

"But this is where he usually keeps the boat?"

"Yes. We've been watching this guy for three years, and I've never seen him do so much as gas the thing up at the Downtown Marina."

"Was Dane—?"

"Didn't see him at all. And Mr. Eye-Patch isn't exactly difficult to spot in a crowd."

"Anyone still watching the boat?"

"Yes, but until we get a warrant . . ." Hitchcock shrugged.

"You know we'd be turned down again," Lefebvre said. "Not enough to go on yet."

"You sure your snitch said here?"

"Yes." Lefebvre looked back toward the yacht, as if this conversation no longer interested him. Hitch bristled over the dismissal.

"Call came in anonymously?" he asked.

"He already told us it did," Rosario said, impatient with Hitch's mood. Hitch gave her a dark look, but she ignored it.

Lefebvre's attention remained with the yacht. "Is that yacht moored legally?"

"What, you want to leave Homicide and join the Harbor Patrol?" Hitch asked.

Lefebvre turned to Rosario. "Is that yacht—"

"How the hell should we know?" Hitch interrupted.

"No," she said. She turned to Hitch. "I like to sail," she said, "but in case you're wondering, no, I don't want to join the Harbor Patrol, either."

Lefebvre quickly hid a smile, but Hitch noticed his amusement. "You might end up working there anyway," he snapped at his partner.

Lefebvre started walking down the dock, toward the yacht. Leaving Hitch behind, Rosario hurried to catch up with him. "Why are you so interested in it?" she asked.

"Rats with wings," Lefebvre said.

"What?"

"Seagulls," he said, walking a little faster. "They usually stay put for the evening, right?"

She then saw what he saw, that birds were gathering around the yacht. "Maybe the bait shop—"

"That's what I noticed. The birds are ignoring the bait shop and going for something on the boat deck. And whoever's belowdecks hasn't come out to see what they're interested in."

"*Amanda*," she said, reading the neat lettering on the stern. "Somebody has bucks. She's a beauty."

She said that before they came close enough to see what was aboard.

• • •

First Lefebvre saw the blood and then the man lying not far from the hatch. "Call for backup," he said. "Wait here on the dock." He stepped aboard amid noisy birds and flies, shooing them off as he moved cautiously toward the body.

Hitch had the only radio. He was still sauntering along.

Rosario shouted to him to make the call.

Lefebvre quickly checked the victim—the body was cold. As he headed for the companionway, he saw Rosario stepping aboard. He sighed with exasperation. "Put your hands in your pockets and don't step on any of the obvious pathways—or in the blood."

"I know enough not to mess up a crime scene," she said testily, but obediently put her hands in the pockets of her slacks. She stared at the dark, open gash on the victim's throat and turned pale.

Lefebvre watched her, then said, "If you're going to be sick—"

"I won't be."

He said nothing else to her; he had already turned to look down the companionway. He swore when he saw the girl's body, then drew his gun and moved awkwardly down the steps, doing his best not to disturb the bloodstain patterns. Rosario took her own weapon out and came closer.

"Oh, no," he heard her say. "Oh, no. Oh, no."

More faintly, from the docks, Hitch's voice. "Christ almighty!"

Rosario shouted, "Get on that radio, you fucking asshole! We've got at least two dead—one's a kid."

Lefebvre kept moving toward the battered door to the head. He pushed on it—it opened only a few inches; something heavy was on the other side. Through a narrow, splintered slit that had been hacked into the door, he saw more blood—and then the boy. Lefebvre quickly holstered his weapon, got down near the floor, then reached inside. He pushed in a little farther and touched skin—cool, but not the cold of the bodies behind him.

For one brief instant, the memory of the cooling skin of another young man flickered across his thoughts, but he closed his mind to it.

Not this time, he swore to himself. Not this time!

And in that moment felt a faint pulse.

He turned to Rosario and shouted, "Still alive! Get an ambulance here!"

Even as she began relaying this to Hitch, Lefebvre saw the ax. He grabbed it, and heedless of Rosario's shout about prints, swung it hard but with precision, striking the wood near the upper hinges. With the fourth swing, the door began to give—he dropped the ax and turned, catching the door's weight, slowing its outward fall. He gently lowered it, and with it, the boy.

Lefebvre gathered the unconscious young man in his arms, keeping pressure on the bloodstained towel at the boy's throat, holding him close to warm him, speaking to him in a low voice, a desperate litany of "Stay with me, keep fighting, come on!"

Rosario found a sleeping bag among some camping gear near the companionway and brought it over. She covered the boy with it, helping Lefebvre bundle him within it, but when she touched the boy's skin, Lefebvre heard her sharp intake of breath.

"Lefebvre," she said gently, placing a hand on his shoulder.

He shrugged it off. "Stay with me!" he repeated to the boy, bending closer to him, as if shielding him from her lack of faith.

"Lefebvre," she tried again, but when he would not relent, moved closer, holding on to a boy he knew she believed to be dead, silently adding her own warmth to his.

4

The boy was awake, and watching him.

Two days earlier, the first time Seth had awakened, it was as if from a nightmare. He had looked wildly about the room, his face contorted in terror and pain; he batted his swathed hands in the air as if warding off blows. One of the doctors and his mother had tried to calm him, but their efforts seemed to further upset him.

Lefebvre had said one word: "Easy." Seth turned toward the sound of his voice, ceased struggling, and quickly went back to sleep.

The doctor, after subjecting Lefebvre to a long and considering look, gave orders that the detective should be allowed to stay by the boy as long as he liked, any time he liked—provided Mrs. Randolph had no objections? Lefebvre thought she hid the smallest trace of resentment before answering, "No, of course not. Detective Lefebvre saved my son's life."

Now Lefebvre sat at the side of Seth Randolph's hospital bed, hoping for another miracle—that the boy would be able to identify his attacker. Seth had lived. That, he told himself, was miracle enough. The boy's vocal cords had been damaged, but a slightly deeper cut would have severed a major artery and killed him. A laceration on one shoulder had required stitches. His hands were covered in bandages, but the doctors thought he would eventually recover most of the use of his fingers. He had lost a lot of blood; this would undoubtedly cause him to suffer weakness and fatigue. Those, of course, were only the physical injuries.

He was the son, Lefebvre had learned, of Trent Randolph—the first of the victims they had found on the *Amanda*—a wealthy local industrialist, divorced, and recently named a member of the police commission. The case had been making headlines all week, resulting in more interference than progress toward its resolution. Other than bloody footprints, and a report that someone had heard a powerboat with big engines near the area, the police had little to go on.

Lefebvre surprised his boss and most of his coworkers by taking a less active investigative role than expected, insisting on staying at Seth's side. Elena Rosario came by every day. She thought she understood why he kept watch over the boy. Lefebvre knew she didn't, but never corrected her notion that he had formed some sort of bond with Seth during the rescue. It was, after all, not entirely untrue. It simply wasn't the whole truth. Yesterday she had come by a little later than he expected, and he found himself checking his watch and looking at the door every few moments until her arrival.

Seth's mother, Tory Randolph, also came by every day. Today she had stayed until about half an hour ago. While Lefebvre knew she would have wanted to be here for this occasion—the first time since his surgery that Seth had awakened for more than a brief moment—he was not sorry she had left. Once she learned that she couldn't hint Lefebvre out of the room, they fell into a pattern of strained civility and long silences.

She was, he thought dispassionately, a beautiful woman. Her hair was auburn, and its thick, loose curls perfectly framed her pale, heart-shaped face. Her brows were dark, thin lines above long-lashed blue eyes. She wore stylish clothes that flattered her shapely figure. Yet her manner gave him an almost instant dislike of her—her lack of quiet irked him, and all his instincts told him that her need for attention was insatiable.

He thought he should probably feel more sympathy for her, but he was not convinced that she was good for Seth. Although Seth did not seem to be aware of his surroundings during the last few days, he was restless when she was near, as if responding to her anxiousness.

Lefebvre thought there was a fine line between her concern for the boy and her own fear of suffering another loss. He did not blame her for clinging to Seth—the funerals of her ex-husband, Trent Randolph, and daughter, Amanda, had been held just today—he simply believed that her strained emotions were having an adverse effect on her son.

Lefebvre alone had the opposite effect on Seth. Perhaps, Lefebvre thought, Seth remembered his voice from those seemingly endless moments on the boat while he held him, or in the ambulance, or after the surgery. Lefebvre was not a talker, but he talked to Seth. He did not tell him stories or talk of himself, but in the hours when they were alone in the room, Lefebvre spoke to him, his voice soft and low, urging Seth to live.

Until now, the moments of waking had always been the same—brief and panic-filled until Lefebvre spoke to him. Once, when Lefebvre had been away from the boy's bedside for a few hours, he had come back to find Seth's arms restrained. He released them and called Rosario. He gave her what he had never given anyone else—the key to his condo—and asked what he seldom asked of anyone else—a favor. Would she please pack a few things for him in an overnight case? She had responded immediately, and without asking questions.

And he had not left Seth's room since. A friend from the newspaper had brought him a couple of "outside meals," but Irene Kelly knew him well enough not to pester him for the story. The guard at the door had apparently reported these visits, though, because after the first one, his boss, Lieutenant Willis, complained about the time Lefebvre was spending at the hospital.

"You've been trying to get me to take time off, right?" Lefebvre asked.

"Yes, why don't you take that little plane of yours and get out of town for a while—maybe fly somewhere like Vegas—you know, someplace where you can relax for a few days?"

Lefebvre could think of nothing he would find less relaxing than a trip to Las Vegas. "So you're saying I can have the time off?"

"Of course."

"Fine, I'm on vacation then."

So far—to Willis's irritation—he had spent the first few days of it in Seth's room.

And now Seth was awake—calm, and truly awake. Lefebvre considered calling a doctor or a nurse to the boy's bedside, but he found he could not walk away from that steady regard.

"Hello, Seth. Don't try to talk, okay? Your vocal cords have been damaged, so it will hurt if you try to speak."

Seth reached toward his throat, then held out his hands, staring at the bandages.

"Do you remember how you got hurt?"

Unable to move his head much, he shook it slightly, a puzzled expression on his face.

"Don't be worried about that. It's not unusual for an injured person to—"

But suddenly Seth's eyes widened, and he tried to speak. He winced, but still Lefebvre thought he knew the one word the boy had tried to say.

Lefebvre's hands tightened on the bed rails. "You want to know about Amanda?"

Seth mouthed the word "yes."

"I'm sorry, Seth. Amanda and your father—"

But even before Lefebvre spoke, Seth had read his look. Tears began rolling down the boy's face.

"I—maybe I should get the nurse." Lefebvre started to move away, but felt a bandaged hand on top of his own and hesitated.

Seth gestured toward him, brows raised in question.

"Who am I?"

He tried to nod and winced—the damage to his throat had made the motion painful.

"Philip Lefebvre. I'm a detective with the Las Piernas Police Department."

Seth wiped at his tears. Lefebvre reached for a tissue, to help the boy dry his face, but Seth tapped at Lefebvre's hand in some urgency.

Seth covered his left eye, mouthing something.

Lefebvre moved to a nearby cupboard and took out a board a speech therapist had left. It had large letters, numbers, and a few short phrases on it—an aid for communicating with patients who could not speak after surgery.

"You tap my other hand when I'm pointing at the correct letter," Lefebvre said.

He began slowly tracing his hand over the alphabet, almost Ouija-board style. When he reached the "P," Seth tapped.

"First letter, *p*."

Seth touched the word "yes" on the board, then put his hand back on Lefebvre's, eager to proceed.

Slowly but surely, working together, they spelled out a word. P-I-R-A-T-E.

Lefebvre stared at him a moment. "You were attacked by a pirate?"

Awkwardly, Seth moved a bandaged hand to "yes" on the board. Seeing Lefebvre's incredulous look, he covered his left eye again.

"My God," Lefebvre said, suddenly realizing what Seth was saying. "You were attacked by a man wearing an eye patch?"

Seth's relief at Lefebvre's understanding was visible.

"A patch over his left eye?"

Yes.

"You're certain?"

Another yes.

Working patiently, Lefebvre focused on getting a description of the man, and gradually one developed. A white male, medium build, dark hair and clothing. Seth was unsure of his attacker's age, but thought he was around Lefebvre's age—maybe a little younger or older. Seth indicated that he had seen the man for only a few moments, but believed his father may have known him.

From the moment the eye patch was mentioned, Lefebvre suspected that Dane was the killer. None of the other elements of the description changed that suspicion. He knew that more evidence would be needed to bring Dane to trial, but for once, the police might have enough to get a search warrant.

He needed to establish a time frame. He knew that when he had arrived at the yacht, neither Trent Randolph nor Amanda had been dead for long. The coroner's report had confirmed that impression. He also believed that the killer had struck quickly and had not lingered aboard the *Amanda*. There were several indications of this—the attacker had not herded his victims belowdecks; bloodstain patterns showed that while Amanda died belowdecks, she and her father had been attacked above. There were no signs that anyone had been restrained, and except for damage to the door of the head, no signs of prolonged struggle or resistance. The killer had been in and out, not staying around to rob the victims or to steal any of the yacht's equipment.

Again working with the board, he asked about the time of the attack. Seth thought it had been between eleven forty-five and midnight. Lefebvre remembered that a witness had heard a big-engined powerboat in that section of the marina at about that time. Carefully structuring his questions, he learned from Seth that the man who had attacked the Randolph family came aboard from another boat. A powerboat.

"Did you see the name of the boat?"

No. He looked away.

"Don't worry, Seth. What you've told me tonight is very helpful. I think we can catch the man who did this."

Seth looked at him uncertainly.

"Yes, I mean it," he said. He was not just comforting the boy. Seth had already been more useful than many other crime victims would have been under far less traumatic circumstances.

He saw the boy was tiring, but ventured one more question. "Do you know how to use a computer?"

Yes, Seth answered, but held up his bandaged hands.

"The speech therapist and your mother want to get you one that will let you communicate without using your fingers to type—they can wire these computers now so that they will read movement from muscles in your arm, for example. We can deal with that later—for now, just concentrate on getting stronger, all right? We'll talk again when you've had a little more rest."

Seth looked toward the chair where Lefebvre had been sitting, then anxiously back at the detective.

"I'm not going anywhere, if that's what you're asking."

Seth mouthed the word "thanks," then closed his eyes.

When he was sure Seth was sleeping soundly, Lefebvre called Elena Rosario.

"Are they still watching Whitey Dane's boat?"

"Yes. And Whitey, too."

"Has he been anywhere near the *Cygnet* in the last few days?"

"No."

"Do we know what time it came into the Downtown Marina that night?"

"No, but I could ask around. Maybe one of the live-aboards will remember. You working again?"

"Sort of. Listen—I think Dane just became our prime suspect in the Randolph case."

"What?" she asked, startled.

"Seth woke up. I asked a few questions."

"And you got a mute witness to talk to you."

"Yes. Come by and I'll tell you all about it."

A search warrant was issued, and although the *Cygnet* didn't look as lovely when they finished, the crime scene unit found crucial evidence there. Whitey Dane protested that he had not been aboard the boat for days, that he never took it to the Downtown Marina, that it must have been stolen from the Marina South. While the boat had been made to look as if it had been hot-wired, the police didn't buy his story. The boat was not far from its home, and none of its expensive gear had been taken.

The decks had been washed, but luminol tests showed bloody footprints. And although the weapon was not found, a pair of bloodstained deck shoes were discovered hidden in a footlocker. An uncommon and expensive brand of deck shoes, of a style which exactly matched—as surveillance photos showed—those worn by Whitey Dane on several occasions. Careful collection of trace evidence in the locker and shoes yielded small amounts of hair and fiber evidence as well.

Whitey Dane was arrested for the murders of Trent and Amanda Randolph and the attempted murder of Seth Randolph. The D.A. wanted him held without bail, but the defense argued that he had no criminal record, that he had business interests in the community, and that there were indications that the boat had indeed been stolen. Judge Lewis Kerr, in a move some considered uncharacteristically harsh, set bail at two million dollars. Dane made bail in less than twenty-four hours.

5

The room was too crowded, and the camera lights made it overly bright and warm. Lefebvre wanted the television news crews to leave. He wanted everyone to leave. But Tory Randolph was holding court, charming the press, the captain, the members of the police commission, and the others.

He was especially uncomfortable to see Polly Logan here. The platinum blond television news reporter always managed to get herself assigned to stories about his cases. He had thought it was coincidence until she had asked him out. He had politely refused, and although she had never asked again, when she showed up to cover stories now, he often found her glancing his way, directing a camera operator to shoot footage of him, and positioning herself as close as possible to him—to an extent that gave him the creeps. She often muttered catty remarks about Irene Kelly of the *Express*, perhaps jealous of Irene's closeness to him. His friendship with Irene would never be understood by someone like Polly, he knew—like many of his coworkers, Ms. Logan suspected they were more than friends.

As if his thoughts had tapped her on the shoulder, Polly Logan turned to look at him. She smiled. He nodded, then looked away. He watched Irene, who seemed tired today. Her father was ill—cancer—and she was caring for him. She did not play the martyr about this, as some might have. He tried to picture Polly Logan or Tory Randolph bearing such a burden so quietly, and could not imagine it.

Most of the other members of the media were captivated by the Tory

Show, as he had started to think of this press conference. When the reporters realized that Seth still couldn't speak, they had focused on his surviving parent, camera operators dutifully recording her as she starred in the role of concerned mother—a beautiful, tragic figure, hovering over Seth, making statements about the credit due to her brave boy, who had helped police capture the man who had killed her daughter and her husband.

"Ex-husband, correct?" Irene asked. Lefebvre suppressed an urge to smile.

Tory said—with a little catch in her voice, and lifting a tissue to a dry eye—that divorce was just a legal term, but in her heart she had never stopped loving Trent Randolph and considered herself a widow. She continued her planned speech, ending by skillfully reminding the assembled reporters that her son, heir to the Randolph Chemicals fortune, would become one of the wealthiest young men in Southern California when he reached his majority. He could almost feel her distress whenever Polly asked her camera operator to get a shot of anyone else, especially him.

Lefebvre despised Tory, but over the last three weeks he had carefully hidden that. He had not been so successful at hiding it from Seth, who he thought sensed it and sympathized with him. Seth, he had come to realize, was an excellent observer. Lefebvre was the person most often in his company, and Seth hadn't hesitated to study him, picking up on nuances of his behavior to a degree that was at times unnerving to the detective, who was much more used to being observer than observed.

The formal portion of the conference ended, but Polly Logan and some of the others asked Tory to pose with the newly appointed Homicide Division captain—Captain Bredloe—as well as the members of the police commission.

The doctors and a few reporters left, but there was still a crowd in the room. Most were from the PD—Willis and two other lieutenants, as well as a few uniforms, a couple of guys from the crime lab, and several detectives—including Hitch and Rosario.

Something was happening between him and Rosario, he admitted to himself. Not surprisingly, Seth had picked up on that, too. Now proficient at utilizing the special equipment that allowed him to type on the computer without using his fingers, Seth had urged Lefebvre to ask her out. Maybe he would. He was not living here, in Seth's room, as he had during those first two weeks, but he still spent many hours at a time at the young man's bedside. He found he rarely thought of Seth as a boy now, although just this moment, while others laughed and talked around him without actually talking to him, Lefebvre thought he looked more fragile than usual.

Lefebvre had done his best to stay in the background during this press conference, but in recent days the media had made much of his role in the rescue of Seth and in the case against Whitey Dane. Some of his coworkers resented it, made a play on the sound of his name and called him "The Fave"—not in a complimentary way. Their resentment made some aspects of his work difficult, but otherwise, it didn't bother him much. Others from the department, people who would not normally have had much to do with him, now sought him out. Most of that was, he knew, strictly political—a desire to be seen with the golden boy of the moment—and all of it sickened him.

Turning his back on them, he moved toward Seth, who was clearly wearing down—Seth still tired easily, a result, the doctors said, of having lost so much blood on the night of the attack. In one bandaged hand, he was cradling a rubber ball his physical therapist had given him, barely able to curl the hand around it. Even so, he weakly squeezed it, doing his best to regain strength in his fingers.

Seeing Lefebvre approach, Seth smiled. There was a knowing look in his eyes, one that said he knew Lefebvre was displeased with all the hoopla.

It was at that moment that the alarm on someone's watch played a little tune. It was shut off almost as soon as it sounded.

Seth's already pale face lost all color—the look in his eyes became one of sheer terror. The ball dropped to the floor. Lefebvre hurried to his side.

"Easy," he said, but this time Seth would not be soothed. Lefebvre saw a kind of desperation in him that had not been there since his first days in the hospital—the way he looked when he awakened from nightmares. "Seth, it's all right."

Seth shook his head, reached out to hold on to Lefebvre.

"What's wrong?" Tory asked. "What's wrong with him?"

Television cameras and lights turned toward the bed, and Polly Logan repeated the question, in a less frantic tone.

Fear, Lefebvre thought. "A little too much excitement," he said. "Perhaps it would be best if we let Seth rest."

"Detective Lefebvre is right," Captain Bredloe said. "We need to let the boy have a chance to recover. I'm sure everyone here understands that Seth's health must be our first concern."

Lefebvre's respect for the new captain increased when Bredloe suited action to word and courteously herded almost everyone out of the room, including Polly. Irene moved a little more slowly, watching Lefebvre and Seth with open curiosity. She met Lefebvre's eyes and seemed to realize that if she pushed to stay around now, she'd anger him — and risk losing future co-operation from him. He was glad she didn't say anything to him as she left. It would have only increased some of the friction he was encountering in the office, and Polly would have complained about unfair access for the *Express*.

Rosario, under Hitch's watchful eye, didn't look back at Lefebvre as she left. Even Tory Randolph found herself gently escorted away on the captain's reassuring arm.

Lefebvre reached up, smoothing Seth's hair in a calming gesture. "Better now?"

Seth still seemed frightened, but he nodded, turning to the computer. Lefebvre moved to read the screen:

`He was here just now. In this room.`

"Who?"

`The killer.`

"Whitey Dane?"

Seth shook his head and typed furiously.

`No. Wrong man.`

Lefebvre wondered briefly if this was some sort of setback brought on by the excitement of the day, but when he looked back into Seth's eyes, he saw the young man's need to be believed. "Tell me more," he said.

Seth looked relieved and began typing again:

`Doremi.`

6

Lefebvre paused, making sure Seth was sound asleep, then quietly stepped out of the room. The stocky guard was away from the door, chatting with the nurses down the hall. He saw Lefebvre's fierce scowl and hurried back to his post.

"How's he doing?" the guard asked, looking as if he wondered if Lefebvre had had all his shots.

"He's asleep. If he awakens, Officer, you will please ask one of the nurses to let me know—a nurse, or anyone else, but you remain here at all times— understood?"

"I'll stay right here, sir," he said nervously. "Uh, where will you be?"

"On the patio, outside the waiting area—just over there." He pointed to a tinted glass door at the end of the hallway. "I need a little air. I won't be long."

As he stepped out into the warm evening, he sensed movement to his left. Another door to the patio, leading to a separate corridor, swung softly shut. He walked toward it and pulled it open, but whoever had been on the patio must have moved into the nearby stairwell. He listened, heard footsteps going down the stairs, and walked back outside. He returned to the door he had used to enter the patio and looked down the hallway. The guard was still at Seth's door, looking a little more alert than usual. Lefebvre hoped he had scared the crap out of him.

He took off his suit coat and stretched, looking into the moonlit sky, imagining how it would feel to take the Cessna up into this calm night. He had not flown since the day before the Randolph murders. Perhaps when Seth had recovered, he would take him flying.

He sighed, chiding himself for the thought. He was too emotionally involved in this case. That involvement began the moment he reached through that door on the yacht and felt Seth's pulse. No—a little later, when he held Seth, and perhaps in some small way helped him to live, as he had not been able to help another boy . . .

But that was a long time ago, he scolded himself, and nothing could be changed by thinking about it.

Honest with himself about his own weaknesses, he had tried to stay away from most of the investigative work of the Randolph case, to involve others. But today—what Seth had told him today had shattered the delicate balance he had worked out between his protectiveness of Seth and his obligations to the department.

He heard a door open and turned to see Elena walking toward him.

"Phil? Is Seth all right?"

"Yes. He's sleeping. Did you come to see him?"

She hesitated, then said, "Both of you. I worried about him this afternoon, but knew he would be all right if you stayed. I wanted to stay, too, but Hitch . . ."

"Hitch is worried that his partner spends too much time with Lefebvre and always watches how she acts around him now."

"Yes, I thought you had probably picked up on that." She moved closer, standing a few inches from him, at his side. She did not touch him, but he felt his skin warm at her nearness. It would be easy to touch her, so simple to lean a little closer.

"Seth has picked up on it, too," he said, moving a little farther away.

"Seth?"

"Yes, but I think little escapes Seth."

"Little concerning you."

He shrugged.

"Are you sure he knows?"

"Knows what?" he asked, angry with himself for letting this conversation begin, let alone reach this point.

She was silent.

Lefebvre, you are an asshole, he told himself.

She began to walk away and he heard himself say, "Have you eaten?"

• • •

He took her to the Prop Room.

The place was crowded. "I've never been here before," she said, looking around at the various airplane paraphernalia that covered the walls—including the propeller mounted on the wall behind the bar.

"Unless you count a couple of guys from the Air Patrol, it's not a cop hangout."

"Which is why you like it."

"One reason," he admitted.

A large woman saw him, called out, "Philippe!" and eyed Elena speculatively. After a brief, rapid-fire exchange of French with Lefebvre, she pointed to an empty back booth. They made their way through the crowd.

"I didn't know you spoke French," Elena said as he sat opposite her.

"My parents and sister live in Quebec. When Marie"—he indicated the woman he had spoken to—"lived there, she and my sister were friends."

"So you're French-Canadian?"

"My parents are Quebecois. I was born in the U.S., despite my father's best efforts to get my mother back to Canada when she went into labor. I was born in Maine, so you see how close it was."

She laughed. "And your sister?"

"Yvette was born in Quebec, so my father had nothing to be ashamed of there."

"You have other brothers and sisters?"

He looked away but answered, "No."

She was studying him, he knew, seeing the evasion. He pretended to be engaging in the cop's habit he had already observed in her—the habit of staying aware of one's surroundings, of the people who moved in and out of any room. But he knew she was watching only him.

He tried to impartially consider what she was seeing. That he was older, undoubtedly. She was about eight or ten years his junior—somewhere in her early thirties. She was probably deciding he was too old for her. While he was tall and slender—too thin, some would say—he was not at all handsome. His features were harsh. He was intelligent, but not a conversationalist, not a charmer. It occurred to him that most women would have liked a quieter place to dine, decorated with something other than airplane parts.

"It's not a very fancy place—" he began.

"It's comfortable."

"Yes," he agreed. "The food is plain here, but good. The steaks are the best in Las Piernas. I should have asked before—are you a vegetarian?"

She shook her head. He signaled to Marie, who quickly came to take their orders. They waited in silence until she brought their wine. Searching for another topic of conversation, he said, "Tell me about your family."

"I have two brothers, one fifteen years older, the other, twelve years older—they refer to me as 'the retirement package.' My parents were both forty-five when I was born—they're no longer living. I'm close to my brothers, though. They both live in Santa Barbara."

He studied her, just as she had studied him, all the while wondering why he had no gift for flirtation. After years of spurning overtures, of letting subtle and not-so-subtle invitations go unanswered—he found himself curiously unwilling to waste this chance. There was something waiting to begin here, but how to make that beginning? He might compliment her on her green eyes and dark hair—tell her that he liked the way she wore her hair tonight, perhaps? Not pinned up, as usual, but falling in soft curls across her shoulders. But why should she care what he liked, after all? Did any woman really want a man to say such things? Certainly, no woman would want a man to tell her that her skin was the color of walnuts. Walnuts were wrinkly things—nuts, for God's sake. What a poet you are, Lefebvre! A real smooth operator. Still, to his eye, her skin was just that lovely, creamy brown color—

He realized she had stopped talking and was looking at him with—impatience?

"You're wondering what I am," she said.

"Pardon?"

"I'm used to it."

"I'm sorry, I don't know what you're talking about."

"Oh." She blushed.

You see? he told himself. Walnuts do not blush. Of all the things—

"I saw you looking at my skin."

Now he blushed.

She smiled. "You were thinking, let's see . . ."

For an awful moment, he wondered if she would somehow guess.

"You wouldn't put it like Hitch did," she went on. "So you wouldn't say, 'What kind of goddamned mutt are you, anyway?'"

"Mutt?" he repeated blankly.

"I admired his directness, actually. So much better than being told I'm 'exotic.'"

The look on his face must have made her realize that he hadn't been thinking about her ethnicity at all, because she faltered, then said, "Oh," again—this time, a sound of both pleasure and embarrassment.

"I wasn't—"

"I know," she said quickly. "I mean, I see that now." She hesitated, then rapidly forged ahead. "You're lucky to know both French and English. Even though your last name is French, when people read your ID card, they probably don't expect you to speak the language—"

"They don't even know how to say my last name," he said, looking mildly amused. "And I know I cannot ever teach most of them to say it—the sounds aren't found in English, so..." He shrugged. "I'm known as 'Ley-feb,' 'Le-fever,' 'La-five,' 'Luh-fave.' Usually I tell them it almost rhymes with 'ever,' and then they're really confused."

"Tell me how to say it."

"The way my cousins in Maine say it? Or the way my father said it?"

"The way you say it."

He smiled. "Phil."

"No, come on."

"Okay. 'Luh-fevre.' A short *e*, then a soft 'vre' sound." He repeated it. She tried it.

"Almost. You're rolling the *r*—you're making it Spanish." He said his name a few more times.

She repeated it back until he said, "Yes, now you have it. Now—you were about to tell me more about your name. Rosario."

"You rolled the *r*'s perfectly! You speak Spanish, don't you? English, French, and Spanish?"

"Yes, but just those three."

"*Just* those three," she said mournfully.

"The French of Quebec, the English of California, and the Spanish of Baja California. There are undoubtedly Europeans who would tell you I don't speak any of those languages properly."

"When people read 'Rosario' on my badge, they definitely expect me to speak Spanish. I'm trying to learn Spanish, but the last people in my family who spoke the language came to California not long after Junípero Serra."

"But you are not only Hispanic," he said.

"That's exactly it. Without telling you my whole family history, let's just say I'm one of those people who could mark about four boxes when asked to indicate ethnic origins. African American, Chumash Indian, Spanish, Mexican, Irish, Greek . . . Maybe Hitch is right—I'm a mutt."

"An American," he said. "Like me—true no matter what side of the border I was born on, I suppose."

She smiled. "Yes."

They were silent again, but this time it was more companionable. She asked him how he came to know of this place, and he told her about being a military pilot and saving for the Cessna, searching for just the right one, and finding it—becoming more animated as he talked about flying.

When they had finished eating, he looked across at her and said, "Thanks for coming here with me."

"My pleasure."

Another silence stretched out, then she asked, "Phil, what was bothering you tonight—at the hospital?"

He frowned. "It's this—probably half the department knows every detail that can be known about Whitey Dane's appearance and habits, right?"

"Sure," she said, surprised by the question. "All of us who've been part of the investigations connected to him, anyway."

"And he has a number of affectations, right?"

"Like the patch, you mean? I've heard he's not actually missing an eye," she said. "I've even heard that he used to wear the patch on the other eye."

"It's not just the patch. For example, he sometimes wears vests."

"Yes, usually. Complete with a watch on a chain."

"Not a wristwatch." He said it flatly.

"Not in a million years. You must have read about that in the files—he carries an old Hamilton railroad pocket watch on a gold chain and tucks it into a vest pocket. Makes a big show of winding it and taking it out and looking at it."

"He's never been seen wearing an electronic watch?"

"No—like you say, one of his affectations. Like the patch."

Again he was silent.

She waited.

"Don't mention to anyone that I asked about a watch, all right?"

"Sure."

"It could be . . . it could cause a lot of problems, and be dangerous to Seth."

"What?"

"Just don't talk about it—not to anyone, not even Hitch."

"I said I wouldn't, and I won't," she said with some exasperation. "What's this all about?"

He looked down at his hands, debating how much to tell her. He had so little to go on, and the implications . . . "I'll take you back to your car," he said.

He could see that she wanted to tell him to go to hell, but after studying him for another moment, said, "Okay." They argued over the payment of the bill, which allowed her to discover that he was a little old-fashioned in some matters, and very stubborn.

"Do you have to go in early tomorrow?" he asked after they had driven in silence for a while.

"No, sleeping in. I have a late-night surveillance with Hitch on one of our other cases."

Again he fell silent, thinking he should apologize to her, but not wanting to reopen the topic of the Dane case. He dropped her off at her car and watched her drive away. He had not been able to think of the sort of words that might have tempted her to stay with him a little longer, and deciding that it was useless to wish for what was beyond his reach, he started to get out of the car. He noticed something small and white on his passenger seat. A business card. He picked it up and saw that it was hers. In bold blue strokes, she had written her home address and phone number on the back. He sat for a long time, tracing its edges with his fingertips, then started to put it away in his wallet. He hesitated, then tucked it into his shirt pocket instead.

"Anyone come by?" he asked the guard.

"No, sir. And I've checked on him a couple times—he's asleep."

Just as Lefebvre was about to enter Seth's room, he saw the door to the patio open slightly, then quickly close, as if someone had started through it and changed his mind. He walked with quick strides toward the patio, stepping outside just as the far door closed. He ran to it, yanking it open. He could see no one, but again heard footsteps on the stairs. This time, they were hurried. He followed as quietly as possible. The footsteps stopped, and Lefebvre slowed his own steps, creeping closer to his prey. A series of small, high-pitched sounds filled the stairwell:

Do-re-mi-do-re-mi-do-re-mi

Lefebvre ran toward the sounds, heedless of any noise he was making.

He reached the bottom of the stairwell and came out into the hospital lobby. He quickly scanned the room: A pair of doctors, wearing scrubs, talking to each other. A receptionist. Five people huddled together in one set of chairs, as if praying together; a family, it seemed. None of them looked as if he or she had just sat down. He turned around and saw a bank of elevators—one car just starting to ascend. And beyond the elevators, a series of hallways. He made a quick check of these, but realized his quarry was long gone.

Or was he? He thought of the elevator and ran back up the stairs. If the attacker had returned while Lefebvre searched the lobby and hallways—how much resistance would that guard offer?

Heart pounding, he raced to the fourth floor, immediately went out onto the patio and crossed it to the other door. Yanking it open, he looked toward the door to Seth's room—the guard's chair was empty.

"No!" he shouted, causing the nurses to stare at him as if he were a madman.

But in the next instant, the guard came out of the room, and seeing Lefebvre, said, "Oh, you're back. He just woke up. I think he wanted me to find out if you were still here. Of course, since he can't talk, I'm only guessing . . . hey!"

Lefebvre pushed past him into the room.

Seth smiled when he saw him, then raised a questioning brow.

"You're okay?" Lefebvre asked, still shaken.

He nodded, then pointed to Lefebvre, asking a silent question in return.

"I'm fine."

Seth seemed skeptical, but gestured toward a chair.

"Yes," Lefebvre said. "Yes, I'll stay awhile—I have a phone call to make, but I'll be right back."

Seth gestured to the phone next to his bed.

"What, you think you get to be privy to all police business now?" Lefebvre said, trying to keep his tone light. Seth smiled, but Lefebvre did not think he looked convinced.

He apologized brusquely to the guard, then using the phone at the nurses' station, called the homicide desk and asked to be patched through to the team currently on surveillance of Dane. No, Dane had not left his house. Yes, they had seen him with their own eyes—had him in sight right now.

He had pissed them off with the last question. It could not be helped.

The guard's replacement had come on duty in the meantime. Lefebvre felt more sure of this man's alertness and abilities. He went back into Seth's room and bent himself to the task of distracting Seth from his memories and fears. He failed miserably at this, until he began to tell him about his dinner with Elena.

7

Lefebvre nodded to Pete Baird as he went to his desk. Baird, the only other detective in the homicide room, nodded back and continued working, his head bent over a file. There was a thinning spot on his crown—Lefebvre dispassionately considered the likelihood that Baird would be bald within a few years.

He didn't think Baird disliked him, but would not have worried if he did. He knew that his coworkers' feelings about him were mixed. He was not a gregarious person, as Baird was. Among some of his fellow detectives, he knew, his success was probably more resented than admired, in part because he was a loner.

If he could cope with Baird's talkativeness, Baird would make a good partner on this case. It was not that he would be especially interested in Baird's thoughts about it—Baird did not solve cases with his mind, although Lefebvre was sure there was more going on under that thinning hair than most people believed. Baird solved cases with doggedness. Doggedness was undoubtedly what had brought him here so early in the morning. Many times Lefebvre had seen Baird's persistence pay off; Baird often solved cases that had discouraged supposedly smarter detectives.

Lefebvre's last assigned partner had been his mentor, Matthew Arden. When Arden retired, he convinced their lieutenant that Lefebvre would work best without a partner, and no lieutenant since then had insisted on pairing him with anyone.

But although there were a great many differences in their style of work and in their personalities, Lefebvre believed Pete Baird was trustworthy. Lefebvre did not for a moment doubt his honesty. Looking around the room at the other desks, he realized that there was no one else of whom he felt quite so sure. It would be good, Lefebvre thought, to tell someone else that perhaps Whitey Dane was not the one who had attacked the Randolphs.

But what would he say, after all?

Pete, I have no idea who the killer is, but it isn't Dane—even though all the physical evidence and the witness's description point to him. I know he's a suspected crime boss we've been trying to arrest for several years, and probably has been involved in murder many times over, but he's not the man we want for this one, the only one to which we can connect him. I base this on how frightened Seth became at the sound of a watch—a watch that many thousands of people may own, but which I believe may belong to a member of our own police department.

Ludicrous.

He would spend the day trying to learn more, to come up with something more solid—and answers to the questions that had plagued him all night. Those questions, and his fears for Seth's safety, had denied him any sleep.

At least the guard who had come on duty at eleven was more capable than the previous man. Lefebvre was equally confident about the man who had the next rotation. He had called the officer who took over this morning, intimating that new threats had been made against Seth. He would try today to get the guard on Seth's room doubled, and to get the hospital to lock the door between the patio and the stairwell. The hospital night-shift security guard had been unwilling to do so.

At his desk, Lefebvre took out his notebook and reviewed a list of initials he had made during the long night. Once again he pictured himself in Seth's room and tried to recall exactly who had been present when the watch beeped. With the exception of a few reporters, Tory Randolph, and Seth himself, they were all members of the Las Piernas Police Department or police commissioners. Lefebvre still strongly resisted the idea. He told himself that other evidence still indicated Dane.

Then he thought of the sound of the watch in the stairwell.

Whoever wore the watch had seen Seth's reaction and had returned, probably to finish what he had started on the *Amanda*.

Why, Lefebvre wondered now, was the watch set to go off a few minutes before eleven?

Gazing off into space as he recalled the previous evening, he soon came to an answer. The guard's shift changed at eleven. Any member of the department could easily learn which officers had guard duty at the hospital. With very little research, the attacker would know that the least alert guard was on duty from three to eleven. And near eleven, as the shift changed, both guards would be on hand—presenting two guards to overcome at Seth's door, instead of one inattentive man who often strayed away from it.

He went back over the description Seth had given of his attacker. Eliminating only those who most obviously differed from that description, Lefebvre narrowed his list of potential suspects. He reviewed the remaining names.

Two were on the police commission: Dan Soury and Michael Pickens. Soury, who chaired the commission, had a thick, full beard. He could not have grown that out so rapidly in the weeks after the murders. He crossed Soury off the list.

Three were from the Homicide Division: Captain Bredloe, Pete Baird, and Vince Adams. He recalled that Bredloe and Randolph had been at odds on occasion, but Lefebvre did not know of any disagreement that would have led to murder. No matter how he tried, Lefebvre could not picture Bredloe in the role of the attacker. Besides, Bredloe was tall and broad-shouldered, and Lefebvre thought Seth would probably have described the attacker as a larger man if Bredloe had been the one.

Baird and Adams had investigated a homicide case believed to be connected to Dane, but had not been able to come up with any solid evidence. They weren't alone—Lefebvre himself was working on such a case.

Lefebvre started to cross off the name of Robert Hitchcock, Elena's partner. Then he realized that he could not account for every moment of Hitch's time on the night of the murders. A long shot, but still . . .

The next three men on his list—Dr. Alfred Larson, Paul Haycroft, and Dale Britton—all worked in the crime lab. Larson managed it, Haycroft worked for him, and Britton was part of the crime scene unit that had examined both the *Cygnet* and the *Amanda*. Britton had seemed quite taken with Tory Randolph, while Larson and Haycroft had been ill at ease during their part of her show in Seth's room yesterday.

The last three men on his list were uniformed officers. Earl Allen, Duke Fenly, and Ned Perry. He was well acquainted with "the aristocrats," as Earl and Duke were known. They were large men, often called upon to help transport violent criminals. Again, too large, thought Lefebvre. Still, he would need to take a closer look at their activities on the night of the murders. He knew very little about Perry, only that he had been one of the first to respond to their call for backup on the *Amanda.* He had seemed uneasy in Seth's room, but Lefebvre had been uneasy, too—so he wasn't ready to hold that against him.

He decided to start with the uniformed officers. Their movements would be the easiest to check. He went downstairs and asked for their schedules and records of calls between about eleven o'clock on the night of June 3 and one in the morning on June 4—roughly the time of the murders. The sergeant who supplied the information didn't hide his curiosity over the request, but didn't hesitate to comply with it. Lefebvre ignored the curiosity and thanked him for his help.

Looking at the logs, he noticed that Perry and his partner had been busy with a nearby domestic violence call during the time of the attack on the *Amanda.* Duke and Earl had been near the downtown area, arresting a felon on a parole violation. Their time had been completely taken up with these activities. Relieved, he crossed all three names off his list.

While he was downstairs, he put in a request for an additional guard on Seth's room, but despite his arguments of urgency, the sergeant told him that they were stretched thin now, and if he could manage it at all, tomorrow would be the earliest—if the request was approved by higher-ups.

Lefebvre hid his annoyance and went back to the homicide room.

He found it much more crowded and filled with the hum of conversation. He returned a few greetings, then sat down at his desk and took out a pen and paper. His notebook was full of disjointed reminders, notes made in the anxious hours of the previous night. Seeking an orderly approach to the problem, he started to make a list of the avenues he would pursue from here.

The first of these was to take a look at the physical evidence against Dane.

This brought to mind a problem that had nagged at him throughout the night—the anonymous tip he had received, telling him about Dane's supposed meeting with a triggerman—the one that had brought him to the marina in the early hours of June 4. If Dane had not killed Trent and Amanda Randolph, then Dane had been set up, and the informant who had called Lefebvre was very likely the murderer. What bothered Lefebvre most was the awareness that this was not the first time he had been contacted by the informant.

On two other occasions, he had heard that obviously disguised voice— the caller had spoken as few words as possible, almost as if he had been sending a telegram. Just before midnight, on a night when he had been working late at his desk, going over department files on Whitey Dane, Lefebvre had received the call. "Dane on *Cygnet* paying shooter. Returns to Marina South soon. Slip three-zero-five."

Even if he had never heard the weird, altered voice before, even if two previous tips from that same caller had not led to important arrests, Lefebvre would have gone down to the marina. But because he thought of this informant as reliable, that night he paged Elena and Hitch. Yes, they said, Dane had a boat called the *Cygnet* and moored it in slip number 305.

If Seth had not heard the watch, Lefebvre never would have questioned the snitch's information. Over the last few hours, he had wondered about the previous cases. Although he remained convinced that they were good arrests, he made a note to look at those files as well. Perhaps there was some link between them, some person within the department or commission who was connected to all the cases.

He looked over the list of names again and wondered how long it might take him to ferret out the man he sought. For Seth's sake, he hoped it would be soon. He neatly folded the page, placed it in his top desk drawer with the pen, and locked the drawer.

Lefebvre felt a certain pride in the Las Piernas lab. A year or so ago, there had been pressure to close it down and to rely on the county forensic science services. He had nothing against the county lab, but they were overburdened and would be far less convenient to use. And the thought of losing scientists like Paul Haycroft was one he'd rather not contemplate.

Haycroft was studying photographs of blood-spatter patterns when Lefebvre walked into the lab. Although both Larson and Haycroft had solid, broad-based experience in a number of areas of forensic science, this was Haycroft's specialty. The department's success in solving cases where bloodstains were present was higher than average, and Lefebvre knew this was due in part to Haycroft's ability to interpret the evidence.

Haycroft looked up as he heard Lefebvre approach, and seeing him, smiled. "Hello, Phil. Decided to take a little time away from the boy and help us solve murders, eh?"

"The thought has occurred to me, Paul," Lefebvre said. "But actually, I need to see if I can come up with anything more on the Randolph case."

Haycroft's brows rose. "You don't think we have enough to prosecute Dane?"

Lefebvre shrugged. "I would like to feel satisfied that we are doing our best to make sure the man who attacked Seth and his family is punished."

Haycroft sighed. "I'm relieved to find someone else who feels that way. When we put Mr. Dane away, I'd like it to be for good. I suspect he is more clever than many of us believe. In fact—well, let me show you something."

He put the photos away and rose from his desk. Lefebvre followed him as he went to the property room and signed for the box for the Randolph case. He took Lefebvre to a microscope with a video camera and monitor attached to it. Haycroft sat at the microscope itself and motioned Lefebvre to sit in front of the monitor. He found a labeled slide and set it up for viewing. After some minor adjustments, he said, "There. I've got it at about four hundred and fifty X."

On the monitor, Lefebvre saw two thin parallel lines with a row of dark marks between them, the darker row looking somewhat like beads on an invisible string. "Hair or fiber?"

"Hair," Haycroft said. "From the inside of the shoes—the bloodstained shoes we found on Dane's boat."

"Inside of the shoes, but not from the outside?"

"Right. This is just a sample, of course. Several of these were recovered from inside the shoes."

"You found these hairs?"

He shook his head. "No, Dale Britton had the good sense to look for hair and fiber evidence. He was on the mobile crime scene unit that day, thank God. We found these inside the shoes. One of our trace evidence technicians did the identification work."

"So is this hair Dane's?"

Haycroft laughed. "Only if he is a cat."

Lefebvre looked away from the monitor. "A cat?"

"Yes, among other indicators, that medulla pattern—the pattern of the material in the middle of the hair shaft—tells us this is from a cat." He pointed to the row of dark marks on the monitor.

Lefebvre stared at Haycroft in disbelief. Reading his look, Haycroft said, "Yes, once we had identified it as cat hair, I asked Vince Adams if Dane had a cat. And he told me what I suspect you also know."

"That Dane is highly allergic to cats." Lefebvre paused, then asked, "Did Detective Adams have anything more to say about this?"

"Yes. He told me to keep my mouth shut."

Lefebvre frowned. "But—"

"I told Al about it anyway."

"Good. And what did Dr. Larson say?" Lefebvre was sure the lab's director would be concerned.

"Al had two theories. One was that Dale or Vince—who found the shoes—contaminated the evidence. They both own cats, you see. For that matter, so does Dr. Larson. But he didn't process the scene. Dale and Vince were there."

"Locard's Exchange," Lefebvre said. "'Whenever two objects come in contact with one another, there is always a transfer of material across the contact boundaries.'"

"Yes," Haycroft said, pleased that Lefebvre could quote this tenet of forensic science.

"Because of static electricity in his clothing, Vince Adams picks up cat hairs on, say, his cuffs. He later touches the shoes on the *Cygnet* and the hairs transfer to them."

"Something like that, yes. When I asked how he handled the shoes, he admitted that in order to preserve the blood evidence on the outside, he had carefully placed his hands on the inside of the shoes. He was wearing gloves, but still, he could have transferred hairs to the shoes."

"You said Dr. Larson had two theories."

"The second is that Dane intentionally placed cat hairs in the shoes to eliminate himself as a suspect."

"A little far-fetched?"

"If it were anyone but Dane, I would think so."

"Yes, I see what you mean."

"In any case, don't let the boss know I talked to you about this, all right? Or anyone else, for the time being. Al's actually going to try to match the hairs up to Dale's or Vince's cat, but both of them are touchy about it." Haycroft smiled. "Dale had to let Al comb his cat, of course—Al's his boss. But he resented the implication that he was sloppy on an important case. Dale's a little—well, lacking in physical coordination at times. He'll trip over his own two feet. But when he's concentrating on a case, that clumsiness disappears. He's never careless when it comes to handling evidence."

"And Vince?"

"Oh, Vince was so mad about it, he told Al he'll have to get a court order to come anywhere near his cat."

"Al?"

Dr. Al Larson, who had been staring into a microscope, gave a start. He looked up at Phil and said, "Oh! How long have you been standing there?"

"Not long. Can you spare a few moments?"

He hesitated slightly, then smiled and said, "Sure. I could use a break. Let me buy you a cup of coffee."

They moved to a small break room, aglow with the light from a wall of vending machines. Lefebvre declined Larson's offer of coffee, then waited while the other man got a cup for himself. As they sat down at one of the empty tables, Larson said, "What's on your mind, Phil?"

"Trent Randolph."

Larson's smile disappeared. "I liked Trent Randolph very much," he said quietly. "I can't tell you how difficult it has been for me to work on this case. He was brilliant. And to have a scientist on the commission . . . a terrible loss."

"How well did you know him?"

"Personally? Not well. After he was appointed to the commission, he spent a great deal of time here, though. So he was well acquainted with the lab and everyone who worked in it—he reviewed the whole lab and had wonderful suggestions—and resources. He even donated equipment."

"Didn't you resent that a little? Not the donations, but having some newcomer from the commission reviewing your work?"

Larson pushed the coffee cup away. "Not in the least. I invited him to do so. I knew what Michael Pickens was trying to do to this lab."

"Commissioner Pickens wanted it shut down."

"Yes," he said. "Move everything to the county. I saw the chance to have an ally, someone who would be able to give an informed and respected opinion to the commission."

"And Randolph was that ally?"

"Absolutely. Pickens is no scientist. Randolph was able to silence his objections quite easily. And he was able to help us acquire funding that we've needed for years. Until Randolph came on the scene, Pickens always made sure we were shortchanged. He kept us from obtaining new equipment, then complained that we weren't able to do the job because our equipment was outdated."

"Politicians," Lefebvre said.

"Exactly! But Randolph outmaneuvered him. He got O'Connor from the *Express*—you know him?"

"I've met him once or twice," Lefebvre said.

"Trent Randolph got that old man in our corner, and between the two of them, they put Pickens on the defensive for once. So the recommendations for the budget looked a little different than they had for the last few years—and we got our funding."

"Is that funding secure without Randolph on the commission?"

Larson moved the paper coffee cup to the center of the small table, the coffee still untouched. "We'll be fine this year, but who knows what will happen without Trent?" He frowned, then added, "I've only talked to you about the funding, but he was—he was more than that to us. He was a colleague. And a man of integrity."

Lefebvre waited.

Larson suddenly looked him directly in the eye and said, "I know why you're asking."

Lefebvre told himself to keep his face impassive, to stay calm. "Oh?"

"It's the boy," Larson said.

Lefebvre didn't answer.

"Don't be angry with me for suggesting this, Phil, but there are those around here who think you're too attached to Seth Randolph—a little too *devoted*, let's say. Staying overnight in his room and so on. I won't repeat the crudest comments—"

Lefebvre felt an impulse to let his fist fly into Larson's face. With an effort, he held his temper, but Larson must have read something of the intent in his eyes, because the lab director turned pale and beads of sweat broke out on his forehead.

His voice cold, Lefebvre said, "Are you implying—"

"I'm simply warning you that there are rumors. Just a word to the wise—okay? I don't even know who started them. Besides, most of them are saying you're after the ex-wife."

"Tory?" He nearly laughed.

"Yes, after all, she's a beautiful woman and—"

Lefebvre suddenly stood, and Larson went another shade of white.

"First you suggest I've molested a young witness," Lefebvre said quietly, "and then you insult my tastes. And you will not say—"

"Forget I said anything at all!" Larson said just as Dale Britton stepped into the break room, carrying a clipboard and looking owlish.

"Sorry to interrupt," he said, "but I need your signature on this, Al." He leaned across Lefebvre's vacant chair with the clipboard and knocked the coffee cup over. Larson came to his feet, but not in time to prevent the lukewarm liquid from splashing over his lap, staining the front of his pants.

Britton was still apologizing to his boss when Lefebvre left the room.

Lefebvre returned to his desk some time later, so lost in anger that he pulled the top drawer open before he realized that he had not unlocked it. The list he had made earlier was missing from the drawer. He felt a cold knot form in the pit of his stomach. He looked up to see Pete Baird watching him.

"Have you been here all morning?" Lefebvre asked.

"Look," Pete said, "you work your way, I'll work mine. Just because I've been working from my desk—"

"That's not what I meant," he said hastily. "I just wondered—did you see anyone approach my desk while I was gone?"

"All sorts of people. Look." He pointed to the desk tray. As usual, during the morning hours various bulletins and paperwork had been placed there.

Lefebvre didn't miss Baird's look of amusement. Ignoring it, he said, "Has anyone used my desk or looked through it?"

The amusement faded. "Exactly what are you getting at, Lefebvre?"

"I had some paperwork here. It was in this drawer. It's gone now."

"And you think someone from this squad took it."

Too late, Lefebvre saw his mistake. "No, I just wondered if someone might have used the phone and accidentally picked up the paperwork."

"No one has used your frickin' phone. Or sat at your desk. Or taken anything that belongs to you."

"I must have mislaid it, then," Lefebvre said, and closed the drawer. When he tried to relock it, he found the lock was broken.

Baird continued to watch him, frowning. Lefebvre left the squad room without saying anything more to him.

He went downstairs, trying to walk off some of the tension he was feeling. If he had any doubt that someone within the department was involved in Trent Randolph's murder, that doubt was gone now. He wandered near a pay phone in the hallway and got as far as fishing coins out of his pocket. He stopped before pulling the card out of his shirt pocket. Elena had a late-night surveillance assignment tonight. She might be sleeping. He did not know what he would have said to her anyway.

He went to the Records Department and requested the files for the two previous cases for which he had received calls from the anonymous tipster, hoping that they might help him discover something about the identity of the caller.

"Give me an hour or so, okay?" the harassed clerk asked. "I just got a huge list of files to be pulled for Captain Bredloe. When we take his up, I'll have someone bring these two to your desk."

"No," Lefebvre said quickly, surprising the clerk. "Just hold them for me here, please. Give me a call when they're ready."

"It's no trouble, I'll be up there anyway."

"Just give me a call."

He left, hearing the clerk mutter behind him.

He was halfway up the stairs when he heard a familiar voice in the break room.

"Fuckin' Lefebvre." Pete Baird.

Lefebvre paused on the stairway, not wanting to walk by the open doorway.

"That asshole asks me if anyone has been using his desk—'maybe using the phone,' he says. Like the anal little prick wouldn't know if someone sat there. Says someone might have picked up some paper he left on the top of the desk, but he's looking in the drawer, right? Now, number one, he locks his fucking desk all the time 'cause he thinks the rest of us are so fucking interested in his caseload, we're gonna ignore our own cases to spy on Mr. Hotshot. So you know it's his desk drawer he's freaking out over, and not the top of his desk. And number two, it would be easier to find paper in the only stall on a diarrhea ward than on the top of Lefebvre's desk."

The others laughed, and someone razzed Pete about the messy state of his own desk. Lefebvre told himself to ignore their childishness and began to climb the stairs again just as Pete Baird stepped out of the break room and looked down at him.

Baird blushed, obviously aware that Lefebvre had heard his loud comments. Lefebvre looked straight at him, thought about his wanting to confide in this man only a few hours earlier, and turned to go back down the stairs.

Baird followed him, and from behind him, put a hand on his shoulder. "Lefebvre—"

Lefebvre shook the hand off and kept walking.

He was on the sidewalk when a slender, blue-eyed brunette hailed him. Irene Kelly hurried after him. "Hello," he said. "How are things at the *Express?*"

"Are you okay?" she asked.

He felt a nearly uncontrollable urge to tell her to follow him to a restaurant, to tell her everything he knew. But even as he thought this, he realized that he could not bring himself to talk to a reporter about mere suspicions, especially ones that would damage the reputation of the entire department. "Just tired," he said.

She studied him, then said, "Can I give you a lift somewhere?"

Behind her, he saw Vince Adams step out of the building. Adams noticed who he was with and gave him a look of disgust.

She followed Lefebvre's glance and said, "They're just jealous of the attention you get, you know."

"It doesn't help me to have them jealous," he said.

"What's bothering you today?"

He smiled. "Do you really care, or are you looking for a story?"

Her chin came up. He thought, wryly, that he had just given Baird the same look of disappointment.

"Sorry," he said. "I'm in a terrible mood. Come by tomorrow and maybe I'll be better company."

"Lunch?"

"Sure."

She started to walk off, then paused and said, "Take care of yourself, Phil."

He walked with no set purpose. When he realized that he was some distance from the office, he hailed a cab.

"Where to?" the driver asked.

He started to say, "Police headquarters." Instead, he reached into his shirt pocket, found Elena's card, and asked the cabdriver to take him to a corner near her address. He would just take a look at her neighborhood, he told himself. Get a sense of where she lived.

She unlatched the last of the locks and opened the door, standing back as she said, "Come in." She was wearing a short, silky yellow robe, and her hair tumbled down over her shoulders. She looked drowsy—sleep-softened and warm.

"I've awakened you," he said as he stepped into her apartment.

"I've been thinking the same thing for weeks," she said, and began loosening his tie.

8

"It's a good plan," she said, straightening the tie she had removed several hours earlier. She moved her hands into his hair.

He traced the curve of her spine, not ready to let go yet. "I'm not sure. If it weren't for Seth—"

"I know." She looked up into his eyes. "Whatever you decide."

He pulled her closer, held her to him, and said, "Promise me you will be careful."

"I will. You too."

Reluctantly, he let her go. "I'll leave first. If you see anyone follow—"

"I'll page you."

He saw the worry in her eyes. "Elena—"

"I'll be fine. Don't make me one of your problems."

He smiled, thinking of how, despite all the tension and trouble in his life right now, she had made him feel good, had eased some ache within him. "Sometimes, *mon ange*, you really are quite ridiculous."

"What's an 'ange'?"

"Angel."

He left hearing the warm sound of her laughter.

He did not step out into the street until he had studied it for a moment. Seeing no sign of anyone watching the building, he walked a block south. He unbuttoned his coat and kept his hand near his weapon. He continued for a few blocks, to a coffee shop. He used a pay phone there to call Lieutenant Willis.

He was surprised when the lieutenant answered over a speaker phone—the lieutenant disliked using the speaker. "Lefebvre? Glad you called." His voice sounded tinny. "Captain Bredloe and Pete Baird are here in my office. The captain wants to talk to you."

He heard Bredloe's voice, a little closer to the phone, and deeper. "Everything okay with you, Phil?"

"Yes, but—actually, I was calling to ask the lieutenant for a few days off."

There was a pause, then Bredloe said, "I happened to overhear—there was an incident here this morning—"

Lefebvre heard a chair squeak and pictured Baird shifting in discomfort. So Baird was getting his ass chewed out. "Nothing of any importance," he said quickly.

"We haven't seen you since then, and your car was still here, so we became a little concerned."

"I went for a walk, that's all."

"For seven hours?" Baird's voice said. "The *Express* must be getting one hell of a story out of this one."

"Detective Baird," Bredloe said repressively.

The picture became clearer in Lefebvre's mind. "I'm afraid Vince Adams may have misled you. Except to disappoint Ms. Kelly when she asked for my time, I haven't been talking to reporters today. I didn't realize I had caused so much concern by holding that brief conversation with her."

This time more than one chair creaked.

"I owe Detective Baird an apology," Lefebvre went on, perfectly capable of returning Baird's insults, but knowing that a man like Pete Baird would feel worse if he got conciliation when he expected revenge. "I was irritable this morning. The walk helped—taking a little time to myself helped. I realized that Lieutenant Willis made a good suggestion to me a few weeks ago, and I ignored it. So I called Matt Arden and he has invited me to fly out to the desert to spend a few days with him. If you've no objection, I'd like to go."

"You do need a real break, Phil," Willis said. "You're either working or with the kid. You've been too involved in the Randolph case."

"Exactly. Although to be honest, I would feel easier about going if we increased the guard on his room."

"Why?" Bredloe asked sharply.

"Once or twice, I've thought I've seen suspicious-looking individuals in the hallways," he said, glad to be able to be truthful about that, at least. "Nothing definite, but it occurs to me that Dane had no reason to attack when he thought Seth might die. Now that we've held this news conference, everyone knows that Seth is doing better and can communicate with us—but by making that information public, we've increased the danger to our only witness. I'm going over to the hospital this evening, but I can't be with Seth all the time."

"What he's saying makes sense," he heard Bredloe say to Willis. "Let's double the guard at the start of the next shift."

Lefebvre caught a cab. He took it back to headquarters, but didn't enter the building. He retrieved his car and began a series of errands, the final one to Mail Call, a store where he rented a private mailbox. He talked for a moment with the owner and made a few arrangements with him. He picked up his mail, then drove over to the hospital.

He sat in the car for a few moments, to give himself time to consider how he would tell Seth that he was leaving Las Piernas for a few days. Earlier, from Elena's apartment, he had called Matt Arden. Matt had immediately agreed to help and urged Lefebvre to move out of range of the killer. Lefebvre, unwilling to run away, had at first refused to leave Las Piernas. After some argument, though, the old man had finally persuaded Lefebvre that it would be best for him to come to the desert just long enough to meet with an outside investigator. To bring anyone into Las Piernas would only alert the killer, he said—Matt would use his connections to make sure Lefebvre told his story to someone they could trust, but Lefebvre must tell Seth's story away from the department.

The moment he walked into Seth's room, Lefebvre began to reconsider his plan to leave Las Piernas. Seth looked worse than he had in days—pale and tense, with dark circles under his eyes. Although his mother was with him, he did not hide his relief at seeing Lefebvre.

Tory Randolph immediately launched into an exhaustive list of grievances, most of them having to do with what she considered the premature breakup of the gathering the day before.

Lefebvre, watching Seth, suddenly said, "No, don't—"

But he was too late—Seth angrily knocked a stack of books to the floor.

She rounded on Seth. "Why did you do that?" she asked angrily.

"It's the only way he can interrupt you," Lefebvre said, bending to pick up the books.

"I asked him!" she said.

Lefebvre stood. "Well, then—read his answer."

She read the computer screen aloud. "'You don't listen to me. He does. He stays.'" She looked at her son, then began to cry. "Oh, Seth—"

Apparently accustomed to her tears, he ignored her.

"I'm thinking of going away for a few days," Lefebvre said quietly.

Seth mouthed the word "no," then in frustration, pointed to the screen.

Please don't go. Not now.

Tory turned and walked to the far side of the room, saying nothing.

Again Seth pointed to the screen. He had typed one word:

Scared.

He erased it before his mother walked back to pick up her purse. She bent to kiss his cheek. "I'm going to get a cup of coffee. I'll come back later."

When she had left, Lefebvre sat quietly beside Seth. Seth tapped him on the hand and wrote: Sorry. Selfish of me. Ashamed.

"Don't be. I'm scared, too."

When will you be back?

"I don't think I'll go after all," Lefebvre said. "Not just yet."

Lefebvre decided to call Matt and tell him that he would wait until Monday to fly out there. By then, Seth would probably feel a little more at ease and the guard on his room would be heavier. Matt wouldn't be happy, but he couldn't disappoint Seth. He would at least take care of one of Matt's requests—he would stop by the lab and take another look at the bloody shoes that had been found on the *Cygnet*. Matt wanted to know if the shoes looked new or worn.

"When your mother comes back, I'm going to go over to my office for a few minutes," Lefebvre said. "But I won't be gone long—I'll hurry back, and I'll stay here with you this evening."

When he saw Seth's look of relief, he said, "I'm sorry—I should have stayed with you last night, too."

You can't be here all the time.

"No, but I could have stayed here last night. Will you be okay until I get back?"

Yes.

But he seemed anxious. Lefebvre began talking to him about the Cessna and asked him if he thought he might like to learn to fly when he was feeling better. Seth said yes and began asking him questions about the requirements for a pilot's license.

With his typical perceptiveness, Seth wrote: You miss flying. Haven't done it because I've kept you grounded here with me.

"I do what I like," Lefebvre said. "I stayed here because I like spending time with you—you know that's true. I'll get to fly again soon enough."

Take me with you someday?

"As soon as you are well enough to leave here, you can be certain I'll take you up."

And Elena?

"Are you playing matchmaker again?"

Seth smiled at him.

"Yes, Elena, too. If I can convince her to come along."

She'll like it.

Tory returned then, her makeup repaired, her manner reserved. Lefebvre took his leave.

It was dark by the time he parked in the underground lot at department headquarters. He sat in the car for a moment, hesitant to go inside. The building had changed, he thought. Yesterday, it was a place where he felt completely at home. Today, it was an enemy's lair.

"You are being foolish," he told himself. "Almost everyone in there is your ally, not your enemy."

But that, he knew, was also foolish.

He looked about him but saw no one. Still, by the time he reached the property room, his nerves were stretched taut.

The evidence technician smiled as she handed the sign-out sheet to him. He had just finished signing his name when he heard her say, "Back already?"

"Yes," he said, trying for a smile—then paused when he saw his own name already on the sheet—supposedly signing for the Randolph case evidence at 6:01 P.M.

An excellent forgery of his signature.

The tech turned away from him to help an officer who was checking in evidence from a drug bust. With cold fingers, Lefebvre lifted the lid of the box. It was empty except for one item—a wristwatch.

He shut the lid and managed to say to the tech, "Not your usual night, is it?"

"No," she said absently, still concentrating on the incoming evidence. "This is Bill's shift, but he had to go home." She glanced over at him. "He was probably looking kind of green around the gills when you saw him."

Lefebvre didn't answer.

"You're not looking so great yourself," she added. "Must be something going around."

"Must be." He walked away without taking the box.

"Hey!" she called. "Don't you want—"

"Changed my mind," he said, hurrying out of the building.

He held down the urge to race through traffic and drove back to the hospital at a sedate pace, not wanting to attract police attention to his car.

He tried to seem casual as he walked through the hospital lobby, cautiously looking around him, wondering how long it would be before a call was made to Internal Affairs saying he had stolen the evidence in the Randolph case.

The guard on Seth's room was away from his post, talking to the nurses at the nurses' station. When he saw Lefebvre, his eyes widened, and for a moment Lefebvre thought he might be placed under arrest by this incompetent jerk. But the guard merely took up his place at the door of the room, avoiding eye contact with Lefebvre.

Lefebvre was surprised to find the room almost completely in darkness— only the soft glow of Seth's computer screen provided light. By it, he could see the boy's sleeping face.

He sat next to the bed, holding his head in his hands. He thought of paging Elena, but if IAD learned of it, she would fall under suspicion, too. He might have only a few more minutes of freedom; he could not just sit here. Keep moving, he told himself.

"Seth?"

The young man didn't stir.

"Seth?" he said, a little louder.

When there was still no response, he reached to gently waken him.

The boy's skin felt cool beneath Lefebvre's hand. No, not cool. Cold.

"Seth!" He felt for a pulse. Seth had none—his own was racing.

"No," he murmured, disbelieving. "No . . ." Panicking, he looked for the call button—but suddenly remembered the forged signature, the stolen evidence.

What did that matter if Seth could be helped? he asked himself angrily. Nothing else mattered! He must get help, call a doctor—

But he knew he was too late. His experience with death was too thorough to allow him to believe that anything could be done for Seth. Still, he fumbled for the control button on the bed that turned on the lights and pressed it. In their stark brightness, his hope faltered. With a trembling hand, he raised the lids of Seth's eyes. There was no pupil response to the light.

"Seth," he said again, but now it was a sound of loss. He heard himself make a low, animal cry, and for a time was aware of nothing other than the boy lying still and cold and alone in the bed, and the crushing weight of his failure to protect him.

"Forgive me," he said again and again. "Forgive me."

He gradually became aware that he was weeping and grew angry with himself for it. Wiping his face, he forced himself to observe the room as a professional. The small harness device used to operate the computer had been removed from Seth's arm. The call button for the nurse was on the floor beneath the bed. Near it, he found a pillow—he glanced at the other bed and saw that the pillow had been taken from it. The pillow had been torn near the center—perhaps bitten. He also saw bruising on Seth's arms and marks near his nose and mouth.

He felt a white-hot anger burn through him, a desire for vengeance unlike any he had ever known before.

He heard voices in the hall. He hurriedly turned off the lights and moved to the closed door. The so-called guard was chatting with a nurse. "Need some help with that?" he heard the guard say to her. There was the scrape of the guard's chair as he stood, the sound of his footsteps moving away.

Lefebvre quietly moved out of the room and out to the patio door. He used it to escape down the stairwell, just as the killer had escaped him the night before. Sickened that he had not caught him then, he made his way to the car.

He looked back toward the window of Seth's room, saw it was still darkened, and with a sense of emptiness unlike any he had ever known, he drove away.

9

He stared at the pencil lead, placed it on the page, and then lifted it again. How to rate today's performance?

At times, he had achieved nothing less than an eight. At others, he barely merited a one. Those hours, for example, when he had lost track of Lefebvre. Terrible, though hardly his fault.

He decided that he would need to patiently await the final outcome before giving himself a rating. Waiting patiently would add points; jumping to conclusions would lower his score.

He never doubted the importance and necessity of his work, but that did not mean that he was pleased with every aspect of it or even took joy in it. He was quite critical of himself. Knowing that his special calling would always be a lonely business, he not only had to keep his triumphs to himself, but there was no one with whom he could share his disappointments.

In truth, the entire Dane episode had been a disappointment. Had his plans succeeded as intended, a great deal of trouble would have been spared. God was indeed in the details—one small element out of place could ruin the most elaborate plans.

The watch. If the boy had fought instead of hiding on the yacht, he would have been dead long before he heard the watch. If he had not recognized the sound of the watch yesterday afternoon, he would have been allowed to live. And Lefebvre! Such a brilliant career, and it would end in shame. Because of a watch.

He shook his head and sighed deeply, genuinely sad about Lefebvre.

To console himself, he carefully turned to the first page of the notebook and began reading.

As always, it cheered him.

10

Lefebvre flew above the dense fog that blanketed the mountains on that moonless summer night. Solo in the Cessna, with a cloud carpet below, a canopy of starlight above — on another night he would have been calmed by the view, lulled by the droning of the engine. Not tonight.

Tonight he was distracted from the night sky by memories of Seth, lying cold and still in the hospital bed. He had thought himself accustomed to seeing the dead, until he had seen the body of the young man.

Not a young man, really. Not yet. Not ever.

The boy, he amended. The boy who had trusted him.

Against such thoughts, the drone of the plane's engine became a drill, burrowing into his mind, looking for secrets. He needed to get away from talk and noise and pursuers.

The engine coughed and caught, coughed and caught — once, twice, three times. And then, with a horrifying suddenness, the drone was gone.

Without another cough or sputter or miss, the Cessna's engine died.

At first, he was disbelieving. He was an experienced pilot. This couldn't be happening to him. Not tonight. Not tonight of all nights.

He feathered the propeller to reduce drag on the plane, tried to restart the engine. Nothing. Tried switching fuel tanks. Nothing.

What was wrong?

Had he missed some problem in preflight? Tonight he had found some comfort in the rituals of preflight, rituals he performed religiously. But he could not deny that he had been upset, distracted. He kept seeing the boy, dead—kept wondering if the others had found the body yet and how much lead time he would have before they came looking for him. Wondering if Elena would be safe, would be wise enough to keep her distance from him.

Even in that anxious state, though, he had made sure he had enough fuel to reach his destination. He had topped off the Cessna's tanks himself.

He checked the gauges—he still had plenty of fuel. Then what the hell was wrong?

He went through the Cessna's checklist, item by item, fighting the urge to panic. Nothing worked.

He tried to restart again. No response.

Nothing made sense! Helplessly, he watched the altimeter fall.

No, he pleaded. No! Please, God, not now! Not now!

The plane was losing altitude, dropping into the clouds, the darkness below. He did not need lights to know what lay waiting for him.

Trees. Tall pines and unforgiving rocky canyons—mountain slopes.

Don't come in fast, he told himself. He slowed the plane to a stall. The fog beaded into water on the windows, enveloped him in white silent darkness.

His mouth went dry. He knew a moment of nearly unbearable loneliness, then calm, as his thoughts returned to Elena and the boy.

The young man, he amended.

The left wing went first—wrenched off by a pine tree. Once again—though briefly—Lefebvre's world filled with noise.

TWO

Ten Years Later

1

"It's in our jurisdiction," the sheriff's deputy said as he led the way to the wreckage. "I guess we had to give it to you because the deceased is a Las Piernas police officer."

Frank Harriman didn't respond. Nor did Ben Sheridan. However excited this green kid was to be associated with a crash investigation, they both knew that the San Bernardino Sheriff's Department homicide detective who had brought them here was more than happy to have this case off his hands. Cliff Garrett was currently waiting in his air-conditioned car at the top of the steep incline they had just hiked down.

As they made their way in the sticky afternoon heat, the young deputy had taken one horrified look at the prosthesis on the lower half of Ben's left leg and started up to meet them. He had reached for Ben's elbow, and Ben had told him in no uncertain terms that if he touched him, he'd find out just how well a one-legged man could do in an ass-kicking contest.

Frank had thought Ben was a little hard on the kid. Fifteen minutes later, he wished he had volunteered to referee.

"Jesus, what is that thing?" the deputy had asked, staring at the prosthesis. "It looks like a shock absorber getting it on with the end of a ski or something."

"Does it?" Ben asked.

"Yes, sir, it sure does."

Ben turned to Frank and said, "Garrett gave you a radio?"

Frank nodded.

"Call him and tell him there was no one here to lead us to the Cessna."

"Oh, no!" the kid said. "That's why I'm here. That's my job."

"Then do it," Ben snapped.

The deputy didn't seemed fazed by this; he shrugged and started down an uneven path. Two seconds later, he turned and said, "You going to be able to—"

"Don't ask him that," Frank warned.

"I used to go surfing in Las Piernas," he said as they finally reached the shade.

When Frank said nothing, he added, "You probably don't think a guy from the Inland Empire would know much about surfing, but I haven't lived here all my life."

"A rambling man," Ben muttered.

"Exactly," he said. "I've lived all over Southern California. Even San Diego." He turned to Frank and asked, "You're a homicide detective in Las Piernas?"

"Yes," Frank answered, slapping at a mosquito, wondering why the shade wasn't offering more relief from the heat.

"Really? You're a detective?"

"Really. You want to call Detective Garrett from your department and verify it?"

"No, sir, it's just—" Their guide stopped, taking a moment to look him up and down. "They let you—you know, wear hiking clothes on the job down there?"

"No."

"But you can wear them when you're not in your own jurisdiction?"

"No. Are you with the reserves?"

"Yes, sir, how'd you know?"

"In Las Piernas, that's on the test for detectives. Identification of Reserve Officers."

Deputy Whatever continued on as he mulled this over, giving them a little peace. A few minutes later, though, he let loose with a loud and pungent fart.

"For Christ's sakes!" Ben said angrily.

"Sorry." The kid grinned. "No charge for the bug repellent."

Eventually, they could hear other voices up ahead.

"Deputy," Frank said then, "I just realized that I am without one of the authorization forms I'll need for this investigation to be taken over by Las Piernas. It's vital that I have it. We can find the site from here—but would you please return to Detective Garrett and tell him that I need a Universal Transfer of Responsibility Form Eighty-five-dash-seven?"

"I don't know if I should—"

"Maybe I should go," said Ben. "I don't know if I'll be able to make it back here on my bad leg, but—"

"Don't even think of it!" The deputy repeated the form number and took off.

"Universal Transfer of Responsibility Form?" Ben asked as soon as the deputy was out of earshot.

"I thought the 'Eighty-five-dash-seven' was a nice touch, myself. Which one is your bad leg?"

Ben smiled.

Frank called Garrett on the radio and warned him that the deputy was on his way. "You'd better take a long time finding that form, Cliff," he said, "or I may require lots of cooperation from a certain San Bernardino homicide detective. You want to hike down here again to help?"

Cliff laughed and asked how the mosquitoes were, then agreed to keep the deputy busy.

They had no trouble finding the others; they followed the sound of their voices until they saw the coroner's assistant, several sheriff's deputies, and a tall, dark-haired woman in lightweight coveralls standing in a small clearing. Frank recognized the woman—they had worked together on a previous case. Was that the real reason Carlson had sent him out here?

"Hello, Mayumi," he said to her. "How's life with the NTSB?"

She turned and smiled. "Frank! Good to see you again." She quickly sobered and said, "Sorry it has to be under these circumstances."

"Thanks, but I never knew him, so—"

"Of course not," she said.

This quick reassurance puzzled him. He glanced at the other men. They seemed a little tense. What was going on?

"You weren't in the department in Las Piernas ten years ago, were you?" Mayumi was saying.

"No, I was still working in Bakersfield then," he said, and saw the others visibly relax. What the hell was that all about?

"Where's the wreckage?" Ben asked.

"Not far. I'm Mayumi Iwata," she said, extending a hand. "I'm with the National Transportation Safety Board."

"Forgive me for not introducing you, Mayumi," Frank said. "This is Dr. Ben Sheridan. Ben's a forensic anthropologist. He'll be doing the work on recovering and identifying the remains."

"Oh, yes, the coroner's office told us you would be coming here with Frank." She introduced them to the coroner's assistant and the others. One of the older deputies, a man named Wilson, looked back in the direction of the road and asked, "Where's the chatterbox?"

Frank and Ben exchanged a look.

"Frank sent him on an important errand," Ben said.

Wilson laughed. "You have our undying gratitude." He gave them the sign-in sheet for the scene, noting the time of their arrival, then reached into a canvas bag and brought out some gloves. "You'll need these. There's quite a bit of poison oak down there."

"I begin to see why Cliff was so happy to hand this one off," Frank said with a laugh, but noticed that Wilson suddenly seemed uneasy. Probably one of Cliff's friends. Frank decided to stick to business. "Who was first on the scene?"

"I was," Wilson said. "A couple hikers with a dog wandered through here. We don't get many through this ravine, because most of the time the little creek that runs through here is dry. I don't think they would have seen the wreckage if it hadn't been for the dog."

"Did the dog disturb the remains?" Ben asked.

"No, and the hikers didn't either. The dog kind of scratched at the door of the plane. Hikers called him back, and I guess they—well, they freaked out when they realized what it was and came running out of here. We almost couldn't find it again. Hadn't been for the dog, I don't know if we would have. We took statements from them and let them go on home— didn't realize what a mess . . ." His voice trailed off, and he colored slightly. "Well, let's take you on over there."

Again, Frank felt as if the others were waiting for him to react to something, that there was more going on here than the little Carlson had told him.

He mentally reviewed the brief, unpleasant phone conversation he'd had with his lieutenant. Carlson had paged him just as he had settled into a deck chair at his cabin, cold beer in hand. Frank had objected to being called on a day off; Carlson told him he didn't care who was up next on the roster, Frank was only a few minutes away from the scene. Besides, the lieutenant told him, Lefebvre, the presumed victim of the crash, had not only been a Las Piernas homicide detective, he had been involved in one of the old cases he had just assigned to Frank. The Randolph cases.

"What Randolph cases? I don't have any Randolph cases."

"You do now. Discuss this with no one. You and Sheridan have a very simple task today. Just let me know what you find in a careful search of whatever's left of that plane." He had added that Cliff Garrett would be by to drive them to the scene, then hung up.

Lefebvre's name had seemed vaguely familiar to Frank. He supposed that someone who had worked with Lefebvre when he was with the department must have mentioned him, but he could not remember who might have done so or what had been said.

They picked up a couple of duffel bags, including one with supplies for Ben—courtesy of the San Bernardino Coroner's Office—and began following Wilson.

"San Bernardino called us right away," Mayumi said as they walked. "As you know, Frank, if a plane is missing, we start a file at that time."

"When you say 'missing'—that might not be known immediately, right? The pilots of these small planes don't always file flight plans, do they?"

"No. Eventually, though, family members or friends will report that a pilot didn't return home on time or didn't reach a planned destination. But you're right, flight plans aren't always required, and obviously one wasn't filed in this case—"

Obviously? But before Frank could ask about that, Wilson said, "The file you start—is this data about the plane or the pilot?"

"Both," Mayumi answered. "The plane's registration number, manufacturer, model, and age are included, along with information about the pilot's health, experience, drug or alcohol consumption, and possible state of mind. So are any flight plans, communications with control towers, checks on the weather conditions that day, and other data. When any wreckage is found, the registration number is checked against the list of missing planes—its file can be matched very quickly, especially if the plane is from the local area."

"And this one was on your local list," Ben said.

"Yes. When we checked this registration number against our records, we found that ten years ago, this plane went missing—and that it was owned and piloted by Detective Philip Lefebvre. That's why we called Las Piernas right away."

They climbed a small rise overlooking a dry gully. What remained of the Cessna lay below, so covered with leaves, pine needles, earth, and vines,

Frank was amazed that the hikers had been able to see what their dog was after. Most of the left wing was broken off; Mayumi told them they had found it about twenty-five yards back. There were little numbered yellow flags on wires scattered in a pattern behind and near the plane; locations where debris had been found or from which measurements had been taken. "Lots of small hardware scattered along here," Mayumi said. "Mostly from the wings and tail." He half listened as she spoke. He was looking at the fuselage. He wasn't thinking about small hardware.

He had brought a notebook with him, and he took it out now. He began making crude sketches, noting the position of the plane. He could tell that the scene had already been mapped and measured by the sheriff's department and Mayumi. He didn't care; he started sketching because the process helped him think.

He thought about Lefebvre and wondered who he had been and what those last few moments of life had been like for him. Peaceful or terrifying?

This is an NTSB case, he told himself. If a Las Piernas cop hadn't been at the controls, his department never would have been called in. Frank might not have been the one to take that call if he hadn't been up here — or maybe he was sent because he was with Ben. Given the age of the remains, a forensic anthropologist was needed, so Ben might have been called by the San Bernardino coroner anyway.

Mostly, though, the investigation would be Mayumi's problem — figuring out what had happened, what had caused this crash. He knew that most of these light plane crashes were caused by inexperience, overconfidence, or other pilot error. What had been Lefebvre's error?

The plane had landed on its belly and lay slightly askew. The right wing was buckled back, the right side of the cockpit caved in, the nose buried. The fuselage had taken a beating, but even so, it was relatively intact. Although it was dented and scraped, Frank saw no large tears or holes. There were stains where muddy water had reached the lowest portions of the wreckage.

He moved closer to the plane. Some of the covering vines had been cut away and a portion of a window cleaned. Mayumi assured him that they had both videotaped and photographed the scene before disturbing it. Frank cautiously approached the window and peered in.

He saw the body, or what remained of it, immediately. Directly in front of him, it sat at the controls. A seat belt was strapped across the headless form. One side of a bright blue nylon jacket was stained with large brownish-black patches of dried blood. Here and there, the jagged edges of broken ribs pierced the jacket, corresponding roughly to the impact from the right. The radius and ulna of one arm protruded from a sleeve; dark dried sinew still covered them. He did not see hand bones or a skull.

Once they knew remains were present, Mayumi was saying, they had called the coroner. Her voice seemed separated from what lay before him, as if she were the narrator of a documentary film.

With the help of Wilson and one of the other deputies, Frank pried the cockpit door open. A dry, musty smell greeted him. Ben stepped forward and shone a flashlight over the interior. Spiderwebs were everywhere. The material of Lefebvre's pants had not fared as well as the jacket; mummified leg bones stuck out of a pair of boots.

"Luckily, it seems to have stayed fairly dry in here," Ben said. "And I don't see many signs of scavenger activity. No entry point large enough for most of them. Insects, spiders, mice . . . maybe a wood rat . . . that seems to be about it. We may want to look for a wood rat's nest. Wish I had Bingle up here with me."

"Bingle?" Wilson asked.

"Ben is also a cadaver dog handler," Frank said. "Bingle is one of his dogs. He might be able to find bones carried off by other animals."

"There has been disarticulation as the ligaments have decomposed, of course," Ben said, absorbed in his study of the remains.

Wilson peered in, stepped back with a little shudder. "What I can't figure out is, what tore his head off?"

"He wasn't decapitated," Ben said absently. "Nothing's at the right level to act as a guillotine." He slowly moved the flashlight beam across the floor. He paused as it lit a mandible—the horseshoe of lower teeth jutting up into space—then moved on. "There."

A skull stared back at them. Gauzy webs filled the eye sockets, giving the appearance of pale eyelids. A long-legged brown spider, annoyed by the light, scurried out of the nasal passage.

"The skull wasn't taken off," Ben said. "It fell off after the neck muscles decomposed. Skulls only stay on upright skeletons on television."

Ben kept moving the light, and they saw a dust-covered nylon bag stowed toward the back of the cabin. The spiders had been at work there, too. The bag was draped in cobwebs.

"Think anyone has been in here since the crash?" Wilson asked.

"Doesn't look like it," Frank said.

"So, you can see that we didn't open this up before you got here, right?" Wilson asked.

"What do you mean?" Frank asked, looking at him sharply.

Wilson turned red again. "I mean, you can see all the dust and every-thing—you can tell we didn't go inside, right?"

"What are you getting at?" Frank asked.

"I'm just wondering—you know—about the money."

"What money?"

"The money Lefebvre was paid for killing that witness. You know, the kid."

2

Wilson's remark led to questions, and then Frank remembered long-ago talk of the case, but not from Las Piernas. The story of a cop who had taken a bribe to kill a witness—and then supposedly disappeared—had briefly made headlines and television news in Bakersfield. But Frank had been a patrol-man then, pulling long shifts in a department that was dealing with its own problems. In those days, he had thought of Las Piernas as nothing more than an extension of L.A., a place where any weird-assed thing could hap-pen, and so he had paid little attention to the stories about Lefebvre.

No one at the scene was able—or willing—to tell him much. Mayumi didn't have the complete NTSB file yet, but promised to send a copy to Frank as soon as she got back to her office in Gardena. Even Cliff Garrett claimed to only vaguely remember the case—which had taken place "downhill" ten years ago. "Bad news for the Las Piernas Police Depart-ment," Cliff said, "but not our case. I had my own cases to worry about then, just as I do now." Frank had said as much to himself when he remem-bered mention of the case, but he sensed that Cliff knew more and was sim-ply dodging involvement.

Over the next few hours, Frank never heard more than a half-told tale that made little sense to him. Lefebvre, they said, had been a homicide de-tective in Las Piernas. He was supposedly paid a large sum (recollections varied on this point, the amounts ranging from ten thousand to two million dollars) to steal evidence and kill a witness—a teenager. He had killed the witness while the kid was in his hospital bed, supposedly under the watchful eye of the Las Piernas police. "Guess the wrong officer was watching him," Cliff said. Lefebvre fled Las Piernas in his Cessna that night and hadn't been heard from since. Until today, everyone thought he was drinking piña coladas on some distant beach, laughing at Las Piernas's failure to catch him.

No large sums of money were found hidden in the wreckage of Lefebvre's plane, and nothing that resembled stolen evidence was discovered. Carefully working their way through the wreckage—all the while taking photographs, making notes—Frank and the other investigators found little to go on. Among Lefebvre's effects were his pilot's logbooks, a wallet, a small notebook, a cheap ballpoint pen, a set of keys, and a badge holder with his police ID. Most of these items were in a zippered side pocket in the jacket. In an inside pocket, near where the heart had been, Frank found a business card–size piece of paper, too blackened by bloodstains to be read. He bagged it and marked it for the lab's documents examiner.

No duffel bags full of cash. No luggage. Not even so much as a change of clothes or a toothbrush. The nylon bag held nothing but a set of rusting tools.

Mayumi confirmed that the last entry in the flight log was dated June 22, the night Lefebvre made his escape from Las Piernas ten years ago. There were no remarks of note, except that it showed that Lefebvre had filled the tanks before taking off.

"So it seems unlikely that he ran out of fuel," she said.

"Any ideas on what caused the crash?"

She smiled. "Far too early to say."

He looked through the wallet. It held a driver's license, two charge cards, and forty-three dollars. There were also two credit card receipts. One was dated June 21—the day before Lefebvre had left Las Piernas—from a restaurant called the Prop Room. The total bill was high enough to make Frank wonder if the restaurant was pricey or if Lefebvre had met with someone else the night before he disappeared.

The other receipt was dated June 22, from Las Piernas Aviation Services, for fuel for the plane.

He showed the fuel receipt to Mayumi.

"Hmm. That matches what he wrote in the log. Unless he developed a fuel leak, he had more than enough to make it over these mountains."

Frank studied the photos on the license and the ID. Lefebvre stared back at the camera with dark eyes, his expression solemn and intense. His hair was dark and cut short. His cheekbones were high, the face slender. The nose was slightly crooked. A hard face, Frank thought. According to the driver's license, ten years ago Lefebvre would have been forty-two. It showed his height as 6'1", his weight 170. Frank knew that weight and stature figures on licenses were notoriously incorrect—men made themselves taller, women, lighter—and that Ben would need time to measure and examine the bones to determine the dead man's probable age and stature. He glanced between the photos and the skull, tried to match the skull with the face in the photos. He couldn't. He handed them to Ben.

"Too bad he didn't smile in the photos," Ben said. "The skull has a chipped front tooth."

"Maybe that happened when it fell off his neck and rolled across the floor."

"No, the chip looks antemortem. Filed smooth by a dentist at one time." He pointed to a crack on the right side of the cranium. "But this fracture is perimortem, I think—it shows no healing and was probably a result of the impact of the crash."

With gloved hands, Frank gently turned to the last few pages of the notebook. The pages were a little moldy, but intact and legible. They were filled with neatly penned notes, apparently regarding several cases. There were phone numbers, dates, and other numbers that appeared to be house or apartment numbers. Nothing that looked like the combination to a safe with two million bucks in it, Frank thought, but you never knew. He went through the wallet more carefully, found nothing.

The air inside the plane was hot and close. Frank moved outside the wreckage, found a large, flat rock in the shade, and sat thinking while Mayumi continued examining the crash site and Ben and the coroner's assistant finished inventorying and removing the remains. He tried using his cell phone to call Carlson, but couldn't get a signal in the ravine.

When they were on their way back, he tried again. The call was routed to the Wheeze—Louise Oswald, division secretary. Frank suppressed a sigh of impatience when her voice came on the line. The Wheeze never had to search hard for a sense of her own importance.

She told him that the lieutenant was in a meeting, but would speak to him when he returned. "He asked me to tell you," she said, lowering her voice, "not to discuss this case with anyone—repeat, *anyone*—until then."

"In that case . . ." he said, and disconnected. He knew she would undoubtedly make him pay for that later, but it gave him some small satisfaction on a day that was damned short of it.

By the time he took Ben home and drove to headquarters, it was after nine
that evening. Frank looked up at the building that housed the Las Piernas
Police Department, sought a particular window, and found it. The light was
on in Carlson's office.

"That better be you and not the cleaning lady, you asshole," he muttered,
and pulled into the parking garage.

He first stopped by the property room to turn in the box of Lefebvre's effects he had signed for at the scene and completed a set of chain of custody
forms.

Then he went upstairs to Homicide. The Homicide Division was an open
room with a dozen battered desks pushed up close to one another. Computers competed for space with aging office equipment. The walls were beige, or
what had once been beige. Paint was low on the city budget priorities. A wide
hallway led to interrogation rooms. Four enclosed offices stood along the wall
opposite the hallway door. The lights were on in one of the offices.

Frank nodded a greeting to a couple of detectives who were talking to a
crying middle-aged woman. Her face was heavily swollen on one side. He
did not pause near them, but went straight to Carlson's office. He entered
without knocking, shutting the door behind him.

Carlson, startled, pushed away from his desk. His chair rolled back with
the sudden movement—so far back, he was more than an arm's length from
the desk. He had to use his feet to scoot the chair back into place.

"Sit down, Frank," he said, red-faced.

"No thanks," Frank said quietly.

Carlson was uneasy. He had once seen Frank Harriman knock a man out
cold—without ever raising his voice before throwing the punch. And there
were other reasons he sometimes questioned Frank's stability.

"Sit down, Detective Harriman—please," Carlson said.

Frank knew that Carlson wasn't one of those people who found it hard to
say "please"—he just found it hard to mean it. Frank let him sweat it for a
moment before he took a chair. "I don't like being set up," he said.

"You weren't—"

"I don't like being set up under any circumstances, but walking into that situation less informed than San Bernardino *and* the NTSB—hell, less informed than a reserve officer—"

"Yes, well, I'm sorry, that couldn't be helped."

Frank didn't bother to hide his disbelief. "There was no reason to keep me in the dark. And Ben Sheridan should have been informed—"

"Never mind Sheridan. Here . . ." He opened a desk drawer, pulled out a thick stack of files, and held it out. Frank didn't move. Carlson set the stack down on the desk. "You'll have to take them eventually. I'm assigning Lefebvre's case to you."

"That looks like more than one case file to me."

"As I told you earlier today, you have the Randolph cases, too. We believe they are all related."

Frank still didn't move to take them. "Before today, Lefebvre's name was nearly meaningless to me. I vaguely recalled hearing a news story about him years ago. Don't you think it would have been better to let me know that this was not only high profile, but also that someone as notorious as Whitey Dane had a connection to the case?"

Carlson shrugged. "So the killer is a man we've been after for a long time. If Lefebvre hadn't murdered Seth Randolph and stolen the evidence against Dane, you might not have remembered Dane's name either. He would have been locked away years ago. As a matter of fact—"

"As a matter of fact, you decided to send me to that scene without breathing a word about any of this. For God's sake, why not send someone who knew the background on the case? I know you saved a little mileage on a pool car, but—"

"I didn't decide to send you just because you were nearest the scene!"

Frank watched as Carlson struggled to control his temper. After a moment, Carlson said, "Even if you had been in Las Piernas, you're the one I would have sent up to the mountains precisely because you are one of the only detectives in Homicide who has been with this department less than ten years. I needed at least one person who would be able to approach that wreckage without a lot of preconceived notions about the pilot of that plane."

"This is ridiculous. The other detectives in this department can be trusted to be professional."

"Where Lefebvre is concerned, no. Not anyone who was around here then. Lefebvre's name is universally despised in this department—and the sooner you understand that, the sooner you'll see why you must be the one to take the case. None of the others could have viewed the scene objectively—including Pete Baird."

"With or without Pete, I deserved to know what I was walking into."

Carlson shifted in his chair, making sure he had a firm grip on the desk before doing so. "Yes," he said, "in retrospect, I concede that's true. At the time—perhaps I allowed my own dislike of Lefebvre to influence my response to the situation." He sighed. "To tell you the truth, I would have been happy if Lefebvre stayed missing. Now this will all be raked up again." A sudden suspicion came to him. "You haven't discussed this with your damned wife, have you?"

Frank leaned forward just slightly. Carlson leaned back. He kept his grip on the desk.

"I don't think I could have possibly heard you correctly."

Carlson looked down at his desk again. "I want to reiterate that this is not to be discussed with the press."

"Who around here has ever leaked anything to the press?"

Carlson colored. Not so long ago, he had received a formal reprimand for discussing a sensitive investigation with the *Express*. He had evidently counted on the fact that Frank's marriage to a reporter would always make him the first person the department suspected of leaking stories to the paper. Fortunately for Frank, Carlson's efforts to divert suspicion for the leak had backfired.

Carlson cleared his throat. "I'm only saying that I dread what this department will inevitably be put through as a result of reopening old wounds. I gather you understand my concerns?"

"I've got a few of my own. Once everybody up there realized I didn't know jack shit about my own case, they didn't have much to say. What little I heard from them doesn't make sense, and now—"

"The basics are simple. We believe Lefebvre stole evidence and killed a teenager who was a witness in a capital case. Word on the street was that he was paid handsomely to ruin the case—half a million dollars."

"Half a million, huh? Nice to have an official figure."

"You found it?" Carlson said eagerly.

"Only if he spent all but forty-three bucks of it gassing up the plane."

Carlson looked ludicrously crestfallen. "What do you mean?"

"I mean either Lefebvre stashed it somewhere, had a confederate, or never had it in the first place. From what I saw today, I'd say he never had it."

"Perhaps it was stolen from the plane—"

"Doesn't seem likely." Frank described the scene.

Carlson sat brooding. He began making a low, tuneless humming noise, a sound he made whenever he was inwardly debating something. He was unaware that his coworkers referred to this as "Carlson's thinking noise." The office joke was that it would have driven everyone crazy if he'd made it more often.

"Cliff Garrett said that Lefebvre was a department hotshot," Frank said by way of interrupting the humming.

"He was a fine detective," Carlson agreed. "One of the best."

"A friend of yours?"

"Don't be ridiculous. I was in uniform then. Not very likely I'd be fraternizing with a detective." He shifted in his chair—undoubtedly he had suddenly recalled that Frank often socialized with uniformed officers.

Harriman was silent, studying him. Carlson had never spent much time on the street, and Frank suspected he hadn't been very useful during the time he was in uniform. Hell, he wasn't very useful now. "So you didn't know him at all?"

"He was a loner," Carlson said, shrugging. "Afterward, we realized how much he had really held himself apart from others in the department."

"So he had enemies—even before the kid's death?"

"Not really. He was someone we were proud of," Carlson said. "If you want to know why, take a look at his record." He smiled smugly. "In fact, your wife seemed to be rather fond of him."

"Is there something you'd like to come right out and say?"

"No, not at all," Carlson said, quickly losing the smile. "She was a crime reporter then, and naturally she wrote about him. A lot. I'm sure she was devastated when you told her he was dead."

"I haven't told her."

"I suppose Louise conveyed my level of concern about the sensitive—"

"Setting aside your dire warnings about discussing the case, I haven't had the chance to talk to Irene today. She's up in Sacramento, covering a political story. She won't be home until tomorrow. But you were talking about Lefebvre—at least, I think that's who you were talking about."

Carlson went back to making his thinking noise, then abruptly said, "You don't believe Lefebvre ever had the money. Why not?"

"He wasn't a stupid man, right?"

"Not at all."

"So, being a cop, he'd know you could trace his movements if he used his credit cards, right?"

"Certainly."

"And so this man who supposedly has a half a million in cash, who knows you can put a trace on his credit cards, buys gas for a plane on one and only pulls forty-three bucks out to cover his other expenses during his great escape?"

"But if he hid the cash in Las Piernas—"

"He's coming back here, where his face has already been on television and all over the newspapers?"

"No, I suppose not."

"There's no sign that he stopped off anywhere between here and that mountainside, right?"

"Right," Carlson said. "We checked every possible landing strip in the local area. But we don't really know when that airplane crashed, do we?"

"Not definitely, but the logbook and other indicators say it was the night he left town. No one saw him after that?"

Carlson shook his head.

"Even if he was dumb enough not to take all of the money with him," Frank said, "he would have carried a couple hundred, don't you think? How long can a man hide out on forty-three bucks? What's he planning to do, write a book called *How to Lie Low on Pennies a Day*?"

"You mentioned the possibility of a confederate."

"Same argument. Why does he take off with only forty-three dollars?"

"Perhaps he anticipated we would catch up with him, thought he might be questioned, and decided that this would make him appear to be innocent."

Frank shrugged. "Even two hundred out of this rumored half-million would have looked innocent."

Carlson had been frowning, but now a slow smile came over his face.

"What?" said Frank, mistrusting any of Carlson's smiles.

"Read the files. The ones for Lefebvre and the Randolphs."

"Lieutenant, just because—listen, he could have asked for a wire transfer to a foreign bank account. I'm just saying he didn't have it with him, that's all. After this beginning, I don't think— I'm requesting that you put someone else on this case."

"Your request is denied."

"Shouldn't this go to IAD?"

"We have discussed this with them. For the time being, this will proceed as a homicide investigation. Unfortunately, the two members of IAD who originally investigated the case have retired—and one is deceased."

"Natural causes?"

"Yes," Carlson said, narrowing his gaze. He apparently decided that Frank was not being flippant and continued. "Because all the current IAD investigators were involved in the Dane case, they will be assigning someone new to IAD to handle their part of the investigation—someone like yourself, who was not with the department at the time. Until then, you are in charge of investigating Detective Lefebvre's death. Naturally, if you discover evidence implicating him—or any other member of this department—in wrongdoing, we will make that available to IAD."

Carlson lifted the stack of files and held them out again. "Read these. If you still want someone else to take over the case—you may talk to Captain Bredloe on Monday morning with my blessing."

"I may talk to him on Monday morning with or without it." Frank took the files and walked out. He noticed that the other detectives had left. He sat down at his desk and locked the files away without looking at them, knowing Carlson was watching him.

Carlson stepped out of his office, locked it, and marched over to Frank, briefcase at his side, walking with his typical stiff-assed gait. What does this guy do to relax? Frank wondered. He pictured Carlson at home, practicing drills in the living room while his CD player blasted *The Complete Works of John Philip Sousa.*

"I don't want to be accused of letting you walk into another situation without fair warning," Carlson said. "So there's something you should know before you step into the captain's office on Monday."

Frank stood, forcing Carlson to look up at him. "Oh?"

"There are times, Detective Harriman, when you fail to show me the level of respect you owe a superior."

Frank didn't answer.

"You've felt safe in doing so, because the captain has always been something of a protector of yours, hasn't he? Perhaps you should know, then, that I've already told him you were my choice for the Lefebvre case. He said he was in complete agreement and asked me to give you the other cases as well."

He turned on his heel and walked out.

Frank listened to the fading sound of Carlson's soldierly footsteps on the old linoleum.

He glanced toward Bredloe's office, sat back down at his desk, and unlocked it.

3

He pulled into his driveway, feeling tired and depressed. He never liked working on cases involving the murders of children. Adding a police commissioner and a homicide detective into the mix made this set of cases even less appealing. The cases were all cold; memories would be hazy. Physical evidence was an even bigger problem.

He looked at his watch. Irene had probably already gone to bed in her hotel room in Sacramento. He wished he had called her earlier, from work. He wanted to hear her voice, to listen to her talk of ordinary things.

As he stood on the porch, he was surprised to hear the dogs scratching at the inside of the front door. He had left the two of them in the care of his next-door neighbor; Jack usually kept them at his house whenever Frank and his wife were away. He hadn't told Jack that he would be coming back early; Jack would have expected both Frank and Irene to be gone overnight. He wearily wondered what sort of havoc the mutts might have wreaked in the house while he was gone.

But although they greeted him warmly, the two dogs—a shepherd and a Lab mix adopted from the pound—didn't act as if they had been cooped up all day. The cat was nowhere in sight, but that didn't mean he was hiding— Cody had probably staked out a place on the bed. Not so long ago, Frank would have come home to an empty house. He smiled to himself, thinking that these were the least complicated strays Irene had brought into his life.

As he made his way down the hall, he saw that a light was on in the living room. His steps slowed—there was no way in hell he had left that light on.

The dogs passed him, trotting back without a care. He relaxed a little, then followed them.

He saw the cat first—the gray giant blinked at him from the armchair.

Then he saw his wife, asleep on the couch, and felt the tension that had been with him since that afternoon ease a little. He quietly moved closer.

She slept on her side, a strand of her dark, straight hair falling over her face. She wore a short, silky, dark blue kimono—if her eyes had been open, he thought the color might have come close to matching them. The kimono fell about mid-thigh on her long, slender legs. He followed their curve and smiled to himself, seeing that this enticing ensemble was completed by a pair of everyday white cotton socks—a toe peeked out of a hole in the left one.

He moved closer still, until he was next to her. He wondered if he should call her name, so as not to startle her. He stayed silent.

She must have sensed his presence, though, because she opened her eyes and smiled drowsily up at him. "Surprise," she said sleepily.

"Yes," he said, gently brushing the strand of hair away. "When did you get in?"

She turned her face to his palm and kissed his hand. "About nine. Caught a late flight. I was trying to wait up for you."

"How'd you know I'd be home tonight?"

"Ben called. I asked him if he wanted to leave a message, but he said he'd talk to you on Monday."

"Hmm," he said, bending to taste her mouth. She reached up to pull him closer, making the kiss longer, slower. He stroked his hand along the back of her leg, down to her ankle—and took a sock off.

She pulled away and said, "Damn!"

"What's wrong?"

"The socks." She was blushing. "My feet got cold. Real sexy, right?"

He was already pulling the second one off. "I'm the one with too many clothes on."

"You're right," she said, reaching for his belt.

Just after dawn, he awoke with a start from a nightmare in which he was trapped in a small, vine-covered Cessna, unable to get out. Not even Lefebvre had been in such a situation, he knew, but the dream had disturbed him. He tried to fall asleep again, but his thoughts continued to turn to the cases. He watched the room lighten as he debated whether he should try to catch a little more sleep or just get up.

Irene stirred next to him. "Frank? What's wrong?"

"Nothing. Just a dream. Go back to sleep."

But she turned to study his face and asked again, "What's wrong?"

He hesitated, then said, "None of this goes to the newspaper, okay?"

She nodded.

"Do you remember a man named Lefebvre?"

Her eyes widened. "Phil Lefebvre?"

"Yes. Used to work Homicide."

"Yes! Have they found him?"

Again he hesitated, mentally kicking himself for going about this wrong.

"He's dead," she said, reading his silence.

"Yes."

He saw her look of dismay and said, "I'm sorry—I didn't know you were close."

"Not close, really. I don't think anyone was close to Phil—well, I shouldn't say that. He was just—intensely private."

"But you liked him."

"Yes. Better than anybody else I met in the PD in those days." She was quiet for a long moment, then said, "I guess down deep, I hoped he was still alive. What happened to him?"

"His plane crashed in the San Bernardinos."

"I thought they looked for it."

"They did, but the wreckage of small planes that crash in remote areas isn't always easy to see. I was talking to the NTSB investigator about it. She said they estimate that there are over one hundred and fifty missing small aircraft in the Sierra Nevada mountains alone."

"To think that he's been up there all this time . . ."

He felt her shudder and pulled her closer. After a moment, he asked, "Did you cover the story of his disappearance?"

She shook her head against his shoulder. "Not once he was accused—in absentia—of killing Seth Randolph." She looked up at him. "You know about that?"

"I'm learning more. Carlson has assigned the Randolph cases to me."

"Wow. That's—" She mentally calculated. "Ten years ago. Why do you keep getting assigned to cold cases?"

He shrugged. "Everybody in Homicide has been handling old investigations lately. The murder rate is down."

"I know, I know. We've run stories on it. Everyone's arguing over where the credit for that should go."

"I'm just saying that the department has more time to reinvestigate the old ones and we have more tools now—new technologies to help solve them."

"But there are new cases—you and Pete just seem to be getting more than your fair share of the old ones."

"You can probably guess why."

"You're getting them because you've been clearing them—you're good at it."

"We've been lucky with the DNA on a couple of them."

"Save the humility for your speech at the department awards banquet."

He laughed.

Her brows drew together. "You don't get these cases because you're good at them, right? You get them because Carlson wants you to fail."

"If that's true, this time he'll get what he wants. I can't tell you how excited I am to be working a ten-year-old case in which all the physical evidence has been stolen—and apparently ninety percent of the department has a personal ax to grind with the alleged thief."

"Lefebvre didn't steal it."

"I'm not saying he did—but what makes you so sure he didn't?"

"It wasn't like him. Totally unlike him. Except for flying that plane, the guy had no life outside of the department."

"I thought you said you didn't know him that well."

"That's not what I meant. We were friends, and I knew things about him, but I didn't *know him*. No—don't give me that look. What I mean is, Phil was one of those guys you could never really get to know. If you followed him around all day, day after day, you might get some idea of how his mind worked, and know that he was absolutely devoted to his job, or begin to see this—this sort of quiet sense of humor he had. But you would never get a word out of him about his past, or learn if he had the hots for someone, or much of anything else about the man underneath all of that."

He was silent, thinking over what she had said, when she added, "There were two times when he seemed really happy to me and when I actually thought, 'He does think of me as a friend, because he's letting me in on this.' Once, when he took me flying."

"Oh, Christ—you went up in that little Cessna with him?" He thought of the wreckage he had seen—of both pilot and plane—and felt his stomach clench.

She bristled at his tone, then seemed to realize the direction of his thoughts. "I know you've just seen the worst possible results of being in that plane, but, Frank, I swear to you, he was a terrific pilot. He flew in the military and had lots of hours flying solo in that Cessna. He was careful, and safety conscious. He wasn't a hot dog." She paused, then said, "I got to know Phil when I was caring for my dad—when I was first starting to realize that my dad wasn't going to recover from the cancer. I had some really rough days with that, and on one of those, I ran into Phil. It was one of his rare days off. He took one look at me and said, 'Meet me at the airport.' And he took me up. It was great. He was so in love with flying, it was contagious."

"So—do I want to know about the other time you saw him happy?"

She hit him with her pillow. "You're as bad as Vince Adams and those other clowns in Homicide."

"I am one of the other 'clowns,' remember?"

"No, you are not. Vince was always so sure that I had something going on with Phil. He made remarks. It was bullshit, but it pissed me off—you know what I think Vince's problem is?"

"Forget about Vince. Tell me about this other time Lefebvre was happy."

She fell silent, all the fight of the moment before draining away. "The only other time," she said quietly, "was at the hospital. He had waited there for hours while they operated on Seth Randolph. After that, he kept waiting—the doctors weren't sure the kid was going to pull through, but Phil never left his side. At first I thought it was Phil's dedication to the job. You know—if Seth came around, he wanted to be there to ask questions. Anyway, I was there when the doctor told him that he thought Seth was going to live. He was so happy—I was there, Frank, and I saw his face. I saw how he looked when the doctor said that. Lefebvre didn't want that boy to die, and he never could have murdered him. Whoever says that is full of crap."

"Maybe something changed—"

"I was there," she repeated. "I don't know why Seth was so important to him, but if you had seen them together, you'd be as certain as I am that Phil Lefebvre would never have hurt him, let alone kill him."

"Is that the position the Express took?" he asked.

"No. I was pulled off those stories. John Walters was news editor then, and he thought I was too close to Phil to be objective. It made me madder than hell, but around that same time my dad took a turn for the worse—to be honest, I was too busy with him to think of anything else."

"When was the last time you saw Lefebvre?"

"The day he left town." She frowned. "Was that the day his plane crashed?"

"Probably." He watched the play of emotions on her face, then asked, "What aren't you telling me?"

"It will be in the reports you have. I was interviewed—some might say grilled—by the LPPD about my last conversation with him."

He sighed with impatience.

"All right, all right. He seemed upset. But not so agitated that I thought he was about to kill the kid whose life he saved! And I just remembered something else—something I told Vince Adams about a dozen times, and he ignored me. Phil said he would meet me for lunch the next day, which shows he planned to come back right away, right?"

"Yes, but he told other people he was flying out to see Matt Arden for a few days."

"What did Arden say?"

"He said Lefebvre had called him, but just to talk about old times and to ask how he was doing. He said Lefebvre hadn't mentioned any plans to see him."

She fell into a brooding silence. He let it stretch, caught up in his own thoughts. He wondered how well anyone had really known Phil Lefebvre.

"Did you know Elena Rosario?" he asked Irene.

"Who?"

"Narcotics detective who was with Lefebvre the night they found the Randolphs. She quit the department right after Lefebvre went missing."

"No," she said, "not really."

He would have asked more, but the phone rang.

"Harriman," he answered.

"Frank—good to have you back."

"Hello, Pete. How'd you know I was home?"

"Partners have no secrets, right?"

"Who told you—Carlson?"

"That asswipe? You've got to be kidding."

"Then Cliff called you."

"Cliff and I go way back, you know?"

"Terrific."

Pete missed the sarcasm. "So he told me you and Ben found Lefebvre. I hope you pissed on his bones before you packed them up."

Frank was silent.

"Listen," Pete said uneasily, "no need to take that wrong. I want to help you out here. I called to invite you to breakfast. Me and some of the other guys who were around back then thought we'd bring you up to speed."

"It's Sunday. I didn't get yesterday off, and I don't want to spend Sunday working."

"But—"

"Cold cases, Pete. They can wait."

"Well, we're all together here at the Galley."

"All? Who's with you?"

"Vince, Jake, Reed—a couple of other guys. Why don't you come on down and join us? Then the rest of the day is yours."

"The day's already mine."

"Frank, c'mon," he said. "Let's get this over with and behind us, okay?"

Irene was tracing her hand along his spine. He looked down at her; her hand stilled.

"I don't know, Pete," he said, and the hand began moving again.

"Frank, I'm asking this as a personal favor."

Frank covered the phone, but before he could say anything, she was out of bed and putting on the blue kimono.

"I'm sorry," he whispered.

She looked back, shrugged, and said, "Me, too," before walking out of the room.

He heard her turn on the shower.

"Frank?" he heard Pete say.

"I can't be there sooner than an hour," he said into the phone.

"Aw, for God's sake, Frank. It's only ten minutes from your place."

"An hour. And next time, *partner,* call me first—not last." He hung up and hurried down the hall, wondering if her temper had led her to lock the bathroom door.

But she opened it before he reached it and said, "Get a towel."

He laughed. "What a relief—if you didn't grab a towel for me, I guess you weren't too sure of me."

She smiled, slipped the kimono off, and stepped into the shower.

So he had been wrong, he thought, but couldn't bring himself to feel bad about it.

4

They were all detectives, he realized, as he walked toward the table. A half dozen of them. They stopped talking when they saw him approach. There was a moment when, just as they looked up at him from their cups of coffee, their faces reflected how angry they were. He was surprised by the intensity of it and certain it wasn't because he had kept them waiting. Five of them—Pete Baird, Vince Adams, Reed Collins, Ned Perry, and Jake Matsuda—worked in Homicide with him. Vince and Reed were partners, as were Ned and Jake. Although they had their disagreements here and there, Frank thought of all five of them as friends—the closest of these his own partner, Pete. During an average week, he spent more waking hours with Pete than he did with Irene.

He knew little about the sixth man—Bob Hitchcock—although he had seen his name in the case files he had read last night. Hitch was a heavyset man, with sagging jowls and small eyes. His hair was cut short, bristling gray over his round head. A few times, Frank's team had played against Hitch's in the amateur ice hockey league they were in, but Hitch never got much ice time. He had come over to the house once, when Frank and Irene had held a barbecue after a hockey tournament—but he hadn't stayed long. Pete had once told Frank that Hitch used to be a good player, but he was out of shape now.

Pete broke the silence, smiling and saying, "Frank! You made it. Pull up a chair."

Hitch smiled—a phony smile, Frank thought—and came awkwardly to his feet. He held out a hand that looked like five sausages attached to a water balloon. "You may not remember me, Frank. I'm Bob Hitchcock. Most of these guys call me Hitch." Although his palm was damp, his grip was firm. Frank forced himself not to wipe his hand off before he sat down next to Pete.

Hitch gestured toward the table, where the remains of their breakfasts congealed unappetizingly on heavy white ceramic plates. "We waited for you like one hog waits on another," he said, and gave a little laugh.

"You still working Narcotics?" Frank asked.

"Surprised you remember that," Hitch said, pleased. "No, I'm in Auto Theft now. I'm close to retirement, so it's kind of nice to just be able to spend the day taking phone calls and saying, 'Gee, that's too bad—yeah, here's the police report number for your insurance.'"

A waitress came by and cleared away the dirty plates. She asked Frank if he wanted to order something. Eyeing the plates, he asked for a cup of coffee.

Another silence fell.

"You wanted to talk to me about Lefebvre?" Frank asked.

"Don't even say that name," Vince snarled.

Frank leaned lazily back in his chair. "Then this will take less time than I thought it would."

Vince leaned forward, but Jake Matsuda held up a hand. "You weren't in Las Piernas when it happened, Frank," he said quietly.

"Which, I'm told, is exactly why I got the call. Were you in Homicide then, Jake?"

He shook his head. "I was in uniform. In fact, I spent some time guarding Seth Randolph's room. But even if I hadn't—we all suffered because of what Lefebvre did. The Randolph case was high profile. Seth Randolph was a young hero, as far as everyone in town was concerned. We got attached to him, too. He was a good kid—"

"And he was going to help us nail the biggest bastard in town," Pete said.

"Yes," Jake said, "but even if Whitey Dane hadn't been a part of it, the public had sort of adopted Seth."

"We all felt that way," Ned Perry said. "The department had adopted him, too. Like Jake, I was in uniform back then. My unit was dispatched to the marina on the night Trent Randolph and his daughter were murdered. I'll never forget that night as long as I live. When Lefebvre came off of that yacht with that kid, we thought we had three dead. No one thought Seth would make it, and when it looked as if he might—well, we were all rooting for him. The kid had guts—he had fought off Dane. And he was willing to testify against him."

"Which is something a hell of a lot of grown men weren't willing to do," Pete said.

"People who were going to testify against Dane seldom made it to court," Vince said. "If they didn't change their minds about what they saw or suddenly lose their memories, they had a way of disappearing."

"But this time, it was a cop who took the payoff," Pete said. "And he killed this kid."

"How do you know he killed Seth Randolph?" Frank asked.

Pete made a sound of exasperation. "I thought you read the files."

"You've had ten years to think about it. I've had less than twenty-four hours. Humor me."

"He was the last person to go into Seth Randolph's room before the kid's body was discovered," Vince said. "The guard reported that Lefebvre was in there for a long time."

"The guard that had been talking to nurses all evening? The one Lefebvre had reprimanded in front of the nurses on the previous evening?"

"You did read the files," Pete said.

Frank nodded.

"Not everything," Vince said. "Or you'd know that Lefebvre signed out the evidence and returned the box with nothing but a watch in it."

"What do you suppose that was about?" Frank asked.

Vince shrugged. "Who knows? The guy was the biggest fuckin' fruitcake on the force."

"He acted crazy?"

Vince hesitated, then said, "Naw, he was just odd, you know? A loner. Never went out for so much as a beer with anyone in the department. Never saw him with women, even though sometimes women came on to him. God knows why. Ask your wife about it."

"Damn it, Vince!" Pete said. "See if you can rent some sense from somebody. Frank—ignore him."

"No insult intended," Vince said with a smile. "Besides, Frank, that was before the two of you got together. She wasn't supposed to be a nun all those years, right? I mean, some women have a thing for—"

"Shut the fuck up, Vince," Pete said.

"Nothing to get upset about," Vince said. "Ugly as he was, women went for him. Remember that TV reporter who was practically stalking the guy? Even Hitch's partner wasn't immune to him."

"Rosario the Lesbo?" Hitch said. "You gotta be kidding. The other guys in Narcotics used to call her 'Twenty Below,' because that's how cold you felt if you tried to get next to her. But you seem to have been real interested in everybody's sex life, Vince. Weren't you getting any back then?"

Pete laughed. "No, he wasn't. I remember, Vince—you were splitting up with Blond Bitch Number Three then, right?"

"Oh, man," Hitch said, "I remember that one, too. San Onofre."

The others laughed, even Vince. Hitch turned to Frank. "You ever see that nuclear power plant on Interstate Five?" He cupped his hands in front of his chest. "She had a pair of knockers that made those twin domes look like anthills."

"I thought we were here to talk about Lefebvre," Vince said, and had to put up with another round of laughter.

"So Lefebvre worked in a department where everyone hated him?" Frank asked.

"No," Pete said. "You're getting the wrong idea. Nobody hated him until after he killed Seth Randolph."

"Nobody?"

"He could be a little abrupt," Hitch said. "He pissed a few people off."

"But we all thought he was a good cop," Pete said.

"Good?" Ned Perry shook his head. "We thought he was great."

"He's right," Reed said. "You'd have to be a priest—a very old priest—to have as many sinners confess to you as Phil did. And Phil wasn't physical— he never so much as touched 'em. He had a brain, too."

"He got a little too smart with that brain," Pete said.

"I was just starting in detectives when this whole thing broke," Reed said. "I used to really admire him. Until he took that payoff, he won the department all kinds of praise. That made it worse, really."

There were nods of agreement from everyone but Hitch and Vince.

"Not that I don't just live to see you guys," Frank said, "but I was having an enjoyable Sunday morning until Pete called. Okay, so I came down here. But nothing you've told me is big news to me—except the part about Vince's ex."

Everyone but Vince laughed.

"The point," Pete said, "is to let you know what this means to us. It's going to be bad enough that the guy's name is before the public again. This is going to rake up a lot of ill will. The department doesn't need it."

Frank eyed him skeptically. "There's more to it than that."

"No, there's not. Look, Cliff said you didn't find the payoff money, and he thought maybe you had some questions—were leaning toward trying to clear Lefebvre's name."

"Now we're getting warmer."

"So you haven't recovered the money," Hitch said. "That doesn't mean he was innocent. Everything else pointed to him—the fact that he was the last one to see the kid, the fact that he was the last one to handle the evidence. Those two facts alone are enough to make it clear that he's the killer. You don't settle this quickly, you make life miserable for all of us. No one is going to be happy with you if you start making this out to be something more than it was. It will just give the *Express* an excuse to make us look bad."

Vince, Pete, and Ned voiced their agreement at length. Jake and Reed stayed quiet.

"What if he was innocent?" Frank asked.

"He wasn't," Vince insisted. "Get that through your head, Harriman."

Frank turned to Matsuda. "You feel that way, Jake?"

"I don't think it's at all likely that anyone other than Phil Lefebvre killed that boy, Frank. And I think Hitch is right—no good will come of bringing it all up again."

Frank looked at Reed, who was resolutely staring into his coffee cup. "You, too, Reed?"

Reed shrugged, still not meeting his eyes.

Pete, on the other hand, returned his stare, reading him. "Aw, shit," he said.

Frank smiled. "Thanks for your concern," he said to the group.

"Shit," Pete said again as Frank stood and dropped a couple of dollars on the table.

"You're not going to—" Vince began, but fell silent when Pete grabbed his arm in warning.

"Not going to let you pressure me?" Frank said. "No, I'm not."

"Look," Ned Perry said, "no one wants you to compromise an investigation. We're just asking you not to drag it out unnecessarily."

"Believe me," Frank said, "until this morning, I didn't feel any particular urgency about this set of cases."

He walked away. Behind him, he heard Pete say, "Shit."

5

Frank looked through the file on Lefebvre until he found the phone number for Lefebvre's parents, in Quebec. The coroner's office had obtained dental records and identified the remains from the wreckage as those of Las Piernas Police Detective Philip Lefebvre, aka Philippe Jean-Michel Lefebvre, age forty-two. Cause of death to be determined, but preliminary findings indicated massive injuries received in the crash.

Frank hated this part of the job—notifying parents that their son was dead. That Lefebvre was an adult son who had been missing for ten years would not, he knew, make it any easier for them to hear of his death. He was further dismayed to read a note near the phone number: the Lefebvres refused to communicate in English.

He rubbed his forehead, feeling a headache coming on. He couldn't use just anyone to translate the news of Phil Lefebvre's death to his parents. It was hard enough to give someone that kind of news in a language you both knew. He looked for the number for Lefebvre's sister, Yvette Nereault.

Same notation.

"Hey, Pete—we have any French speakers in the department?"

Pete shrugged and said nothing. Pete had been shrugging at him all morning. He was ready to shove Pete's neck down into his shoulders to save him the effort for the next one. He sighed and said, "I've got to make a next-of-kin notification here. Lefebvre's parents are French-Canadian."

Pete stayed busy with some paperwork on his desk.

"Great. Very considerate of the family. Maybe someday someone will have to call your elderly mother in Rome, New York, and ask her to get one of her English-speaking neighbors to come over—so that we can tell her in Italian that we hated her son so much, we talked about pissing on his bones."

Pete flushed red, but still said nothing.

Frank picked up the file and locked his desk, deciding he'd try calling Lefebvre's sister anyway, and make the next-of-kin call from a more private phone. As he was leaving, Reed Collins called out, "Frank."

It was the first time anyone had spoken to him all day. The others frowned at Collins for breaking the silence.

Reed ignored them. "Try Mike Tran in Gang Prevention."

"Thanks," Frank said.

"Don't thank me yet. For all I know, Vietnamese French and Canadian French may not be anything alike."

"Thanks, anyway."

He suffered another setback when he learned that Tran was on vacation. He decided to go outside the department and called Guy St. Germain—a friend who had grown up in Montreal. Guy said he'd be glad to help and invited Frank to come to his downtown office.

A former pro hockey player, Guy had then followed a family tradition and gone to work in banking. Frank had met him through Irene—he dated Irene's best friend, so the couples went out together fairly often. And Guy had been aiding Frank's efforts to learn to play ice hockey—a game he'd been unaware of while growing up in Bakersfield.

"What a sad business you are in," Guy said as Frank settled into a soft leather chair in the banker's office.

"Notifying the families is one of the worst parts of the job," Frank agreed.

Guy shut the office door and took a seat behind a large desk. "I'll use the speakerphone—even though you may not understand the language, it's better if you hear the tone of the other's voice, I think." He dialed the number. Three tones sounded, and even before the English explanation was spoken, Frank knew what they meant.

"Disconnected. Hell, I could have saved you the trouble."

"You've had all the trouble," Guy said. He tried the sister's number.

A man answered. Frank heard Guy ask for Yvette Nereault. A rapid exchange occurred in which he thought he heard the word "California." Then he heard Guy say something about the Las Piernas Police Department.

"The Las Piernas police?" he heard the man ask in English.

"*Oui*—" Guy answered, but before he could say more, the man hung up.

"What happened?" Frank asked.

"I asked for Yvette Nereault and was told that she was not at home, but the man who answered was her husband. I asked when she would be back and he said not for a week, that she was in California. I said that I was calling on behalf of a friend who was with the Las Piernas Police Department, who needed urgently to contact her. You heard what happened after that."

Frank sighed. "This family is understandably upset with the department."

"Why?"

"Strictly between us?"

"Of course."

Frank gave him a brief summary of the case.

"Phew!" Guy said. "So they must believe in his innocence."

"I'm not so sure their faith is misplaced. And the notes on the case indicate that persistent inquiries were made of the family during the first year or so after Lefebvre disappeared—some members of the department thought Lefebvre would hide out in Canada."

"So they feel harassed and have no love of the Las Piernas police."

"Right. But I need to do my best to tell them that we've found him. Are you willing to try again?"

"Sure."

"Maybe we can convince him to get in touch with his wife and ask her to call us—to let it be her decision."

Guy dialed the number again. He spoke very rapidly when Nereault answered, and Nereault allowed him to go on at some length. Frank heard him mention Montreal and then the Buffalo Sabres and, from Nereault's disbelieving and then excited tone, realized that Guy was gaining ground. He also realized that however excellent Detective Tran's French might be, unless he had played pro hockey, he wouldn't have made such a hit with Nereault. Eventually, Frank heard Guy mention "Detective Harriman" and then Philippe Lefebvre.

"So you didn't work for the department when my brother-in-law disappeared?" Nereault said in perfect English.

"No. I was working in another city then."

"Philippe is dead, isn't he?"

"Yes," Frank answered.

There was a long silence.

"Yvette knew it. She knew it then. Her parents—that was another matter."

"Can you tell me how to reach them?"

"Do you know a spiritualist?" Nereault said. "Sorry—that was in poor taste. They have been dead for eight years."

"I'm sorry."

"Don't be. I can't say that I miss them. And even Yvette has come to see that they were not—well, that does not matter. Whatever one thinks of them, it is a shame that they died thinking their son was a crooked cop. But to tell the truth, for many years, they had thought worse of him than that. Philippe had been dead to them for a long time, you know."

"No, I didn't—"

"And now you tell me he is really dead. Who killed him?"

"His plane crashed in the mountains."

"Who killed him?" Nereault asked again.

"I'm trying to learn the truth about what happened to him," Frank said. "If someone killed him, I'll do my best to find out who it was."

"I'll tell you who it was," Nereault said. "It was one of you. One of your Las Piernas Police Department fellows, that's who. You should watch your back, Detective Harriman, especially if you are going around saying that Philippe might have been innocent."

He spoke in French to Guy for a while, then said, "You may be surprised to learn that my wife is not far from you at the moment. She is in Las Piernas."

"What brings her here?"

He hesitated, then said, "She would not want me to discuss her business with you."

Frank waited.

"Let's say she is visiting a friend. A good reason to be there, no? A woman named Marie. You can ask for Marie at a place near the airport. A little restaurant called the Prop Room."

"The Prop Room?" Frank asked, remembering the receipt among Lefebvre's effects. He knew of the place and had seen it mentioned in the files on Lefebvre, but he had never been there himself.

"Yes," Nereault was saying. "And if she acts upset, you have to tell her you threatened me with torture before I would say a word. And you better bring your hockey defenseman friend with you. She likes speaking this language even less than I do."

●●●

"Want to have an early lunch near the airport?" Frank asked Guy when Nereault had hung up.

"Actually, I'm very curious about this place. A friend tells me it's the only place in town where one can find genuine French-Canadian cuisine."

During the drive to the restaurant, Frank said, "After he spoke to me in English, he spoke to you in French again."

"He asked if I thought you were an honest man. I told him yes. He said that Las Piernas is not healthy for honest policemen, and that if I am really your friend, I would encourage you to go into another line of work, so that you could live to see your children."

"Very dramatic, but not an accurate picture of the Las Piernas Police Department."

"You're right, of course. But perhaps from his perspective —"

"Yes, I understand that. I can't blame him for being down on the department. But saying Lefebvre was framed is one thing — saying he was murdered is another."

"Yes, it is something else entirely," Guy said, and seemed lost in thought.

A large woman stood near the door, clutching a handkerchief. She dabbed at her eyes as they approached, then said, "You are from the police?"

"I am, yes," Frank said, and started to pull out his badge. But she had already turned her back on them and motioned to them to follow her through the restaurant. Although it was just after eleven, the place was already starting to fill up. She seated them at a relatively quiet booth near the back. "Yvette said to ask you to have your lunch. She will sit with you a little later."

Guy ordered a hearty stew and ate it with gusto. Frank ordered a sandwich, but as he looked around at the aircraft paraphernalia decorating the walls, he thought of the wreckage in the mountains, of Lefebvre spending one of his last evenings here, and lost his appetite.

"I would think," Guy said, observing this, "that by now a dead man wouldn't stop you from eating."

"Most don't," Frank admitted.

"But this one is different?"

Frank traced his right thumb over the knuckles of his left hand. "Yes, I suppose so. Every now and then a case bothers me more than others.

Maybe this one bothers me because Lefebvre was in the same line of work."

His pager went off. He saw that it was Ben Sheridan's number. He excused himself from the table and went outside to return the call.

"My search group is going up to the mountains again next weekend," Ben said. "We're going to take the dogs to the crash site."

"Didn't the coroner's office call you? The identification is in. They got it from the dental."

"I know, I was there. I spent the morning going over the remains with the coroner. The trauma from the crash caused Lefebvre's death, but the NTSB will have to tell you what caused the crash."

"So why are you going up there?"

"Two reasons. First, it's a good training opportunity for the dogs. And the other—a hunch. I suspect scavengers carried off some of the smaller bones and anything else that was small and loose and of interest to them. And almost anything that can be carried off is of interest to a wood rat. So if there's a wood rat's nest nearby, who knows what we might find in it? Maybe there will be a key to a safe-deposit box built into it."

Frank smiled to himself, imagining Carlson's face if he told him Lefebvre's accomplice was a wood rat. "Call me if you find anything, but as you know, I have my doubts about this payoff story. It may be nothing more than a rumor." He was about to hang up, when he thought of the chilly atmosphere in the squad room and said, "You don't have anybody from LPPD in your group, do you?"

"No, not at the moment. Why?"

"Do me a favor. If anyone asks—especially Cliff Garrett—you're just looking for bones, okay? I'd rather not start a treasure hunt up there."

"Sure. I'm with you—no need to have dozens of people digging up the wilderness."

When he walked back into the restaurant, a woman was sitting in his place across from Guy. Yvette Lefebvre Nereault was tall and slender, and looked to be in her late forties. Although her features were nowhere near as plain as her late brother's, Frank could see the family resemblance. Especially in her dark, intense eyes, which were, at the moment, red-rimmed and puffy from crying. Still, she regarded him steadily as he approached, and he began to wonder if Lefebvre had looked at suspects in that same way. If so, it was not difficult to see why Phil Lefebvre had had success in getting confessions.

Guy introduced them to each other, and when she didn't budge, scooted over so that Frank could share his side of the booth.

"So my husband the bag of wind told you exactly where to find me, eh?"

"I appreciated his help."

She gave a harsh bark of laughter. "I'm sure you did."

"Did he tell you why I was trying to reach you?"

She looked away for a moment, her lower lip trembling. She drew a steadying breath. "He said you found my brother."

"Yes."

"Well, then, perhaps the Royal Canadian Mounted Police and every other law enforcement group between here and Hong Kong can sleep better tonight. Their enemy is dead after all."

Frank said nothing. She stared hard at him, then said, "So, is it true? My husband said you believe in Philippe's innocence."

"I told him I am not sure of his guilt."

"Not quite the same thing, but at least you are honest with me about it."

She spoke to Guy in French for a moment, then said to Frank, "He tells me your wife knew my brother. What is her name?"

"Irene Kelly."

"Irene Kelly," she repeated slowly. A small smile of private amusement briefly crossed her face. "I know this name. In fact, at one time . . ." Her voice trailed off, and the look of amusement was gone. "It's nothing."

"Did he mention her to you?"

But Yvette's attention strayed to the large woman who had met them at the door. The woman walked up to the table, and Yvette introduced her as an old friend, Marie, and indicated that she should sit down beside her. "Ten years ago Marie was a waitress here. Today she owns this place."

"The food was excellent," Guy said. "I haven't eaten so well since I was last in Montreal." Seeing her look between Frank and his nearly untouched sandwich, he said something quickly in French. It caused both Marie and Yvette to look at Frank with expressions of disbelief.

"C'est vrai," Guy said.

"What did you tell them?" Frank asked warily.

"That my brother's ghost troubles you and has taken your appetite," Yvette said.

Frank felt his headache returning.

"Holy God, it's so!" Marie said, turning white. "This table—this is the very one where he sat with her, that last night."

"With *her?*" Frank asked even as Yvette shot her friend a quelling look. "Who was here with him?"

Marie said nothing.

"Who?" he asked again.

Marie crossed her arms. She looked away.

"If he didn't kill Seth Randolph," Frank said, "let me help you clear his name. We already know he ate here the night before he died. I read the file—the owner of the restaurant was questioned, and so were the staff. Everyone said that Lefebvre ate here often, and was probably here that night, but no one could recall anything remarkable about it."

Marie glanced at Yvette, then said, "I was mistaken. He was here alone."

"If you know something—"

"I don't."

"All right—perhaps he was here earlier in the week with someone else," Frank said, not believing for a moment that Lefebvre had dined alone on that last night. "What did this woman look like?"

"There is no time for this," Yvette interrupted. "I am only here a few more days. Will I be allowed to arrange for a funeral for my brother? Or will you make me wait another decade to bury him?"

Frank gave her the information she would need to contact the coroner. "If you would like me to take you there—"

"No . . . no, thank you," she said.

"Where can I reach you while you are here?"

"Marie can always reach me."

He waited. She returned his stare, then slowly she began to smile.

"You know, Philippe used to be the only one who could get me to say what I did not want to say to him." She hesitated. "Do you have a good memory?"

He nodded.

"If I give you a phone number—"

"Yvette!" Marie warned.

"If I give you a phone number, you must promise not to write it down. Not anywhere. I would not want the people I am staying with to be bothered—or worse—by the Las Piernas Police Department."

"All right."

She gave him a local number.

He gave her his card. "My pager number is on there. Please let me know if I can be of help. And please let me know when and where the services will be held."

"So that he can be buried with full police honors?" she asked bitterly. "I should take him back to Quebec. He never should have left."

"Why did he live here, so far away from the rest of the family?" Frank asked.

She hesitated, then said, "He never got along well with my father. He left home when he was eighteen and went to college in the U.S. He was born here, you know. A U.S. citizen. Whenever he was angry at Philippe, my father used to call him '*L'Américain*.'"

"Yvette and Bernard were born in Quebec," Marie said proudly.

"Bernard?" Frank asked.

"My younger brother," Yvette replied. Turning to Marie, she said something in rapid French, speaking angrily and in a low voice.

Marie blushed. "Excuse me," she said, and stood up.

"Marie! *Pardon* . . ." Yvette called to her, but the other woman walked away.

Frank glanced at Guy, who gave a small shrug.

"I didn't know you had another brother," Frank said to Yvette. "If you'll let me know how to reach him—"

"Bernard died a long time ago," she said softly. "A hunting accident."

Frank waited, and silently willed Guy to do the same.

"Philippe came home from college for Christmas that year," she said, reminiscing. "And Bernard—Bernard had missed him and never let him have a moment's peace. Bernard and I were both excited—we had not seen Philippe for two years. When Bernard begged to be allowed to join Philippe and a few of his friends on a hunting trip, my father said no, but Philippe took him along anyway." She shook her head. "It was nothing new for Philippe to defy my father. And Bernard had gone hunting with Philippe many times before. But this time—the others said that one of the laces of Bernard's boot became loose. That is how I lost my younger brother, you see? Because of a bootlace. Bernard leaned his rifle against a fallen log, then placed his boot on the log to retie the lace. Only—the log moved a little. The gun fell and went off, and he was killed. Philippe did everything he could to save him, but there was not the slightest chance he could have done so."

"How old was Bernard?" Guy asked.

"Sixteen."

"The same age as Seth Randolph," Frank said.

She looked sharply at him. "So . . . you see it, too—penance, *non*? A way to redeem himself." But in the next moment she smiled cynically. "If the police are right, what a Judas my brother must have been!"

6

Whitey Dane sensed the presence of his chief assistant and lowered the newspaper. The other man had not cleared his throat or cast the slightest shadow over the page Dane had been reading. After twelve years in his service, Myles would never have been guilty of such a disturbance of his boss's peace. At twenty-eight years of age, Myles's manners were far more refined than those of the teenager who had indentured himself to Dane those dozen years ago.

"Everything to your satisfaction, Mr. Dane?" he asked.

"Yes, Myles, thank you. You may take the rest away."

Built like a linebacker, Myles nevertheless moved gracefully and silently as he removed the fine bone-china plate and crystal wineglass. The tall, dark-haired man was dressed entirely in white. All the assistants who cared for Mr. Dane when he was on his yacht wore white. Their sailing clothes were spotless.

Myles nodded at another assistant—a younger man, but also of hefty build. The young man quickly and thoroughly rid the linen tablecloth of any crumbs. Myles glanced around the cabin to make sure his master—for he thought of Mr. Dane as his master—did not want for anything that might be necessary for his comfort, then left.

When he was sixteen, Myles had eluded Mr. Dane's security guards and approached a surprised and not especially pleased Mr. Dane. Although

Dane, not quite as slow as his guards, was training a gun on him by then, Myles asked for his help. Mr. Dane listened and soon relieved Myles of a major burden—his drunken, abusive father—and made it possible for Myles's mother and two younger brothers to leave the rathole they were living in. Myles moved into Dane's mansion.

Dane had simply used Myles as muscle at first, which Myles was pleased to provide. But one evening, after he had given a year of loyal service to his eccentric employer, Dane had called the brawny street kid into his library, where he sat before a warm fire, reading a book that Myles would later realize contained a play by George Bernard Shaw. Mr. Dane had looked up from his book and stared at Myles. An elderly member of the staff had once told Myles that Mr. Dane could see more with one eye than anyone else could see with two. Myles hadn't understood that when the old man said it, but he did when Dane studied him that evening. Mr. Dane said that he had decided to play Pygmalion. At that point, Myles had had no idea what Mr. Dane meant. That was before he acquired what Mr. Dane referred to as "polish." Myles had also acquired a measure of pride in himself, and a devotion to Dane no dog could have matched.

That afternoon Myles did not betray his concern over Mr. Dane's lack of appetite, although he knew Mr. Dane's chef would be nearly inconsolable. Myles's years in service to Mr. Dane had taught him to read the most subtle indicators of his master's moods, and Mr. Dane's almost untouched luncheon was a sign far from subtle. He knew the reason for Mr. Dane's pensiveness, of course.

Myles handed the plate and glass to an underling. He took time to wash his hands, carefully drying them and checking his manicure before returning to his master's side.

Mr. Dane had not returned to reading his paper. He was standing now, looking toward the open sea. Without averting his gaze, he made a little sign to Myles, who in turn signaled the others to leave. This was speedily accomplished, but it was some time before Mr. Dane spoke to him.

"Myles—you have had an opportunity to read the *Express* today?"

"Yes, sir."

Dane reached into his vest pocket and removed his Hamilton watch. He opened it, wound it carefully, and replaced it before saying, "Then you know which article most interested me?"

"Yes, sir. The one about the wreckage of a plane."

"Oh, not just a plane."

"No, sir."

"'Identity of the pilot withheld pending notification of the next of kin,'" Dane quoted.

"They've found him, sir."

"Presumably. His plane, anyway."

"Shall I check to see if progress has been made on the identification, Mr. Dane?"

"Later, perhaps."

Myles waited. He knew not to rush Mr. Dane.

"Tell me, Myles—do you anticipate any problems?"

"Difficult to say, sir."

"That is not the answer I wished to hear."

"Which is what makes it difficult to say, sir."

Dane smiled. "Why, Myles! Unexpected wit."

"I apologize if I seemed . . . impertinent, sir."

Dane waved this away. "What is your evaluation of the situation?"

"That we need to monitor events, sir. Until now, we worried that he might be able to bring some pressure to bear. We have probably long been out of danger. Ten years—"

"There is no statute of limitations on murder," Dane said testily.

"No, sir. But as we did then, we may rely on certain individuals who will have access to any . . ."

"'Recovered evidence'?" Dane sneered.

"To any object or obstacle we may wish to have removed."

"Are we as sure of our situation now as we were then?"

"More certain than previously, sir."

Dane raised an eyebrow.

"Much more certain," Myles said.

Dane brooded for a time. "I don't share your level of confidence, I'm afraid. Too many of our acquaintances have been convicted of crimes I'm not so sure they committed. Not that they were innocents, mind you—and admittedly their operations were less subtle and clever than ours—but our failure to discover how they were trapped disturbs me greatly."

Myles remained silent.

"You do realize, Myles, that I would feel so much more at ease if the dismissal of charges ten years ago had come through our efforts and not those of some unknown?"

"Yes, sir."

Eventually, Dane sighed. "I don't think I'll sail today after all," he said. "Being in this marina makes me think of that bastard Trent Randolph.

What a damned nuisance that man's death turned out to be!"

"Yes, sir," Myles said. "May I do anything more for you before asking for your car?"

"No, thank you, Myles."

Mr. Dane was unhappy. Myles vowed to be extra vigilant in matters connected to the discovery of Lefebvre's plane.

He would do just about anything to receive one of Mr. Dane's smiles.

7

Frank told Carlson that the next-of-kin notification had been made and watched the other man hurry over to the Wheeze with ready-made press releases. As he returned to his desk, he noticed that most of the other desks were empty. Pete and Vince were still in, but neither acknowledged his presence.

Their silence no longer bothered him. In his present mood, he welcomed it. He reread the file on Lefebvre and the reports taken on the night of the attack on the *Amanda*. He focused on Elena Rosario's report, which told of Lefebvre attacking a door with an ax in order to rescue Seth Randolph, the reports of Lefebvre's movements on those last two days of his life, the autopsy report on Seth Randolph.

Each reading raised more and more questions in his mind. Lefebvre's family members could have easily distanced themselves from him when the accusations were made, but they had been fiercely loyal. Even Lefebvre's parents were uncooperative with the Las Piernas police when he disappeared.

He looked at Lefebvre's photo, wishing he had the power to read the man's character from it. There was so little to go on. That, he realized, said something on Lefebvre's behalf—if he had been a bad cop, where were the signs of it?

Where were the tales from anywhere in his past to indicate that he would be inclined to take a bribe? To arrange the killing of such a key witness, would Dane dare to approach someone he had never dealt with before? Nothing in the Internal Affairs investigation indicated that Lefebvre would have been ready to cross the line—no reprimands, no signs of dissatisfaction with his job, none of his partners from his days in uniform saying they suspected him of being on the take. Instead, it seemed the worst accusation anyone could make was that he was a loner.

But was he? He had been friendly to Irene. And despite Marie's denials, Frank was certain that Lefebvre had met a woman at the restaurant on the evening before he died.

Frank focused on the events of that day—June 21. Several witnesses said that at the press conference, Seth suddenly seemed upset. No one knew why. The press conference ended, and the room was cleared—but Lefebvre stayed behind. That night Lefebvre the loner dined with a woman at the Prop Room. A date or a business connection? Was the woman an emissary from Whitey Dane? Did she hire Lefebvre to kill Seth that night?

After thinking it over, Frank discarded that idea. Lefebvre would not hold such a meeting in a public place, let alone in one where he was so well known. He had paid for the meal with a credit card—knowing such transactions could be traced.

There was some connection between the woman and Yvette. At lunch today, Yvette was the one who had prevented Marie from naming the woman—Yvette had protected the woman's identity. But the only woman whose name had been mentioned in connection with Lefebvre was . . . Irene.

Had Irene been afraid to reveal just how close she had been to Lefebvre?

He thought of Yvette's recognition of Irene's name, that look of amusement.

He dialed Irene's work number. The line rang once, twice, three times, then went to her voice mail. He hesitated, suddenly aware that he was about to ask her if she had lied to him. He hung up.

He sat for a long moment with his hand on the receiver. Maybe he'd ask to be taken off the case after all.

He glanced down at the photo of Lefebvre, then looked around the office. Vince was staring at him. Some of the others had returned, but they ignored him. If he bailed on this case, would any of these men take the time to find out what had really happened to the Randolphs and Lefebvre?

He turned back to Lefebvre's record.

Money was widely assumed to have motivated Lefebvre to murder Seth.

But instead of the multiple reports of a payoff that Frank had expected, the files showed only one anonymous tip. Reed had taken the call and noted that the voice was mechanically disguised. Anyone with an ax to grind could have made that call. He began to see why the numbers he had heard up in the mountains were so varied—the rumors about the payoff amount had probably originated in-house. He had seen this sort of thing many times before, squad-room know-it-alls making sly remarks to one another, innuendos that soon were believed to be fact. This case had all the ingredients needed to excite the gossips—a fallen department star, envied for his success, supposedly turned into a hired killer for Whitey Dane—rumors must have been flying.

But Frank was more and more convinced that there had been no payoff. Nothing in Lefebvre's financial records indicated money trouble or even big spending habits. He was at top pay for a detective. As in his military days, he saved more than he spent. He owned a small condo, which he had bought for a song. His only other big expenditure had been the purchase of the Cessna, and Internal Affairs documents showed that Lefebvre had saved over years to buy it and had chosen it carefully. The man had been conservative with his money, lived simply, and was not burdened by debt.

Lefebvre was not at all the typical target for bribery or a hired hit. A large enough sum might tempt any man, but given what he had learned about Lefebvre, it was hard for Frank to imagine that Lefebvre would have been the easiest person for Dane to approach. Why not bribe one of the lower-paid guards? Or send in a professional killer dressed as a hospital staff person?

He was struck by the degree to which the investigation had always focused on Lefebvre; apparently, no other suspect had been considered. He could easily see how this had happened, but still thought the investigators guilty of poor detective work.

His phone began ringing with calls from reporters. Someone must have tipped them off about who was handling the investigation. He gave a polite but standard "no comment on open cases" to all of them and referred them to the department's public information officer. After the sixth call, he picked up the files and moved to the break room. Once his voice mail was full, the calls would transfer to the Wheeze's desk.

He poured a cup of coffee and began looking through the coroner's and lab reports. The physical evidence in the Seth Randolph case was of little use; the autopsy had not provided any surprises. The boy had been held down and suffocated with a pillow, and judging from the direction of the pressure, it was likely that the killer had been right-handed. Seth's hands had been too injured from the previous attack to allow the boy to defend himself—no skin from the attacker had been found beneath the boy's fingernails.

Trace and fingerprint evidence were inconclusive. Many people had been in and out of the hospital room during the previous twenty-four hours, including Lefebvre.

Frank also noted that Seth's computer files had been erased. He would have to ask Henry Freeman, the department's computer expert, if there was any chance that the files could be recovered. He knew that sometimes this could be done, that the erased files might actually still "reside" on the computer's hard drive, but he wasn't sure what was involved in locating and restoring them.

He finished his coffee and went back to his desk. As he sat down, Frank glanced at Vince Adams, who was now involved in completing paperwork. At the time of Seth Randolph's murder, Vince would have been paying alimony for an ex-wife and child support for four kids. Frank recalled what Pete had said at breakfast—in addition to the payments to his first wife, Vince was beginning divorce proceedings with his third wife. Attorney fees and court costs, setting up a separate household—and the costs from the two previous marriages already on his back. He would have had all those expenses, and at a lower salary grade than the one he had now. Were there others in the department who might have found Whitey Dane's offer too tempting to refuse?

He became aware of some new tension in the room and followed the gaze of the other detectives. The Wheeze was coming toward his desk with a skirt-stretching stride, and he found himself thinking that she could teach Carlson how to march. Maybe the two of them could form a private drill team.

Some of his amusement must have shown on his face, because she raised her brows. They had been recently re-dyed, he noticed, a process she went through every few weeks. Now, as always on the first day or two after she had them done, her brows were alarmingly dark—a cue for Pete to stalk behind her, doing Groucho imitations behind her back.

The Wheeze was a tall, brittle woman in her mid-fifties, slender and conservatively dressed. She wore her (also re-dyed) ash-blond hair pulled back into a chignon. He supposed that if her mouth had been a little less wide, her eyes a little less hard, she might have been a handsome woman. Irene had met her once at an office party and said, "When none of you are watching, she goes into Bredloe's office, tries on his hat, and sits in his chair."

Looking up at her now, Frank thought she probably strapped on the captain's gun while she was at it.

She was carrying a small stack of pink telephone message notes by the fingertips of both hands, as if she were parading a consecrated host through the squad room. She snapped them down on his desk without saying a word, turned on her heel, and headed back toward the captain's office.

"Walks on water," Pete muttered.

"Easy for her," Frank said. "It freezes under her feet."

Pete gave a muffled snort of laughter and grinned at him—then looked up to see Vince scowling at them. Pete said, "Oh, for God's sake," then stood up and walked out of the room.

Frank sorted through the slips. Most were calls from reporters—one television reporter, Polly Logan from Channel 6, had called eleven times. Frank knew the obnoxious woman and smiled to himself when he thought of the Wheeze doing battle with Logan. The smile faded when he came across a message from Yvette Nereault. She had called to say that Lefebvre's funeral would be held on Wednesday morning.

He stood up and walked toward Bredloe's office. As he approached, he could hear the murmur of voices through the captain's half-open door.

"He can't see you right now, Detective Harriman," the Wheeze said.

"I'll wait, then," Frank said.

She started to object, but Bredloe's deep voice called out, "Frank? Come in—you should see this."

Frank entered the office and shut the door behind him to keep the Wheeze from eavesdropping. He discovered the captain was alone—the low voices were coming from a small television.

An aerial shot of the mountainside where the wreckage had been found was on the screen. There was little to be seen—it was basically a shot of the trees above the ravine. As the reporter's helicopter hovered, he spoke of how difficult it would be for searchers to spot the Cessna.

The scene suddenly changed to a hospital room, and Frank was startled to realize that he was seeing Seth Randolph and Philip Lefebvre on one of the last days of their lives. The sound had been cut out, so he could not hear what Lefebvre was saying to someone else in the room. He was hovering near Seth, who looked pale and frightened. Over the brief shot, a news anchor's voice said, "When asked if any evidence in connection with the murder of Seth Randolph was recovered at the scene of the crash, the Las Piernas Police Department refused to comment."

"They've shown that same ten-second clip a dozen times," Bredloe said, turning the set off. "Must be the only one they saved."

He walked slowly toward the windows along one wall of the room. He was a tall man in his late fifties, about six foot eight, and built like a bull. Unlike Carlson, Bredloe had worked patrol in the toughest parts of the city before he made detective. While there had been times when Frank disagreed with Bredloe's decisions, he had always respected him, not just because of his experience, but because he believed that Bredloe did all he could to make the department the best it could be.

After a moment of silently staring out over the city, he seemed to remember that Frank was in the office. "Have a seat," he said, and returned to his own chair. "Lieutenant Carlson tells me you want to be taken off the Lefebvre case. If that's true . . . ?"

Frank hesitated briefly, thinking of Irene, then said, "No, sir."

"No?"

"If you had asked me on Saturday night, when I spoke to Lieutenant Carlson, I would have told you I didn't want it. But I've changed my mind."

"Why?"

Because too many cops wanted me to join them for breakfast the next day, he thought. To Bredloe, he said, "I'm not sure you'd like my answer."

"You know me better than that."

"Yes—I apologize."

Bredloe waited.

"Because of the possibility that Lefebvre looked guilty but wasn't."

Bredloe seemed ready to object, but apparently thought better of it. He stood and began to pace near the windows. He took three or four turns before he said, "You won't find a lot of support for that theory in this department."

"Believe me, sir, I know."

With a small smile, Bredloe nodded toward the squad room. "It has been a quiet day out there."

"I don't imagine that was true any time I stepped out of the room."

The smile broadened. "No, it did get a little noisier then."

Frank said nothing.

"I have no doubt you can cope with a little friction. After all, you've dealt with that sort of heat before now. Selfishly, I depended on your ability to do so when it was decided that you should be the one to handle this investigation. That wasn't the only consideration, or even the first consideration, but I won't deny it was a factor."

Frank shrugged. "Thanks for the faith, but popularity contests aside, I may not be able to learn much. Ten years—"

"I don't expect miracles."

Frank was silent.

"If you had already decided to stay with the case," Bredloe asked, "what brought you into my office?"

"Lefebvre's funeral arrangements."

Bredloe frowned, and Frank suddenly wondered if he had made a mistake in bringing Lefebvre's funeral to the captain's attention; perhaps the captain, like the others in the department, wanted only to distance himself from the pariah—dead or alive. Deciding it was too late to turn back now, Frank recited the information on the note.

When he finished, Bredloe turned back to the windows, staring out with an unseeing look. "Is the family asking for—?"

"No. Not a thing. They—they're quite bitter toward the department, sir."

"Yes, I remember how difficult they were. Refusing to speak English, even though they obviously understood it. They clearly hated us. And yet you are invited to attend Lefebvre's funeral."

"I asked to be invited," Frank said.

"Still—"

"I'm sure they expect me to give the information to the rest of the department, so that any of his friends who want to attend—"

"He had no friends in this department," Bredloe said calmly.

"So I've been told. But I don't want to assume anything."

"No, of course not. Ask Louise to send out a memo. I'll have Public Relations prepare a press release. Thank you for keeping me informed."

It was said in a tone of dismissal. Frank stood to leave. He had his hand on the doorknob when Bredloe said, "Matt Arden, perhaps."

Frank turned back to him. "Matt Arden?"

"Friends in the department. Matt Arden was one. On the other hand, I always thought Matt lied to us."

"About what, sir?"

Bredloe looked toward him. "About Lefebvre's plans to visit him."

"I'm fairly sure he did lie, sir."

Bredloe seemed startled by this response. "What makes you say so?"

"Lefebvre had no reason to tell you he was on his way to see Arden if he intended to disappear."

"It gave him an excuse to be out of town."

"He could have told you he was going somewhere else, to see someone unknown to the department. Made up a name, a place. Instead, he told you that he would be with someone you knew. Someone you could easily contact. Why didn't he just disappear? Why not leave you waiting for him to return to his condo or make you search for his car? Instead, he tells you he's flying his own plane—and he *does* take off in it. If you were planning to kill a witness in a capital case, would you act that way?"

"No," Bredloe said. "But—"

"Would you make sure the guard saw you go into Seth Randolph's room just before you killed the boy?"

Bredloe shook his head, then said, "But Lefebvre made sure no one saw him leave."

"What if the boy was already dead when he went in?"

"Then why not tell someone?" Bredloe said angrily. "Why not summon help immediately? Why flee?"

"I don't know," Frank admitted. "This gets into pure guesswork. But maybe—maybe he felt he needed time or thought he was being framed."

"Framed!" Bredloe shouted. "By someone in this department?"

"All right, all right," Frank said, making calming motions. "Let's back up a few steps. Arden lied to you. Why?"

The captain fell silent.

"There were three of you who heard Lefebvre say that he was going to visit Arden, right?"

"I don't recall," Bredloe said.

"According to the file, you, Lieutenant Willis, and Pete Baird were in the room when he called in, and you heard him say he was going to spend time with Arden."

"Yes—now I remember. On the speakerphone in Willis's office."

"Right. Anyone else in the room with you?"

Bredloe frowned in concentration. "I don't think so. Why?" he asked warily.

"I'm just wondering who or what scared Arden into lying."

"Scared Arden? Are you implying—"

Frank held his hands up. "I'm implying nothing, sir. I'm just saying that Arden, who had spent years in this department and probably knew Lefebvre better than any of you, was extremely uncooperative when it came to helping you find Lefebvre." A sudden thought struck Frank. "When you said Matt Arden lied, you meant—you thought he knew where Lefebvre was— that he was helping to hide him."

"Yes," Bredloe said.

"You thought a man with Arden's reputation was hiding a man who had murdered a witness?" Frank asked incredulously.

"We could understand how that might have happened! Lefebvre was his protégé, really almost like a son to him."

"But he made this protégé of his out to be a liar—and none of you questioned it at the time—or spoke up if you did."

"We thought Matt was lying. We had him watched for months, thinking he'd lead us to Lefebvre."

"But he didn't."

"No."

"I'm not saying I blame you for suspecting Lefebvre, Captain. Other evidence made him look bad—it still does. But you've had your doubts, haven't you?"

After a long silence, Bredloe said, "Yes. Yes, I suppose I have. But there was so much to indicate Lefebvre—believe it or not, at first I couldn't accept the idea that he was guilty. But the evidence against him was overwhelming."

"I'm just getting my feet wet on this one, Captain. I have a long way to go. Like you, I think Arden lied—but for a different reason. I think he was scared into lying. And I want to know who or what scared him."

"Scared Matt?" Bredloe said with a small laugh. "That in itself is unbelievable. Matt Arden is probably the toughest old son of a bitch I know. Even now—and he has to be almost eighty."

Frank hesitated, then said, "With your permission, sir, I'd like to personally invite him to Lefebvre's funeral."

"I can't see any harm in that. Louise can give you his number."

"I'd prefer to get it out of the files, sir, or through the DMV."

"Detective Harriman—" Bredloe said angrily.

"And I'd ask, sir, that you keep our conversation absolutely confidential. In fact, I'd prefer the others thought I whined to you about the silent treatment, or asked to be taken off the case, or better yet—that I told you I had no hope of learning anything more."

Bredloe rubbed at his forehead, as if trying to relieve a headache. "For now, I will not discuss this with anyone. But I will use my own judgment about this case, Frank. If you are right, then of course we must consider that someone else has Seth Randolph's blood on his hands, that someone else allowed Dane to escape punishment for the murders. And if that someone is in this department, I'll want a full-scale investigation of the matter."

• • •

Frank looked up Matt Arden's number in the file and dialed it. He got a phone company recording saying that the number was disconnected or no longer in service. But he remembered that it had been ten years since the number was entered in the file and thought the area code might have changed. He checked with information—and discovered he had guessed right. He redialed.

On the fourth ring, an answering machine picked up the call. A gravelly recorded voice said, "This is Matt. Can't come to the phone. Leave a message. . . ." There was the sound of someone fumbling around in the background and a muttered, "How do I record the damned beep on this thing?" and finally the beep itself.

"This is Detective Frank Harriman with the Las Piernas Police Department. Please call me as soon as possible." He left his pager number and hung up.

He looked up to see that although the squad room was more crowded now, he was still on the receiving end of the scowl-a-thon. He saw Bredloe leaving his office—even the captain frowned at him as he went by. Frank shrugged it off—Homicide was never a goddamned sunshine factory on the best of days.

He felt restless, though, and made a sudden decision. He gathered the files before locking his desk. He headed down to his car, where he looked up Lefebvre's old address on a Thomas Guide map of the city.

He had seen the place where the man had died. Now he wanted to see where he had lived.

8

Hidden in the shadows of the parking garage, hunched down behind the front seat of his van, the Looking Glass Man stared into the rearview mirror—but not at an angle that would reflect his own face back to him. He watched Frank Harriman, who sat in his car with the dome light on. The Looking Glass Man had intentionally parked across the aisle from Harriman's car when he learned that the detective was handling the Lefebvre case.

Harriman troubled him. He felt a moment's fury toward Bredloe for assigning Harriman to the case.

Harriman wouldn't rush things. He would be thorough. And he was just a little too good at his job to make the Looking Glass Man feel safe. Perhaps it would be best to simply remove Harriman from the equation.

The Looking Glass Man had been fortunate this afternoon, lucky enough to be in the homicide room when Harriman had gone in to talk to Bredloe. Harriman had aggravated Captain Bredloe, and the Looking Glass Man doubted Harriman had done so by talking about funeral arrangements. The others knew about the funeral before Harriman had left Bredloe's office, of course. The Wheeze, miffed that Harriman had shut the door to a realm she considered her protectorate, had immediately gone among the other detectives and told them that Harriman was trying to get the captain to provide an honor guard for Lefebvre's funeral.

This had caused some outrage—sadly, the expressions of it had not allowed the Looking Glass Man to make out Bredloe's occasional muffled shouts while he stood near the wall of Bredloe's office.

Still, he thought he understood why Bredloe was upset. He was upset as well, though not for quite the same reason. Trying to discover what Harriman was up to, what line of investigation he was using, meant following him here. That alone had put some pressure on the Looking Glass Man to act hastily.

He smiled to himself now, acknowledging that over the years he had become adept at handling such pressure. He preferred to plan in advance and had any number of contingency plans ready and waiting. But if he had to think on his feet, he could do so.

The dome light in Harriman's car went out, and the man heard the Volvo's engine start. He was preparing to follow Harriman when his pager vibrated.

He shielded the pager's light from view and read the number on it. It was not a phone number, but a code. After checking it against a list of similar codes in his electronic organizer, he broke out in a cold sweat.

Anxiety overtook him, his fears rising like a buzzing swarm of bees inside his head. He held his hands to his temples, lowered his face between his knees to keep from fainting. A neatly bundled stack of newspapers on the floor of the van—papers he had planned to take to the recycling center after work today—caught his eye. He calmed immediately.

Under other circumstances, he would have mentally enumerated the reasons he found pleasure in seeing the bundle: (1) the papers faced the same way, with the folds neatly aligned; (2) the lengths of twine that bound them were exactly the right length to hold them neatly without creasing them; (3) the papers were stacked in order of date of issue, oldest to newest, with the most recent on top, and within each day's issues the sections were in the proper alphabetical order; (4) it represented his good intentions, because recycling was the socially and environmentally correct thing to do.

During that moment of high-pitched anxiety, though, this particular bundle brought him more than pride in good citizenship—it brought him inspiration. For the front page of last Saturday's edition of the *Las Piernas News Express* carried a local news story that made him think of a place. He had already considered going there to further test a device he had recently made. It might hold the answer to his current problem.

He would have to act quickly.

Fortunately, not entirely without preparation.

9

As he drove toward Lefebvre's condo, Frank called several local television stations, asking if they had any footage of the press conference in Seth Randolph's hospital room. None had much more than what he had seen in Bredloe's office. Since no one actually went looking for tapes when he called, he thought he might be talking to the wrong people—getting the brush-off from production assistants who didn't want to be bothered with his request.

He needed help from someone inside the business. He thought of a friend of Irene's, Marcia Wolfe, a news editor at an L.A. station. He remembered that she used to work for Channel 6 in Las Piernas. He gave her a call.

"Try Polly Logan."

Frank groaned. "I've been trying to avoid her."

She laughed. "I know, she's got more bad miles on her than a Baja road race, but she knows you're married to Kelly, so she'll leave you alone."

"She has some history with Irene?"

"Yep, but I'm not even going to go there."

"Okay, but why should I talk to Logan? She's just a face, right?"

"And a very expensive face it is—and I'm not talking about what they pay her. Somewhere in Beverly Hills, a plastic surgeon thinks of her every time he starts up his Rolls. But aside from all that, if there's anyone who has footage of Lefebvre, it's going to be Polly. I know for a fact that she has a personal collection on the guy."

"A personal collection on Lefebvre?"

"She had a major crush on him. Never took her camera off him if she could help it. I started out over at Channel Six, and believe me, I saw so much of that guy's mug, we began sending crews out with her just so we could verify that more than one detective worked for the LPPD."

He thanked her and called Logan.

"Yes, I can help you," she said. "But what will you do for me in return?"

"You know I can't discuss the case itself with you," he said. "Lieutenant Carlson—"

"That pompous twit—never mind. I suppose you'd be in trouble if he knew you had called me about the tapes?"

"Probably."

"Well, we'll have to be discreet, then. This will take some time, and I'm about to leave on an assignment. How can I reach you later?"

He gave her his cell phone number.

"It might be late," she warned. "How late can I call?"

"Anytime," he said, envisioning Polly Logan thinking of his number as a personal hotline to the LPPD Homicide Division. Maybe he'd have to get a new cell phone.

The condo was in a large, gated complex, but Frank had no difficulty following another car through before the electronic gate rolled closed. He figured that "gated community" ran second only to "one size fits all" when it came to phrases that offered Americans a false sense of security.

He drove along the street that formed the outer circle of the complex, then made a series of turns that took him past a shallow, artificial lake with a fountain in the center. He passed an empty tennis court and then a fenced playground, where a half-dozen small children were playing on swings, a sandbox, and a slide under the watchful eye of young mothers. Not far from them, some slightly older children, perhaps fourth or fifth graders, were playing basketball.

He parked in a visitor's space near the playground, then walked some distance through the complex, until he found Lefebvre's street. He could have parked closer, but he wanted to get a feel for the place. He wondered if Lefebvre had ever taken walks like this one—or had he simply parked in his garage and gone up to his bed each night?

He should look up real estate records, he supposed. Get the names of people who had lived here for ten years or more. The files he had read indicated that not many of Lefebvre's neighbors knew anything about him;

those who did knew two things: he was quiet and he was a cop. Frank decided he would ask around, anyway.

He had a hard time imagining a man as private as Lefebvre in such a place, with shared walls and a condo association. But perhaps it was all he could afford—at the time Lefebvre had bought his condo, a modest single-family dwelling in this part of Southern California went for the price of four houses in almost any other state.

Perhaps Lefebvre had done more of his living away from home. There was his love of flying—Frank decided he would try to talk to pilots and workers at the airport, people who might have been closer to Lefebvre when he was relaxed and enjoying himself.

He came to a building that was somewhat set apart from the others, at the end of a cul-de-sac. The address matched Lefebvre's. He was walking along a shrubbery-lined sidewalk, toward the last unit near the back, when a skinny, dark-haired boy rounded the corner at a run, pointed at Frank, and shouted frantically, "Stop him!"

Startled, a second passed before Frank realized that the boy was pointing toward the ground near his feet, and looked down just in time to see a small reddish-brown mop of fur scurrying toward him.

A guinea pig.

He blocked the rodent's path with a judiciously placed shoe, apparently confounding it, because it came to a halt. He scooped it up just as the boy came up to him. Frank thought he was probably about eight or nine. For reasons he couldn't name, the kid seemed familiar. The boy stopped as suddenly as the guinea pig had and held up his hands, looking at Frank with pleading brown eyes.

"You'll be able to keep hold of him?" Frank asked as the animal began squirming, making high-pitched beeping noises.

"Oh, yes," the boy said softly, taking it from him. The guinea pig calmed immediately.

The boy started to walk away, then turned and said, "Thank you."

"You're welcome."

He walked a little farther, then came back a few steps and said in a low, conspiratorial voice, "You won't tell anyone, will you?"

"Won't tell anyone what?"

"About My Dog."

"Your dog?" Frank asked, looking around. "Is he loose, too?"

The boy shook his head and sighed. "My guinea pig's name is My Dog. I'm not allowed to have a dog, and so—" He shrugged.

Frank kept himself from laughing—an effort he made because the kid was so serious. "So what is it I'm not supposed to tell?"

The boy studied Frank, then said, "You don't live here, do you?"

"No," Frank said.

"We can't have pets," the boy said.

"But you do."

"No, if we could have real pets, I would have a dog. I mean—I love My Dog, but he's not a dog. And I'm not even allowed to have him."

"I have two dogs," Frank said.

The boy studied him again, then said, "Why are you wearing a gun?"

Frank's jacket was closed, so he was surprised that the boy had noticed the weapon. "I'm a policeman."

"Let me see some identification," the boy said—then added, "Please."

Frank smiled and pulled out his badge and ID. Without touching the holder, the boy studied them carefully.

"Have you come to arrest me?" he asked.

"No—oh, you mean because of the guinea pig? No."

The boy's brows drew together, and he seemed to silently debate something with himself. But then he shook his head and said, "I am not allowed to talk to strangers." He began to walk away.

"Wait—" Frank called. "Have we met before?"

The boy shook his head again, then hurried around the corner. Frank followed slowly and caught a glimpse of the kid climbing the stairs at the end of the building two at a time. He heard a door close. Lefebvre's old unit.

Those brown eyes, that serious face.

He climbed the stairs faster than the boy had and rang the bell.

He heard muffled voices and footsteps approaching the door. He heard the latch and waited for the door to open.

It didn't. He realized that he had heard it being locked, not unlocked.

He knocked again. There was no sound from the other side of the door.

He moved to the top stair and sat down. He pulled out his cell phone and called the number Yvette Nereault had given him—the one she made him promise not to write down. The phone rang in the apartment, but there was no answer, not even from a machine. He hung up, and the phone in the apartment stopped ringing. He tried again. Again the phone in the apartment rang. Again it stopped when he hung up.

He considered annoying the hell out of Yvette just by making the phone ring or camping out on the stairs, but he couldn't bring himself to do it. He pictured the kid hiding in the condo, afraid of him. And thought of all the harassment the department had already given this family. He had no warrant, no real reason to be here. He began the walk back to his car.

Where had he seen that kid before?

The boy's eyes made him think of Lefebvre—was the kid Yvette Nereault's son? No—he talked of living here, not in Quebec, and he did not have her accent. Perhaps some other relation to her? Living in Lefebvre's home—he made a note to check property records to see who owned the condo now.

Maybe he was just seeing Lefebvre everywhere. Besides, it wasn't as if the boy was Lefebvre in duplicate—many of his features weren't at all like Lefebvre's. Lucky for the kid, Frank thought wryly.

As he rounded the building, the sensation of being watched made him look up at the rear windows of the condo. He saw the kid staring down at him, his face solemn. Frank waved to him, but the boy didn't wave back.

10

After more than ten years of escaping detection—years of constant vigilance—after thousands of hours spent developing contingency plans and making complicated preparations—the Looking Glass Man began to fear that his elaborate plans would all fall apart here, at a bus station.

He needed nothing more than a frequently used pay phone. The contempt he felt for the persons he encountered at the downtown terminal was increased when he failed to find a working phone that was not already in use.

He glanced at his watch, tried to calm himself. Bredloe routinely put in long hours and could often be found in his office as late as ten o'clock. No need to panic. If he could not find a phone here, then he could go elsewhere—to a shopping mall or even the airport—to find one that would suit his purpose.

He walked out of the building and found a less popular bank of phones situated closer to the parking lot. The parking lot's toll booth was nearby, and the phones were within view of the attendant—he thought this might account for the fewer signs of vandalism on these phones.

Although the attendant was busy with the rush-hour exodus from the lot, the Looking Glass Man did not want to take unnecessary chances, and turned his back to the attendant's booth, so that the logo on his coveralls—Las Piernas Security—faced her. The heat of the day had not subsided, and the coveralls were warm. The wig he wore beneath his billed cap made his own hair damp with perspiration—his scalp began to itch unbearably. So did his upper lip, but he dared not scratch at his small, false mustache for fear of dislodging it. Even the sunglasses were a nuisance, but he consoled himself with the thought that he would not need to wear the disguise much longer.

The one item he would have been pleased to wear—gloves—would have been far too conspicuous. He would now have to touch surfaces a great many other hands had touched. This caused him more discomfort than the itching of his scalp.

His plans were complex, and in many regards experimental, and yet he did not fear failure. Thus far, with the exception of this minor problem of finding a usable pay phone, every step had been carried out with remarkable efficiency. In fact, if all went well, when he was ready to leave, he would not even be required to pay for parking—he would be within the "first thirty minutes free" allowance and save one dollar. A pleasing thought, indeed.

He removed a small device from one of his capacious pockets. Shuddering slightly, he picked up the receiver with his bare hand and fit the device over the mouthpiece. Trying not to think of the contaminants on the push buttons, he dialed a phone number. He pictured Captain Bredloe's cell phone ringing, imagined the captain supposing that his wife, Miriam, was calling. Wouldn't he be surprised!

"Captain Bredloe?" he asked when the call was answered.

"Who is this?"

"I have information you need."

"Who is this? How did you get this number?"

"I'm afraid I can't say—"

"This is a private telephone. Call 555-5773 if you have information for the police."

"Please don't hang up! This is about Lefebvre."

The captain said nothing, but the Looking Glass Man knew that he had the other man's attention. "I don't want the same thing to happen to me that happened to Lefebvre," he went on. "That's why I want to talk to you and only you. I need protection, Captain . . ."

"I'll put you in touch with the detective who's handling the case," Bredloe said. "He can offer you confidentiality and protection if you need it."

"No! You or no one—I can trust no one else in the Las Piernas Police Department. Do you want to know what really happened to the Randolphs? Come to the Sheffield Club tonight at six-thirty. Come alone."

"If you have something we should be interested in, you'll have to get it to me another way."

"I'll prove to you I know what I'm talking about. There was only one item left in the box of evidence—a watch."

There was the briefest hesitation before Bredloe said, "You could have read that in the newspaper."

"No. You know that information wasn't released. The Sheffield Club, six-thirty."

He disconnected, then removed the device that had altered his voice from the mouthpiece. He placed it in a plastic bag so that it would not contaminate his clothing with bacteria from the phone. He took out a small packet containing a disinfectant hand cleaner and used it to wipe his hands. He noticed that the shiny plated surface surrounding the phone's keypad reflected his image, and could not resist wiping a small portion of it so that he could better see himself. He lowered the sunglasses and marveled at his changed appearance.

Reluctantly, he turned away and walked back to his van.

11

When it came to self-control, Irene thought irritably, Frank Harriman was a damned black belt. Usually, this wasn't much of a problem between them—she was well aware that she held the record for getting him to lose his temper, and vice versa—although she would have readily admitted to having a much shorter fuse. Once, when they had snapped at each other in front of his mother, Bea Harriman had said disapprovingly, "You should have known what you were getting into when you married an Irishwoman, Frank."

He had smiled at Irene in a way that had made her suddenly blush from head to toe and said softly, "Oh, I knew." They had said quick good-byes to his mother, left the house, and less than an hour into the drive home, rented a motel room.

Now, as they ran together along the beach, she grinned as she recalled that evening, but when she glanced over at Frank, he seemed lost in his own thoughts—and they didn't seem to be happy ones.

Throughout dinner, he had been tense, alternating between seeming ready to talk to her about something and not meeting her eyes. Not at all like him.

She thought she knew what his problem was. Just before he came home, she had received a call from Rachel, Pete Baird's wife. Rachel let her know that Frank had been getting snubbed at work. Irene was angry that his coworkers were so childish, but was also surprised that he had let it get to him—that wasn't like him, either.

Once or twice, she had looked up from her plate and caught him studying her. Then he would quickly look away. Talk to me, you big lug, she thought. But he didn't.

She was tempted to goad him into saying something, but she decided he didn't need more hassles at home and resolved not to push him this evening. She would just try to help him relax.

The beach run with the dogs was a ritual they followed on any evening when they were both home, and it usually would have helped him to relieve tension. But as this evening's run came to an end, he seemed more ill at ease than before.

Wondering which tactic to try next, she headed up the wooden stairs that led from the beach to their street, Frank and the dogs behind her.

"Have you ever been to a place called the Prop Room?" he asked.

She stopped and looked back at him. "The French-Canadian place near the airport?"

For some reason, her response seemed to trouble him. "Yes," he said. "Have you ever been there?"

"No. A couple of guys at the paper said it's great, though. Want to try it sometime?"

"I had lunch there with Guy today. He came along as a translator."

"Oh. Is this about Phil?"

"His sister knows the owner. We met with his sister today."

Now she was sure she understood what was wrong with him. "Oh, no— you had to give the notice?" She knew he hated that part of the job, telling a family of the death of a loved one.

"Yes."

"I thought Phil's sister was in Canada."

"She's down here for a while."

She shook her head. "I can't believe they didn't give that task to someone who knew Phil."

"Probably better that they didn't. The people in the department who knew him aren't exactly weighed down by fond remembrance. Besides, it's my case."

"Still, I'm sorry—that must have been difficult for you."

He looked away, as if uneasy with her kindness.

"Was it hard on her?"

Frank shrugged. "She had already assumed he was dead, and her husband passed the word on to her before I met with her, but—yes, I think it was hard on her."

She came back down the stairs and looped her arm through his. He seemed, for the briefest moment, to want to move away from her—but just as she wondered if he thought it was too hot out to walk arm in arm, he seemed to make some silent resolution and put his hand over hers.

She was puzzled. Had she done something to make him angry? But this wasn't really anger, it was—what? She didn't know.

They walked in silence, but when they were almost back at the house, he said, "Lefebvre dined at that restaurant the night before he left town."

"The night before he died?"

"Presumably, yes. The night before Seth Randolph was killed."

She called to the dogs, who had loped beyond the house. Where was he going with this?

"The owner of the restaurant said a woman dined with him that night."

She looked up at him then—studying him. Understanding began to dawn.

"It was the day of the press conference—that evening," he was saying. "It's so close to the time he disappeared, I thought it might be important. Or if it isn't—well, I'd like to know that it isn't."

She quickly left his side to put the dogs in the backyard. She turned around, her hands on her hips. "Rachel said the other guys in the department weren't talking to you today."

"They weren't," he said, apprehensive now.

"Oh, yeah? So why am I hearing an insinuation?"

"What insinuation?"

She folded her arms across her chest. "Don't fuck with me, Frank."

"Lower your voice."

"Answer the question," she said, twice as loud.

"Let's go inside. Let's not have this discussion out here on the front lawn."

"You started this discussion in the great outdoors, we can finish here."

"Irene—" he pleaded, glancing at the house next door. "Do you really want Jack and all the other neighbors to have to listen to this?"

"I don't give a rat's ass if they pop popcorn to enjoy with the show!"

"Damn it, Irene—"

"You're wondering if I had dinner with Phil after the press conference. You're wondering if I've—if I've what? Cheated on you before we were together? No—no, that's not it. You aren't that crazy." She considered his questions, not one by one, but as a whole, their direction. "You keep talking about the night before he disappeared. You think—you think Phil and I had some kind of secret, right? About what, Seth Randolph?"

He looked away. "I made a mistake."

"A *mistake?* My God . . . you thought that I've known something about the murder of a sixteen-year-old boy and kept it to myself for ten years? You could believe that of me? Jesus, why am I even trying to talk to you!"

"Irene—" He took hold of her arm, but she shook him off angrily. "God damn it," he said. "Irene, it's my job."

"Oh, really? I have a job, too, so I guess I'll phone in a story—"

"Come on, be reasonable!"

"So now I'm the one being unreasonable? Bullshit! We have rules, Frank, and you've broken them. Don't expect me to shrug that off."

"Look—"

"No, *you* look. A little while ago, I could have sworn I was talking to my husband as his wife—but come to find out I'm secretly being questioned by the Las Piernas Police Department regarding a murder case! Next time let me know who's talking to me—the flaming asshole who works for the PD or the flaming asshole I married." She stormed into the house, slamming the front door behind her.

Her anger squeezed the breath from her, made the house feel too small. The phone was ringing, Frank's pager was beeping, and she kept right on walking, kept right on going, until she was out in the backyard, on the damned patio he had built, seeing the damned garden he had planted. She heard him come in through the front door. She needed to get away from him, from this house, this yard. She kept moving, along the side of the house to the gate, then, taking the dogs with her, headed back to the beach.

Deke and Dunk, at first cowed by her anger, now seemed unable to believe their luck.

She couldn't believe her own.

12

Bredloe was parked five blocks away from the Sheffield Club when his cell phone rang. For a moment, he feared it was the anonymous caller, making a last-minute change in arrangements or canceling altogether. But it was one of the sharpshooters.

"We're in position, Captain."

"The dogs are out?"

"Yes."

"I hope the members of the bomb squad were discreet."

"Yes, sir. Sheriff's department dog handlers showed up dressed as security guards—even had a van made up. No explosives were found."

Bredloe mentally reviewed his hasty preparations: The bomb squad had checked for explosives. Tactical officers were in place in key locations outside the building, and two marksmen were positioned within. A helicopter unit was ready to join in on any pursuit. Other units were standing by. And he was wearing his Kevlar vest.

"You weren't seen?" he asked the marksman.

There was slight hesitation before the SWAT officer answered, "I can't be one hundred percent certain on that, sir. But no, sir, we don't think we were seen."

"I appreciate your honesty, Lieutenant. We're probably on a wild-goose chase here anyway. Civilians have been cleared from the building?"

"We sent the last of the construction crew home an hour ago."

"And no sign of our caller?"

"Not yet, sir."

"I'm on my way, then."

Bredloe stepped onto a plywood ramp that led away from the covered wooden sidewalk, ignoring the handbills that had been plastered everywhere. The narrow passageway from there to the building had been opened only four days ago, and would probably be closed again soon. The Sheffield Club was an active construction site, and only a brief moment of recent limelight had made it accessible to the public.

He didn't know how the anonymous caller had obtained his cell phone number, but he was even more concerned about the fact that he knew about the watch—the caller had been right, it was a detail of the Lefebvre investigation that had not been released to the public. Perhaps the caller had learned of it through a careless comment by a property room clerk, or more seriously, a deliberate leak within the department. He felt almost certain that the caller himself was not a member of the department, because he had asked Bredloe to come here alone.

An urgent invitation to come alone to an empty building? Only an amateur—someone who had watched too many B movies—would have issued it. No one in his department would believe for a moment that someone who had reached his rank would truly come alone. And so he had felt relieved, because the invitation must have been from an outsider. Annoying that the man—if indeed it was a man, for the voice had been altered—had discovered his cell phone number. Obviously the caller had some contacts within the department.

He thought of the caller's distorted voice, tried to remember all that he had said, the phrases he had used. Bredloe had tried to see if it could be traced. It was—to a phone booth outside the downtown bus station. By then, the caller was long gone.

He might have ignored the call, considered it a crank, had it come at any other time. But the phone had rung not long after he had taken a look at some of the documents and evidence in the Randolph cases. He had been made uneasy by Frank Harriman's questions, uneasy enough to begin suspecting that someone in his department had framed Lefebvre.

He was convinced that the call was a crude trap, and had set a more sophisticated trap of his own. While he doubted anything would come of it, he still found himself hoping the caller would follow through. These days, most of his time was spent pushing papers, dealing with department politics, and coping with personnel problems—like the ongoing conflict between Carlson and Harriman. It was good to be involved more actively. He knew the tactical commander and others thought he had lost his mind, but that was just too damn bad. All his "political" work in the department was paying off—if, on rare occasions, he chose to do something on a whim, they had to live with it.

Reaching the entrance to the building itself, Bredloe pushed gently at the brass handle on the old oak door. The door, which should have been locked, opened easily. He hesitated, wondering if the caller had unlocked it earlier in the day, if the construction crew had erred, or if his own team had been a little careless.

He stepped inside, standing still while he let his eyes adjust to the darkness. Although the late summer afternoon was still warm and bright, little warmth or light filtered into the old building.

The Sheffield Club, founded by one of the city's leading families before the turn of the century, had once been a private establishment for the city's wealthiest merchants. It had survived the 1933 earthquake that flattened much of downtown, but by the 1950s, the club had found other quarters, and the building had been sold to the first of a long series of practical businessmen who saw no need to preserve its original charm.

Now the Sheffield Club was the pride of the Historical Preservation Commission, which had found a local investor willing to spend the money needed to restore it—and to retrofit it to meet current earthquake standards.

Bredloe's wife, Miriam, was on the commission, so he had received constant updates on the project over the dinner table at home. Although it appeared to be little more than a brick shell at the moment, he knew that workers in the building had made several discoveries. While replacing the flooring in the building's entry hall, they had uncovered an elaborate, sun-shaped mosaic depicting a golden chariot pulled by winged horses and driven by a half-clad muscular young man. Miriam had shown her husband a photograph of it one evening and assured him that the fellow could be none other than Apollo, but Bredloe pointed out his resemblance to Hector Sheffield, one of the wilder Sheffield sons—a fellow he had learned about while helping her prepare a lecture on the shadier side of Las Piernas's history.

Hector-Apollo had not been the only discovery, though. Just last Friday a press conference had been held on the second floor of the three-story building to show off another treasure—a mural on the north side of the second-floor gallery that surrounded the entry, a richly colored painting of a mythological figure whom Bredloe had continued to refer to as Neptune, even after Miriam told him the name of the work—according to a tarnished brass plate not far from it—was "Poseidon." Until a few weeks ago, the ancient god of the sea and the plate bearing his Greek name had been hidden beneath some cheap paneling. When they attended the press conference, Miriam had been so relieved that her husband did not recognize a resemblance between the god and any reprobates from earlier generations of the Sheffield family, she didn't correct Bredloe's stubborn use of the Roman name.

He had felt completely at ease strolling around the Sheffield Club with his wife on Friday.

But on Friday, Lefebvre's body had still been waiting on a mountainside, silent and undiscovered. On Friday, no one had come into his office hinting that Lefebvre had been framed. On Friday, he would not have agreed to meet an anonymous caller at the Sheffield Club, with or without the precautions he had taken today.

He knew it was not just the coolness of the air inside the building that was sending a chill down his spine.

"I'm here," he announced, his voice reverberating in the darkness. He turned on his standard-issue police flashlight. Its beam glinted off the golden floor tiles. Bredloe wanted to be sure the two marksmen who had hidden themselves on the second-floor gallery knew where he was—and did not mistake him for the caller. He thought it highly unlikely that the caller was in the building.

Still, if need be, the flashlight could also serve as a weapon—it was heavy enough to inflict damage on an attacker. He held it in his left hand, away from his body—unwilling to let it serve as a personal bull's-eye for someone aiming a gun. Bredloe kept his right hand near his own revolver.

Had the caller been scared off?

He heard a sound.

Upstairs, Bredloe thought, somewhere along the gallery. He knew the marksmen were there, but they would be silent. Was the caller up there? He didn't like the idea of a potential enemy standing somewhere above him. He took a small step forward and moved the flashlight, directing the beam upward, near where he thought he had heard the sound. Eerie shadows cast by scaffolding loomed before him, mixed with strange gray reflections as the light played off plastic sheeting draped here and there in the entry hall. He thought he saw a face, then realized it belonged to Neptune.

"I'm here," he said again, and heard the question echo back to him, his voice sounding loud in the emptiness.

There was no answer. He took a cautious step out onto the mosaic.

Instantly, the area was flooded with light. He crouched low, gun unholstered, then realized he had set off some sort of motion detector. Security cameras were catching his foolish reaction. If the cameras had audio capabilities, he thought, they must be picking up the sound of his heart thudding in his chest.

He heard a brief, faint, rustling noise and saw a paper airplane sailing down from the second-floor gallery, making a vertical loop before gliding to a stop near Apollo's golden curls.

Bredloe stayed where he was, angry now. "All right, Tactical, so he hasn't shown. Is this your idea of a joke?"

The snipers slowly moved into view. "Is there a problem, sir?" one of them asked.

The lights went out again, apparently because no further motion was detected.

"Sir?" the SWAT officer called.

"You knew about these motion detectors?" Bredloe called up in the darkness.

"Yes, sir."

He wasn't going to let them know he had been riled. "Nothing. Return to your posts. Let's give him a little more time."

He heard them moving.

He waited. The building was silent.

The airplane still lay on the tile. It annoyed him to think that a situation this serious could be reduced by those hot dogs into fun and games. He walked out to the center of the mosaic, causing the motion detectors to light the entry again. Keeping his eyes on the upper level, he bent to pick up the airplane, setting the flashlight down just long enough to tuck the paper into his jacket pocket. As he picked up the flashlight, the lights above him went out again, which puzzled him—he was still moving, so the detectors should have kept them on.

Suddenly he heard a mechanical sound from somewhere on the scaffolding, and then a loud bang behind him. He caught a brief glimpse of shadowy objects falling from above, like bats suddenly stirring from a cave, and tried to move out of their path—but the first of the bricks struck hard on his back and shoulders, making him shout in pain. He heard the tactical team shouting from above as he moved his arms up, trying to shield his head, but this only caused his forearms to be broken and his fingers smashed, so that he fired the gun even as his hand lost its grasp on it, and dropped the flashlight almost in the same instant. He doubled over, crying out for help, stumbling forward, and still the awful rain continued, bruising and breaking him. One glancing blow to his head hit hard enough to bring him dizzily to his knees, the next felled him completely, so that he sprawled against the white wings of Apollo's horses, staining them with his blood, and lost consciousness as tiles of the sun god shattered all around him.

13

Pete Baird met Frank at the entrance to the waiting room. He looked shaken, and Frank was afraid that he had arrived too late.

Pete had been paging him, leaving messages on his home answering machine. Frank had heard Pete's voice on the machine as he had followed Irene into the house, saying, "Bredloe's at the emergency room at St. Anne's—he might not make it," and Frank had hurriedly picked up the call. Only twenty-five minutes had passed since then—but maybe it had been twenty-five minutes too many.

Pete must have read the fear on his face, though, because he quickly said, "No—we haven't had any more news yet."

"He's still in surgery?"

"Yeah. It's not looking good. Head injury and all kinds of bone fractures and cuts and bruises and God knows what else. Head injuries worry them the most. Miriam hasn't even been able to see him yet—she's really shaken up."

Frank looked across the room and saw Bredloe's wife, pale and silent, staring toward the doors that led to the surgery center. Next to her was Chief Ellis Hale himself, who sat stone-faced while one of his aides tried to calm a distraught Louise Oswald. Not far from them, several men from the division huddled together, speaking in low voices. Lieutenant Carlson, Jake Matsuda, Reed Collins, and others. They had seen him enter, but he had not been met with scowls or coldness—not even from Carlson. Like Pete, they had apparently decided to cease hostilities for the moment.

Frank turned back to Pete. "Was Miriam with him when it happened?"

"No—I thought she might have been, when I first heard it was the Sheffield. Captain had his picture in the paper over the weekend, 'cause he went with her to some shindig they had there on Friday. So I figured she had taken him back to the building for some reason—but that turns out not to be the case."

"What happened?"

"The captain had a whole operation set up down there, and on short notice." He described the precautions Bredloe had taken.

"So what was this anonymous caller meeting him about?"

"He wouldn't tell anyone. According to the Wheeze, she came back from running an errand for him at a little after five o'clock, and he was on the cell phone with someone then. She locked her desk up and was ready to call it a day when the captain asked her to get Tactical on the line—one of many calls." He paused, eyeing Frank speculatively. "She said he'd been acting weird ever since he talked to you."

"Like everybody else in the department, the captain was upset about the Lefebvre case," Frank said. "Now that you've remembered I'm working it, are you going to stop talking to me?"

Pete shrugged. "I wish you'd face facts, but—no, I was ready to call a truce anyway. Besides, Rachel found out I wasn't speaking to you, and—let's just say I thought I was going to need to check in here myself."

"Remind me to thank your wife the next time I see her. But tell me more about what happened to the captain. Any idea who called him?"

"No. Pay phone at the bus station—too many prints to make it worthwhile dusting for them. The lab found one little area on it that had been wiped down and figured that the caller cleaned up after himself."

"So Bredloe gets a call and just trots off to the Sheffield Club?" Frank asked. "That doesn't sound like him."

"No, but that's just item one on a long list of things we haven't figured out. We're not even sure what happened after he was there. First, he keeps setting off the motion detectors and cameras in the entryway—all of which, we learned, was just installed today. So because of the lights attached to the motion detectors, it goes bright and dark and makes the marksmen's work more difficult—they hardly adjust their eyes to darkness and suddenly it's bright again. Then the captain says something that makes no sense to the marksmen—is this 'their idea of a joke.' Next thing they know, there's this sound, and a pile of bricks falls down on him from some scaffolding."

"The building had been searched, though—"

"All done by remote."

"What? Remote-control bricks?"

"No—but there was this gizmo beneath the pallet they were on. Kinda like a miniature jack. Small, but strong enough to tip the pallet. It straightens up and suddenly the bricks are at an angle and falling. Lab hasn't had much time to study it, but they think it's homemade—not something commercially available."

"So with luck they'll be able to track down the sellers of the components."

"Right. And track the buyer from there."

"The cameras didn't catch anyone setting up that device?"

"Well," Pete said uneasily, "that's another problem. Those cameras and motion detectors just arrived today—at the end of the day. Battery operated. And guess what was being taped on the machine? Nothing, that's what. It was a dummy setup. I mean, the monitor worked, but the tape machine didn't."

"What did the security company have to say for itself?"

"You mean 'Las Piernas Security'? There is no such security company. No one ordered those cameras or lights or monitor."

"The construction crew allowed this phony company to have the run of the place?"

"Did a very good job of faking city papers, they claim. Apparently there had been complaints about building security all along."

"Not hard to see why."

"Something else—nobody can figure this out—there was a little remote-controlled fan."

"What?"

"This other little gizmo reacts to a signal and turns a small fan on. But we can't figure out what the fan was supposed to do."

"So no one saw the cameras being installed?"

"Saw it, paid no attention. And although we got a description on the installer, it was pretty vague. White male, medium build, thirty to fifty—yeah, I know, but the age guesses were all over the place—light brown hair, brown eyes, mustache. About all we have to go on, though."

"What was the range on the remotes?"

"Not all that far—lab says he was probably less than a block away the whole time."

They became aware of a small commotion and saw a doctor wearing scrubs walking toward Chief Hale and Miriam Bredloe. He escorted the two of them to another room. All conversation in the waiting area stopped. When they returned, it was clear that the captain's wife had been crying. The chief's expression was grim.

The Wheeze moaned loudly and Frank heard the chief snap, "Get that fool woman out of here," to the aide. The aide complied, hustling her away so quickly, she didn't seem to notice Frank's presence as they went past him.

With Miriam, Hale was all solicitude, gently guiding her to a seat next to him, speaking to her in soothing tones. Frank was relieved to see her grow visibly calmer.

"She doesn't have any friends or family with her?" he asked Pete.

"Her sister is driving down from Tulare, so it may be a few hours before she's here. We asked about friends, but to be honest, I think she was still in a state of shock then. The chief has been good to her, and she knows we're all here for her, too."

Another half hour passed. Miriam Bredloe gradually began looking around the room. She saw Frank and beckoned him to come nearer. He approached as the chief watched him with apparent interest. Frank nodded a greeting to him. The two men seldom came in contact with each other.

"Thank you for coming here," Miriam said. "Is Irene with you?"

"No, I'm sorry, she's not," he said uneasily. *She's mad as hell at me.*

Miriam Bredloe turned to Hale and said, "Detective Harriman's wife shares my love of old buildings. She's written stories about the commission's work for the *Express* and has done a great deal to help us save a number of Las Piernas's treasures from the wrecking ball. We've become friends."

"You don't say," the chief murmured, seeming to regard Frank a little more closely. Frank wondered if Chief Hale was among those who thought wrecking balls represented progress, or if he thought Irene must be the type of woman who kissed up to the boss's wife—an idea that would have made Frank laugh out loud under any other circumstances.

"My husband was going to meet an informer in the Sheffield Club tonight," Miriam said. "Louise—not that I think she's very sensible in a crisis—but Louise seemed to think you'd know which one it was."

"Me? I'm sorry, Miriam—I don't. I wish I did."

"Oh," she said, clearly disappointed. "I guess Louise was mistaken."

"Louise sometimes . . ." Glancing at the chief, Frank decided not to finish the sentence.

"You don't have to explain," Miriam said. "This isn't the first wild idea she's had."

"Harriman," the chief interrupted, still studying him. "You're handling the Randolph cases, aren't you?"

"Yes, sir," Frank said, surprised not only that Ellis Hale knew such a detail, but also that he didn't refer to it as the "Lefebvre case."

Hale frowned and glanced toward Carlson, but said nothing more.

"Your sister is on her way?" Frank asked Miriam.

"Yes, but I don't think she'll make it down here much before midnight."

"Harriman," the chief said, "perhaps you should call your wife and tell her that Miriam here could use another female—a sensible female—by her side tonight."

"If Mrs. Bredloe would like that, sir—certainly." He wondered if Irene would answer the phone if he called.

"Oh, yes," Miriam said. "Thank you."

"One other thing," the chief said.

"Yes, sir?"

"Trent Randolph was a man I thought of with respect, and he was a friend of this department. When I think of what he might have been able to do as a commissioner had he lived . . ." His brows drew together, deepening his frown. "I was supposed to meet with him before he left for that trip to Catalina with his children. I was forced to reschedule—and Trent offered to cancel the trip so that we could meet that same day. You don't know how many times I've wished I'd agreed to that offer. But I told him to enjoy his weekend with his kids and set up a meeting for that Monday. I never saw him again."

"I'm sorry, sir."

"Not half as sorry as I am, that's for damn sure. When Trent's son was murdered . . ." He faltered and fell silent, suddenly looking tired. Several moments passed before he seemed to shake off his memories and the mood he had fallen into. The chief glanced at Carlson again, then said to Frank, "Your father was in law enforcement, wasn't he?"

"Yes, sir. Bakersfield PD."

"Then no one needs to explain to you the importance of resolving this matter quickly."

"The matter of Lefebvre's guilt or innocence?"

"Don't mention that name to me!" the chief snapped.

Taken aback, Frank said nothing.

Miriam straightened in her chair. She stared at the chief in disbelief and said, "Ellis, I wouldn't have expected that from you."

The chief's face flamed red. He seemed more embarrassed than angry, but Frank found himself wishing that Miriam had not come to his defense.

"Call your wife, Detective Harriman," Hale said brusquely, then stared at him, as if daring him to react to this curt dismissal.

It rankled, but he wasn't about to let Hale know that. Keeping his voice cool and even, he said, "Yes, sir," and walked away.

He had to walk outside the building to get a signal for his cell phone. He called home and got the answering machine—not a good sign.

"Irene? It's Frank. Are you there?" He waited, but she didn't answer before the machine cut the call off. He had left a note for her, telling her where he was and asking her to listen to the messages Pete had left on the answering machine. He wondered if she had even seen the note—or bothered to read it. Maybe she had been too busy packing.

As he tried to decide what to do next, his cell phone rang. The caller ID display on the phone showed his home number. "Irene?" he answered.

"How's Bredloe doing?"

"Not good. There may be brain damage, and he might not even—" The words seemed to sink in for the first time as he said them. He suddenly felt his throat tighten and couldn't go on.

The silence stretched, then she said, "Do you need me to be there?"

"I know you hate hospitals, but Miriam's here with nothing but—nothing but flaming assholes from the department around her."

"That *is* an emergency. I'll see you in a few minutes."

They didn't talk about their argument, though he could tell she was still angry with him. But long after the others—including the chief—left, they stayed with Miriam. Frank was glad Irene was there to comfort her—and to help him keep his own hopes up.

Those hopes suffered a setback a little before ten o'clock, when he first saw Bredloe.

The captain had been moved into the intensive care unit. He had not regained consciousness. Frank tried to tell himself that he had seen crime victims survive more terrible injuries, but he had not known those individuals personally or seen them before they were hurt. He could not reconcile the Bredloe he knew, always a strong and healthy man, with the pale, stitched, and bandaged one lying so still on this hospital bed, attached by tubing and wiring to machines and medications.

The doctors seemed to think that their work to save the captain's life had gone well and were optimistic about his chances for survival, even if they avoided predicting what impairments the head injuries would cause.

An orderly handed Miriam a large plastic bag, explaining that it contained the clothing her husband had been wearing when he was admitted. Frank watched as she peered into the bag, then reached to support her as she nearly fainted.

"Let Frank look through it for you," Irene suggested as he guided Miriam to a chair.

But Miriam shook her head and began sorting what remained of the bloodstained and battered clothing from inside the bag. She separated the contents, placing them on the chair next to her own, then tenderly folded each item before putting it back in the bag. The pants were completely ruined, obviously cut away by ER doctors hurrying to treat his wounds. His shirt had not fared much better. She was smoothing the stained but relatively intact suit coat when she paused, then reached into an inside pocket. She removed what Frank at first thought was a document of some kind. She held it up, a puzzled look on her face.

"What in the world was he doing with this?" she asked.

As Frank drew closer, he saw the reason for her question. What he had thought to be a document was a fancy paper airplane.

14

The Looking Glass Man double-checked all the blinds and curtains. He secured all three dead bolts on the front door, pausing to polish his fingerprints from their gleaming brass surfaces. He did not do this because of
concerns regarding evidence—it was perfectly natural that his own fingerprints would be found in his own home. He simply did not like to see any
sort of smudge on the locks.

Satisfied with these and other safeguards, he moved to the back of the
house, to the large walk-in closet off his bedroom. The light was already
on—triggered by a motion detector in the bedroom itself. He took a moment to survey the perfectly polished and aligned shoes, to admire the shirts
on their hangers—all facing the same way, each buttoned up to the second
highest button on the front. They were arranged by color, lightest to darkest,
and each was spaced exactly three-quarters of an inch from the shirt next to
it, so that they never touched and therefore never wrinkled or creased a
neighboring shirt. He glanced at the side of the closet that held his more casual clothes and adjusted the neatly ironed pair of blue jeans so that it was
more precisely centered on its hanger.

The switch for the closet light was in the "on" position. It was always in
this position. He pushed slightly on one side of the switch plate, which, like
the switch itself, was nothing more than camouflage. The plate swung away
to reveal an alarm keypad. He entered a code and heard a series of bolts
click in the ceiling above him. He moved a small step stool to the middle of
the closet floor.

He pulled down on the access door to the attic, which was unlocked. He did not place a lock on the door because he did not wish to draw attention to it. He returned the step stool to its place, then lowered the ladder built into the access door. Carefully, he climbed until he could reach the true barrier to the attic: a heavy, steel-plated hatch. He lifted it, reaching for the switches for the lights and ventilation system inside the attic before climbing higher.

He smiled to himself, just as he always did when entering this room. He still used other sites as needed, but after the Randolph killings he felt it had become imperative that he acquire a permanent residence over which he was the only landlord, the only man with keys to the front door.

The element of risk did not excite him. He disliked risk. That was why he needed a special house, a house that would seem like any other house from the outside. He had patiently waited for a house in this tract, where every fifth or sixth home was of a style with a high-pitched roof. It was, in fact, the very neighborhood where Wendell Leroy Wallace had once lived. Wallace had been a man with the kind of genius that the Looking Glass Man admired. Like Wallace, he needed a place to build unique devices.

Not that anyone looking at the house from the street would be aware of the extraordinary activities taking place within it. Even from the inside— unless one knew where to look—the house seemed average.

Far less important to him than the house itself was this attic room. He bought this house because of the pitch of its roof. He ran the numbers in his head—the pitch of the roof was 12/12—the attic was fifteen feet high under the ridge and sloped steeply to zero at the walls—a lovely space of eight hundred square feet where the headroom was over seven feet. He found construction nearly as fascinating as destruction.

He ate and slept and bathed in the house, but these were activities he could have carried out in any house. Some said a man's home was his castle, but he preferred to think of his home as a moat, a large defense system protecting the real castle—this attic with its hidden treasures.

He had done almost all of the work on the attic himself, a fact that pleased him for many reasons—one being that his participation reduced the need to eliminate more than two skilled workmen after they had completed their part of the project. It had not been difficult to arrange the deaths of a roofer and his helper at their next job site. People expected roofers to fall off roofs in the same way they expected race car drivers to crash.

He regretted the necessity, of course. He did not enjoy killing. Murder was always a last resort, to be avoided if at all possible. The roofers—although they *did* fail to obtain the proper building permits for the work done on his property—weren't really criminals. Even though that permit business technically made them lawbreakers, he counted them among the innocent. Until today, only six of his victims had been innocent. Bredloe made the seventh.

He cringed, realizing that he was guilty of an inaccuracy. Bredloe was still clinging to life, and Bredloe could not, therefore, be counted as a murder victim. Not yet.

Careless thinking. Careless thinking easily led to careless actions. He did not have a perfect record. He knew this. It was the source of most of his unhappiness.

He pulled the ladder up after him, secured the access door and hatch, and reset the alarm from a pad inside the attic. Should anyone enter the house while he was up here, he would have plenty of time to destroy any incriminating materials. The mere thought of finding it necessary to do so made him shudder.

He took his newest notebook from its hiding place in one of the small safes in the attic floor—the compartment under the loose carpeting in the northeast corner of the room—and placed it on the immaculate desk in the middle of the room. He selected a mechanical pencil from a line of three of them in the top drawer of the desk.

He closed his eyes for a moment, mentally reviewing the events of the day. He had been forced to act hastily—haste was not the same thing as carelessness, merely an invitation to it. He must make certain that any errors were corrected. This was his first opportunity to reflect on all that had happened today . . .

He had been paged while watching Harriman. The page had not been sent by a human caller. Years ago, he had made a change in the software used in the property room. The people who worked in Property were like most people who used computers. They used them in the same way they used their refrigerators and television sets—as long as the computer functioned and did what they expected it to do, they did not investigate its inner workings.

So when he made the small change in the program, it went unnoticed. The property room staff was totally unaware that whenever anyone asked for evidence from certain cases, the property room computer sent a message to his own computer. And when his computer received the message, it dialed his pager number and left a code indicating which evidence had been requested and the name of the person making the request.

Today it had indicated that Bredloe was looking at the evidence the department had gathered against Lefebvre. When he realized which evidence in particular the captain had studied, his sense of alarm had increased.

It would not be easy, he had realized, to lure Bredloe away from the office. An intensive investigation would be launched into any attack on the captain of the Homicide Division. Seeing the newspaper article about the unveiling of the mural had reminded him of the Sheffield Club, and suddenly he had known where he would ask Bredloe to meet him. The Looking Glass Man had attended the event—not knowing at that time how useful it would be.

It had not been difficult to gain access to the building. The disguise had been effective. He already knew that security at the site was lax. No one on that job would question someone who was carrying equipment *into* the building. He had entered unnoticed while most of the workers were washing up and putting their tools away.

He was able to install the cameras and lights within thirty minutes. It was the end of the workday—the Sheffield was already nearly empty. While he ran cables to a monitor—which would only appear to be taping what was seen by the cameras—he checked to make sure no one was nearby. Then he used a pallet jack to position the load of bricks and put the remote-controlled lift in place beneath the pallet itself.

He made sure that the ramp from the publicity event was still accessible and that Bredloe would be able to enter through the front doors. The most difficult aspect to arrange was the single whimsical note—the paper airplane. He had worried that the small fan—a second remote would trigger its operation—would be discovered before he was ready to launch the plane. He dared not try a test launch there, and feared the plane would not perform as he hoped it would—in the science of paper airplane flight, every room was different, with drafts and thermal factors that could ruin everything.

Though he had installed the fan that afternoon, the plane had been ready to go since Saturday, when the department grapevine was buzzing with rumors about Lefebvre's plane being found. He had intended the paper plane for Frank Harriman, a final little touch to be used at some future date if necessary—but the Looking Glass Man had decided to use it now, curious to see if Harriman would make the connection between it and the Cessna. But today's flight had not, after all, been such a bad experiment.

With everything in place, he had made a single phone call—at that dreadful bus station!—and the captain was on his way.

He had been pleased with all the mechanical aspects of the plan and could not help but feel a sense of pride in his quick thinking. He was not so foolish as to believe his problems were over now. But he had been able to contain the damage that might have been done. He sighed, saddened that his work on behalf of justice require the sacrifice of a man like Bredloe. This, he decided, must be how a victorious general felt in the aftermath of battle—exhilarated by the achievement but mournful over the loss of life among his troops. Like a general, he must concentrate on the ultimate and worthy objective. Some lives might be lost, but many others would be saved. By his own reckoning, he had already saved hundreds of lives, spared all kinds of suffering and deprivation.

Yes, he thought, I am a general. At war with Judge Lewis Kerr.

The Looking Glass Man acknowledged that he was driven by hatred, not of a race or nation—that kind of hatred he found abhorrent—but rather of a single individual. He did not consider this hatred an imperfection, and his hatred of Judge Kerr did not make him unhappy. On the contrary, he knew his anger toward Kerr fueled all the finer fires of his existence. At its onset, that anger had been a remedy for pain, and seeking relief, he had fantasized Kerr's death at his hands a thousand times over. Each hour, it seemed, brought some new vision of Kerr's demise: a delivery of food poisoned with undetectable substances, a prescription that had been altered, household "accidents"—an electrical problem or a small but smoky fire—a shove into traffic or down a flight of stairs. He had seen so much murder in his career, it was not difficult to consider methods that might end another man's life.

These visions of Kerr's death brought a certain measure of delight, but none seemed to correspond with the Looking Glass Man's notions of a fitting punishment, and so he hesitated to implement any of them. Sadly, he would only be able to kill Kerr once and must not squander his chance.

Over the years, though, as his anger burned on—hollowing him, hardening him—he became glad for the reluctance that had made him delay the pleasure of slaying Kerr—for in that time he learned of a magnificent opportunity, a perfect event to bring matters to an appropriate close, an event that was now not so far away. A plan had slowly emerged, and he prepared. He learned his craft, honed his skills. And took comfort in the good he was doing while he waited.

He had bided his time in the service of justice. It had become a challenge, a true challenge, to make certain that the worst criminals set loose by Kerr's idiotic rulings were later caught again and prosecuted successfully. It mattered not at all to the Looking Glass Man that the criminals were never guilty of these later crimes, that these later crimes were ones he himself had planned. No, that was the joy of it! He wrote the script, managed the stage, set the props, and ultimately, directed the action. If someone else got the credit for capturing these lowlifes, it didn't trouble him. After all, the arresting officers were just another set of players. The last thing he wanted was the limelight.

And so certain anonymous tips nearly always led to arrests, and then convictions, because he orchestrated events to ensure the best outcome. He did his best to ensure that the evidence was in place, that witnesses would be present, that anything that had gone wrong in the first trial would not go wrong in the second.

He frowned as his thoughts strayed to Trent Randolph and to Seth and Amanda. He thought of Lefebvre and suddenly shivered. Was there some divine message here? A warning from the cosmos, perhaps? Some reason Lefebvre's body had been found now, of all times, when he was within reach of his long-awaited goal?

Lefebvre! Even now, Lefebvre caused him trouble.

He stood and walked over to a short row of file cabinets, precisely positioned in an area that would support their weight. The drawers of the cabinets were labeled by date. He unlocked one and pulled the second drawer open. He did this every day—came to this room, opened a file cabinet, and read from a file. Sometimes he could read one in a day; other files took several days to complete. He read them in order, oldest to newest, and back again. This ritual kept him focused on his calling.

He had been collecting information on Kerr for years now. He doubted Kerr himself had such meticulous records of his own actions. Tonight's reading was the final section of a lengthy transcript of court proceedings. It was a case in which Kerr dismissed all charges against a man who had asked his ex-wife and young son to drive with him to visit the child's paternal grandparents—then taken them to a remote area and shot and killed them both. Judge Kerr claimed the evidence against the man was gathered in an improper search. The transcript was just the sort of thing the Looking Glass Man needed to read right now, because it reminded him of why he must fight this good fight. He carefully replaced the file and went back to the desk.

He opened the notebook to a new page, ready to begin to write up this latest event. He would start with the moment his pager went off, when he was in his van watching Harriman look at maps in his car. He placed the tip of his mechanical pencil in the middle of the first square, then lifted it again as a new question occurred to him.

Where had Harriman been all afternoon?

15

He watched the taillights of the Jeep Cherokee as he followed Irene home. They had left Miriam in the care of her sister, who had arrived—remarkably energetic after her long drive—a little before eleven-thirty. Irene had followed him to the department, where he had taken a moment to examine the paper airplane. Wearing gloves, he had gently unfolded it, looking for writing or any other enclosed message. There was none. The plane had been made with over a dozen folds, and a section of the tail had been shaped by cutting curves into it. He had filled out paperwork describing when and where the plane had been found, then placed a copy of it with the plane in an evidence locker, where it would remain secure until the lab examined it.

Now, at last, he thought, they could call it a day.

They were stopped at a light when his cell phone rang.

"Hi—it's Polly Logan. If you come by right now, I can show you the tape."

"Now? It's after—"

"I do know how to tell time, Frank. You said I could call anytime, and it's now or never. I'm not sure how my station manager will feel about my showing this to you, so I'd rather not have a lot of folks around while you're looking at it—all right? You know where the station is?"

"Yes."

She gave him directions to a back entrance. "And don't tell the doofus at the gate that you're a cop. He's a wannabe, and he'll keep you there all night. Besides—"

"The station manager."

"Right."

He tried calling Irene's cell phone number, but got her voice mail. He hung up without leaving a message. He sighed in frustration. She probably didn't have it with her—she disliked it and had only recently agreed to carry one at all.

This was not the time to complain to her about it, he decided.

He pulled alongside the Jeep at the next intersection and motioned to Irene to roll down her window.

"I'll make sure you get home safely, but then I'll have to take off. I've got to meet with someone on the other side of town."

"They've given you another case?"

"No, more of the same. This just worked out to be the only time I could get together with this person."

"'Person,' huh? Must be a woman. If you're going in the other direction, don't worry about following me home. I'll be okay."

He found himself unable to resist saying, "I'd feel better if you had your cell phone with you."

She shrugged. "I'll be okay," she repeated, a little impatiently. When she saw his reluctance to let it go, she added, "Besides, Big Brother, you can ask the comm center to track the Jeep's LoJack signal if you're worried that I'm heading out of state."

"Before you decide that the LoJack in the Jeep is there just in case I want to abuse my mighty police powers, I'd remind you that Ben had it installed long before we bought the Jeep from him."

"Don't take everything I say so seriously, Frank. And you don't need to watch over me every minute. I'll be fine. I'll call you when I get in, if it will make you feel better."

Afraid she was feeling hemmed in, he said, "All right. I'll be home as soon as I can. Listen—I'm sorry this meeting came up. I was hoping we could talk."

She shook her head. "Not a good time to do that anyway. I'm beat."

A car pulled up behind her and the driver tapped his horn—the light had changed. She moved off, waving to Frank as she drove through the intersection.

He watched until he could no longer see the Jeep's taillights, then made a U-turn.

• • •

If someone had hauled away the satellite dishes and painted over the mural that adorned one side of the Channel 6 studios, the building would have looked no more exciting than a warehouse. The mural showed the "News Where You Live Team" in smiling, bright-eyed, larger-than-life scale. He noticed that Polly Logan's portrait was also younger than life.

The gatekeeper was a cheerful, middle-aged man whose girth was wedged nearly miraculously into a tall armchair. Frank wondered how, if a pursuit were necessary, the fellow would ever get to his feet.

When he gave the man his name, the gatekeeper responded with a knowing smile and said, "That Polly is something, isn't she?" He handed him a clipboard, then went back to reading a crumpled copy of *Hustler*. Frank wrote his name illegibly and handed it back. The guard didn't look at it. He picked up a phone and dialed a number.

Frank's cell phone rang while the guard was talking to someone inside the building.

"Hi," Irene said. "I made it home, safe and sound."

At that moment, the guard leaned out and handed him a visitor's badge, saying in a loud voice, "Here you go, lover boy, a pass to see Polly Logan. But a word to the wise—with the stuff that's going around these days, you'd better wear a rubber—that broad has laid more pipe than the local plumbers' union."

He heard Irene disconnect.

He drove through the gate, parked in the nearly empty lot, and tried calling home. He got the answering machine. "Irene, I know you're there. Please pick up the phone."

Nothing.

"You aren't going to let one loudmouthed knucklehead cause us problems, are you?"

He heard her pick up the receiver—and set it right back down in the cradle.

He swore, turned the phone off, and headed for the building's back entrance.

The cloying scent of Polly Logan's perfume hit him before he saw her. She stood waiting for him, a blond beacon at the end of a dimly lit hallway—a narrow figure clad in a dark blue suit and high heels that would have made a stilt-maker proud. At six four, he was a tall man, but he thought he was only about half a foot above being eye-to-eye with her. In this semidarkness, she bore at least some resemblance to the woman on the mural. He knew better. In her efforts to stay in front of the camera, Polly Logan must have spent most of the money she had made there on cosmetic surgery. The results were now in the waxworks stage—her blue eyes had that wide-open, perpetually startled look that was a by-product of too many facelifts, her mouth and chin so stiff as to make a ventriloquist's dummy's seem more supple, and her satiny, wrinkle-free face was, alas, perched atop her original, aging neck, making her look as if her head had been transplanted to the wrong body.

"Frank," she said, extending a hand, "good to see you."

The hand was smooth but dry and bony, so that he felt as if he were grasping an albino bat's wing. He let go before the bat did. "I appreciate your willingness to help me out."

"I'm sure I'll be able to think of a way for you to return the favor," she said with a smile.

He thought he might have grimaced in response.

She didn't seem to notice and sauntered toward a door at the end of the hallway. "Come along, I've set this up in one of the conference rooms."

She aimed a remote at a television set attached to a VCR. When the set came on, she immediately pressed a volume button, so that the sound was nearly muted. "I don't want to attract a lot of attention to what we're doing in here," she said. "Not just because you're a cop, but because—well, I've taken a lot of crap around here about keeping these."

"These?" he asked, wondering how long he'd be trapped here with her, watching videotapes.

"The original footage, I mean. The clips I copied to make this one for you." She smiled. "A labor of love."

"How long is the final product?" he asked.

"Two hours," she said, and pressed the play button on the remote.

The first few minutes were made up of footage from about a dozen years ago, she explained. "I shot most of this myself."

Fleeting images of Lefebvre went by. There was an almost voyeuristic quality in them that Frank found unsettling. Most of the time Lefebvre clearly wasn't aware he was on camera. The woman was all but stalking him.

"He had the most interesting eyes," she said softly, after a close-up.

The rest of the tape had been shot by other camera operators. Frank glanced at Polly as she narrated in a low voice. "This was after he solved the Berton case." Then "This is at the courthouse, after he testified against Hunter." She gazed at the screen, caught up in memories, giving a running commentary that prevented him from hearing the soundtrack of the tape.

He half listened as Polly droned on. When the press conference in Seth Randolph's room came on the screen, Frank found himself distracted to see Irene, ten years younger. Although younger, she had dark circles under her eyes. She seemed tired, he thought, a little down, and—what was that quality he saw in her face? Vulnerability. Yes, she seemed more vulnerable then.

The camera went back to Tory Randolph, but Frank was still thinking of Irene. He remembered her comments about getting to know Lefebvre during her father's long, final illness. Rough days. But for all this, when the camera next was on her, he saw a familiar impishness in her eyes—she was calling out a question.

"Ex-husband, correct?" she asked on the tape.

He could see the amusement of some of the other journalists before the camera went back to Tory Randolph, who was saying something about not thinking of Trent Randolph as her ex-husband. Frank shook his head. From reading the files, he knew that within a few months of this press conference, Tory Randolph remarried. She married Dale Britton, a man who had worked in the crime lab. They had already met by the time of the press conference—Britton had been one of the criminalists on the case.

Polly had asked him a question, he realized. "Pardon?"

"Tory—have you ever seen such a stage hog?"

Nothing he saw on the tape made him think she was wrong, but he didn't answer.

The camera went back to Seth Randolph for a moment. Knowing how little future Seth had—knowing the futures of many of the people he was now watching—Frank found the tape unsettling. Lefebvre and Seth Randolph would die violently the next evening. Lefebvre, obviously a hero at this point, would be in disgrace during the ensuing decade. Irene would bury her father and suffer other ordeals, including being held captive in a small room—an experience that would leave her far too claustrophobic to stay calm in a room as crowded as the one on the tape.

She would also marry Frank—although she might, at the moment, count that as another ordeal.

Polly Logan would fail miserably at recapturing her youth—a bird that was already well on the wing ten years ago. As he watched, he was surprised by how much footage she had kept of this press conference—it was much more extensive than what had gone before on the tape. When he commented about this to her, she said, "I kept all of it, because it was the last time I ever saw him." Tears started rolling down her expensive cheeks. "And the things they said about him! Look at him! Does he look as if he wants to harm that boy? No! He's more protective of Seth than Tory is!"

Frank had to agree. The brief shots he had seen in Bredloe's office on the afternoon news were, he realized, misleading. And when Seth's reactions were shown in context, rather than in the brief segment he had seen before, he could see that the boy trusted Lefebvre—had turned to him for protection, in fact.

Hearing Polly sniff, Frank offered a tissue to her. She thanked him, wiped delicately at her eyes, then murmured, "I loved him, you know." She blew her sculpted nose. "Not requited, I'll admit."

"No? You didn't ever go out together?"

She shook her head, looking more miserable than ever. "No, not even when *I* asked *him*. He turned me down flat. He was too busy panting after your wife."

"I don't blame him," he said evenly. "She was single, after all."

"Your loyalty is refreshing, and of course you're right—she was *very* available in those days."

She glanced up at him, saw the hard look that had come into his eyes, and said, "Don't get bent out of shape—I didn't mean anything by it." She gave a short, bitter laugh. "God knows, I can't cast any stones."

He thought of the boy he had seen at the condo and asked, "Do you know of anyone else Lefebvre might have dated?"

"Other than Irene? No. Except for trying to go after her, he was married to his work."

The tape started hissing, and she removed it from the VCR and held it out to him. "This copy is yours, if you'd like it."

"Thanks," he said. "This is a real help. And thanks for your time this evening." He said this politely, even though he was irritated with her. If she had simply given him the tape or sent it to him at the department, he could have gone home much earlier. Instead, she had forced him to attend this private screening with her, while she grew maudlin over a man who had not, apparently, returned her affection.

Her devotion to Lefebvre did not puzzle him—long ago he had realized that some people never really wanted what they could have. Some women would fall in love with priests, with gay men, with men who were in love with other women—precisely because they were unobtainable. This devotion at a distance seldom ended with the beloved's death—after all, nobody was more unobtainable than a dead man.

"When I heard you were on the case," Polly said, looping an arm through his as she led him out, "I knew Phil stood a chance."

He halted. A vision of Lefebvre as he had found him—dried remains in the wreckage of a plane—flashed before him. "A chance?"

She urged him forward. "Yes, to be proven innocent. It would have been important to him." When they were almost at the building's exit, she said, "I always hoped he'd come back alive. I thought I might be able to get him to take a second look, you know what I mean?"

"Sure."

At the door he gently extricated his arm, said good night, and made his way back to the car. As he shut the car door, he could smell her perfume on his suit.

Perhaps she didn't get all that plastic surgery to keep her job, he thought. Maybe she was trying to bookmark a page in her life, trying to stay at a certain point in the story, so that Lefebvre would come back to her like a reader who had only temporarily set her aside and find his place.

He turned his phone on, and it beeped twice to indicate that he had a voice-mail message. He retrieved the call, which had been received about five minutes after Irene had hung up on him.

"Frank, I'm sorry. Call me as soon as you have the phone back on—wake me up, I won't care. Call me. I keep thinking about Bredloe and—just call and let me know you're safe, okay?"

He glanced at his watch. It was after three in the morning.

He drove home without calling.

She was awake. She met him at the door, drowsy but intent, and without saying a word took his face in her hands and kissed him long and hard. He made a small, low sound of surrender, and she pulled him closer. She stepped back a little, wrinkled her nose as she caught the scent of the perfume, but didn't remark on it. He started to say something, but she stopped him with another kiss, this one softer, sweeter, coaxing.

"Enough talk," she said.

16

The story of the attack on Bredloe made the front page of the *Express*. A much smaller story about Lefebvre's funeral appeared on one of the inside pages. Frank had just finished reading it when his phone rang.

"Harriman," he answered.

"How dare you give that man a special police funeral!" a woman screeched.

"Excuse me?"

"This is Detective Frank Harriman—am I right?"

"Yes, it is."

"This is Tory Randolph-Britton."

He could see her in his mind, or at least her image as she appeared on the tape he had viewed the previous night. "Trent Randolph's ex-wife?"

"I never thought of him that way!" she said, as if she had just watched the same tape and knew her lines. "But yes, I was married to Trent, and Amanda was my daughter, and Seth was my son. My son—do you understand? And you are about to give my son's murderer a funeral with—with bagpipes and things!"

"No, we're not. It's a private funeral. No special treatment by the department."

There was a brief silence. "Are you sure?"

"Very sure. Do you mind if I ask who told you otherwise?"

"Friends of my husband."

"Trent Randolph's friends?"

"No, I . . . I remarried. My current husband was a member of the police department for a time. He still has many friends there."

"Dale Britton."

"Yes. Do you know him?"

"Your husband had left by the time I was hired here. But I can assure you that his friends were mistaken about the funeral."

"Oh. Well—I'm quite upset about all of this."

Wondering if the Randolph cases could possibly become more of a nightmare than they already were, he said, "That's understandable. Anyone in your situation would be upset."

He heard her draw in a steadying breath. "Dale told me they'll be reopening the investigation into the murders."

"The cases have never been officially closed—but yes. In fact, I was hoping I could talk to you at some point—"

"Of course! I've been wondering, you know, if anyone was going to call me. Are you the detective assigned to my husband's and children's murders?"

"Yes, I am. I've only had the cases since late Saturday, though, so I'm just getting started."

"We must definitely meet soon, then. Dale and I will take you to lunch today."

"Thanks for the offer, but I'm afraid I won't be able to make it for lunch," he said, not because he already had plans, but because he didn't like the way she was trying to take control. "Are you free at all this morning?"

"Oh . . . Dale has business meetings . . . but I'm the one you probably really want to talk to, right? I mean, *I'm* the one who has suffered the most in all this. No one has been hurt more than me."

"I'd appreciate any time you can spare," he said, working to keep his voice neutral, trying not to betray his disgust. "I can meet with your husband later."

"I'm just leaving for downtown, but I'll be free later this morning."

He arranged to meet her at ten-thirty at a coffee shop not far from the newspaper, then called Irene. "Want to have lunch together?" he asked. "I'm going to be downtown."

"Still not convinced we've patched things up?"

He hesitated, then said, "Have we?"

"No, but we're making progress."

"I'm all for progress. Meet me for lunch."

"What brings you this way?"

"Just between us?"

"Of course."

"Going to meet with Tory Randolph. Tory Randolph-Britton."

"Oh, you poor thing. A front-row seat for the *Me Show*, starring Tory. God, she's a bitch."

"Tell me how you really feel about her."

She laughed. "It's awful, I know. I really wanted to feel sorry for her—I mean, what happened to her family was terrible. But she *uses* it to gain attention for herself in a truly repulsive way. No wonder Randolph dumped her—I think it's a shame that she ended up with his money."

He felt a mild shock—it suddenly dawned on him that in all the files and notes he had read on all of these cases, no real time had been spent on a question that had to be considered in any murder investigation: Who benefits by this death? In both the *Amanda* murders and Seth's murder, obvious suspects had been pursued—even though a lot of money was at stake, and neither Dane nor Lefebvre would inherit.

"Tell me what you know about that, Irene. The money went to Tory?"

"Not immediately, and I'm sure her ex-husband never intended that she'd get any of it. But apparently his will was poorly worded. Trent Randolph knew how to make money, but he didn't know how to bequeath it. Which was a pity for his company's stockholders."

"Why?"

"Randolph Chemicals was a bigger company ten years ago than it is now, and its future looked rosy. The first blow came when Trent was murdered, because he was the driving force behind the company. Everything was supposed to go to his children, but Amanda was dead, too. So Seth inherited everything, but of course, he was underage—so it stayed in trust, and he never took control. Unfortunately, because of some problem in the way the trust was set up, Seth's estate ultimately went to Tory."

"And now she shares it with a former member of the department."

"Yes. Dale Britton—he quit the department before they officially dated, but she definitely met him through the investigation. Weird, huh? He went from Crime Lab Technician II to CEO when he said, 'I do.'"

"Are you telling me Britton runs Randolph Chemicals?"

"Not now—but he did for a short time. He has a degree in chemistry, but no real background in business or manufacturing. That didn't stop Tory from making him president of the company."

"What happened to the company?"

"In the beginning, it looked as if it was going to be a total disaster—stock price fell and lots of their best employees abandoned ship. Some of that started when Trent Randolph was killed, of course. So just when the company was starting to recover from that setback, Tory insisted on making her new hubby the boss. Luckily, Britton was smart enough to see that if he stayed at the helm, the value of all that stock he married into was going to be a big zero. So he managed to keep some key people by 'retiring' and letting wiser heads rule. Things improved, and the two of them aren't hurting for bucks, but Randolph Chemicals never regained all the ground it lost."

"I can't help but feel a little sorry for Tory Randolph," Frank said. "To lose two children to murder—especially after Seth survived the first attack—"

"For almost any other mother, that would be true. I felt bad for her, too, until I saw how much she gloried in the attention she was getting. It was awful. You'll be around her for more than ten seconds, so I know you'll have a chance to see what I mean."

He stopped by the lab, feeling a little awkward when he saw Alfred Larson and Paul Haycroft examining the paper airplane.

"Frank!" Haycroft said, smiling at him. "We were wondering if we should call in the NTSB on this one, too."

"Don't let him give you a hard time," Larson said. "It's a good piece of evidence. Thanks for taking the time to bring it by from the hospital. It should have been recovered by one of our people, of course, but I don't think they could bring themselves to treat Captain Bredloe as if he were just any other victim of an assault. How is the captain? Any word?"

"Nothing new," Frank said. "Call Pete if you'd like—Miriam said she'd call him today if there was any change."

"And not you?" Haycroft asked in surprise.

"No—I've got a full day ahead of me today, and Pete's working here in the office. Carlson has vowed to suspend him if he doesn't clear his desk off."

Haycroft laughed. "I'm afraid your lieutenant is fighting a losing battle."

"So—you think you can learn anything from this?" Frank asked, indicating the plane.

"Possibly," Haycroft said. "We've taken a look at the paper—it's a better grade of twenty-pound bond, but unfortunately it isn't all that special—it's a type sold in many stationers and office supply stores. As you know, the more unique something is, the more helpful it is to us. I don't know that this will lead you to the attacker, but it might help us nail him once you've found him. There are these cutout areas in the tail section, and if he hasn't taken out his trash or gone to the recycling center, we might match the cutout places to the paper that has been removed. And, of course, the plane isn't folded in an ordinary way."

"Folded with real precision," Larson said. "The attacker isn't sloppy."

"Which means we no longer suspect Pete Baird," Haycroft said, and Larson laughed.

"Pete's desk may be messy," Frank said, regretting that he had told them about Pete's run-in with Carlson, "but his work isn't."

"Of course not," Larson said quickly. "Your partner's track record proves that. But the person who folded this also gave it a unique design, or at least not one that just anyone would fold when making a paper airplane." He handed Frank a sheet of paper. "If I asked you to make one, what would you do?"

Frank folded the classic design.

"Yes, in half, then the nose and a pair of wings. A few folds. But this is more elaborate. Perhaps not as fancy as the ones engineering students design for college competitions, but closer to those than the one you just made. Making a simple plane wasn't good enough. It gives us an insight into his character."

"It explains the fan, too," Frank said.

"Exactly!" Haycroft said. "He wanted the plane to fly toward the captain, but since he didn't want to be in the building, he couldn't launch it himself, so he thought up this mechanism."

"Ingenious, really," Larson said. He explained that the cameras and lights had been set up by the attacker. "So it looks as if he knew what the captain might do to protect himself and created distractions."

"And drew him out into the middle of the mosaic, where Bredloe made a better target."

"Yes," Larson said. "We've given this information to Vince Adams and Reed Collins. They're handling the investigation of the attack. Apparently, there's very little to go on."

Haycroft said, "You didn't come down here just to ask about the plane, did you?"

"No, I didn't. I've wanted to talk to you about Trent Randolph, but I think that may have to wait until later. My more immediate interest is in Dale Britton."

Larson and Haycroft exchanged a look. Haycroft shook his head. "Rather awkward, isn't it?"

"You could put it that way."

"His involvement with Mrs. Randolph was my fault, I'm afraid," Larson said.

"You can't blame yourself for it," Haycroft protested.

"I introduced them," Larson said. "She was always hounding me—waiting for me outside the building, cornering me every chance she could to nag me about the investigations. She was calling here constantly, and I seemed only to infuriate her. One day she stopped me as I was walking out to the crime scene unit van. Dale was with me and I introduced them. He was much more patient with her—I could see that he had a calming effect on her. So I began to let him deal with her, and before long, he was the one she asked for when she called."

"Is he still in contact with you?"

"No, I haven't spoken to him since he resigned," Larson said. "He kept coming back late from lunch, and eventually someone told me that these long lunches were with Mrs. Randolph. I asked him to stop seeing her—concerned that if we ever managed to bring charges against Whitey Dane, his lawyers would claim she was influencing the investigation. Dale resigned instead."

"So you haven't talked to either of them lately?"

"No," Haycroft said. "Why do you ask?"

"Someone in the department is contacting Dale Britton—at least his wife claims they're getting updates about the Lefebvre case. Not very accurate ones, but he obviously has some connection here."

Al Larson frowned. "I suppose that's to be expected, but I can't say it makes me happy."

"I'll see if I can learn more from her this morning," Frank said, glancing at his watch. "I'd better get going. I'm supposed to meet her at ten-thirty."

"Good luck, Frank," Haycroft said. "Of all the questions you might have about Trent Randolph, you'll have the answer to one of them by ten thirty-five—you'll know why he got a divorce."

17

She was standing outside the small café, talking on a cellular phone. Her face was turned slightly away from him, so she did not see him yet and did not know that he had seen her stomp her foot in impatience with her caller.

She was in her late forties, he thought, although doing her best to look much younger than that. She had succeeded to a greater degree than Polly Logan. She was still a beautiful woman, and he wondered briefly if Amanda would have grown up to look like her. But Frank could not reconcile the file photos of smiling, carefree Amanda with Tory Randolph-Britton.

She was slender and dressed becomingly in a dark silk suit. As he approached, she watched him appraisingly and began to smile. If it hadn't been so blatantly predatory, he decided, it would have been more attractive.

She put the phone away and extended a well-manicured hand. "Detective Harriman? I'm Tory."

"Thank you for agreeing to meet with me on such short notice," he said. Her clasp was cool and firm, and she held his hand a little longer than necessary.

"*Anything* I can do to be of help to you, Frank—it is Frank, isn't it?"

"Yes. Let's go inside."

The owner greeted him by name and gestured toward a booth.

"You come here often?" Tory said, then giggled. "Sorry, that sounds like a bad pickup line."

"My wife works not far from here," he said. "So, yes, I'm here fairly often."

"Oh." She lowered her lashes and began tapping her nails on the gleaming wood of the tabletop.

A waiter came and Frank ordered a coffee. Tory ordered a double latte and a croissant. "I shouldn't, but I feel like being bad," she said, smiling.

"Tell me, how did you meet your husband?" he asked.

"We met in college—oh, do you mean Dale?"

"Let's start with Trent."

"Trent, I met in college—at San Diego State. He was crazy over me then. In those days, he couldn't believe his luck. He was this nerdy science guy, and—well, let's just say he wasn't my only admirer."

He smiled, hoping it didn't look as phony as it felt.

"Yes indeed. You may not believe it to look at me now, but I was quite a beauty in my day. Won a pageant—just a little local contest in El Cajon, but still—"

What the hell, he thought. No use insulting her—chances were, she could provide information he couldn't get from anyone else. "I have no trouble believing you could have won any contest you entered. I take it marrying Trent was the only reason you didn't go on to state competition?"

"Oh, there were some who thought I could have taken it all."

"And I would be sitting here having coffee with Miss America. Imagine that."

She laughed, clearly delighted. "Well, who knows, right?"

Their orders arrived. It wasn't hard to see the way to her heart, so as soon as the waiter walked away, Frank said, "Trent Randolph must have been the envy of every man on campus."

"Oh, yes. But I didn't do so badly, either. He was a handsome man, but he wore glasses—not real thick ones, but still, most girls didn't notice him. To be honest, he was a big old clumsy geek when I met him. A chemistry major—and a computer freak!"

Let her keep talking, he told himself.

"My mother thought he'd never go anywhere, but I guess I showed her, didn't I? He had a quality about him that I saw right away. He was smart, he was ambitious, and he was—oh, a leader. And after I had a chance to teach him not to wear such dumb-looking outfits and got him to start wearing contact lenses—let me tell you, there was a bona fide hunk underneath that geek."

"He was lucky to have your help."

"Damned straight he was! I was no small part of his success. And what does he do? Has himself some midlife crisis and runs off with the first bimbo to lean her tits over his mouse pad."

Frank recalled the scant information in the files about Trent Randolph's girlfriend. Another person who had been overlooked by the investigation—she had been dumped by the man not long before the murders. Trying to learn more while letting Tory believe he was sympathetic, he asked, "This home wrecker worked in your husband's office?"

"No, but he met her there. Some blond bimbo from an import business. Tessa. As in she had him by the Tessa-ticles. He walks out after seventeen years of marriage to chase after a woman who wasn't all that much older than Seth. It broke the kids' hearts. When I think of what we did to them . . . not knowing . . ."

She fell silent and tears began rolling slowly down her face. He offered her a tissue, and she took it with a muttered thanks. For the first time since he sat down across from her, he thought she might be thinking of someone other than herself. An unconcealed, sudden sadness had taken hold of her, and he found himself feeling relieved that perhaps she was not as utterly self-involved as he had thought her to be. He did not admire her, or even like her, but sorrow softened her.

She drew a hiccuping breath and said, "Do you have children, Frank?"

"No, I don't."

"If I had known what was going to happen to them . . . I'm not sure I would have—no, that's not true. I don't regret bringing Seth and Amanda into this world. Not for one minute. That would be like—like making their deaths all that mattered. And that would mean I had let their killers win, do you see?"

"Yes, I think I do," he said, beginning to see the fighter in her and wondering if Trent Randolph had perhaps once loved her for more than her beauty.

She wiped at her eyes, studying him. "I believe you do. So you see, that's why I make such a damned nuisance of myself as far as the police in this town are concerned. I have hated two names for the past ten years: Philip Lefebvre and Whitey Dane. They robbed me in the worst way. I thought Tessa Satel had robbed me of my husband—but that was nothing—I think Trent and I would have patched things up, given a little more time. But Whitey Dane robbed me of all the time I ever could have had to do that, and took Trent away from me in a way that made Tessa look downright charitable. And he robbed me of my daughter, and ultimately arranged to rob me of my son. He took my *future*."

"You got to know Phil Lefebvre?"

"Lefebvre," she said with disgust. "I suppose I should feel relieved, knowing that Seth's murderer crashed his plane while he was trying to run away—and that his ass has been rotting on some mountainside all this time—which is almost enough to make me think about getting religion, because if that isn't divine justice, I don't know what is. But . . . but . . . it didn't feel as good as I thought it would. And I think that must be in part because he still got away with destroying evidence and letting Whitey Dane roam around free as a damned bird."

"Did he ever mention—"

"But that's not the worst thing he did," she interrupted. "You know what he did? Lefebvre allowed Seth to think of him as his friend. His friend! My son loved that man. Loved him. He'd rather have Lefebvre there than me—Seth made that plain enough. I understood. After the terrible things Seth went through on that boat, my son was scared. Who would protect him? Lefebvre. The man who had saved his life. The man who was in there, day after day, gaining Seth's trust. Comforting him, helping him, talking to him. Seth didn't care what he went through in that hospital as long as his good friend Lefebvre was there at his side."

She leaned over the table and said angrily, "I would have to have Detective Lefebvre come back to life and kill him again and again and again and again to feel any better. Because I trusted him, too. And no one—not even Trent and his bimbo—ever betrayed my trust more terribly."

She sat back suddenly and gave a short laugh. "I haven't let you ask me a damned thing, have I? Go ahead—what can I tell you?"

"That last time you saw Lefebvre, was he agitated?"

"To say the least. He talked about leaving—I heard later that he spread some story around the police department about seeing a friend, but the friend didn't know anything about it. Seth panicked, begged him to stay."

"He communicated with Seth using a computer?"

She nodded. "I still have it."

"You have it?" he asked, startled. He was sure he had seen the computer listed as evidence. "I thought—"

She blushed. "Well, Dale got it for me. I mean, he asked for it for me, and they released it to me. There were no fingerprints on it—at least not ones that could have proven anything—and everything was erased from it. But it was—I don't know, the only way I could communicate with Seth during that time when it was just the two of us. My link to him. I wanted to keep it."

"Has anyone used it since the night Seth died?"

"No, not unless it was someone in the lab. Dale was the one who checked it when they brought it in, and I don't think anyone else worked on it."

"Tory, sometimes files can be recovered even when it seems they've been erased. Would you mind if I had an expert take a look at the computer?"

"You really think they might be able to find something on it?"

"I don't want to mislead you—they might not. And it has been a long time, so . . . I can't promise anything. But I have so little to work with right now that I've got to try every possible means to recover evidence."

She suddenly seemed uneasy. "There might be some private conversation on it."

"There might be," he agreed. "As well as enough information to prove once and for all who murdered your son."

She didn't jump at that, but sat quietly, watching him. Knowing she had long been convinced that Lefebvre had killed Seth, Frank was trying to come up with another way to persuade her when she said, "All right, I'll bring Seth's computer to you."

"Thank you," he said.

His surprise must have shown, though, because she smiled and said, "You're wondering why I agreed."

"Yes, I guess I am."

"Because I had two children, Frank, not one. Seth talked to Lefebvre about that night several times—went over and over his description of Amanda's killer and what had happened. If you can find files that have been erased, you might find those, too, right? I know it's a long shot, but if you had that again, you might be able to do something about Dane, right?"

"I might," he agreed, not thinking there was much hope in it.

"Good. What else can I do for you?"

"The other questions I have may be a little more difficult to answer, because you and Trent were divorced at the time of his murder," he said. "I thought you might know if your ex-husband had any enemies other than Whitey Dane—does anyone come to mind?"

"Is someone else in on all of this, too? Hiding the evidence against Dane?"

"I'm just exploring every possibility."

She frowned. "I guess everyone knew that one of the other commissioners had it in for him. Trent had embarrassed the guy. Let's see, what was his name? Soury? No, that one was friendly to Trent. It was . . . Pickens! That was his name!"

"Michael Pickens?"

"Yes, he's the one. I'll ask Dale—"

"Actually, I'd appreciate it if you didn't."

She looked puzzled.

"I know you must want to confide in your husband, and that's perfectly understandable. But you've told me that he has contacts in the department, and word from those contacts could reach Commissioner Pickens—"

"As if Bob Hi—as if his friends in the department are the type to hobnob with commissioners!"

So Bob Hitchcock had called Britton. Acting as if he hadn't noticed the slip, Frank said, "Even so—there is a difference between helping an investigation and interfering in an investigation. I cannot stress how important it is that you allow me to do my job without being concerned that the person I need to talk to has had time to prepare answers or that a former member of my department is involving himself in the process. I'm sure your husband's motives would be the best, as would yours, but it will cause problems. I don't want anyone to be able to get away with murder because we failed to follow the rules the courts have set down for us."

"You mean—someone could get off on a 'technicality' because I talked to Dale?"

"The case might not even go to court if a D.A. believes there is a rogue investigation going on, or that someone who benefited from the deaths of your husband and children influenced the investigation."

"Benefited!"

"That's the way the court may see it."

She crossed her arms, a mulish expression on her face. When he didn't back down, she relented. "Oh, all right."

His pager went off. Mayumi Iwata at the NTSB.

18

Several times during the ninety-minute drive to San Bernardino, Frank had to force himself to ease his grip on the steering wheel. He told himself to relax, that he didn't know anything for sure yet, that Mayumi had simply asked him to come out to the hangar where Lefebvre's Cessna was being studied. But he knew she would have told him about a simple finding of pilot error or mechanical failure over the phone.

Don't jump to conclusions. But that, he thought, was like asking a three-packs-a-day man not to worry about being asked to come in for a second chest X-ray.

He tried to distract himself. He thought of calling Irene and decided against it. He hadn't told her where he was going when he canceled his lunch with her. Although he wished Mayumi's call had come an hour later, he knew Irene wasn't adding the canceled lunch to her list of grievances — given their occupations, sudden changes in plans for reasons unprovided were commonplace. They had long ago accepted the fact that they could not always talk to each other about their workdays. They had prided themselves on respecting certain boundaries around their jobs. He knew she still hadn't completely forgiven him for crossing the line.

On the seat next to him was the videotape Polly Logan had given him. He hadn't managed to watch it again yet. He wanted to see it without Polly's commentary, to study the people who had surrounded Seth Randolph at that time. He could have locked it in his desk drawer, but he felt strangely uneasy about doing so. He decided to keep it with him. He'd take it home tonight, watch it after going over to visit Bredloe.

Thinking of Bredloe make him think about the paper airplane, and he wondered if there were paper airplane experts. He knew there were paper airplane competitions, but was there some kind of national paper airplane association? It would be far from the most absurd organization he had ever heard of.

He remembered reading about an annual contest among local engineering students to make the best paper airplane. Maybe the man who attacked Bredloe had learned to make paper airplanes in college. It wasn't hard to believe that a man with a background in engineering could have made the device that toppled the bricks.

Mayumi must have been watching for his car, because she was waiting for him just inside the hangar. She gave him a visitor's badge, then led him to a large work area where the Cessna was being examined.

It was a sight that unexpectedly disturbed him. On the mountainside, he had seen the plane as little more than a vine-covered tomb and had been interested only in who and what had been buried within it. But now the plane itself was at center stage—Lefebvre's means of escape held captive. Frank could not rid himself of the notion that he was viewing an autopsy. The Cessna stood gutted—stark, battered, lifeless—delayed from its final disposition for the sake of an examination. A lone corpse, its damage too demanding—distracting observers from the remaining traces of its former beauty.

What had failed? What had brought on the beginning of this end?

"It will be a while before we release any official report of our findings," Mayumi said, "but I wanted you to know what we've learned right away."

He heard the anxiety in her voice and gave her his full attention.

"We have many factors to consider in an accident investigation," she said. "The pilot's experience, his state of mind, his health. The plane itself, especially its maintenance."

"The pilot is supposed to log all maintenance, right?"

"Yes. There are three required logbooks—the pilot's log, the propeller log, and an engine and airframe log. If a pilot so much as replaces a screw on his plane, it should be logged. Some pilots are better than others at keeping records, of course. Lefebvre was meticulous. And, I should add, meticulous in the care of his aircraft. Routine maintenance was performed on or even ahead of schedule. He didn't push a single component of this Cessna past its life expectancy. He took measures to ensure that this machine was in prime condition."

"Irene—my wife—knew him. She told me he really loved flying, that it was what made him happiest. She also said he was cautious."

"I can tell you that's true without ever having met him. You could have guessed it from his logbooks. When we were first notified that he was missing, we looked up what records we could and talked to people who knew him—not just friends and family, but his mechanic, other pilots, and so on. So even before I read these logs, I already knew that he had many hours of both military and civilian flying experience—he knew what he was doing. The logbooks confirmed that, but they tell me more. They tell me that he wasn't just a weekend flier. In fact, until the first week of June in the year of the crash, Lefebvre never let more than a few days go by without flying."

"The first week of June?" Frank asked. "You're sure of that?"

"Yes. There are no entries dated between June third and June twenty-first."

"The attack on the Randolph family happened just before midnight on June third," Frank said. "Lefebvre saved Seth Randolph's life that night—in the early hours of June fourth, and he was with the boy almost constantly after that. Until Seth Randolph was killed—on the night of the twenty-second."

"My God."

"You're saying he completely put aside flying during that period?"

"He completely put aside something he loved." She gave a small shrug and said, "That's not a term you'll find in my report, of course, but—I'm trying to get a picture across to you. I want you to see the kind of care that went into this plane, the hours he spent in it—I'm telling you, it was a love affair. He put a lot more time into its upkeep than most men put into their marriages." She smiled wryly. "Which may not be saying much. The man who taught me to fly told me that the reason pilots spend more time with their planes than their wives is that there are more women than P-51s."

Frank laughed. "Oh, sorry. Being the female trainee of a man who valued vintage military aircraft more than women must have been a pain."

"Nah," she said. "I was used to it. He was my dad. Anyway, Irene was right—Lefebvre was a cautious flier. We know he checked the weather before he took off that night. We know he filled his tanks. He also had relatively sophisticated navigational equipment aboard this plane, and he clearly knew how to use it."

"So you don't believe it was pilot error."

"That's not why I told you all of that—but no, I don't believe it was pilot error. I know why the plane crashed, but I wouldn't have ruled out pilot error just because he loved to fly and did the maintenance. Pilots make mistakes—even experienced pilots. Or they become incapacitated—have heart attacks, strokes, you name it."

"But you don't think it was a health problem or you wouldn't have paged me to come down here—so tell me, why did it crash?"

"Because someone else wanted it to."

He said nothing—his mind quickly retracing steps over a path of implications he had hoped he wouldn't have to consider seriously.

"You aren't especially surprised, are you?" Mayumi said quietly.

He shook his head. "No, I guess I'm not. I've had nothing more to go on than the sort of thing you just talked about—gut feeling, mostly. I haven't been able to make the pieces fit the way everyone in the LPPD seems to insist they do. Killing a teenage witness, going for a bribe—nothing in Lefebvre's background matched up with that." He paused, remembering his conversation with Yvette Nereault, of her unwavering faith in her brother. "Tell me more about what happened to the plane."

"Let me back up a little," she said. "When the NTSB starts an investigation, we're concerned with more than determining the cause of any one crash—we study crashes so that we can improve safety. If there's some design flaw or manufacturing problem in an aircraft, we want to know. When any aircraft crashes for unknown reasons, we notify interested third parties to the investigation—the aircraft manufacturer, the maker of the engine and of the propeller and so on. They help us to investigate. We send parts to them, they send field investigators to us."

"That's why the propeller and engine are missing?" Frank said, looking toward the plane.

"Right. Here—come over this way." She walked toward a series of photographs pinned to a corkboard display. The first group was of the crash site and the plane as it was found there. "I put these up here to help explain it to you." She pointed to the next group of photos—close-ups of the propeller.

"We start by looking at the propeller. Experts study the scratches on it—are they chordwise, spanwise, and so on. The scratches tell us if the plane was developing power at the time of impact and if the pilot had feathered the propeller."

"Feathered?"

"Turned the windmilling blade into the wind, to reduce drag. When we took a look at Lefebvre's propeller, we learned that he used that procedure and that the engine was not developing power."

Frank looked at the next set of photos. "The engine?"

"Yes. We sent it back to Mobile, Alabama. To Teledyne. They were able to start it."

"To start it! After it had been through a crash?"

"Yes. Not at all uncommon to be able to do that when the problem isn't the engine per se. This one isn't badly damaged—only picked up a few dents. But look at these close-ups."

"It looks as if there's some charring," he said. He glanced back at the photos taken of the wreckage in the mountains. "But no sign that any other part of the plane caught fire. Was this one just local to the engine?"

"Yes," she said approvingly. "A small engine fire. That will be important later. It's the only thing that saved your evidence."

He looked at the next group. "The carburetor?"

"Yes. And that's where we found our molasses."

"Molasses?"

She moved to a table and picked up a glass vial. She held it up to the light so that he could see the small amount of crusty brown material in it. "Most of this went to the lab, but I saved a little to show to you. I thought it might be oil varnish at first, but I sent it in for identification. It's sugar."

"The fire caramelized it?"

"Right. Without that, we might not have found it. Over ten years, moisture might have washed it out."

"So someone dumped sugar into his fuel tanks?"

"That seems to be the case. He flew for a while, and then the lines started to clog. It fouled the carburetor and the engine coughed to a halt. That bit of hardened sugar tells us what caused the crash, but we have another indication that someone tampered with his plane."

"In case the sugar didn't work?"

"The second has nothing to do with causing a crash, but may have a lot to do with the amount of time the aircraft was missing—the emergency locator transponder. It sends out a signal for a number of hours if certain g-forces are applied—which happens in a crash. If the ELT had been working, we might have been able to locate the plane shortly after it went down. I'm not saying that was guaranteed—especially since he was in rough terrain. But an ELT can certainly help. Lefebvre's ELT was externally mounted. So someone could have tampered with it."

He frowned. "Tampered with it . . . because if Lefebvre survived the crash but needed medical attention, a delay in locating the plane might lead to his death."

"I can't help but think that might have been the case."

"Jesus, that's cold."

"Yes."

"But you're not sure anything was wrong with the ELT?"

"Not absolutely. There is no sign of damage, and after ten years that battery would have been dead no matter what. But the curious thing was, the battery was long past its expiration date *before* the crash."

"And Lefebvre wouldn't have let it go."

"His maintenance logs say he routinely checked the battery and had just replaced it that May. I can't believe he replaced it with an old one."

"No. Mayumi—is there any way to trace the purchase of the battery?"

"I've got someone working on it."

She walked him to his car. He looked back toward the building and said, "What will happen to it?"

"The plane? Depends in part on what his heirs want us to do when we're finished. Probably be sold for scrap. I try to think of it as organ donation."

He smiled and thanked her for her help with the case. He started to get into the car, then said, "Mayumi, if anyone else from my department calls about this—"

"I'll be away from my desk. Maybe even on vacation. Yes, I've thought about what all of this means, too, Frank. You've got more to worry about than I do."

On the way back to Las Piernas, he thought of facing Yvette Nereault and telling her that her brother had been murdered, just as she had always believed. He thought of the men who had met him for breakfast that first morning back from the mountains—including his own partner—and their clumsy attempt to pressure him into forgetting about Lefebvre.

He grew angry thinking of their disparagement of a good cop—even the chief had made Lefebvre's name taboo.

Suddenly he thought again of the paper airplane in Bredloe's pocket and heard Nereault's warning echoing through his mind:

"You should watch your back, Detective Harriman, especially if you are going around saying that Philippe might have been innocent."

19

He called Pete to get an update on the captain's condition. Pete told him that Bredloe had briefly regained consciousness several times during the afternoon. The captain hadn't been awake long enough to really talk to anyone, but his doctors seemed pleased that he had managed a slurred version of Miriam's name when he saw her at his bedside.

Frank decided to stop by the hospital before heading home. Bredloe probably wouldn't even know he was there, but it seemed important to Frank to take the time to visit him. If nothing else, he could give Miriam a chance to eat dinner or offer to bring something to her if she wouldn't leave the room. Irene wouldn't be able to join him; on Tuesday nights, she covered city council meetings.

As he pulled into a parking space at St. Anne's, his pager went off. Ben Sheridan's cell phone number. Frank called the anthropologist.

"Frank? Glad you called back so quickly," Ben said. "I'm just coming back from the mountains."

"I thought you weren't going up there until the weekend."

"I wasn't, but I didn't have any classes today and I was curious. So Anna and I took the dogs up to the site."

Anna was Ben's girlfriend. She was also an experienced dog handler and often helped Ben on searches. "You found something or you wouldn't have paged me."

"Well, not much in the way of remains—a few small bones. But we found a wood rat's nest and located something that might be sort of interesting in it. Lefebvre's watch."

"His watch? Are you sure it's his?"

"Inscribed to him from his sister, Yvette, on the back. In French, by the way. Even better, I've got made-for-TV evidence for you here."

"What do you mean?"

"You know how it works on TV," Ben said. "A bullet passes through a victim and conveniently hits a clock or breaks his watch, so you learn the time of death—right? Only it wasn't a bullet, just good old impact. Plenty of that in a crash. So it stopped Lefebvre's watch. The watch is an old-fashioned but very nice Omega. An analog dial. With little windows on the face that show the day and date."

"Are you telling me you can determine the time of the crash from it?"

"Not exactly. The watch was smashed up on impact, and the minute hand and crown are missing—probably in the debris the NTSB picked up on the cockpit floor. Your lab should be able to see the impression of the minute hand on the face even though it's gone. The face is a little dirty, but you can still see 'Fri' for Friday and 'Jun' for June and the number twenty-two for the date. The hour hand is on nine."

"Which means Lefebvre died the same night he took off. The NTSB learned that already, I think, but this helps to confirm that. It should probably go into their report, too."

"So—I guess it wasn't so exciting after all."

"No—it is. I'll tell you why the next time I see you. I've got to check out something in the property room before I know more. Are you hanging on to the watch?"

"I'll be giving it to the county coroner. I'm working for him at this point. But I'll call Mayumi Iwata and let her know about it."

"Good. Thanks a lot. Oh—one other thing. Do you know the name of the engineering professor who's in charge of the paper airplane competition at the university?"

"Ray Wilkes. Do you need to talk to him about something?"

"Yes, are you friends?"

"I haven't known him for long, but I like him. The first time I came on campus openly wearing my prosthesis, he stared—but not in the way most people do. He named the make and model of everything in my rig and complimented me on my choice of prosthetist. Turns out he runs the campus program for students interested in going into prosthesis design. Want me to ask him to give you a call?"

"Thanks, Ben. Have him call the cell phone."

As he hung up, he saw Chief Hale walking out of St. Anne's. Frank locked his car, hesitated briefly, then called out to the chief. Hale's aide had already opened the door to the chief's car, but Hale waited, scowling as Frank hurried over to where he stood.

"If I could have a word alone with you, sir?"

"What is it?" the chief snapped.

"Alone, sir," Frank said, glancing toward the aide.

Hale seemed about to refuse, but then said, "Wait here," to the aide and began walking. Frank followed him as he took quick strides back toward the hospital. The chief moved on a determined course, not stopping until he reached a walled area near the emergency room. He went through a gate as if he owned the place, and Frank saw that they were in a small garden, an outdoor waiting area for families of patients. At one end of the garden was a fountain with a religious statue at its center—a serene woman Frank guessed to be St. Anne, although he wasn't sure. There was a bench near the fountain. Hale moved to the bench but did not sit down. He frowned at the statue for a moment, then turned to Frank and said, "Well?"

Now that he had the chief's attention, he wasn't sure where to begin. Hale was obviously not in a receptive mood.

"Well?" the chief said again.

"The NTSB contacted me today. I drove out to where they are studying the wreckage of Lefebvre's plane. They've made some preliminary findings that I thought you should know about, sir."

"How odd," the chief said.

"Sir?"

"How odd, Detective Harriman, that the chain of command in this department has been changed and no one saw fit to tell me about it. So now you report directly to me and not to Lieutenant Carlson?"

Frank considered saying nothing more. Carlson wasn't up to handling a problem like this, and Bredloe—the man he would have gone to under other circumstances—was in no condition to help. Frank had decided to approach Hale because he trusted him. He knew Hale tried to run an honest department—that was part of why Frank liked working for the Las Piernas PD. But this was the second time in as many days that the chief had rebuffed him after a mention of Lefebvre's name. Tired and frustrated, Frank felt his hold on his temper slipping and clenched his teeth to hold back a suggestion about where Hale could put his organization chart. If he couldn't talk to Hale, to hell with it.

Hale watched his reaction, smiled, and said, "As long as you have me here, Detective, let's hear it."

"I need to know that I'm speaking to you with absolute confidentiality," Frank said.

Hale looked surprised, but said, "All right. Now what's the trouble?"

"There is definite evidence that Lefebvre's plane was sabotaged, sir. Lefebvre was murdered."

Hale sighed. "I'm sorry to hear that. But those who do business with men like Whitey Dane shouldn't expect to live forever."

"But we can't assume—"

"Lefebvre was cozying up to the wrong side!" he said angrily. "Obviously the man who hired him killed him."

"With all due respect," Frank said, again struggling to control his own temper, "there is another possibility. It's possible that Lefebvre was not working with Dane, that someone else within our department stole that evidence and murdered Seth Randolph. And Lefebvre as well."

"Ludicrous."

"Lefebvre had an excellent record and no motive to kill Seth Randolph. If he was working for Dane, why did he call attention to the *Amanda* on the night Trent and Amanda Randolph were killed?"

"No one believes he was working for Dane then. He was obviously recruited later, when Dane saw that he had access to the boy. As for motive—Dane had enough money to make it worthwhile."

"To make it worthwhile to someone, yes. But not necessarily Lefebvre."

"Do you suppose we just drew his name out of a hat ten years ago? It was not simply that he fled, you know. He was the last person to handle the evidence against Dane and the last person to enter Seth Randolph's room before the boy's body was found. You know those are the facts, Detective Harriman."

"I'm not saying I understand all of his actions on that night, sir—but to ignore the possibility that Lefebvre was framed is to endanger other members of the department now."

"Such as you?" Hale asked sarcastically.

"Such as Captain Bredloe."

"Harriman, really—"

"The paper airplane, sir. It has to be connected. A mistake on the part of—"

"Detective Harriman," Hale said, leaning so that he was only a few inches from Frank's face. "I'll tell you who's making a mistake. You are." He straightened, then began pacing, muttering to himself. "Paper airplanes! For God's sake—"

"Captain Bredloe and I had been talking—arguing, really—about Lefebvre not long before the captain left for the Sheffield Club. Many members of the department knew that—I think Lefebvre's killer knew it. Not much later someone used that paper airplane to lure the captain out to where he'd be hit by the falling bricks."

Hale rolled his eyes. "God grant me patience! You find a paper airplane in a suit pocket and you're ready to call in the paratroopers. Bredloe could have picked up that paper airplane anywhere—anytime. He could have made it himself."

Frank stayed silent. He thought of arguing that even the lab believed Bredloe's attacker made the plane, but obviously Hale's mind was made up.

"You asked to speak to me in confidence," Hale said. "I will respect that request, in part because I know you have done good work for this department. We've had our ups and downs with you, but you've got the gift. No, don't look surprised to hear me say that—and don't expect I'll ever admit I did. I don't think of it as voodoo, you know. But I've been on the job too long not to know it when I see it. You've got it. I'll tell you who else had it—Lefebvre. For all the good it did him."

"I'm gratified by your comments, sir, but—"

"You should be. But don't think that makes me feel all warm and fuzzy about you, Harriman. You're a damned pain in the ass. And if you think I enjoy working with a pain in the ass, maybe you don't have such great instincts after all."

"It's not just my instinct that tells—" Frank began, but Hale interrupted again.

"If you are about to tell me that your instinct tells you that traitor was innocent, spare yourself the trouble. I have an assignment for you, Harriman. The assignment is for you to reread the case files so that you know what the hell was going on here ten years ago. Now, if that's all . . . ?"

"Sir, I have read them, and forgive me, but I can't say the investigations were up to the department's usual standards. I can't help but wonder why we didn't look at who benefited from Randolph's death, why we didn't ask—"

"Because, Detective Harriman," Hale bit out, "as you'll see from the files, we had evidence and witnesses and all those other dumb little elements of a murder investigation that bring criminals to justice. I'll admit we only did our poor best before a creative thinker like you came along, showing us how paper airplanes are more important than all that, but somehow, by God, we closed cases!"

Accepting defeat—for the moment—Frank said, "I take it you have no objection to my telling the family what I've learned from the NTSB?"

The chief hesitated, then said, "Why not? Even if you don't, the NTSB files will soon be a matter of public record in any case. But do you mean to tell me you would tell those French hotheads before you'd give this information to your own lieutenant?"

"They're Quebecois, not French, sir. Given our—let's say our lack of sympathy—"

"Sympathy! I'll be damned before—"

"I'm just saying that under the circumstances, I haven't found the family to be unreasonable."

"You also haven't answered my question."

"I believe they can be discreet."

"And Carlson can't, eh? Well, he's proven that, I suppose." Hale studied him. "You don't like Carlson much, do you?"

"No, sir."

Hale laughed. "Honest to a fault. Good night, Detective Harriman. Read those files again."

He began to walk away, then turned back toward Frank. "The files only tell part of the story, you know. They won't tell you what this department suffered. Budget cuts, community mistrust—those were bad. You know what was worse? We couldn't hold our heads up. That was the worst. The loss of morale, of pride. Not to mention the guilt—I felt it, Bredloe felt it, and so did Willis. You didn't know Willis, but he was Lefebvre's lieutenant. I don't think he ever got over feeling that he was in some way responsible for Seth Randolph's death and all that followed. He retired not long after that. Died the same year he retired. I can promise you this, Detective Harriman—I will not let this department be put through something like that again. Not by anyone."

20

Myles waited patiently while Mr. Dane finished feeding the swans. Dane would not sit down to his own dinner for another hour. The household was on its summer schedule now.

Dane scattered the last of the food pellets, then turned and held out his hands. One of the younger servants came forward immediately—Derrick, blond and blue-eyed, a little wasp tattooed just behind his right ear—and washed and dried Mr. Dane's hands very carefully. Dane smiled at him and Myles felt a little jealousy. He did not betray this in any way.

Dane took his silver-handled walking cane from another young man, then dismissed him and the others. He beckoned to Myles to walk with him. This was a special privilege, and Myles already felt both comforted by the invitation and ashamed of his earlier stab of envy.

Mr. Dane began by talking of general business matters. Mr. Dane no longer involved himself in the drug trade—at least, not in any direct fashion. He made a certain amount of money from it, but only by controlling more direct participants. He had divided his territory and now amused himself by playing the bystander, watching his successors murder one another's associates in a quest to reunite that territory. That would never happen. Mr. Dane would not allow it to happen.

And he had made it clear that the violence was not to spill over into areas where he had forbidden it. When one of the leaders of these two groups failed to abide by this rule, Mr. Dane had him brought to a meeting place and told him not to defecate where he dined. Mr. Dane had asked Myles to translate the phrase into language the young man would comprehend. Myles, misunderstanding, merely told the young man, "Don't shit where you eat."

But Dane said, "No, Myles, he doesn't understand what is *said* to him, because I have already said that I did not want altercations to take place near any establishment in which I had an interest. I believe *experience* is the only language he'll understand."

And so, as Dane watched, they had fed the man a cathartic, and after the inevitable event occurred, forced him to swallow the results. He did not live long after that, though the cause of death had more to do with asphyxiation than with anything ingested. Dane promoted the man's second-in-command—a witness to the lesson—and there had been no difficulties of a similar nature since.

Mr. Dane had grown tired of such people, he told Myles. Their stupidity wearied him. He now focused his attention on various business enterprises, mostly real estate and import-export concerns. He was a silent partner in a great many small establishments in the city. He told Myles that over the past ten years, he had learned that there were opportunities everywhere—and plenty of stupidity as well. "But the latter—on the part of another—often creates the former for me, so I must not complain."

Myles was pleased that, so far, he was able to answer all of Mr. Dane's questions this evening.

"And were you able to learn anything more about the incident at the Sheffield Club?"

"Yes, sir. The story being given to the media is inaccurate. The police are claiming that they are unsure of Captain Bredloe's reasons for being there, even hinting that he was there because his wife is on the Historical Preservation Commission. But Captain Bredloe clearly expected some attack—there were SWAT team members on hand and a bomb squad checked the building before he entered."

"How curious."

"Yes, sir. We are trying to learn more. I should also mention that there is a rumor within the department that this has something to do with the investigation of Detective Lefebvre's death."

Dane brooded over this, then said, "What about the NTSB report?"

"We have had difficulty there, sir, but one of our associates is saying that they have found evidence of sabotage."

"Surprise, surprise," Dane said, yawning delicately. "By whom?"

"Person or persons unknown. They do not, of course, pursue criminal investigations. That is left to law enforcement. In this instance, to Las Piernas."

Dane watched the swans for a time, then said, "Have you made any progress on the other matter?"

"The court cases and police files will be given to me tonight. I'll study them in depth this evening. It will take another day to get the district attorney's files."

"And you have prepared information for me about Detective Harriman?"

"Yes, sir. When would you like that report?"

"Oh, tomorrow will be soon enough. Bring it to me after you return from your assignment. Now, tell me who you have for me this evening."

"Tessa is here, sir, as you requested. She has already dined, also as you requested."

"Yes, she's lovely in bed, but I can't stand to listen to her talk. Probably what drove Trent Randolph to leave her. You know, although Tessa would have been an invaluable asset to us if she had been married to the man, I'm really glad that she wasn't able to snare him after all, aren't you? I just don't think Trent was the sort of fellow who'd share his wife with me."

21

Frank waited in the hall outside a faculty office in one of the engineering buildings. He idly studied posters and displays that were by and large beyond his comprehension, listening to the drone of a professor's voice in a nearby classroom. He shifted the cardboard box he was carrying—a little wider and shallower than a shoebox—to the other arm.

Dr. Ray Wilkes had left a message on his voice mail, saying that he was leaving Wednesday afternoon for an out-of-state conference, but if Frank needed to talk to him before he returned next Monday, he could come by the university this evening. "I teach a summer session extension course tonight; we'll finish up at about nine-thirty."

Frank had heard the message after a depressing visit to Bredloe. The captain's bruises were showing more vividly now, worsening his appearance. And Miriam, past the initial shock and reassured that he would survive, was more fearful about the long-term effects of his injuries.

When he had heard Wilkes's message, he thought of the chief's sarcastic remarks and briefly considered calling the professor to tell him that he appreciated the offer of help, but that things had changed and he was no longer pursuing that line of investigation. Instead, he stopped by the lab and talked a night-shift tech into letting him sign out the paper airplane.

He had also called Yvette Nereault. Unlike the day before this time, she had answered the phone. He told her what he had learned from the NTSB and asked her to please not discuss it with anyone outside the family.

"It's a great injustice," she said. "Not to me, but to Philippe. I am amazed that you worry that anyone would care about anything I might say. For ten years, we who loved him have been saying that Philippe was murdered. No one listened to us in all that time, so I don't know why they should start listening now."

"Because now there is proof. I won't lie to you—my chief thinks your brother was killed by the people who supposedly paid him off."

"But you don't, do you?" she said. "You'll forgive me if I sound astonished, Detective Harriman, but you see, this is something new to me—a member of that department who has not condemned Philippe out of hand. So—if you continue to work to clear Philippe's name, I will keep quiet."

He had gone home, fed the dogs, and taken them for a run. He watched part of Polly Logan's tape before heading out to the university. Without her commentary, he got a better feel for Lefebvre.

Students began filing out of the classroom, and soon he heard other groups of them coming down the stairs at the far end of the hall. He saw an elderly gentleman in a three-piece suit and bow tie step out of the classroom. He carried a large valise. The man walked toward Frank, peering over a pair of half-glasses as he approached.

"Professor Wilkes?" Frank asked.

The man's lips pursed and he shook his head. "No, I'm sorry. I'm Professor Frost. Can I help you?"

"Thanks, but no—I have an appointment with Dr. Wilkes."

"Then I can only hope you believe that patience is a virtue, young man, because my esteemed colleague will undoubtedly be late for it." He continued to stroll down the hall.

The building began to empty out. Soon it grew quiet again. Frank found a plastic chair that someone had left in the hallway and dragged it down to the professor's door. He sat down and looked at his watch—nine forty-five. Folding his arms around the box, he leaned his head back against the wall and closed his eyes.

He awoke with a start when he heard another group of students coming down the stairs. He still had the box and opened it to see that the plane had not somehow been removed. He checked his watch again and saw that he had dozed off for only about ten minutes. He stood up and stretched, watching as the students—four men and two women—walked toward him. The young men were all dressed in a similar way, wearing sports coats over colorful shirts, and carrying backpacks. The clear leader of this group seemed to be a little older than the others, a grad student perhaps. He had the complete attention of his peers, although Frank couldn't make out what he was saying. He apparently made a joke that was a hit, though, because they suddenly broke into laughter. As they came closer, the leader seemed to notice Frank for the first time. He suddenly looked chagrined and said, "Detective Harriman? I'm so sorry!" He hurried forward and extended a hand. "Ray Wilkes. Forgive me, I lost track of time."

"He didn't *lose* track of time," one of the female students said. "He doesn't recognize the fourth dimension."

Wilkes sighed dramatically. "Wounded again, Jill. Now, you'll all have to excuse me. Detective Harriman has been waiting for me for half an hour."

"You're with the police?" Jill asked Frank.

"He's not in trouble, is he?" one of the young men asked at nearly the same time.

"Yes, he's with the police," Wilkes said, unlocking his office door. "No, I am not in trouble—and yes, we'd like some privacy." He smiled. "Scram."

They invited him to join them at the on-campus beer bar when he finished, invited Frank, too. Wilkes took a rain check, reminding them that he still needed to pack for the conference. Finally, after a prolonged chorus of "Bon voyage," "Are you sure you don't need a ride to the airport?" and "Good night, Dr. Wilkes," they left.

"I apologize again," Wilkes said to Frank, inviting him to take a seat in the tiny but neatly organized office. "Now, how can I help you?"

"I need your expertise on a matter concerning an open case, but I have to ask that this matter remain absolutely confidential."

"Certainly, I understand—otherwise your investigation may suffer. I promise I won't discuss this with anyone else."

Frank hesitated, then said, "Ben said you're the organizer of the paper airplane contest on campus—is that true?"

Wilkes was openly surprised. "Yes. It's one of the School of Engineering's contributions to the university's Spring Festival. Mercury Aircraft gives cash prizes to the winners. It's also an assignment in some courses."

"So it isn't just for fun?"

"Oh, no. I mean to say, it's fun, but there is a lot more to it than that. A paper airplane contest is a great way to teach the students about aerodynamics—lift and drag, the effect of thermals, stabilizer and wing design— and much more. For many of them, it's the first time they've designed something as part of a team. Coming up with an original design is always harder than they imagine it will be."

"Are there specialists in this field? Expert paper airplane builders?"

"Yes, absolutely. May I ask why you need one?"

"You know of the attack on one of our captains?"

Wilkes nodded. "I read about it—horrible. A remote-controlled lift top-pled bricks onto him, right? To be honest, when Ben called, I thought you might have wanted me to examine that device."

"That might not be a bad idea, but I'm here tonight because of a paper airplane. The captain had this one in his pocket." Frank extended the box to Wilkes. "We think it was used as a lure, so that he was positioned where the bricks would fall—but since the plane is so unusual, I wondered if it was also a signature of sorts. I'm hoping you might recognize the style."

Wilkes opened the box and took the plane out, then shook his head. "Unfortunately, I do recognize it."

"Unfortunately?"

"This is a textbook paper airplane, I'm afraid. Literally." He set the box on his desk, then scanned his bookshelf. He pulled out an oversize paperback, a book called *Winging It.* "For the classes, we use this one by Bray and Killeen, one by Blackburn and Lammers, and a few others." Without needing to use the index, he opened the book to page 98 and handed it to Frank. There was a large photograph of a paper airplane, a plane nearly identical to the one found in Bredloe's pocket. Instructions for making it began on the next page.

"So it's not unique," Frank said, disappointed.

"Dinterman's Stunt Flyer," Wilkes said. "I would have given a failing grade to the student who turned this in—an F for plagiarism and for failing to make progress in the class. We show them how to make this one during the first week of the course. We even demonstrate it at the festival."

"So dozens of people know how to make this?"

"More than dozens, I'm afraid," Wilkes said ruefully. "A little over a hundred at the very least."

Frank studied the folding instructions in the book for a moment, then said, "This looks like origami—aerodynamic origami. It can't be that easy to learn."

"Oh, no—most people won't fold it as precisely as is necessary. I will say this much for your airplane maker—he or she is patient and loves precision. You can see that in the quality of the work."

"Tell me more about this Stunt Flyer—what is it supposed to do?"

"Acrobatics. The plane is designed to slowly loop its way downward from the height at which it is launched. It's not designed for distance, but you won't have to run after it, and it stays in the air longer than most."

"So it would be ideal for use in an enclosed space," Frank said.

"Yes."

"How many paper airplane contests are there each year—locally, in Las Piernas?"

"In Las Piernas? One. Ours. This year's was our third event."

"Only open to students?"

"No—anyone can enter. The event is actually several contests—prizes for distance, duration—that's time aloft—aerial acrobatics, and so on. Within each, there are categories of competition. We have faculty, student, and public competitions. The same man takes the faculty competition every year, so we may start handicapping."

"You?"

He laughed. "No. Professor Frost." Seeing Frank's smile, he asked, "Do you know him?"

"We met briefly this evening. But about the contest—do you have any lists of competitors? Entry forms perhaps?"

"Yes, both, if you need them." He moved to a file cabinet, halted, and said, "I probably shouldn't be giving this information to you, but—well, Ben speaks highly of you. Can I trust you not to sell the names and addresses to a mailing list or telephone solicitor?"

"I'm only looking for one name—I'm not sure whose name it is. But I suspect the attacker is someone who knows the captain, so maybe he learned how to fold this plane here. Maybe somewhere else, but I'd like to give this a shot."

Wilkes pulled three thick folders out of a drawer. "I do wish I could stay around to help with this."

Frank declined Wilkes's offer of a ride to his car. The air had cooled considerably from the heat of the day, and a walk on this quiet, moonlit night would be pleasant, he decided. It would give him time to think.

He made his way across the campus alone, carrying the plane's box and the three bulky file folders. During the spring or fall, even at this hour, groups of students would have been leaving classrooms, talking in the halls. But now, during summer session, the quad was nearly deserted. He saw a few students walking toward one of the libraries, but no one else. A little later, as he passed an open window near one of the art buildings, he saw lights and heard the sound of steel drums beating, caught a peculiar mix of scents of paint and brush cleaner and linseed oil—someone listening to music while working late in one of the studios.

He took the shortcut offered by a path through the campus sculpture garden. As he strolled past the abstract metal shapes, he wondered if he had jumped to conclusions about the paper airplane. Maybe Bredloe had some other enemy and the paper airplane was just a coincidence. Maybe it didn't have anything to do with Lefebvre's killer—maybe he had assumed a connection that wasn't really there just because he had come from seeing the wreckage of Lefebvre's plane not long before.

He had a sudden sensation of being watched, and halted. He was nearly in the center of the garden, surrounded now by an alien landscape of rising curves and sharp angles—a few of the large sculptures reflected moonlight off their highly polished surfaces, but most eclipsed it, darkening the pathway.

He saw movement out of the corner of his eye and turned quickly—and beheld nothing more than the garden's odd patchwork of shadow and light. He waited. The faint pulse of the drum music reached him, and the distant, intermittent sound of cars on a campus road. He walked a little farther, then quickly stepped behind a tall, flat piece of metal with a single, four-inch hole in it. A placard at the base said the title of the piece was "Mother."

He watched the pathway. Although he had seen nothing more, he now felt sure that someone had followed him. From where? He would have seen anyone who waited in the hall outside Wilkes's office. Outside the engineering building? That was a possibility. There were many places—including inside other buildings—from which someone could have watched his progress until he reached the garden. At that point, the watcher would have been forced to follow him or give up pursuit.

He considered circling back to try to come up behind the follower, but just then he thought he heard a hesitant step. He stayed still, listening, watching.

Again he caught a glimpse of movement, a shadow cast where one had not been a moment ago. He shifted the folders, keeping his right hand—his gun hand—free. Suddenly he heard running footsteps on the path, moving away from him, back toward the art studios. He followed, cautiously at first, leaving the pathway to dart between sculptures, staying low.

He reached the edge of the garden, but did not step out into the open. His pursuer could have used any one of several bordering buildings as his means of escape. Again Frank waited. The steel drum music stopped. Its absence seemed to amplify the silence left in its wake, until a mockingbird began a noisy chant in a nearby ficus. Frank moved back among the sculptures.

He stayed on the grass planted between the works of art, off the concrete path. When he reached the other side of the garden, he studied his surroundings, but now he was as sure that the follower had given up as he had been sure of his presence earlier. Still, he stayed alert on the walk from the garden to the nearby stairs, from the stairs to the adjoining lot, where he was parked. He saw no one, and no other cars were parked near his own. He got into the Volvo's front seat and started the engine.

He was about a block from the campus when he noticed that his left side mirror was out of adjustment.

22

Frank set the files on the dining room table, where Irene had set up her notebook computer. "Mind if I work next to you?" he asked.

"Not at all—but I'm not going to be much of a conversationalist."

"I'm not trying to force you to talk about our argument—"

"No, that's not what I mean. It's just that I have to do some work tonight if I'm going to take time off to go to Phil's funeral in the morning."

"I've got some papers to look through," he said. "I'll keep you company."

She glanced up at him then, perhaps catching something in his tone of voice, and said, "Everything okay?"

He shrugged. "Case is spooking me, that's all."

When he didn't say more, she said lightly, "Well, nothing like a little paperwork to reassure a person—the power of the mundane. Have a seat."

So he sat across from her. Soon she was immersed in her writing, barely aware of his presence. He opened one of Wilkes's folders, listening to the click and tap of the keyboard while she wrote. For a few minutes, he did not read—he simply watched her, by turns taken with her intensity, then amused by the faces she made as she concentrated on the story.

He glanced through the files Wilkes had given him, but did not see any familiar names. A few of the applications were nearly illegible. He thought of Joe Koza, the lab's questioned-documents examiner, and wondered if he'd be able to decipher them. He was reminded that he needed to check in with Koza about the bloodstained business card he had found on Lefebvre's body. By now Joe probably had found time to run laser and other tests that would allow him to read the printing on the card.

As he neared the end of the second folder, he found one application that wouldn't need Koza's expertise. The lettering was so neatly aligned, it seemed impossible that the form had been filled in by hand. The application was for a W. L. Wallace. He found others that had a draftsmanlike quality, but none quite so neat as Wallace's.

He set the folders aside and took out a thick sheaf of photocopies he had made of the small notebook Lefebvre had carried on the plane.

The copies from the notebook made a good-size stack of papers because it had been almost full—Lefebvre had written on one side of each page, then turned the notebook over and started writing on the other side. Frank had been able to copy only two small notebook pages at a time, and the result made awkward reading. At least, he thought, all the blank space left room for his own notes. He knew there were ways to scan things like this into a computer and use a program to rearrange them on a page, but there never seemed to be money in the budget for things like computer scanners. The local high schools had better equipment than the police department did—which wasn't saying much.

Looking through the pages once, then spinning them around to read the reverse side, he began to make a list of the cases covered in the notebook. He decided to ask for files on these. It might help him to learn how Lefebvre had worked. And the names of his enemies.

He couldn't help but notice that the last few pages of writing seem to have been made under some stress. They were in connection with the *Amanda* case. He was especially interested in these. Seth's name was often in them.

Irene finished her work, sent it in by modem, and gave him a quick kiss before going to bed. He was tempted to follow her, but he kept working, sure he was getting close to something now.

He was dismayed when he realized that Lefebvre had started making repeated lists in connection with the murders of Trent and Amanda Randolph—lists of names. Names of members of the department and police commission. What was Lefebvre on to?

He found one exception—one name that he couldn't make sense of. It didn't relate to any name he had seen in the files, and as far as he knew, it wasn't the name of an officer, detective, or crime lab worker.

Doremi. He repeated the name in his head a few times until it began to sing a little song.

Do-re-mi.

But what the hell did it mean?

His thoughts were interrupted by a loud cry, a sound of pain and fear and distress. It was as familiar as it was unsettling—Irene was having a nightmare, crying out in her sleep. He listened, but although he could hear her stirring restlessly, she did not make any other sounds. Still, he put his work away and moved to the bedroom.

She had fallen asleep while reading in bed, and the lamp beside it was still on. The book had been knocked to the floor, as had most of the covers. The dogs had made the most of this latter situation, but a stern look from him was enough to get them to retreat. The cat, who usually slept next to Irene, had moved to the rocking chair—obviously not willing to put up with all the disquiet in the bed.

The room was chilly—a cool ocean breeze came through the open window. He would not close the window—Irene's fear of enclosed spaces prohibited shutting it. He put the sheet and blanket over her again, but by the time he had finished quietly undressing, she had already kicked them down around her feet. As she dreamed, she was breathing as fast and hard as any runner after a sprint.

"Irene, you're safe," he said softly. "It's okay, you're safe."

She murmured something unintelligible, then grew quiet. He was starting to freeze his ass off, but still, he slowly and gently eased into bed. More than once he had been kicked when she took off "running" in her sleep. Recently, the nightmares had not come to her so frequently or as violently as in the past, but he knew the last few days had provided more than enough stress to bring one on. He pulled the covers up again and turned off the light.

She half awakened and said, "You're cold," then snuggled closer to him.

He held her, warming beneath her, stroking her back as he listened to the sound of the nearby sea and then to her soft and steady breathing.

But just before he fell asleep, three notes played in his head—*do-re-mi.*

23

Frank had worried that there would be only four other mourners at Lefeb-vre's funeral: Yvette Nereault, Marie, Polly Logan, and Irene. Now, sitting next to Irene in the last pew of St. Anthony's Catholic Church, he counted forty-seven people in attendance—not a bad turnout for a man no one had heard from for ten years. At first he thought the majority of the small crowd were curiosity seekers, but while he saw two or three people who might fit that description, there were many more who didn't.

Pete wasn't here at the church, but Frank had been able to talk him and Reed into helping with surveillance at the cemetery. Reed would videotape the graveside service, or more accurately, the faces of the mourners, while Pete noted license plates. Frank was hoping that the killer would feel com-pelled to attend, but he kept that hope to himself. He had learned a lesson from his conversation with the chief—he told Pete and Reed that he was hoping that Lefebvre's connection to Dane might show up.

Here in the church, he seemed to be the only one from the department in attendance.

The closed casket near the altar was a plain and inexpensive one, but it was draped in flowers and there were many wreaths and other flowers sur-rounding it. He was puzzled—Lefebvre had been by all accounts a loner, and no one had seen him for ten years. Who were these mourners, and who had sent all the flowers? Most of the names in the guest book were not fa-miliar to him, but he had written them down in his notebook. Did Yvette Nereault have a wide circle of friends in Las Piernas, people who were responding in sympathy for the loss of her brother? He wanted to get a look at the cards on the flowers, but he didn't want to place any additional strain between himself and Yvette Nereault.

He saw her now, sitting in the front pew. Although she was not weeping, her grief was evident. She seemed to be intent on bearing up for the person sitting next to her—the boy Frank had met outside Lefebvre's condo. Another woman sat on the other side of the boy, bending to whisper something to him. The woman was heavily veiled, so Frank could not see her face or even the color of her hair. When she sat up again, he had an impression of both restraint and strength. Marie, the owner of the Prop Room, sat next to her, weeping. On the other side of Marie, an elderly man with close-cropped gray hair and military posture turned and surveyed the church, as if sensing Frank's study of him. But in the next moment Frank realized that the man was making his own study of the mourners. His eyes met Frank's, held for a moment, then continued to scan the crowd.

"Guy's a cop," he whispered, not realizing he had said it aloud until Irene spoke softly in reply.

"Matt Arden."

Frank turned to her. Because she had to leave for work soon after the graveside ceremony, they had driven to the funeral separately. Until now, she had not said anything to him since he'd sat down beside her.

She was still watching Arden and added, "He was Phil's mentor, you know. He's not looking well."

Frank thought the same—the ten years since Lefebvre's death had not been kind to Matt Arden.

"This has got to be so hard on him," she said, but something in her voice caught his attention and he saw how hard this was on her—and that she was trying to hide her grief from him. He put an arm around her shoulders, and understanding the gesture, she leaned against him and let the tears fall. When she started fumbling through her purse, he gave her his handkerchief.

He watched the other mourners and noticed that they did not seem to know one another. They sat a little apart from one another and did not converse.

The priest entered and began the funeral Mass. Frank had been to enough funerals to quickly recognize that this priest, a young man, had had no acquaintance with Lefebvre. He paused to consult notes whenever any mention of the deceased was called for, and never said Lefebvre's name without carefully pronouncing it, like a child who has learned to read a new and difficult word. After a series of prayers, at the point of the Mass where

Frank expected a routine sermon assuring the mourners that Lefebvre was in a better place, the priest said, "Let us take a few moments to celebrate Detective Lefebvre's life by sharing our memories of him. While I did not have the honor of knowing him personally, Mrs. Nereault, Philippe's sister, tells me that some of you would like to share your memories of him. I hope you'll do so now. Would anyone like to begin?"

The result, after a moment's hesitation, was a line at the microphone. One by one, the mourners spoke of family members—of their brothers, sons, daughters, wives—who had been murder victims, and of Philip Lefebvre's dedication in finding the killers. Moreover, they spoke of his kindnesses to their families, of his support that continued through the killers' trials, and well beyond.

Frank took out his notebook and started writing. When Irene saw what he was doing, he thought she might object. Instead, she pulled out her own notebook.

The stories were varied, but had certain elements in common. The speakers often told of Lefebvre persisting long after others had given up. They always spoke of Lefebvre's concern for the families, of how kind and considerate he had been to them. They all stated their faith in his honesty. No one made a direct reference to the accusations made against him after his disappearance, but they clearly believed this man who had helped them could not have been a bad cop. To them, Lefebvre was unquestionably a hero.

No one from Lefebvre's own family got up to speak. At one point, the boy turned around to stare intently at Frank, until the veiled woman noticed and apparently told him not to look back again. A few minutes went by while he looked straight ahead, and then he began stealing glances whenever the woman seemed distracted.

Toward the end of the Mass, Frank heard the church doors open, then a woman's half-hushed voice. He turned to see Tory Randolph making an entrance. He found himself ready to block her way if she started to make a scene. She looked around, saw him, smiled, saw Irene, stopped smiling—saw Polly Logan, and frowned. She then pulled a harried-looking man into the pew across the aisle. The man stumbled over the kneeler as she dragged him behind her, nearly falling into her lap before he regained his balance. He righted himself, but his black-rimmed glasses had fallen halfway down his nose. He used his middle finger to push them up again, inadvertently flipping the bird to the assembled company.

"That's the unfortunate Mr. Britton," Irene murmured. "Pray for him."

24

The Looking Glass Man checked his watch. The church service would be starting now. He had a little more time. It would not do to arrive early. The police always watched for suspects among mourners and spectators.

Frank Harriman would certainly do so. His brows drew together as he considered Harriman. Bad sign that he had gone to the university. The Looking Glass Man did not worry that Harriman could trace him from there—he had never used real information when signing up. Still, he was annoyed that Harriman had even thought to go to the campus. Something must be done about Harriman.

Perhaps an accident in the home. He would bring a few supplies with him today—both Harriman and his wife would be away from the house. First they would attend the funeral and then they would go on to work. There might be a little time to set something up.

Today was a busy day, though. He felt compelled to watch them lower Lefebvre into the ground—he regretted that he had been unable to see the wreckage of the plane, but a burial was better than nothing. From there, he planned to visit St. Anne's Hospital—not because he wished Captain Bredloe well, but because he knew Matt Arden would undoubtedly do so. Arden had been in Lefebvre's confidence. Arden must be watched.

He forced himself to clear his mind of these immediate worries and began to review the blueprints for the targeted building, again confirming the wisdom of his choices in his placement of the devices. He was anxious about this aspect of the work. Placement was a key issue both for effectiveness and avoidance of premature discovery. And it was the one subject Wendell Leroy Wallace had not fully discussed in his notes.

The Looking Glass Man could have learned how to construct such devices from a number of sites on the Internet or from the how-to books that could be found anywhere from swap meets to public libraries. He chose instead to learn from Wallace—that late, local master of the explosive. Wallace had loved precision and neatness, and kept detailed records of his experiments, which made the Looking Glass Man embrace him as a secret soulmate. Wallace had sacrificed himself to his craft some years ago, before the Looking Glass Man had a chance to meet him, but his photocopies of the bomber's notebooks were among his favorite reading materials.

He rolled up the blueprints and carefully stored them. He opened a binder that held a copy of one of Wallace's later notebooks, turning to a section that described devices for use in automobiles. He read for a few moments, gratified that the necessary ingredients would not require a shopping expedition. Then his watch beeped three times, and he knew it was time to go to the cemetery. He looked at the watch with a sense of disappointment.

How he missed hearing *do-re-mi!*

25

The graveside service began under a hot July sun that made the black-veiled woman sway from the heat. No, Frank decided, it wasn't the heat that made her sway. Although she held the boy's hand firmly, she seemed distracted, more upset than at the church. The boy continued to watch Frank. It might have unnerved him to have anyone else regard him so fixedly, but there was nothing hostile or even overly curious in the boy's stare. It was as if the grave between them formed a much deeper chasm, and the boy was willing him to find a place to cross. For what reason, Frank could not begin to guess.

He was wondering again if the boy could be Lefebvre's son when movement several yards away caught his attention. A large, neatly dressed man sought the sparse shade of a jacaranda tree. There was deeper shade nearer to the grave, but the man seemed to want to keep his distance. He was wearing wraparound sunglasses and looked down in a slightly different direction often enough to make Frank briefly wonder if the man was there not for the funeral, but to visit a grave. Something about him made the hair on the back of Frank's neck rise—the way he stood, the way he moved, the way he watched the mourners. Frank looked to see if Reed or Pete had noticed him and saw that they were as attuned to the man as he was. It was then that Frank noticed that the man was looking down and away not toward a gravestone, but to avert his face from the camera whenever Reed moved it toward him.

Reed's presence was not obvious, but the man knew where he was. Matt Arden also knew. Now Frank saw that Arden was watching the man beneath the jacaranda, too.

The large stranger stood straighter and walked away. Pete followed him.

The priest was sprinkling the casket with holy water when a high-pitched, electronic ringing rent the air. As the rest of the group near the grave looked on in irritation and disbelief, Tory Randolph pulled a phone from her purse.

"Hi," she said in a loud voice. "I'm so glad you called me back. I've been trying to reach you about the material for the draperies in the guest cottage. Have you—"

But before she could get any further in her drapery order, the woman in the black veil marched over to her, grabbed the phone from her hand, and pitched it onto the nearby pavement with a force and accuracy that could have won her a place in the Dodgers' starting lineup.

"Hey!" Tory protested. "What do you think you're doing?"

"Today is not about you," the woman said angrily.

"Do I know you?" Tory said.

Frank began moving toward them, wondering if they were going to start a shoving match right here in the cemetery.

"Get out of here," the woman said. "Get out now."

Tory put her hands on her hips. "Just a—"

"Apologize," Dale Britton said to his wife with surprising firmness.

Tory eyed him angrily but said nothing.

"Very well, then, I will." He turned to the veiled woman. "We apologize. It was incredibly rude to create a disturbance at a time like this. I'm sorry, Ms.—?"

"I'll send money for the phone," she said, not telling him her name.

"That won't be necessary. Our condolences to your family."

He took Tory by the arm and steered her toward their gold Lexus. She got into the driver's seat and pulled away from the curb almost before he was able to get into the car. Frank noticed that Britton had slammed part of his suit coat in the door—several inches of dark blue fabric waved along the side of the car as Tory sped away.

The assembled guests murmured, but the ceremony ended without further disturbance. The family group stayed behind as most of the mourners left. Irene moved a little distance away to give the family some privacy.

He looked for Pete, but didn't see him. Pete had apparently followed the jacaranda man. Reed signaled to Frank that he was going, too.

The woman in the veil and Matt Arden were talking with someone from the funeral home, choosing which flowers would be taken with them. Yvette Nereault walked over to Frank. "So—I am saying good-bye to you. I go back home today. You have my phone number there, I know. I'll wait to hear what you learn."

While she was talking, Frank became aware of someone coming closer, to stand next to him. When he looked down, he was not surprised to see the boy.

Yvette said something to the boy in French. He answered, looking stubborn. He moved even closer to Frank.

"Won't you introduce me to your nephew?" Frank said, putting a hand on the boy's shoulder. Yvette Nereault was unable to hide her surprise. The boy gave a small smile of triumph.

Behind them, a woman's voice said, "Don't say another word to him!"

Frank turned to see the veiled woman. Matt Arden stood next to her.

"It's too late," Arden said to her. He studied Frank, then said, "If we can count on your confidence—we can introduce him."

"Confidence from the department?" Frank asked, feeling the ground shift beneath his feet as surely as if he had stepped backward and into the grave.

"Especially from the department," the woman said.

He hesitated. Make a pledge like that to someone whose face he couldn't see? He was fairly sure he knew who she was, and could guess at her reasons for wanting secrecy, but he wasn't willing to offer that promise to a stranger. "I don't know if I can guarantee that under every circumstance—"

"My name is Seth Lefebvre," the boy announced clearly. "I'm not ashamed of it! My father was a hero. That's what everyone said. I'm proud to be Seth Lefebvre."

"Seth?" Frank said, startled.

"Seth," Matt Arden said at the same moment, but in a pained voice. "Of course you're proud, but what you just did is dangerous. You should have let your mother decide."

"He knows," Seth said, looking up at Frank. "You said 'your nephew.' I didn't even tell you. You knew the day you helped me catch My Dog, didn't you? You tried to call on the phone."

"Yes," Frank said. "I wasn't certain, though. Mr. Arden is right, your mother is only trying to protect you from danger." He turned to her. "Elena Rosario?"

"Yes," she said quietly, but not lifting the veil.

"I've been wanting to talk to you."

"And I've been wanting to talk to *you!*" Seth said. "Just ask Tante Yvette."

Yvette Nereault was the only one of the group besides Seth who was smiling. "You know, Seth, I would not need to use DNA testing to know you are my brother's child." To Elena, she said, "He will decide his own course, you know, just like his father. And God help anyone who tries to sway him from it. If you don't mind, Elena, I think it would be best to invite Detective Harriman back to the condo. We should not allow Seth to have his important discussion here in the open."

"It seems I don't have any say in the matter." Elena held out a hand to her son. "All right, let's go, Seth."

Seth didn't budge. "You promise?" he asked his mother.

"Yes, I promise. Now please . . ."

Seth started to move away from Frank but looked up at him and said, "You can come to my house?"

"Yes, I'll be there in a little while," Frank said.

"You know where it is," Elena said acidly.

Frank let that go by. "Yes."

"Good," she said. "Try to make sure you aren't followed."

"Elena," Arden protested, "there's no need to insult the man."

She stiffened, then walked off. Seth called to her and ran after her. Yvette sighed, then followed.

Arden extended a hand. "Don't have much time, and you seem to know who I am, so I won't bother introducing myself. I hear good things about you, Harriman."

"Likewise," Frank said. "No one works Homicide without hearing of the legendary Matthew Arden." He saw that it pleased Arden to hear him say so, and although he wanted Arden to feel at ease with him, he had told Arden nothing less than the truth. He had often heard Pete and the others in Homicide mention Arden's name with near reverence. Most of the current veteran detectives had been trained to do homicide investigations by Arden. But then Frank's last conversation with Bredloe came to mind. They had argued about Arden—argued over Arden's lies about Lefebvre while agreeing that he had lied. "Will you be at the condo as well?" he asked Arden now.

"A little later on. I'm going to try to stop by the hospital, see your captain, if they'll let me. They say he can't talk or anything, but still—Jesus, I hope Bredloe's going to be all right. I knew him when he was in uniform, for God's sake."

"When do you head home?" Frank asked, not wanting to talk to Arden about the captain. He wasn't sure how many details of the attack had been leaked to Arden through his cronies in the department, but he wasn't going to be a source of further information.

"I'm taking Yvette to LAX this afternoon, then driving on from there." He glanced at the others, who were waiting for him. "I'd better get going. Tell that little shit Pete Baird that I said it was good to see him today, even if he is twice as bald as the last time I saw him."

"Arden—" Frank said, as the old man began to step away.

Arden looked back at him.

"We need to talk before you leave Las Piernas."

Arden scowled in disapproval. "You youngsters are too damned impatient. Christ on a cracker! We're in the fucking cemetery, Phil's casket's not even in the ground, and you tell me we need to talk!"

Frank waited.

Arden stared fiercely for a long moment, then gradually his features softened and a small reluctant smile emerged. "Maybe not so damned impatient after all." He sighed. "Yes, we'll have our talk, Detective."

"Thank you."

Arden laughed and walked away.

Frank watched as they drove past the cemetery gates and onto the road beyond, but didn't see any other cars pursuing theirs.

He took a moment to look at the cards on the remaining flowers, writing down names. There was one completely white spray without a card on it. His love of gardening helped him identify the flowers in it, which were mostly gladiolus interspersed with white roses and baby's breath. He frowned; then, taking a small camera from his pocket, he used the last of a roll of film to take photographs of the arrangement. The cemetery workers watched him, their expressions a mixture of disapproval and impatience, as if he were a new brand of ghoul. No, he thought, an old brand. He watched as they lowered the coffin and began the actual work of burial.

"Good-bye, Lefebvre" he said as the coffin was lost from sight. The man deserved better than this, he thought. Then he remembered the gratitude the people in the church had expressed and Seth saying proudly that his father was a hero. "Not such a bad send-off, after all, was it? Something tells me you would have preferred that ceremony to bagpipes." A slight breeze came up, making him shiver. He reminded himself that he wasn't a superstitious man and walked away.

As he started his car, he saw a white Chevy van turn down the lane where the workers continued loading earth over the casket. The van slowed, then stopped. Frank could not see the plates from where he sat.

He waited, but the van didn't move and the driver didn't get out. He put the car in gear and drove closer to get a look at the plates. He saw the number—2E98098. Commercial plates. He couldn't see the driver; a set of curtains had been drawn behind the front seats of the van. He pulled ahead a short distance and parked again. He called the DMV and ran the plates.

A short time later the dispatcher's voice crackled back at him. The van was registered to Garrity's Flowers. Someone with a legitimate reason to be parked at a cemetery.

He pulled away from the curb and headed for the exit. He was out on the street bordering the cemetery when he saw the van behind him. He got held up by a large funeral procession making its way to the cemetery, and stopped to let them turn toward the entrance. The van would be pulling up behind him, and he would get a closer look at the driver. But the van didn't slow. Just as he thought it would rear-end him, it swerved around him and cut across the procession, nearly causing a collision, then turned up a side street. Frank couldn't lose the feeling that the driver didn't want to stop near enough to be seen. He thought of pursuing him, but decided there would be little chance of catching up to him now. He stepped out of the car and walked up to the officer closest to him—the one who had stopped traffic from his direction—and showed him his identification. He was a weary-looking young officer. He had probably worked a regular shift then hired out to do the funeral work, which was contracted separately. "I know you're working privately," Frank said, writing the van's plate number on the back of one of his cards and handing it to the officer, "but could you contact me if the van comes back? I'd like to know who was driving it."

"So would I," the officer said. "Asshole could have caused serious damage." He turned the card over and suddenly seemed more awake. "This a homicide case?"

"Yes. I mean—there's a slight possibility that the driver of the van is connected to a case I'm working. More likely that he's just a jerk in a hurry, with no connection to it at all, but . . ."

"I understand, Detective Harriman. I hope to work Homicide myself someday."

Frank figured this kid was only slightly less green than the reserve officer he had worked with a few days ago. He thought of Lefebvre and wanted to say, "Careful what you wish for." Instead he smiled and said, "That's great. Any help you can give me with this will be appreciated."

"I should have followed him," he said, as if he had failed Frank personally.

"You have a job here. It was probably nothing. Just let me know if he returns."

Frank didn't want to take too long to get over to Lefebvre's condo. Despite her promises to Seth, Elena Rosario might change her mind about talking to him. On his way there, he called Pete on his cell phone. Before he could tell him that he wouldn't be in for a while, Pete said, "Partner, you are brilliant. Damn, am I glad you let me in on this. So is Reed. That will teach Vince to be such an asshole."

"What are you talking about?"

"The guy in the shades who was getting jacaranda sap all over his expensive suit? Myles Volmer. Whitey Dane's number one man. I followed him right back to Dane's lair. And the Organized Crime Unit took one look at that tape and knew exactly who showed up to mourn his old partner Lefebvre. Even Carlson is happy with you over this one. And I'm loving it, because he was giving me and Reed grief about being down there today. Hurry back while the lieutenant is in a good mood. If anyone can tie Whitey Dane to the Randolphs' deaths, I know you can."

Frank was silent. In spite of their disagreements over the last few days, Pete was his closest friend in the department. More than once they had risked their lives for each other. And he was going to lie to him.

"Something wrong?" Pete asked. "Aw, shit—you're still sore about how things have been around here."

"No. Honest to God, Pete, that didn't get to me. But I've got a dozen other things I need follow-up on if we're going to get further with this than a sighting at a cemetery. Not exactly illegal for Dane's guy to show up there."

"No, but it's a start. First real connection we've had to Dane since the evidence disappeared."

"It's definitely worth pursuing," Frank said.

"I knew you'd start to see it our way!" Pete said. "You need any more help, you let me know. No need for you to go it alone from here."

"Sure, Pete," he said. "I'll let you know."

He hung up and forced himself to think of Seth Lefebvre.

26

She was waiting for him outside the building, leaning against the wall near the bottom of the staircase. The veil was gone, but he recognized her by her shape and the dress she was wearing. She was a good-looking woman, with long dark brown hair and beautiful sea green eyes—a winter sea, he thought. There was not the slightest bit of warmth in them at the moment. They bore the marks of her recent grief, but she regarded him coldly. She was lean and strong—the muscles of her calves and arms were so well defined, he wondered if she lifted weights. She wasn't mannish, but there was physical power in her build. She looked as if she was sorely tempted to use some of that power to punch him, as if keeping her arms folded tightly across her chest was all that prevented her from doing so.

"You took advantage of my inability to deny my son's request at his father's funeral," she said by way of greeting. "I don't appreciate that. I know how the game works, and that children are certainly not off-limits, but still—"

He held up a hand. "Hold on—your son approached me, not the other way around."

"After you played up to him the other day."

"I didn't set the guinea pig loose. I didn't even know you were living here or that Lefebvre had a son. Meanwhile, your boy is up there waiting for me and you don't dare disappoint him. Not today."

Her mouth leveled into a thin, tight line.

He sighed. "Maybe you'll feel a little less hostile toward me if I tell you that I have no plan to use your son as a pawn."

"Don't bother, because I won't believe you. Any more than I believe the crap you've given Yvette about believing in Phil's innocence."

"I do believe in his innocence."

She rolled her eyes. "Try that on someone who's never been a cop. I've been there, remember? And I know you can lie like the devil—the laws are set up so that you're free to tell anyone just about anything in order to learn what you want to know. So bullshit Yvette if you like, but it won't work with me."

"You've been a cop, so you know what it's like to bust your ass for someone who is determined to give you nothing but grief."

"Cry me a river. Listen, I know you don't want to talk to my son. Not really. He wasn't even around when the trouble started. He can't help you. So—let's leave him out of it, all right?"

"I'm here because he wanted to talk to me. I'm not out to hurt him. Whether you like it or not, he's learned something about his father today and—"

"Exactly my point—can't you just let him think of Phil as the hero he was? Do you have to take that away from him?"

"Who says I am trying to?"

"Don't give me that act!" she said furiously. "The Las Piernas Police Department has not sent you here to be helpful—I know, I worked for them."

"You should consider rejoining the force. You'd fit right in—not twenty-four hours after I got back from the mountains, the guys I work with had all the answers, too."

"Don't ever compare me with those assholes again!" she said.

This is going nowhere, he thought. Sooner or later, he'd need to talk to her about Lefebvre, and he wasn't exactly doing a fine job of building rapport. He slowly let out a breath, tried to recover his temper. "All right, I won't compare you to them," he said, keeping his voice even. "I know the department hasn't been great where the family's concerned. But if I'm going to clear Phil Lefebvre's name, I'll need your help."

She gave him a look that said she had no faith in him whatsoever, but said, "You have questions for me, ask away."

"Look, we're off to a bad start here—"

"We haven't got any kind of start at all, because nothing is building from here—you understand?"

He didn't say anything. After a moment, he saw the tension in her shoulders ease, saw them lower as she relaxed slightly—as if the effort of main-taining this level of anger with him had gradually become too much for her.

When he saw this change, he began. He asked a few easy questions—yes or no questions, ones to which he knew she would always answer yes: She had been promoted to detective faster than any other woman before, right? Commendations during her patrol work? Then worked in Narcotics? About two years as a detective?

It was an old technique, one she undoubtedly knew of—the person being questioned says "yes," and each time he or she says it, becomes a little less resistant, a little more open to the questioner. Elena unfolded her arms, and he was beginning to think all the fight had gone out of her, when he said, "You were partners with Hitch?"

Her eyes flashed and the arms came back up across her chest. "Yes," she said bitterly.

So much for the "yes" theory, he thought.

He heard a door open, then heard Yvette say, "You will wait in here, Seth."

The door closed again, but he realized that he might not get a chance to talk to her alone again for some time, if ever, and that Seth was growing im-patient. He took the plunge. "It seems no one in the department knew you had a relationship with Lefebvre . . ."

"Which is probably why I'm alive." She glanced over at him and re-lented. "Look, no one knew I had a relationship with Phil because we hardly got a chance to know it ourselves. In one twenty-four-hour period, Phil became my lover, Seth Randolph was murdered, Phil disappeared, and everyone started saying that he killed Seth. One day."

"You were only together—"

"Yes. One afternoon." She swallowed hard. "You don't know how much I wish I could say it was more, but . . ."

He thought for a moment that she might cry, but she held the tears back. She moved to the stairs and sat down.

He sat next to her and waited, taking his chances on Seth's patience.

When she started talking again, her voice was steady, but she spoke in the distracted manner of those immersed in memories.

"That night I'm out on a routine surveillance job and the radio starts go-ing wild. What I'm hearing—what I'm hearing on that radio is unbeliev-able. A call from the guard on Seth's room about a one-eighty-seven, and then he keeps saying, 'It's not my fault—it was Lefebvre.'"

She closed her eyes. "At first, I thought he meant that Phil was dead—

that someone had killed both Phil and Seth Randolph." She opened her eyes again and said, "Well, I guess I was right. But I didn't know that then. I just knew that every damned unit in the city was headed over to the hospital and that the hospital was cordoned off. I talked Hitch into going over there. It got worse and worse by the minute. The more I heard, the more I kept hoping I'd wake up from this nightmare."

She paused and cradled her forehead in the palm of one hand. "I was so scared for Phil—I think some part of me knew that something horrible had happened to him. But I didn't want to believe that, so I kept telling myself, 'Phil will straighten all of this out. They'll reach Phil at Matt's house. He'll be there by now.' But he wasn't. And Matt was lying to them, but I didn't know why."

"Why *did* he lie?"

"He didn't know what to believe, but he knew something had gone wrong—terribly wrong—for Phil. Me, at first I kept my hopes up. Not Matt. Matt didn't know who to trust inside the department, and he didn't have enough to go on to take it to someone outside the department. Later he tried, but no one would take him up on it. Phil looked too guilty."

"So that night Lefebvre's gone, and you're hearing that Matt has denied that Lefebvre planned to visit him?"

"Right. At first, I thought it was because Phil was there and Matt was keeping him safe until he could get an attorney or some proof that he was innocent. I didn't dare call Matt, and he didn't dare call me. That went on for a couple of days until Matt finally got a letter to me through the mailbox."

"The mailbox?"

"Phil got his mail at a private mailbox—at one of those mailbox stores. It took our department sleuths a while to figure that out."

"Okay, now I remember reading something about this in the case file. A place called Mail Call?"

"Right. Earlier in the day, Phil and I had figured out an arrangement so that we could keep in touch by mail if things really started going wrong— we just hadn't imagined how wrong they could go. So he set things up at Mail Call that afternoon, and I stopped by there before I went into work that night and picked up two keys—a key to his box and a key to a second box that was in both our names, where he would send messages to me if phones became too risky. He told Matt we would be doing this."

"I take it the owner of this Mail Call place didn't tell all of this to the detectives who questioned him about Phil's mailbox?"

"No. First, the detectives showed up with a very specific court order—naming only the box number Phil had on his own. Second, they came in with an attitude, so he wasn't cooperative. But I don't think he would have been cooperative no matter how sweet they were, because he had a good reason to be loyal to Phil. He was one of the people at the funeral today, although he didn't speak. Phil met the guy while working on a case—the man's daughter had been killed by her ex-husband. The only reason the ex didn't walk was because Phil caught the case and just wouldn't let go."

"So how much of Phil's mail got delivered to your mailbox?"

She smiled a little. "You know, I'm surprised you figured that out. Those dumb asses who worked this case before you never did. How much? A lot of it. There wasn't a heck of a lot of mail for those guys to paw through. The owner of Mail Call was smart enough to give them the bills, figuring that was probably how they found out about the box in the first place—looking up his credit records. Everything else came my way before the LPPD saw it. Didn't help me, though. The one letter I kept waiting for never came."

"But you heard from Matt."

"At first, I wasn't sure if I was hearing from Phil, or Matt, or both. I got a postcard, addressed to me, but the message area was blank. On the other side was a photo of some chrysanthemums. You know—"

Frank groaned. "Mum's the word."

"I had the same reaction, but I had been so anxious, there wasn't much humor in it for me. I was so angry and upset about Seth, too—Seth Randolph, I mean. I wasn't as close to him as Phil was, but I had spent a lot of time with him, too. We had found him that night, and Phil saved his life, and Seth had struggled to live. So it was . . . it was painful to lose him. I liked Seth."

Enough to name your son after him, Frank thought, but let her brood in silence.

After a while, she said, "So about three days into all of this, my nerves were shot. The first night I made the mistake of saying to Hitch, 'I don't believe Phil would kill that boy,' and I got this rant from him that convinced me that I had better keep my mouth shut. And then . . . then I found that someone had gone through my desk. And I remembered that it had happened to Phil, that someone had gone through his desk."

Seth chose that moment to open the apartment door again. "Mom!" he said, making it a complaint.

"Don't blame your mom," Frank said. "It's my fault we're still out here talking."

Seth gestured to him to hurry in.

In Seth's presence, Elena's stiffness of manner returned. In a low voice, she said, "You do anything to bring him into harm's way . . ."

Frank turned toward her and said, "What exactly do you take me for?"

"Mom!" Seth said again, more insistently.

Frank heard Yvette Nereault say something in French to her nephew, and Seth immediately apologized to his mother. "But I've been waiting for-ever!" he muttered, casting a glance back at his aunt. As if to make up for this small rebellion, he politely asked Frank if he could take his jacket and if he would like something to drink. Frank accepted an offer of coffee be-fore Seth led him to the sofa, then sat beside him.

"It is past noon—you must be hungry, Detective Harriman," Yvette said. "Seth would probably enjoy it if you stayed for lunch."

Elena did not hide her look of consternation. Seth looked at him hope-fully and said, "Can you?"

"Sure, if it's not too much trouble—"

"Not at all!" Yvette said. "Elena and I will fix you something to eat." She turned to Seth and said sternly, "Do not plague him with questions." With that, she dragged a reluctant Elena off toward the kitchen.

As soon as they were out of sight, Seth asked, "Did you know my father?"

"No, I'm sorry to say I didn't have a chance to meet him."

He seemed momentarily disappointed, then shrugged. "Neither did I." He thought for a moment, then said, "You're a detective, right?"

"Yes."

"So was my dad. Matt says my dad was a good detective."

"Your dad was better than good. Is Mr. Arden back yet?"

"Matt? Not yet. He's visiting a friend in the hospital. The policeman who got hurt in the building when the bricks fell on him. Do you know who I mean?"

"Yes. He's my captain."

"Did he know my dad?"

"Yes. He was made captain of the division just before . . ."

"Before my dad died?" he asked calmly.

"Yes."

"Can you take me to see him?"

"No, I'm sorry. He isn't able to talk much right now. He's too badly hurt."

"Oh. Do you know anyone else who knew my father?"

Frank hesitated. "I do, but I don't think they really knew him. I think they're mixed up about some things and wouldn't be able to tell you the truth."

"They're liars?"

"No, they're just mistaken."

He grew thoughtful again. "What they said today in the church—those people—that was true, wasn't it?"

"Yes, I think so. I had never met them before today. But I've read about your father, and everything I've read makes me think they were telling the truth. And there would be no reason for them to lie, right?"

Seth solemnly considered this, then said, "No, because they were in church, and you know . . ." He pointed up.

"Exactly," Frank said, struggling to match Seth's gravity.

"They were sad," Seth added. "Their stories were sad."

"Yes. But even though they were sad, they wanted to tell about how your father had helped them and to say that they were grateful."

The boy seemed lost in thought. Frank hoped that Elena and Yvette wouldn't take his silence as a cue to enter the room. He was fairly sure they were within earshot.

As if he had decided that—for the moment—he had puzzled out all he could about his father, Seth suddenly changed the subject. "Do you have a picture of your dogs?"

"Yes." Frank pulled out his wallet and removed a slightly worn photo.

"What are their names?"

"Deke and Dunk."

He frowned. "Really? Like in hockey and basketball?"

"Yes."

"Who is that with them?"

"My wife. Irene."

He studied the photo, then said, "Do they bite?"

"Irene? No, she's nice."

This information won a slight smile. "You know that's not what I mean."

"The dogs are friendly, too. They might bite someone who tried to hurt Irene, but I'm not sure. Now that I think about it, Irene would definitely bite someone who tried to hurt the dogs."

The smile grew a little.

"Where do you go to school?" Frank asked.

"I don't." At Frank's look of surprise, he said, "I used to, but now I'm home schooled."

"Your mother teaches you?"

"Yes. And sometimes my aunt. She teaches me French and about the history of the Quebecois and Canada. My mom teaches me lots of stuff.

Spelling, reading, math. Spanish—we learn that together. And self-defense. You should teach your wife that, you know."

"Self-defense?"

"Yes, because the dogs are good, but they might not be with her all the time when bad guys are around."

"You have a lot of trouble with bad guys?"

He shook his head, then smiled a little. "But once this kid at school? He was being mean to me all the time, and he tried to hit me, so I flipped him!"

"You mean, with a karate throw?"

"Yeah! All the other kids were going, 'Whoa! I can't believe it!'" He looked a little sheepish. "I didn't break any of his bones or anything, but I got in big trouble. Mom said I can't do that to other kids—I have to use it for my last dessert."

"As a last resort, maybe?"

"Yes. That's what I mean."

"That's not why you're home schooled, is it?"

"You mean, did I get kicked out? No way!"

"Do you like being home schooled?"

He hesitated, glancing toward the kitchen. "Of course. I learn more this way. I'll show you."

He led Frank down a hallway toward the back of the condo, to a door with a hand-lettered sign taped to it: Private—Please Do Not Enter Without Permission. The second s in "permission" appeared to have been squeezed in after consultation with a dictionary.

"This is my room," he said, opening the door.

At first glance, the room seemed to be in utter chaos. Hardly a surface was bare. A piece of clothesline stretched from two hooks in the wall above the bed, and over it a sheet formed a tent of sorts above the mattress. An elaborate Lego structure stood in the middle of the room—a fort, it seemed, judging from the number of green plastic army men on parade within its walls. They appeared to be under the command of a Batman figurine. In one corner, a large and intricate guinea pig abode held My Dog, who gave out a series of dovelike cooing sounds as they entered the room. While Seth greeted him, Frank continued to survey the room.

A Macintosh computer with a screensaver of constellations sat on a desk piled high with schoolbooks. There was a map of the world on one wall, a history timeline on another. "What are all the stickers on the map?"

"I come from those places. I mean, those are places where my grandfathers and great-grandfathers and great-great-grandfathers are from—and all the grandmothers, too. I'm from all over the world. Cool, huh?"

"Yes," Frank said. "Very cool—so's this poster."

The closet door had an old hockey poster on it—Gordie Howe. Long before Seth's time.

"Are you a hockey fan?" Frank asked.

"Yes. That poster was my father's, when he was little." Seth stared at it, frowning—although Frank thought he was concentrating on something other than Howe's photo. The boy moved to a small telescope near the window, fidgeting with it for a moment before he said, "I saw a movie once where someone used a picture to make a ghost come into a house. Did you see that one?"

"No, I didn't."

Peering into the large end of the telescope, he asked with studied casualness, "Do you think there's any such thing as ghosts?"

"You mean the scary kind, like the ones you see in movies?"

He looked up from the lens and nodded solemnly.

Frank thought of the times when, while working on especially disturbing cases, he had awakened with a start—and for a brief half-asleep, half-awake instant felt certain that he had seen a murder victim sitting at the end of his bed. "No," he said. "Do you?"

"Not really," Seth said.

"Are you afraid you might see your father's ghost?"

"Maybe a little."

"Your father was a good man who would have wanted to be with you if he could. He never, ever would have harmed you."

"Even if he knew I had been bad?"

"Even then. He was smart, and he would understand that everybody does something wrong now and then. He'd know that you try to be good."

Seth quietly considered this as he walked around the room, familiar with an unobstructed path of his own design. He straightened a Batman comic book that lay on a small table next to the bed, aligning it with a book about dinosaurs and another about ships. He picked up a portable CD player, flipped the cover open and shut a few times, and set it down. Then he gestured to Frank to come nearer a wall with a series of shelves on it. These shelves held an assortment of objects on them.

He showed Frank his rock collection, a seashell collection, a shed snakeskin that he had found while visiting Matt in the desert.

"Matt's a good friend of yours, isn't he?" Frank asked.

"Yeah. He's pretty fun, but he's been sick lately, so I don't get to visit him so often. He had to have an operation on his heart. He's got a big scar. From here to here," he said with a certain amount of relish as he traced a line from his neck to his belly button.

"Who are your other friends?"

He looked away and shrugged, then said, "You want to see my hockey cards?" Without waiting for an answer, he got down on all fours and pulled a shoebox from beneath the bed. He pulled the sheet from the clothesline, then invited Frank to sit next to him on the bed, where he had already displayed several of his favorite cards. He began an impressive recital of not only player stats but observations on the players' performances in recent games.

"Do you play hockey?" Frank asked.

"No," he said sadly, then added on a more hopeful note, "I might get to play next year." His face fell again. "But I don't know. That might be too late. All the other kids will have a head start on me."

"No, you can always learn to play. I just started playing last year."

"You did?"

"Yes. I'm not a great hockey player, but I have a lot of fun. Do you ice-skate?"

"Yes. I'm a good skater."

"And you watch the game. I think you'll do fine."

"Can I watch you play?"

"We'll ask your mom. The games are pretty late at night."

Seth smiled. "That's one good thing about home schooling. I can sleep in!" He fell back onto his pillow, eyes shut, making snoring noises.

There was a knock at the bedroom door. "Seth!" Elena called through it.

He sat upright and called back, "Yes?"

She opened the door. "Are you hungry? Lunch is ready."

Frank saw a slightly mischievous look come into Seth's eyes. "It can't be!" the boy said. "I didn't hear the smoke alarm!"

"Come on, Mr. Smartmouth." She saw the hockey cards and said, "You must really rate, Detective Harriman." She didn't seem especially happy about it.

Mistaking the cause of her displeasure, Seth hurried over to her and said, "I was just teasing, Mom. You're a great cook."

Her face softened and she ruffled his hair. "Oh, yeah? I did burn dinner the other night, so I guess I deserve a little teasing."

"You were upset—"

She glanced nervously at Frank, then quickly said to Seth, "Matt's back, and you know he has to take Aunt Yvette to the airport right after lunch. So hurry and wash up, okay?"

Seth started to sit next to Frank, then moved to take a seat by his mother. Elena managed a smile and said, "Go on, sit next to your guest."

Seth patted her shoulder and stayed where he was, which made Yvette smile and say something to him in French, which seemed to please him.

"*Merci*," he said quietly.

As they ate ham sandwiches made on thick slices of bread, Matt, Seth, and Yvette kept the conversation rolling. Arden talked about his visit to Bredloe, which had shaken him. He began to reminisce about the captain and their days together on the force. Frank noticed that these war stories were strictly G-rated, with a careful concern for Seth, who was clearly drinking in every word.

"I knew him when he was just a rookie," Arden said. "He went up the ranks quickly—like you must have done, Frank."

"I've only known him as a captain," Frank said, skirting the issue of his own advancement. "I hope he'll be able to come back."

"They tell me he's making progress," Matt said. "If that's progress . . ." He shuddered.

"Frank said the captain knew my father," Seth said.

Elena shot Frank a look of displeasure, but Matt answered, "Yes, he did. Maybe if he gets better you can talk to him about your dad."

Yvette looked at her watch. "We need to get going soon, I think, Matt."

Matt asked if Frank could help him load Yvette's bags into his car. "I'd do it myself, but my damn—er, I'm not supposed to lift anything heavy."

"I'll help you, Matt," Elena said.

"Oh, hell no, Elena. You and Seth should spend time saying good-bye to Yvette—in fact, I'd enjoy spending a few minutes shooting the bull with Harriman about my old friends in the department."

She eyed Arden skeptically, but allowed Frank to carry the suitcases.

"Yvette tells me you're open-minded about Phil," Arden said when they reached the bottom of the stairs. "I can't imagine you'll stay at your present rank if that's the case."

"You want to say something, or am I just going to get the B side of the record Elena keeps playing?"

Arden smiled. "No, I'm not as cynical as she is—and I'm damned cynical. I'm just afraid that you may not realize what you're getting yourself into."

"So I should follow your example and keep my mouth shut for a decade or so?"

Arden's mouth flattened and his face turned red. But after a moment he said, "I suppose I deserve that—at least it must look that way from where you're standing."

"I can't help but wonder why a man with your skills, let alone your clout with the department, couldn't have done more."

"You think I haven't wondered about that very same thing every day for the last ten years? But a man's best choices have a nasty way of being easier to see in hindsight. I'm still not sure I would have done anything differently. Look at it from my perspective—Phil called me and told me a story I wouldn't have believed at all if anyone else had been telling it to me. But I knew him, and I knew he wasn't a fool who would be seeing bogeymen in every corner. But this son of a bitch he told me about is inside the department, has killed a god-damn police commissioner, has perfectly set up Whitey-fucking-Dane, and —worse yet—is now on to the fact that Phil doesn't buy the story that Dane did the killing. That was enough to make me fear for Phil's life. And this is all on my faith in him—you understand? Because Phil couldn't get a handle on who the hell it was, didn't have one single goddamned piss drop of tangible proof. So, yes, I was scared—I admit it. Scared for him. The only thing I could think of was to get him the hell out of here."

They had reached the car by then. Arden opened the trunk and Frank loaded Yvette's bags. "So when he didn't show up at your place, what did you do?"

"Worried, that's what. Worried my ass off. I had told Phil to try to take a look at the shoes in the evidence box—to see if they were new or worn. If they were worn, we could find a way to see if they matched wear patterns on Dane's other shoes, and if they didn't, that might be a way to pry a little doubt into the department's certainty that Dane killed the Randolphs. Where we could go from there, I didn't know."

"Smart, though," Frank admitted, deciding he would see what he could learn from the evidence photos of the deck shoes.

"You think so?" He slammed the trunk closed and turned back to Frank. "Me, I've always wondered if that got Phil murdered. That and my other smart idea—that he should come to see me. If he hadn't scared someone by looking at the evidence or been in that fucking plane, on his way to see me, maybe . . ."

He broke off and quickly passed a gnarled hand across his eyes. After a moment, he said quietly, "That's what I have on *my* conscience, Harriman—did I give Phil a suggestion that got him killed?"

"The killer knew Lefebvre loved to fly. The way the plane was sabotaged—it didn't matter where Lefebvre was going."

Arden didn't seem convinced. "When his lieutenant—poor old Willis—called me at almost midnight that first night and asked if Phil was at my place, I knew something was wrong—really wrong. It could have been the middle of the day and I would have known—I could hear it in Willis's voice. He was upset. If things had gone right, there wasn't any reason for Willis to be upset. So I lied to him. I lied and he told me what had happened to Seth Randolph, and that the evidence was missing, and that it looked like Phil did it—Phil! And I felt the damned room spin, because until that moment I just thought it might be trouble, but when Willis told me that, I swear to you, I knew Phil was dead. I knew it in my gut. And I didn't spend all those years in that line of work without knowing when I could trust my gut, you know?"

Frank nodded.

"Yeah, of course you do. Anyway, talking to Willis, for all I knew, I was on the phone with Phil's killer. So I denied that Phil had said he was coming to see me and prayed to God that Elena would keep her mouth shut, because I had also figured out that we were both in danger. Maybe that was chickenshit of me, Harriman, but it wouldn't have made Phil come back to life if I had told the truth, would it? And until we could figure out who was behind the murders, the only way for us to be safe was to make the killer feel safe. I figured I'd get a chance to look into things when all the noise died down."

"So what happened?"

"I got nowhere. Phil looked damned guilty. So guilty, my so-called legendary rep—the one you've been throwing in my face all afternoon—wasn't worth shit when it came to trying to learn the first thing about the case. They suspected me of hiding Phil or of knowing where he was. I was under surveillance. They didn't want to hear anything I had to say about looking at anyone else."

"Who were his enemies?" Frank asked.

"Phil's? I don't think he had any." He smiled at Frank's open look of disbelief. "No, I'm not kidding. He didn't have any friends, either—at least not after I retired."

"Elena—"

"Naw. I'm not saying he was just playing around with her—that wasn't like him at all. He must have felt something for her. Who knows, maybe it was the real deal between them."

"You seem to be close to her."

"I've come to know her and understand why Phil liked her. And the boy—you know, if he hadn't come along . . ." He shook his head. "You picture the most cynical, bitter bastard you've ever known in your life and multiply him about a thousand times, and you've got a slight notion of what I was like after Phil disappeared. I'd failed a man who might as well have been my son, and the department I'd given most of my life to was treating me like a foul little turd—a creep who was hiding a cop who killed a young witness. Yvette called and told me that Elena was going to have his kid. It was—well, the best news of a pregnancy since the archangel Gabriel made his big announcement, as far as I'm concerned. I love that child. Seth is Phil all over. When that boy was born, I cried like a baby myself." He smiled. "He's taken a liking to you, that's for damned sure."

"It's mutual."

"You would have liked his dad, too, I think. A shame you didn't get a chance to meet him. Elena didn't really get a chance to know Phil, either. He obviously trusted her, and if he had lived, I don't doubt he would have stayed with her. He was a loyal person, and he was choosy about that loyalty of his—didn't pass it down the row like a bag of peanuts at the ballpark the way some of these guys do. You know—the blue brotherhood and all that. He didn't hang out with other cops."

"You must have a guess or two about who killed him."

He shook his head. "Not a one. Not for a lack of trying, but none that makes sense to me."

"Meanwhile, the killer's still out there. That has to stick in your craw."

"For a time it did, but now I figure whoever it was is dead or long gone from Las Piernas."

"How do you figure that?"

"He's been quiet for too long. I'm alive, Elena's alive, even Whitey Dane is alive."

"And Seth isn't allowed to go to school or use the name Lefebvre."

"Okay, so we take precautions where the boy is concerned. But there haven't been similar cases of detectives or commissioners and their families murdered. I think the guy cut his losses after Phil and ran."

Frank thought of the attack on Bredloe, but said nothing.

"All right, so sometimes I think he might still be out there," Arden admitted. "But there isn't much I can offer you on it—can't get near enough to learn a damned thing. You can get in where I couldn't. Look at the records for that box of evidence from the Randolph case. The man who killed Phil took the contents of that box." He sighed. "I couldn't figure out who would want Randolph and his family dead. Tory Randolph had the most to gain, but you'll never convince me that she would have sacrificed her kids to get her hands on that money."

"I agree. Even if I could believe she killed her own children, she didn't have access to . . . no, wait . . . Jesus, she did."

"Did what? You look like you swallowed a damned lemon."

"I was going to say she didn't have access to the evidence. But if she got help from the man she later married—Dale Britton—she could have easily managed it."

"That stumbling clod?" Arden scoffed.

"He worked in the lab. Could he have lasted at that job if he was dropping beakers all over the place? Maybe he's not clumsy all the time."

"Maybe."

"There's a lot to sort out about Dane and Randolph, too. One of Dane's men watched the funeral today."

"The gent under the jacaranda?"

"Yes."

They heard the door to the condo open above them.

Arden lowered his voice. "I wish you luck. Trail is colder than a polar bear's nuts and the department wants this whole business out of sight and out of mind. But if there's anything I can do, you let me know."

He held out his hand and Frank shook it, saying, "It's been an honor."

There was the slightest questioning look in Arden's eyes.

"I mean it," Frank said.

The old man smiled. "You call me if I can help," he said again as the others arrived.

Frank stood apart from the group as Seth and Elena said good-bye to Arden and Yvette. As these two members of Seth's extended family drove away, Frank noticed a white van parked in the guest parking lot which was at the far end of the alley, at the intersection of the nearest street. He started to walk toward it when Elena said, "I guess you'll have to be going now."

"My jacket's upstairs," he reminded her, reconsidering his plan to approach the van on foot. "Seth, would it be okay if I took a look through your telescope before I go?"

"Sure!"

Elena made a sound of exasperation, but led the way.

• • •

"I'm not allowed to spy on the neighbors," Seth said, when Frank lowered the angle of the telescope to look toward the guest parking area. Elena, who was apparently not going to let Frank have another minute alone with her son, smiled from the other side of the room.

"That's a good rule," Frank said. "I just want to see if this would be a good kind of telescope to use at work."

"What do you mean?" Seth asked.

Frank could see only part of the van's plate, but enough to tell that it began with "2JST." It was not the same plate number as the one he had seen at the cemetery.

"I mean that sometimes we have to see things that are happening too far away to see with the naked eye." He looked out onto the parkway between the buildings. Other than a gardener carrying a bulging green trash bag and a rake, there was no one nearby.

"Do you want to borrow it?"

"No, I'll make the police buy their own if they want one. But thanks for letting me try it."

"Thanks for visiting us," Elena said. "Here's your jacket. Say good-bye, Seth."

Seth looked disappointed, then asked, "Can I visit you at your house?"

"Seth!"

"Sure you can," Frank said, putting on the jacket. He smiled at Elena and said, "Don't worry, he's more interested in my dogs than me."

"No, I'm not!" Seth said, laughing, then quickly added, "But they don't bite, Mom, so can I visit them?"

"Seth . . ."

"I won't bother him. He likes me, Mom."

Until that moment, Frank was certain she would refuse. But at these words, she seemed ready to relent.

"That's true," Frank said. "We'd be happy to have both of you over. My wife used to know Seth's dad, and I think she'd be pleased to meet Seth."

"Your wife?" Elena asked. "The woman who was with you at the funeral?"

"Yes. Irene Kelly."

"Irene Kelly—now I remember where I've seen her before. You married a reporter?"

"Yes."

"Man, you must already be on the outs with the department."

"What do you mean, Mom?" Seth asked.

Before she could answer, the guinea pig began making squealing noises, sounds of distress.

"What's wrong, My Dog?" Seth asked, then sniffed. "Do you smell smoke?"

The smoke alarm went off before anyone could answer.

"Are you cooking?" Seth asked his mother.

"No," she said, "but let me check the oven." She hurried out of the room, ignoring Frank as he called after her.

But the acrid scent indicated more than a kitchen mishap. As it rapidly grew stronger, he saw smoke billowing outside Seth's window. Seth's eyes widened in fright. Frank put a hand on the boy's shoulder and kept his voice calm as he said, "Let's all go outside. Why don't I carry My Dog's cage?"

Seth ducked out from under his hand and got down on the floor, scattering toy soldiers.

"Seth!" Elena called out frantically as the air in the condo itself began filling with smoke.

"My treasures!" Seth said, pulling a small wooden box from beneath the bed and tucking it inside his shirt.

Frank grabbed hold of him and lifted him into one arm, and took the guinea pig cage with his free hand just as Elena struggled back to them.

"I've got him!" Frank shouted. "Go!"

Eyes tearing, he felt Seth gripping tightly to him, the edges of the wooden box pressing into his side. They found their way to the front door, coughing. Elena started to reach for the doorknob, but Frank yelled, "No! Feel the door first."

"It's hot," she said, backing away from it, a look of panic on her face.

"The fire ladders!" Seth shouted, squirming.

"Where are they?" Frank asked.

"In the bedroom closets."

"You stay here with your mother. Get down on the floor—more air there!" Handing Seth over to her, he hurried back toward Seth's bedroom, the nearest of the two. The smoke had thickened. He stumbled over toys but located the closet and yanked the door open. He bent close to the floor, but still the smoke made his nose and throat and lungs feel as if he were breathing hot needles. He found the ladder and made his way out to the living room in time to hear glass shatter. Elena had picked up a chair and used it to break out the large front window. It sent a rush of cooler, less smoky air into the room. He hooked the chain ladder on the sill and dropped it down. The distance from the bottom rung to the ground would not be difficult for an adult to manage, but he was afraid the boy would be hurt or might freeze halfway down the rungs, trapping them. "You first," he rasped to Elena. "I'll send Seth down after you."

She didn't argue. Seth held on to Frank as he watched her maneuver her way out. He put Seth on the ladder as soon as she was clear of the window. Seth seemed unafraid of the height, but balked at leaving the guinea pig behind. "My Dog!"

"I'll bring him!" Frank said. "Now go!"

Seth obeyed the commanding tone. Frank reached in the cage, grasped the frightened animal by the scruff of the neck, and forced it into his inside jacket pocket, where it squirmed nervously. He was certain it was going to jump to its death when he was halfway down the ladder, but it seemed to realize the pocket was the lesser of two evils, and after that, was subdued. Elena had already moved Seth away from the building. She held him tightly, asking him again and again if he was all right. Frank handed the guinea pig over to Seth, then used his cell phone to report the fire.

Neighbors had already reported it, though, and no sooner had he hung up the phone than they heard a fire truck. It pulled into the alley and the firefighters immediately went to work. One of them hurried over to them and asked if any of them were injured and if anyone else was inside. Frank told him that everyone was safe and showed the firefighter his identification. "We'll be right here," Frank said. Reassured, the man joined the others. In a matter of minutes, the fire was out.

During those few minutes, Frank made a second call, to the department. He asked for the chief and was put through to Hale.

"Detective Harriman," Hale said, "I hear things are going better today. Are you calling to tell me we're about to arrest Dane?"

"No, sir. I'm at Lefebvre's condo."

"I thought I told you—"

"I know you think it's useless for me to investigate Lefebvre's death, sir, but apparently not everyone feels so sure about that."

"Speak up! What the hell's wrong with your voice?"

"Sorry, sir. It's the smoke. Someone just tried to set fire to the condo while I was in it—there were two other people inside at the time as well—a woman and her son. I'd say more, but I'm not on a secure line."

There was a long silence on the other end of the line. Frank waited.

"Anyone hurt?" Hale asked.

"No, sir, but we had to escape through a window—a fire was set on the stairwell outside the door."

Hale sighed. "No accident then."

"No." He looked toward Seth and Elena, huddled together. "I have a favor to ask, sir."

"Then you'd better hope I'm more attentive to you than you are to me."

"If it's arson," Frank said, "eventually they'll call for a detective. If you won't let me handle this myself—"

"Not a chance in hell."

"Then I need to ask that you'll make sure that Carlson sends Pete Baird. And I need you to back me up when I ask for protection of the identities of the residents of the condo."

"Who are they?"

"I'm not on a secure line, sir," he said again. "I promise I'll come in as soon as possible and explain everything to you in person."

The chief hesitated.

"All right," he said finally. "But I won't be here much longer today. Let me give you a number where you can reach me later this evening—no, wait—better yet, come into my office tomorrow morning at ten. One of my meetings has just been canceled, so I have an opening in my schedule. I take it this can wait until then?"

"Yes, sir."

Hale hesitated, then said, "If that changes, call this number."

"Yes, sir." Frank wrote the number down and thanked him.

"Thanks are premature, Harriman." He hung up.

Frank walked back to Seth and Elena. As he drew nearer, she said anxiously, "If anyone asks, please don't call Seth by his father's name. And don't call me Rosario. I don't usually go by Rosario now—for obvious reasons. After what happened to Phil . . . actually, it was Yvette's idea. Seth and I use the name Nereault. It just makes a lot of things easier."

"You okay with that, Seth?" Frank asked.

He shrugged, but didn't look up from his guinea pig.

"Seth?" Elena asked.

"Lefebvre is a good name," he said.

"Yes," Frank said. "And so is Nereault. Right now, Nereault is a safer name, so is it okay if we tell these firefighters that one?"

"Okay," he said, turning the single word into a song of reluctance.

Any further discussion was halted by the approach of the firefighter who had spoken to them earlier. He took down some basic information from Elena, then said, "I'm afraid the car's a total loss, but most of the contents of the house should be okay. You've got some structural damage though—so we won't be able to let you stay here."

She looked back at the condo, as if only now starting to fully absorb what had happened. Frank put an arm around her shoulders. She leaned against him, her face pale. "What caused it?" she asked the firefighter.

"Someone will be over to talk to you about that soon." He left them to join the others.

"Where are we going to live, Mom?" Seth asked.

She looked back at the broken window, where the ladder they had used still hung, and bewilderedly shook her head.

"Maybe you and your mom could stay with me and Irene for a few days," Frank said.

"We couldn't impose—"

"With your dogs?" Seth asked excitedly.

"I don't know—" she began.

"To protect your privacy," Frank said, hoping she would catch his meaning, "we won't tell anyone where you're staying. Not even your former employer."

His attention was drawn toward the firefighters, who were talking to a slender man in a suit. Frank noticed the man in the suit was armed. He turned toward them and Frank recognized Blake Halloran, an arson investigator he had worked with on previous cases. Halloran recognized him at about the same time and stroked his full, blond mustache in a considering way before motioning to Frank.

"Surprised to see you," Halloran said. "Are you here on business or is Ms. Nereault a friend?"

Frank considered not answering, then said, "Both."

"Hmm. Does your friend Ms. Nereault have any reason to light a couple of fires in her sister-in-law's condo?"

"Two fires?" Frank asked, not correcting him about the relationship between Elena and Yvette.

"One on the stairway, one in the garage. She's not a likely suspect, I admit, being inside the place at the time and all. But stranger things have happened."

"No, she didn't start the fires," he said. "I've been with her all day."

Halloran's brows went up. "Some guys have all the luck."

"We just returned from a family funeral," Frank said.

"Jesus, I'm sorry—"

Frank found himself mildly pleased to see Halloran's look of shame. "Yes, it's been a tough day for them, so go easy. Besides, she never would have done anything to this place—especially not with her boy inside."

"She have any enemies?"

"That's a real possibility, but I don't have any names for you." He handed over his business card. "Anything you come up with, Blake, I'd appreciate hearing about it."

"Likewise," he said, handing Frank his own card. "You see anyone around here this afternoon?"

"Just a gardener."

"Let's see if the lady of the house can help out here."

They walked back to Elena and Seth.

"I'd like to talk to you," Halloran said to her, "if you wouldn't mind letting Detective Harriman keep an eye on your boy for a moment?"

Elena looked back at Frank.

"I'll be right here," he said, then added, "Do you know the name of the gardener who works in this part of the complex?"

"Gardener? It's a whole team—a service that comes through once a week. They come here on Fridays."

Frank looked toward where he had seen the white van parked. He was not surprised to find it gone.

27

The Looking Glass Man stepped into the shower, feeling weak and sick to his stomach. Soon he would have to go up to his attic room and chronicle the unmitigated failures of this afternoon, but for now he must try to cleanse himself. For long minutes he stood beneath the spray, his head bent into the roaring rush of hot water. He closed his eyes to the glaring whiteness of the shower walls and allowed his other senses to become attuned solely to this enclosed world—the sting of the hot water pelting his scalp and shoulders, the wash of warmth and steam over his skin, the roaring of the water in his ears, the coolness of the tiles beneath his hands, the pressure of his own weight against his palms and the soles of his feet. He opened his mouth and let the water sluice across his lips and teeth and tongue and down his chin. But soon the water echoed the refrain inside his skull—

You fool! You fool! You fool!

Elena Rosario was in Las Piernas.

He had thought her long gone. A few months after Lefebvre's death, she had left. But she must have returned, and now she had a child.

He did not understand it. He had never understood her. He had held various beliefs about her at various times, and always he ended up uncertain, unable to discard those beliefs and unable to cling to them.

He had put her out of his mind for years now, and here she was, back in Las Piernas. And living in Lefebvre's home.

He had reacted to that out of fear. There had been so much to be afraid of.

When he had nearly been seen by Harriman at the cemetery, it was bad enough, but while eluding the motorcycle officer, his heart had almost given out. After changing the plates on the van, he had driven to the hospital just to see if there was some little thing he might be able to do for Bredloe. A little something to end the man's suffering. But just as he entered the hallway near Bredloe's room, he had caught a glimpse of Matt Arden going in to see the captain. The Looking Glass Man kept walking, hearing Arden's voice say a dreaded name: Lefebvre.

Arden. Did Arden know? Had Lefebvre told Arden his secrets? He had always wondered about this, but when the years went by without a word from him or anyone else, he had decided that Lefebvre had not taken Arden into his confidence. Arden, he was certain, would have defended Lefebvre's reputation—he had had an almost fatherly devotion to the man. Today, perhaps Arden had only mentioned Lefebvre's name because of the funeral.

Or perhaps not.

In his present state, Bredloe would be of no use to Arden. But perhaps Arden was saying other things to other members of the department? Who was he staying with? Who was he seeing while he was here in town?

And so the Looking Glass Man had decided to follow Arden. And he did—right to Lefebvre's former residence.

His shock had been profound.

For a few wild moments, he allowed himself to consider the possibility that Lefebvre was alive, that he had escaped from the wreckage of the plane, that his bones had never been found, that Harriman was involved in some elaborate scheme to trick the Looking Glass Man into revealing his secrets.

It was in this state of panic that he decided to set fire to the condominium. He quickly gathered the materials he had planned to use on Harriman's home and changed into one of his most useful costumes—the green coveralls of a gardener, an outfit that would allow a person to come close to almost any residence without raising the least alarm from neighbors. A disguise that would let a man carry large green plastic bags full of materials without anyone suspecting him of anything untoward.

This time, the bag was full of gasoline-soaked rags.

He was out in the open, next to the building nearest the van, when he saw Harriman and Arden together. His level of panic skyrocketed. He quickly hid himself, cowering in a nearby stairwell, heart pounding, sure that in the next second Harriman would come running, would pull that gun from his shoulder holster and force him to surrender and confess, force him to fail to achieve his most important goals just as they were within his reach. The secrets would come out then. Everything would fall apart. Judge Lewis Kerr would undoubtedly preside over his case—and make an example of him.

Caught up in the horror of these visions, he had nearly missed seeing Arden drive off with a woman. The woman was a surprise. Was she his wife? Perhaps Arden had married. He disliked not knowing who Arden might have spoken to about Lefebvre.

Harriman was no longer in sight then. He was up in the condominium, perhaps reading some papers Arden had left with him or even talking to Lefebvre himself. Perhaps Lefebvre had built secret rooms in his condominium. He had not seen them when he went to Lefebvre's home during the investigation into Seth Randolph's murder. But he had been able to do only so much with half the department on hand at the same time. He disliked such crowds.

He had always approved of Lefebvre, and for many reasons. They had so much in common. They were intelligent and logical. They loved to fly. They both did their best work alone. That was why, for a time, he had done certain favors for Lefebvre—Lefebvre himself had never known the source of these favors. The Looking Glass Man would not be surprised to discover now that they had more than intelligence and a love of solitude in common. He could easily believe that Lefebvre had also created hidden places in his home. After Arden left the condominium, this possibility disturbed him greatly, until his skin itched from his nervousness. It would be best, he decided, to hurry up and destroy Harriman and any evidence he might be studying.

And so he had started the fires. Once he was sure they were going, he had hurriedly left, not so stupid as to stay and watch, as a true arsonist would have done. No, it was best to be far away in such situations. He had the means of learning the results of his work.

He had listened to the scanner and heard the call. But then had come the announcement that three persons had been in the condominium, including a female and a child. He had risked turning back then, unable to resist the temptation—as weak as any arsonist after all—and had caught a glimpse of Elena Rosario holding a child while Harriman spoke to firefighters.

He had driven away again, chastising himself for returning at all, while reeling from the implications. Elena Rosario, living in Lefebvre's home.

He scrubbed himself until his skin was raw.

The water turned cold, and though he briefly considered punishing himself by remaining in the shower, he shut it off. The room seemed unusually quiet, which made him feel afraid, until he realized that he had forgotten to turn the fan on and the quiet was the absence of its noise. He dried himself and wiped down the shower stall and all the chrome before stepping out, carefully placing his feet on the perfectly aligned bathroom rug.

He looked up into the mirror and saw only the blur of steam and condensation.

As if he weren't really there.

An omen, he decided, shivering where he stood.

But ultimately his faith in himself reasserted itself. Perhaps it was a sign of a different sort—a sign that he remained invisible to those who sought him.

He would need to be more careful, true, but the more he considered it, the fire was not such a foolish idea—after all, he had smoked Elena Rosario from her lair.

28

In the end, Pete had helped him. He tried to keep that in mind now as he faced renewed sullenness in the office.

Frank had stopped Pete in the hallway before he came into the homicide room. Pete had assured him that none of the others knew the details of Frank's afternoon. They knew that Pete had been sent on an arson call, but when he returned long before Frank, he pretended that there had been nothing to it—a questionable case of arson with no one hurt. He gave out no exact addresses and no names. A waste of time, he told them.

"No one asked why I hadn't come back?"

"I told them I talked to you on the phone, that you'd be in later. Reed asked if you had had a chance to see if the face was as good as the figure for the babe in the black veil. I told him she was one of the cop-hating Nereaults."

"Thanks, Pete."

But Pete just shook his head and walked away without another word.

Even before he went to his desk, Frank knew he was in for more of the chill. The men in that room were expert observers. None of them would have missed the change in Pete's mood regarding his partner. It would quickly become contagious.

When he arrived at the scene of the fire, Pete had been concerned for his partner's safety, but that had quickly given way to anger over the fact that

Frank had not told him where he was going that afternoon. He dismissed
outright Frank's theory that someone from the department had been the arsonist, and was infuriated that Frank could imagine such a thing to be true.

"It's Whitey Dane's bunch—you can bet on it," Pete said.

Elena, who had been using Frank's cell phone to call her insurance
agent, said, "What about Dane?"

Pete remembered her, and Frank watched his manner change in the way
it often did with women. Pete was short and balding, yet seldom failed to
charm a woman. He was crazy about his wife—a gorgeous Amazon of a
woman—and as far as Frank knew, Pete hadn't ever strayed after marrying
Rachel. But Baird enjoyed flirting with good-looking women, and he was all
solicitude to Elena. Still, it wasn't until Pete became aware of Seth, and became protective of him, that Frank was sure of Pete. By the time Elena and
Seth moved off to beg the firefighters to allow them to retrieve a few essential items from the condo, Pete was saying, "You know, that kid is as sharp as
his old man."

Frank raised a brow.

"Oh, he's Phil's kid, all right. At the funeral, I thought maybe he was a
nephew, speaking French with Lefebvre's sister and all. Now I see him with
Elena, I see a little of her, a little of him. Has Phil's eyes. And no matter
how I feel about Phil, it's still a damn shame. I mean, a kid ought to know
his dad."

"Yes," Frank said, thinking of the sugar in the fuel tanks of Lefebvre's
plane.

"Tell me what you want me to do for them," Pete said.

So Frank had asked him to keep secrets. Knowing Pete, it was the most difficult of requests, simply because he would honor it, contrary though it was to
his talkative nature. Being trustworthy meant something to Pete, and realizing that, Frank said, "I knew you wouldn't want to hear any of this or be involved in it. I'm sorry. I'm glad you're willing to do this for Seth and Elena."

"I'm doing this because you're my partner," Pete said. "You know what
pisses me off, Frank? How easily you forget that." He walked away.

Frank thought of shouting after him that Pete's own memory hadn't been
so great lately, but held back. For all the satisfaction that might give him, he
had to consider Seth's and Elena's safety.

Frank spent two hectic hours helping Seth and Elena before they were settled at his house. Because of the damage to the stairs and the beams above
the garage, the fire department had declared the condo out-of-bounds. Re-

sponding to Elena's pleas and the careful description of where she had left it, one of the firefighters had brought her wallet out to her.

Frank drove Seth and Elena to a pet store, where they bought a cage and some food for the guinea pig. Next to a drugstore for basic toiletries. Frank dropped off the roll of film from the funeral, then came back for it when they finished shopping at a department store for a few articles of plain but essential clothing. Both Elena and Seth changed out of their clothes at the store—Frank, still reeking of smoke, envied them.

Neither Seth nor Elena had taken long to make their purchases. Soon they were on their way to the house—where the cage proved useful in saving the guinea pig from the attentions of Irene's cat, Cody. Seth and the dogs formed an immediate mutual admiration society. The boy was given the guest room; Elena said she would opt for the couch. Frank showered and changed clothes, but he could still smell nothing but smoke.

The strain of the day was telling on all of them, but on Seth especially, who fell asleep sitting next to Elena on the couch. Frank carried him into the guest room and tucked him in.

"You sure your wife won't mind our staying here?" Elena asked as he prepared to go back to the office.

"No," Frank said. "She'll be happy we're able to do something for Phil Lefebvre's son."

He had tried several times to call Irene to warn her about their guests and had ended up leaving a message on her voice mail at work.

Back at his desk, he quickly sorted through the paperwork that had accumulated on it during the day. He was leaving to go down to the property room when Reed dared to speak to him.

"Going to play hockey tomorrow night?" he asked.

"I'm not sure," Frank said, thinking of his houseguests and all the work that lay before him.

"You sick?" Reed asked. "You sound awful."

"Mild laryngitis. I'm fine."

"Our team doesn't mean shit to him," Vince said, and no one thought he was talking about hockey.

"Vince . . ." Reed said in a warning tone.

"I'll be there if I can," Frank said.

"No, do what you want to do on your own," Vince said. "Besides, you're a lousy fucking defenseman. We won't miss you."

It was true, Frank thought. He'd only been playing a year.

"Make up your mind, Vince," Pete said. "Is he fucking up all your beautiful teamwork or can you manage defense all by yourself?"

"What's with you?" Vince said, obviously feeling betrayed.

Pete glanced at Frank, then said, "Nothing. Lieutenant's been chewing my ass out. But what's new with that? I swear, if I'm ever killed by a bomb, just go looking through the rubble for an ass. If the bite marks on it match Carlson's dental records, it's mine!"

The others laughed, but Vince said, "Jesus, Baird, what the hell are you dreaming up? Who'd want to look for you, let alone hunt for your ass?"

"I see you eyeing it all the time, Vince. In fact, from now on, I'm putting my hockey gear on at home."

Frank shook his head and made his way out of the room as Vince did his best to recover lost yardage. Frank figured that after fifteen years of this kind of exchange, Vince should have realized that he didn't stand a chance. If they stayed true to form, they would ridicule each other unmercifully for another twenty minutes or so.

He revised this thought—not unmercifully, really. If the subject was sexual prowess, stature, physique, hair loss, or nationality, virtually no insult was forbidden. But there were certain taboos. While Pete's first wife was fair game, Rachel was not. Neither was Vince's current—and fifth—wife, Amie. Vince's kids were never the subject of a joke Vince didn't make himself. Three of Vince's four ex-wives could be joked about, but not his second one, Lisa, the one who had spent the last twelve years in a psych ward. Lisa was totally off-limits.

Lisa was so seldom mentioned, Frank had almost forgotten her. If he remembered the story correctly, Vince had married her on the rebound, shortly after the breakup of his first marriage. This second marriage had lasted only a few weeks. Rumor said that she was a cop groupie and had bedded a couple of other members of the department—he'd heard varying stories as to whether this occurred before or after they split up. But she ultimately found life on the other side of the law more exciting—or so she told Vince on one of the many occasions when he had bailed her out. She began using drugs and soon was living on the streets. Among the uniforms, she earned the nickname "Old Faithful," not because she was either, but because any time you saw her, you could be certain of being able to make an arrest—she never failed to have illicit drugs on her person.

Pete had told Frank that Vince—against his own better judgment and experience—had tried to save her from herself again and again. She only got into deeper trouble. She ended up involved with a man who took her along with him to a bank one day—five people, including four members of one family, were dead by the time they left. Witnesses said she didn't seem to be an accomplice so much as a shocked onlooker. She had covered her ears and screamed "Stop!" when the shooting began.

Her partner escaped, leaving her behind, so Old Faithful was still good for an arrest. When she was taken into custody, she was questioned about her role, but she didn't say a word. She wasn't, as was first believed, exercising her right to remain silent—in the dozen or so years since the robbery, she hadn't said a word to anyone. Vince put a second mortgage on his house to pay for a good attorney for her, and the court found her to be incompetent to stand trial.

Again Frank considered the financial burdens Vince had faced at the time of the Randolph murders. And reaching his destination, the property room, Frank wondered if Vince's ex had spent time there. Ten years ago, the current property room had been the city's women's jail, and the property room had been in the basement.

Now women who were arrested were kept at the LPPD only very briefly, in holding cells downstairs, until they could be transported to a nearby county facility.

No attempt had been made to hide the signs of the current property room's past. Although bigger and brighter than the underground area it used to occupy, this wasn't exactly a cheerful setting. At the moment, on one side of the blue bars of case-hardened steel, a uniformed officer was arguing loudly with property room workers about a problem with his paperwork. On the other side of the counter, behind the network of bars, the two women who were working the desk almost appeared to be incarcerated—and seemed to be enjoying the experience about as much.

As he drew closer to the counter, passing under the watchful eye of several surveillance cameras, Frank saw that Flynn, the sergeant who was in charge of the area, had put a new sign over the front desk: Evidence Control. He remembered that Flynn was trying to get everybody to leave off calling it the property room and to start calling it by this new name. He wished Flynn luck. It would be easier to teach an elephant to figure-skate.

The sign looked as if it had been printed by a computer and laminated at a local copy shop. Probably at Flynn's own expense.

Frank didn't envy Flynn. The guy was under a lot of pressure and never got a hell of a lot of support. He had to ride almost everybody to get them to follow procedures, and that created a certain level of resentment. Controlling guns, drugs, money, and valuables such as jewelry—against thieves

both inside and outside the department—presented constant challenges in
security. Legal requirements for keeping and controlling evidence were
complex and ever-changing. Less than five percent of the items held in evidence would ever be used in court. All the same, defense lawyers knew that
evidence control was often where a police department was most vulnerable—one sloppy entry in chain-of-custody paperwork could blow a case
apart.

Frank shook his head. Given its importance, you would have thought
Flynn would get whatever he asked for. But only someone who didn't understand the politics of law enforcement would have supposed such a thing.
The chief knew that city hall and the voters were happiest when they saw
lots of black-and-whites on the streets, so by the time patrol cars and rookies
were paid for, there wasn't a hell of a lot left for paying for detectives, electronic equipment, and crime labs—and there sure as hell wasn't much al-
lotted to Flynn's area.

Which was why Flynn, a veteran of twenty years on the force, most of
them on the city's toughest streets, now spent his days in an abandoned
women's jail. Pete sometimes razzed Flynn by calling him a sailor dying of
thirst, a reference both to Flynn's naval career and to the fact that Flynn
guarded all sorts of valuables while his own budget got cut again and again.
Frank figured it was more like being a minimum-wage teller in a big bank.
You could handle a million dollars, but none of it was yours—and let a
dime of it go missing, you were the one who had to come up with the answers.

Frank looked in at the oddball assortment of desks and filing cabinets behind the front counter. Flynn, a former naval supply officer, was a master at
obtaining equipment on the cheap. He watched the newspaper for notices
of businesses closing facilities or going belly-up, and then contacted their
owners begging for desks and office equipment.

The area still smelled like a lockup, a mix of disinfectant, insecticide,
and all the ripened scents on possessions taken from the people who were
in custody. Unlike the clean and healthy specimens of humanity who got
hauled into jail on *Dragnet*, in real life a lot of the people who got arrested
weren't in such fine condition. A drunken man arrested for assault, for example, might piss in his own pants and follow that up by puking all over
himself—if you were lucky, he did this *after* he was out of the patrol car.
When such folks exchanged their garments for jailhouse garb, Flynn and
his workers were required to keep their personal property safe for a certain
period of time, or until it was claimed by them.

Flynn stepped out of his office now, his scowl enough to quiet the protesting officer.

"Tell you what," Flynn said to the patrolman. "You know so damned much more than any of us, I'm going to ask your boss to transfer you down here so we can all benefit from your enlightenment."

He received a hasty apology from the horrified officer, who quickly walked away.

"Harriman!" Flynn said, seeing Frank. "How's it going?"

"Fine," he said. "How about for you, Flynn?"

"What the hell happened to your voice?"

"Mild laryngitis."

Flynn studied him for a brief moment, then said, "Glad you decided to humor me and come down here to check out that new freezer. Big improvement over the old one." He pushed a sign-in sheet on a clipboard toward Frank. "Save your voice, just sign in and I'll take you back to see it."

Frank managed not to show surprise. He smiled and nodded as if thanking Flynn for being so considerate, signed the sheet, and waited while Flynn unlocked the gate into the office area.

"All the monitors working?" Flynn asked the women. When they said yes, he said, "Then you know how to find me if you need me."

Frank wondered if this was Flynn's way of reminding him that there were surveillance cameras throughout the area.

He followed Flynn past another set of clerks doing computer work. Most of them, he knew, were getting ready to leave for the day. As they went through the next room, he saw a worker engaged in disposing of some unclaimed personal effects. Although it was warm in the room, she wore coveralls, a mask, safety glasses, long gloves, and a scarf tied over her hair.

They walked down the concrete corridor, past a long row of cells with open doors.

"How many cells in here?" Frank asked.

"About fifty-five," Flynn said. "We've rearranged it some, but not much. At least they gave me another place to put the bicycles. Twelve hundred stolen bicycles a year. You think the guy who designed these cells was thinking, 'Gee, I better leave room for twelve hundred bicycles'?"

The former cells were converted to hold evidence and other property under police control. Where once women inmates were held, there were now bags, boxes, and bins of evidence, and bunks had been converted into wide shelves. Each bag or box was sealed with red tape; some were also sealed by the lab's blue tape. Affixed to one corner of each of the containers was a computer-printed tag with an evidence number, case number, booking and citation numbers.

Wondering if the Randolph evidence had been tracked by computer, Frank asked, "When did they stop using a manual system to keep track of all of this?"

"Nineteen eighty-three," Flynn said. "I don't even like to think about what it was like back then."

"You've been in charge for what, four years now?"

"Yes. I came in here, there were no video cameras, you could have a single individual working the desk, you had unescorted personnel wandering back through here, no motion detectors—a damned mess. You want to know something crazy?"

"What?"

"I made most of my improvements based on the suggestions of a dead man. Trent Randolph."

Frank stopped walking.

"Come on, we've got to put on a nice show here. Our voices aren't being recorded, thank the baby Jesus in his diapers, but they'll be watching."

"They don't trust their boss?" Frank asked as they passed an area holding televisions, radios, and stereo equipment.

"You're the hot topic of gossip in the department these days," Flynn said, taking out another set of keys and unlocking a door to another hallway. They passed cells containing weapons. The cells were locked.

"Tell me about Randolph's suggestions. Did you know him?"

"No, not really. But he wrote this set of papers for the commission about how screwed up things were around here when it came to evidence. Guess it caused a hell of an uproar among the brass at the time. You know, here he was a newcomer, and the first of these papers says, 'Hey, fellas, your department is HUA when it comes to evidence control.'"

While Frank doubted that Randolph literally reported that the LPPD had its "head up its ass," he could imagine how unwelcome any civilian newcomer's criticism would be.

"You weren't in charge here until long after Randolph was killed," Frank said. "How did you see this report?"

Flynn smiled and said, "I had the good fortune of taking over from a guy who wasn't organized and who never threw anything away." He paused and opened another door. "Don't slip here in front of the ding cells. The floor is wet. We had plumbing problems thanks to those assholes upstairs. Next week we'll see an end to that."

The "ding cells"—Flynn's old-fashioned slang for a cell where an inmate was kept if she was "dingy"—were the former isolation lockups, solid-steel cells with tiny, thick-plate viewing ports, now used to hold low-value drugs. The plumbing leak had been caused when the inmates of the men's jail on the floor above had pulled an equally old-fashioned prisoners' trick—stuffing blankets down the jail's toilets for the amusement of seeing the chaos it could cause when the plumbing backed up. The department was about to install what amounted to a gigantic garbage disposal to chew up the blankets before they clogged the lines.

"You were telling me about finding Randolph's report," Frank said as they continued on.

"Yeah—well, I vaguely remembered something about it from when Randolph was alive. Chief Hale was pissed as hell about it, but Randolph had been his ally on some other matters, so he was in a tough spot. Plus, Randolph was tight with this old geezer on the newspaper, and nobody wanted that kind of trouble." He paused. "Sorry—forgot about your wife."

They were walking near shelves filled with small boxes. Frank thought his pager went off, but when he checked it, there was no new message. He heard the sound again. He looked up to see Flynn smiling. "We keep all the beepers and cell phones in this section. Listen."

Within seconds, another pager sounded and then another, first from one unseen but nearby location and then from another. Soon, it seemed as if they were surrounded by them. It was as if they had entered a forest full of strange crickets that chirped only one or two at a time.

Flynn laughed. "All the damned drug dealers' customers, still trying to get ahold of them."

Frank smiled. "Just think—in the course of a day, you're hearing thousands in lost sales."

"They'll find someone else to buy from, but I'm happy to know that the previous owners of these things are missing out. Anyway, I was telling you about this report. So, I didn't remember all of this history at first, just that there had been some big brouhaha. But that was enough to make me decide not to mention to anybody about where I'm getting all these notions for improvements. And I know Trent Randolph is long dead, so he isn't likely to speak up and tell everyone I stole his ideas. But then I guess my conscience starts to bother me, so I go to Hale, and that's when he tells me that Randolph was his friend and it's great that I have this report and did I find any others."

"Others?"

"I guess Randolph had the fire of a reformer—you know, he had ideas about everything. All excited about applying scientific principles to the way we do business around here. But I only found the one report."

They entered a room that held several large safes, including one for cash and others for the most valuable drugs. Two large walk-in freezers stood nearby, one with a rosary on it. The homicide freezer.

"You didn't want to tell me about Randolph in front of your staff?" Frank asked.

"Oh, hell, no—I don't care—they don't even know who Randolph was. Seeing you made me think of him, because I've heard you caught the cases. And the Lefebvre case, too, right?"

"Yes."

"Well, that's why we're down here, my boy. 'Cause something damned strange is going on, and you should know about it."

29

"First we gotta put on a show. Let's step into the new freezer for half a second."

Flynn unlocked it and Frank followed him in. Blood samples and other biological materials were already neatly organized within. Just before Frank began to feel unbearably cold, Flynn led him back out again. Flynn gestured to a large metal desk, one that looked as if he had found it on one of his scavenger hunts for equipment. "Let's sit over here. You can angle away from the camera, and for now I'd just as soon do that."

"Okay."

Flynn unrolled what looked like a blueprint for the freezer and put it near the top of the desk. He said, "Point at that damned thing once in a while. Anybody asks, I wanted your opinion about organizing the freezer."

Next he pulled out some photocopies and slid one of them over to Frank. He kept a few others to himself, facedown. Indicating the one Frank had, he said, "What you have there is a copy of an evidence-control log sheet—a sign-out sheet for the most recent date on which the Randolph murder evidence—or I should say, the box that once contained the evidence—has been checked out of here."

"Flynn—hold on. I just walked down here. How could you know—"

"I've been wanting to talk to you since Monday, but for reasons I'll get to, I couldn't let you know that. I didn't know when you would finally be moseying along and finding your way here, but I know you. I knew you'd look at the evidence yourself sooner or later. When I checked on the surveillance cameras out near the front desk and saw your mug in the frame, I figured, 'Yes, there is a God.'"

"Monday . . . because of Bredloe?"

"You always were a bright boy. Yes, because of Bredloe. Look at the log."

"Jesus. Bredloe was looking at the evidence the day he was hurt. That afternoon."

"Yes. He was agitated, you might say. People tell me you pissed him off."

Frank smoothed his hand over the sheet. "Yes, I did."

"Well, don't feel bad. This whole thing about Lefebvre has been the equivalent of a departmental wedgie. The only people who can ignore it have no balls."

Frank looked at the time on the log sheet. "He came down here after arguing with me about Lefebvre. I told him I thought Lefebvre might be innocent."

"Is that a fact?" Flynn said, seeming amused.

"Don't feel compelled to give me grief about that—I'm getting plenty already."

"Oh, I'm sure you are," Flynn said.

"So you were saying—he wasn't in a good mood when you saw him?"

"Oh, that's an understatement. He was in a little better mood when he brought it back. But I think someone saw him with the box and that someone had something to say to him about it—'cause he called me a little after he checked it back in to ask who else in the department knew what was in it."

"What did you say?"

"'Everybody and his grandmother, and probably a few great-grandmothers, too.'"

Frank sighed. "You need to tell Hale about this."

"Already have. You mention the 'L' name to him yet?"

"Lefebvre? Yes, I see your point. But maybe that will change now . . . Anyway, let me know what you're getting at."

"Well, even though Bredloe brought it back in kind of a better mood, as if—you know, as if he had just reassured himself that we weren't hatching some monster's egg in this box all these years—I thought it was a little strange. Your case, and he's not usually one to butt in like that. He's not the kind to interfere."

"No, but like you say, this case chaps everybody."

"Even on high-profile cases, he doesn't try to second-guess his detectives.

Something was nagging at him, you ask me. He checks out a box that only has a watch in it. And then he gets hurt. Almost killed. And that same day I've heard that over the weekend, you found Lefebvre's body in the wreckage of his plane, and there wasn't any stolen evidence with him. I start asking myself if this evidence box is like the pharaohs' tombs or something—you know, Egyptian curse or something like that. People handle it, and"—he snapped his fingers—"so long. Your plane crashes or bricks fall on you."

"Could be coincidence."

"You don't like that any more than I do."

"No." Frank nodded toward the other pages. "What are those?"

"Look at this one first," Flynn said, giving another photocopy to him. "It's a log sheet for the day Lefebvre looked at the evidence for the murders. June twenty-second."

"June twenty-second?" Frank repeated, disbelieving. "I thought Lefebvre worked on the Randolph case. But he didn't look at the evidence until that Friday?"

Flynn smiled. "We're on the same wavelength. I love it when people make it easy for me. You're right. He wasn't really that actively involved in the case per se. I was working bunco—handling mostly forgery and fraud cases back then, so I wasn't privy to everything that was going on in Homicide. But you know how things are—word gets around about cases that might be connected and so on. This was Whitey Dane we were about to nail, after all."

"And lots of cases were connected to Dane."

"Exactly. Dane had his fingers in a lot of pies, and we were interested in him in my section, too. So this case had us all hopping. Way I remember it is, we were all a little pissed off because Lefebvre was taking time off, hanging out with this kid. He was with Seth Randolph all the time. You've probably read the notes by now, so you know the role he played in saving the kid and all that. So here's the department bright boy, baby-sitting when we need him in here."

Flynn paused, mentioned the need to look good for the cameras, and took the time to point to the blueprint. Frank obliged him by appearing to focus on it, but his mind was racing.

"Funny," Flynn said, "what questions occur to you when it's too late. I started asking myself stuff I should have asked ten years ago. What I started wondering was, when the hell did the guy get a chance to get corrupted by Dane? In the hospital cafeteria? He'd only seen the stuff twice. Just after six that evening, and again, a couple of hours later. But then I notice something that really makes me crazy. Look at the signatures."

Frank started to study them, but Flynn already had the tip of his pen pointing at the two examples. "Let an old man who used to work the forgery detail show you. The first time the name is written smaller than the second."

"Not much, though," Frank said.

"Not much to your untrained eye. Let's call these two by the date they were made—call them the 'June twenty-second signatures.' The earlier one, the smaller one, we'll call 'Twenty-two A,' and the other, 'Twenty-two B.'" He flipped over the remaining stack of papers, gave them to Frank, and said, "This is a collection of Phil's signatures, ones I took from different parts of the log, on different days. Now compare them to the ones you're looking at there."

Although the signatures were not identical, Frank knew that it was natural for slight variations to occur in a person's signature. But even without closely examining them he could see that most of the examples Flynn showed him were generally formed in the same way, with characteristics that made them look more like the 22B than the 22A signature. The 22A was, indeed, slightly smaller than the others.

"That's a sign of forgery, you know," Flynn said. "I could show you half a dozen others in those examples—hesitations, the way the capital L in Lefebvre is formed, and so on."

"So if someone forged his signature—"

"Someone else took the evidence."

Frank was quiet.

Flynn said, "You've already come to that conclusion, though."

"Yes. I think people in the department saw what they wanted to see, what they expected to see. So they didn't look too closely. But this forgery of his signature might be the strongest proof of his innocence yet. Have you shown this to Joe Koza up in Questioned Documents?"

"No. He's young and I don't think he's had a thing to do with any of this, but . . ."

Frank nodded. "I'm with you. Wait until we know more before word spreads."

"Exactly."

"I need to see that evidence box."

"Just don't forget about the pharaohs' curse."

"Believe me, I haven't. But I still want to see this famous watch."

"Not much to it. Maybe you can see something there that the of fellows have missed. I hope your luck is better than Lefebvre loe's. And I think I may just know the trick to help you avoid harn.

"That rosary?" Frank asked, smiling.

"I don't doubt it—but that's not mine, believe it or not. One of ou ..erks is so spooked by what's in that freezer, she won't go in there unless she's got that in her pocket. No, we're going to change another little ritual for you." He glanced at his watch and said, "We should be okay now. Let's put the papers away—no one is going to believe we were *that* interested in a damned freezer."

He gave all the photocopies to Frank, who folded them and tucked them inside his suit coat's inner pocket as Flynn put the blueprint away.

"Let's walk out," Flynn said. "I'll explain along the way."

When they reached the beeper forest, Flynn said, "Someone checks that box out of here and bad things happen to him, right?"

"Yes, although I'm not quite as superstitious about it as you are."

"It's not superstition."

"It might not be the watch. I think Lefebvre's enemy was gunning for him before he saw the evidence."

"Okay, but play along with me here. Just in case it's seeing this watch that makes someone crazy, I'm not going to let you check that box out of here."

"But I thought you said—"

"I'll let you look at it, and now that everyone but my security officer has gone home for the day, we aren't likely to be interrupted while you're doing that. I think I'll test a new, manual backup system this evening. And it just might take me a while to get my paperwork into the computer. That's the only way I can figure it—someone has glanced at the signatures in the logbook or hacked into the computer, or one of my clerks is tipping somebody off. I'll figure it out eventually. But in the meantime, your name isn't going to send up any red flags if I can help it."

The property room clerks had, as Flynn predicted, left for the day. The security officer nodded to them from his position at a bank of video monitors.

"Working late, Flynn?" he asked.

"Oh, not for much longer."

They went into his office, and Flynn shut the door. There was a video monitor in here as well, showing changing views from the various surveillance cameras. There was also a computer, and several file drawers, as well as a storage cabinet. From the storage cabinet, he removed a box with blue and red tape on it. A quick glance at the tag told Frank that it was the one for the Randolph case.

"Sign here," Flynn said, handing him an outdated carbonless form.

Frank did as he asked, unable to keep from smiling to himself. "He bends them, but they don't break."

"What—the rules?" Flynn said, giving him a pair of gloves. "You expect me to completely abandon my rules? No way."

Frank put the gloves on, wondering if he should bother with them. Ignoring a little chill that raised the hair along the back of his neck, he cut the tape, then opened the box. He reached for the small, numbered envelope within it.

Although he had known there would be nothing more than an electronic watch in the envelope, he still couldn't help feeling a little let down at the sight of it. He had seen a photograph of it, and he found that the actual article looked even more anonymous. It was one of those complex watches with buttons for alarms and timers, other time zones, and a stopwatch. The battery in it had died long ago, of course, so that the numbers on its face were gone, the face now nothing more than a gray blank, the color of a shaken Etch-A-Sketch. All the same, it didn't appear to be cheaply made.

Tracking down the owner of the watch was more than a long shot, but this was the only thing he had to go on other than Flynn's assurance that Lefebvre's signature had been forged. The forged signature might prove that Lefebvre hadn't signed for the box earlier in the day, but it would be remarkable if it could show who did the forging. Still, it was an unexpected break, so Frank decided he'd take a chance on finding the owner of the watch. Perhaps only a few of the watches had been made after all, and a serial number would lead to some record of purchase. He already had the name of the manufacturer—Time Masters—in his notes. Although he was fairly sure he had the words and numbers that were etched on the back in the files, he copied them down:

WATER RESISTANT
BASE METAL
ST STEEL BACK
TMSR3
CHINA
3458904894

He thought of Ben's discovery of Lefebvre's watch in the woods and remembered a detail from the file. He looked at the band for a moment, then said, "I thought the lab report claimed they had Lefebvre's wrist measurement off this thing. How the hell did they get it?"

"What do you mean?"

"I mean, this doesn't look as if it has ever been worn."

Flynn studied it. "By God, you're right . . ."

Frank remembered reading the reports, the notations about indentations made by the buckle in the leather watchband, the one bucklehole that had been slightly larger than the others, worn places that indicated wrist size based on where the strap had been fastened again and again.

He explained this to Flynn and said, "The wrist strap on this one hasn't ever been buckled. It isn't the same watch."

"Shit," Flynn said. "Shit, shit, shit. Let me pull up the records."

He moved over to the computer, logged on, and went into the evidence control program. He asked for a report on requests made for the Randolph case materials.

The report listed a long group of names. Flynn printed it out, then handed it to Frank. Most of the names were familiar. In addition to Captain Bredloe, there were three detectives—Vince Adams, Pete Baird, Elena Rosario. Three members of the lab—Dr. Alfred Larson, Paul Haycroft, and Dale Britton. He asked Flynn about two other names, ones he didn't recognize.

"Those guys were with Internal Affairs. They're retired now, but I can put you in touch with them if need be."

Frank thought about the list of names in Lefebvre's notebook. The IAD detectives weren't on it. "Probably won't be necessary," he said. "Flynn—anybody else asks to see this—"

"I'll let you know," Flynn said.

30

"A child, you say?"

"Yes, sir."

Myles kept his face impassive, but his knowledge of Mr. Dane made him proceed cautiously. Mr. Dane was not following his usual routine this evening. Departure from routine did not often bode well for his staff. Mr. Dane had refused to hear Myles's report on Lefebvre's funeral until a few moments ago. He sometimes did this—put off what he would consider a treat.

A report on the funeral for Lefebvre was, Mr. Dane decided, a real treat.

"The Las Piernas Police Department may not remember all he did for them," Dane had said when told of the arrangements, "but I certainly do!" He considered and rejected the idea of gracing the services with his own presence, but he could not resist causing a stir.

His instructions to Myles had been explicit. "I want you to hover there, Myles. Don't get close enough to kiss the casket—in fact, stay well out of reach, but make sure your appearance is noted. They'll go positively wild. And it will give us an idea where things stand. You must tell me who is in attendance."

Not long after Myles returned from the cemetery, he reported that he had been seen and videotaped by members of the LPPD. Dane had held up one pale hand and shouted, "Don't! Not another word. You will tell me more this evening."

For the past few hours, Dane had been amusing himself by observing the police surveillance efforts, their virtual occupation of other houses in the neighborhood. "Oh, look! They've convinced the old busybody next door to quarter their troops!" he said gleefully.

He had fed the swans a little earlier than usual, making a show of it, his gestures sweeping. He began conversing with the birds in a lunatic fashion. He had been delighted to think of his little play with the swans being immortalized by the video cameras of the LPPD. "They'll believe I've gone gaga!"

But when Dane finally heard Myles's report, his mood changed.

"Elena Rosario—you're sure?"

"No, sir. Not positive."

"But you heard her voice! It must have been chilling! I swear to you, I horripilate at the very idea—Detective Elena Rosario's voice after all these years!"

Myles now knew without a doubt that he was on dangerous ground. He said nothing.

"Did her fellow law enforcement officers embrace her? Did they welcome—ah!—her resurrection?"

"No, sir. Detectives Collins and Baird were intrigued by the veiled woman, but I believe they left the task of identifying her to Detective Harriman. Or perhaps they believed she was in some way connected to Mr. Arden. She stayed next to him throughout the time I saw her."

"Ah, yes, Arden." Dane brooded for a time, then said, "Tell me more."

Myles described the altercation between Tory Randolph and the veiled woman, which had taken place just as he was leaving. He kept hoping Mr. Dane would find some amusement in it. He did not. Suddenly, Myles remembered another detail he had planned to report.

"Before anyone else arrived at the cemetery, I looked at the flowers brought there from the funeral home. They included an elaborate arrangement of white flowers. All white. No card."

Dane sat up straighter. "Really? Now you interest me . . ."

Myles waited.

"Yes, that is interesting. Did you discover where they came from?"

"Not yet, sir, but we are working on it."

"It is very important to me, Myles."

"Yes, sir. I expect an answer by early this evening."

Dane tapped his fingers on the arm of his chair. After a moment, he asked, "Detective Harriman was delayed in his return to his office?"

"Yes, sir. By several hours."

"Curious . . ." Dane grew introspective. "He does not seem as interested in me as his friends are. Which can only mean that he is not as convinced as they that I killed their precious Trent Randolph. Why?" He looked up at Myles. "What does he know that they don't?"

This aspect of matters had escaped Myles's notice. He was ashamed that he had not assigned someone to follow Detective Harriman from the cemetery. He had someone watching inside the department, of course, but that was not helpful to Mr. Dane now.

"You and I were due to discuss him today, weren't we?" Dane asked.

"The report is ready whenever you'd like to go over it, sir."

"Excellent," Dane said. "After dinner, you and I shall spend time together in the study, discussing Detective Harriman."

"Yes, sir. Will that be all?"

Dane nodded absently. Myles was almost to the door when Dane called him back.

"The boy, Myles. Tell me everything you can remember about the boy."

31

Elena checked on Seth, who was still sound asleep. He had stayed up late the last few nights, visiting with Yvette and Matt—added to all the stress and excitement of the day, he was exhausted.

The dogs had gone out when she opened the door to the room. She had almost lost her balance, because she had been using one foot to block the entrance of the big gray cat—Cody? Yes, that was what Frank had called him. She shut the door behind the whole menagerie—on all but Seth's guinea pig, who was sleeping in his new cage, undoubtedly dreaming of huge tomcats.

She looked around the room and tried hard to summon some sense of anger, of righteous indignation toward Frank Harriman. She couldn't do it. She had seen him talking to Baird, could see there was some sort of friction between them. And although Pete had helped them out, she knew he was one of the ones who thought Phil was guilty.

There, the anger was back.

It lasted until she saw a photo of Frank with two boys who were near Seth's age. The kids were climbing all over him; he was laughing. They weren't his kids, though. She had overheard that much of Seth's interrogation of him before Yvette had dragged her farther into the kitchen. No kids. But there were games for kids to play with here. Frank had shown her the closet that held toys. She couldn't picture him playing with them himself—it was an aunt and uncle's house, then.

She smelled smoke on her hair and decided to take a shower. Carrying the plastic bag that held the basic toiletries she had purchased at the drugstore, she gathered up a towel and a washcloth from the stack of linens Frank had left for them and went into the bathroom.

It was there, for the first time, that she became acutely aware of the fact that Frank's wife lived in this house. Not that she had expected that Irene Kelly lived somewhere else, but Elena had been feeling too numb to really study her surroundings. In the moments when the numbness briefly faded, she was caught up in thoughts about the funeral and the fire, in worries about the future, in questions about whom she should trust.

Now, on the counter, small items became a visual alarm, declaring her an interloper on another woman's ground. No, a couple's ground. Two toothbrushes, a man's comb, a woman's hairbrush. A small bottle of scent, almost full. She opened the mirror door on the cabinet over the sink and saw the his-and-hers mix of deodorants, makeup (very little, she noted), mouthwash, razors, shaving cream, aftershave, hand lotion, cotton balls, aspirin, a box of bandages.

She felt a fierce stab of jealousy toward Irene Kelly. This was not because she had long considered Irene a potential rival or even because she had, at some point during the afternoon, decided that she liked the color of Frank Harriman's eyes. It was because Irene Kelly had this male presence in her life.

Would she think of Elena as a poacher?

Elena began shrugging out of her clothes. Irene had nothing to worry over, she decided. Frank was attractive, but Elena never went after married men. Hell, she really didn't spend a lot of time with men, period—although she had always liked the company of men more than of women. She didn't have women friends. Her friendship with Yvette had been a first, and that one probably wouldn't have been formed without Seth.

She shook her head. No, that wasn't it. She liked directness, and most women weren't as direct as Yvette.

As for men friends, most of the single men she met didn't seem to be able to give up using the pointers between their legs as the compasses for their lives. Telling a man she was a single mom was usually enough to send his compass needle due south.

She'd met a few men she liked, and she had dated, but nobody ever got more than a good-night kiss from her. For a while, she had wondered if she was actually as frigid as the jerks at the LPPD had said she was. But she knew that was not the problem. The problem was, no one ever measured up to her memories of Phil Lefebvre.

She knew it wasn't healthy to cling to memories this way, but it was no use trying to let go. She need only look at her son and the memories of Phil were there, inescapable. In a number of ways, she was more faithful to him than many women were to their living mates. She had said this once to Yvette, who had scoffed and said, "A dead husband is very easy to get along with. He doesn't even snore."

Maybe Yvette was right. Maybe they would have come to despise each other. Maybe they would have already been divorced, and she would have become a single mom anyway, and moreover, had to watch him date other women.

That was too hard to think about. Maybe, after all, they would have been happy, the way Harriman seemed to be with his wife. She had seen the way they supported each other at the funeral. She had envied Irene Kelly for that, too.

What would it be like, she asked herself, to have someone like Frank Harriman as your husband? There was a faint scent of aftershave, of maleness, in the room. She touched a towel hanging over the shower door. It was slightly damp. She brought it closer to her face and inhaled the combined scents of the soap and shampoo he used. She suffered a small shock, a sudden reacquaintance with the distantly familiar, and opened the shower door to see that Frank used the same brands of soap and shampoo that Phil had used.

She felt a chill. It was almost enough to make her close the shower door again, to let her hair stay smoky, to tell the Harrimans that she'd rent a hotel room somewhere.

She laughed at herself. A hotel? She didn't make enough money to set herself up like that, not even in a rathole of a hotel. The afternoon shopping spree had almost maxed out her one credit card. "And this is just day one," she said aloud, turning on the shower and stepping in.

Once the warm water began to sluice over her, she reached for Frank's shampoo, leaving her own in the plastic bag, leaving the one she knew must be Irene's on the tile shelf above her. She washed her hair with it, and as its scent rinsed across her face, the knot that had been tied so tightly somewhere in the middle of her chest loosened and the tears began to flow. She couldn't remember ever crying so much in a single day, and she despised herself for it, even as she let long-denied grief take her where it would go.

So she let herself think of Phil and of what might have been. She fantasized, as she had so often, of Phil at the hospital on the night she gave birth to his son, holding Seth as an infant, how proud he would have been.

She thought of being held by him, of sharing warmth with him.

And as she had done so many, many times, she wondered if he had suffered before he died, if he had been scared, or cold, or lonely. If, from within the wreckage, the very marrow of his bones had tried to call out, asking to be found, only to be utterly abandoned.

"Stop it!" she said aloud, but the scolding only made her cry harder.

Irene had been sent into downtown L.A. on a story that the greenest reporter in the newsroom could have covered, on orders from Wrigley, her boss's boss. She had watched while Judge Lewis Kerr was handed a plaque from the Southern California Women in Law, thanking him for organizing a series of Tomorrow's Women in Law days in six counties. Tomorrow's Women in Law days allowed girls to learn about the legal system by touring courtrooms, meeting with judges and attorneys, and generally being scared out of their wits by the inmates in the women's jails.

Irene liked the program, and liked Kerr, but she was a veteran reporter, and the assignment had been a bit of petty office warfare. She had, not for the first time, considered finding other work. She loved her job, especially on the days when she was allowed to do it. Today wasn't one of those days.

Although the press conference was over at two-thirty, Kerr had been flattered that the *Express* had sent her out on the story, had singled her out afterward, and had extracted a promise from her to attend the upcoming dedication ceremonies for a new wing of the Las Piernas County Courthouse. The fifteen minutes of sunshine he showered down on her ensured that she was going to be totally screwed trying to get back from L.A. through traffic.

The traffic was only beginning. Knowing she was never going to make it back in time to file the story, she called it in—on one of the newspaper's cell phones. She had left her own phone at home when she heard that she would be covering this event. Wrigley would have to foot the bill for this one. She knew the cost of the call would irk the stingy bastard. Keeping that in mind, she described today's event in minute detail. She had never loaded a story up with so many adjectives in her life.

As it turned out, she also paid for her moments of revenge—the battery on the cell phone went dead just before she reached the last bloated paragraph of the story, abruptly ending the call and denying her the chance to check her messages. Cussing out Wrigley for not investing in phones with a longer battery life, she inched her way home, smelling exhaust fumes, watching brake lights, and wondering if the paper in Modoc County was hiring.

At last, after spending nearly three hours covering a distance of about thirty miles, home was in sight. She pulled into the driveway, anxious to get out of the car. She hurried into the house, was snubbed by a preoccupied Cody, greeted the dogs, and went back into the bedroom to change.

She was surprised to hear the shower running; she hadn't seen Frank's car. But he might have parked in the garage or on the street. His clothes were in a pile and smelled heavily of smoke. She wrinkled her nose in distaste. She was putting them in the bag for dry cleaning, wondering why her normally neat husband had just tossed them on the floor, then thought of the shower. Probably washing the smoke smell out of his hair. She imagined him in the shower, smiled, and quickly stripped. She was on her way out of the bedroom when she saw the blue kimono. She smiled again and put it on.

She stepped into the bathroom, heard a woman say, "Honey, are you awake now?"

Honey?

Through a haze of red, she pulled the shower door open and yanked the temperature control so that the water went to one hundred percent cold.

Seth woke up, hearing two women's voices shouting words that would have put him on restriction for weeks.

32

He parked in the alley behind the florist shop, checked his pocket to make sure he had the photos, and got out of the car. The two vans parked at the back of the store were older than the one he had seen. They were white Chevy vans, but they didn't look like the one at the cemetery. Emblazoned in red and green on the side panels and the back door of each was Garrity's Flowers and the florist's phone number (2-4-BLOOM). One of the vans had something in common with the van he had seen—its plate number. Even before he walked around to the front end, he knew the other plate would be missing.

He walked through a narrow breezeway between buildings to get to the front of the shop. A bell rang as he stepped in, but apparently it wasn't heard over Bach's Brandenburg Concerto No. 5, which was playing over a speaker. He allowed himself a moment to enjoy both the music and the earthy scents of potted plants, the sweet and spicy mix of fragrances of roses and other flowers, the bright colors of summer blooms.

There was no one at the front counter at the moment. A set of glass climate-controlled cases filled with orchids and other exotic-looking plants stood behind the counter, and through them he could see an elderly woman working in the back of the shop. He heard her humming to herself as she created an elaborate arrangement.

Frank didn't rush her. An avid gardener, he was quickly distracted by the colorful displays around him. Florists could order from greenhouses, of course, and while his own roses and zinnias and dahlias were doing fine, he couldn't match the variety here. He walked slowly past bins of tulips, lilies, irises, snapdragons, carnations, daisies, and chrysanthemums. He made his way toward another set of climate-controlled cases at the back—these were filled with roses. Wending his way to it, he studied their various shades and shapes, wondering if he should surprise Irene by bringing her a dozen of them, a token of thanks for accepting two houseguests without notice—and a peace offering. It would surprise her—he didn't stop at florists very often; not only because there were plenty of flowers right outside their back door, but also because he preferred to see flowers growing.

The aisles of the shop were narrow, crowded with blossoms, indoor plants, boxes of chocolates, and a limited assortment of other gifts—ceramic mugs with "World's Greatest Granddad" and similar phrases imprinted on them; stuffed animals, mostly overdressed bears; hand-painted T-shirts, seemingly designed with cat lovers in mind. He negotiated his way between a display of Mylar balloons and a large potted palm and was bending to take a closer look at a bromeliad when the bell on the door rang again.

A young man entered the shop. He was tall. Not quite as tall as Frank—six two, maybe. His build was solid and muscular—so muscular that Frank thought his neat blue suit must have been custom-tailored. He had close-cropped blond hair, blue eyes, and a small tattoo on his thick neck just behind his right ear. A wasp.

He walked directly to the counter, apparently not noticing Frank's presence. His posture was ramrod straight, his manner assured.

For reasons Frank could not name, the man made him feel uneasy. He stayed still, watching from his crouched position, hidden behind the palm.

The wasp man used his large hands to beat sharply on the countertop. "Hello!" he called, more in impatience than by way of greeting.

The florist came out, smiling. "Sorry to keep you waiting. What can I do for you?"

The wasp man smiled back. "Excuse me, ma'am. I sounded a little impatient, didn't I? I apologize. I guess I'm a little frustrated, is all. You see, I've been to almost every florist in town, so I hope you can help me out."

Her smile grew at this engaging politeness. Frank felt more wary. He unbuttoned his jacket, to give himself freer access to his weapon. He prayed he was being paranoid.

"I certainly hope so," she said. "You're not wanting something completely out of season, are you?"

"No, ma'am," the wasp man said, laughing a little. "Oh, it feels good to laugh. I haven't laughed much today." He suddenly grew solemn. "You see, we had a funeral today—my uncle's."

"I'm so sorry," she said.

He shrugged his big shoulders. "I really wasn't close to him at all. But my mom loved him, and now she's really upset—not just because of the funeral, but because of a little something that happened at it. You see, someone sent a big, beautiful spray of white flowers—gladiolus, mostly, or so my mom says—but the card must have fallen off of them, because we couldn't find it after the service. The funeral home said they didn't bring them to the cemetery, so they must have come directly from a florist. We checked with the cemetery, and they can't tell us who brought them to his grave. Did you happen to make a delivery of white flowers to Good Shepherd Cemetery today?"

Even from the back of the shop, Frank could tell that the woman was nervous. He swore silently to himself, then, staying low, slowly crept forward. He tried to stay beneath the level of the counter, so that his reflection would not appear in the glass of the cases behind it.

"Good Shepherd?" she repeated.

He's not a cop, Frank thought, edging closer. Not the one who killed Lefebvre. He's too young. Which left the only other person who'd be interested in white flowers. One of Dane's men. This likelihood did not make him feel any better.

The wasp man said, "Yes. Lefebvre. My uncle's name was Lefebvre."

"I—I'm afraid I can't help you."

The wasp man sighed, then walked toward the door. Frank couldn't believe he was giving up so easily—there was something else going on. Did the wasp man have a confederate outside? He hurriedly repositioned himself so that he was better concealed, but not aligned with the woman behind the counter. If he had to fire his weapon at the wasp man, he did not want her to be in the line of fire. He could not see as much of the man's movements, but he still had a good view of the woman and the street outside. There was a Camaro parked at the curb. No one was waiting in it.

He hoped the wasp man was going to leave, that he had learned whatever he wanted to know. But he didn't believe for a minute that it was going to happen that way. He thought of all the names on the police memorial that belonged to guys who had bought the farm just like this, on a night when some walk-in asshole's random or not-so-random act of assholishness turned a trip to a florist or a store or a restaurant into a *situation*, forcing an off-duty cop to act without the usual protections he'd have on the job—no backup, no radio, no Kevlar vest. *Shit.*

Instead of going out the door, the wasp man locked it. As he bent to do this, Frank saw the outline of a weapon beneath his coat. *Shit.*

"Why did you do that?" the florist said. "Can't you read the sign? 'This door to remain unlocked during—'"

"I said, I need your help."

Frank unholstered his own weapon. With his other hand, he pulled out his cell phone, which was set on silent mode, and dialed Pete's pager number. Keeping an eye on the wasp man, who was moving closer to the florist, he entered 77, the last digits of his badge number, which would immediately tell Pete who was calling. Separating each code with asterisks, he followed this with 1199, the radio code for "officer needs assistance," then 211, "armed robbery," then 2-4-BLOOM—driven nearly mad by having to translate the store's phone number into digits before hitting the pound key. He put the phone away.

The wasp man was back at the counter now. "Come on, tell me."

"I told you," the woman said. "I can't help you."

He moved closer to her. "Can't you?"

"No. I mean—yes, we did make that delivery, but the customer didn't leave his name. He paid in cash."

"Describe him."

"You aren't upset about him being illegitimate, are you?"

The wasp man momentarily lost his air of menace. "What?"

"He said that he was Mr. Lefebvre's illegitimate brother. That's why he didn't want his name attached. He wanted to pay his respects but not to upset the family. I thought he was being overly sensitive, but—"

The wasp man reached across the counter, grabbed hold of her blouse, and dragged her halfway over it as he pulled his gun out.

Frank moved forward.

"I'll tell you! I'll tell you!" the woman said. "Please don't shoot me! Please don't! I don't want any trouble!"

"Neither do I," he said, releasing her. "Now tell me—who ordered the white flowers?"

"Please don't shoot me!" she said again, cowering down behind the counter.

"Hold still!" the wasp man shouted at her. "Get your hands up where I can see them!"

She whimpered, putting her arms over her head, as if to shield herself from him.

The wasp man laughed. "Are your arms bulletproof?"

"Ohhh, God! Oh, God!"

"Christ, lady, did you just wet yourself?"

She began sobbing.

The phone rang.

"Don't answer that!"

She sobbed louder.

"Shut up! Shut the fuck up! I just want a little information, for God's sake."

She obeyed, making little hiccuping noises. "He didn't give me his name! I swear to you, he didn't! I told you, he paid cash."

"Describe him to me."

"He was older, in his fifties, I'd say. Oh . . ."

"God damn it! Lady! Wake up! Oh, Christ—do *not* have a fucking heart attack on me, lady!" He shoved the weapon into the holster at his back and began to move around the counter.

Frank wasn't going to wait for another chance.

"Police—freeze!" he shouted, his own heart hammering as the man turned toward him. His voice had come out at about half its usual volume—he had forgotten the effects of the smoke. "Freeze!" he said again.

To Frank's surprise, the wasp man complied. He could see in the wasp man's eyes that he didn't necessarily want to do so—but he responded in the manner of someone experienced with being arrested.

"Hands high! On top of your head! Keep them there. Lock your fingers together."

The wasp man complied.

"You will slowly take two steps away from that counter! Now!"

He moved, Frank's weapon trained on him the entire time.

"Face the door!" Frank moved so that he was behind him but not within reach. "On your knees!"

With only the slightest hesitation, he obeyed.

Frank thought of waiting for backup before removing the weapon—always a tricky moment, one when it was easy to end up losing your own. But not knowing whether Pete had received the message, he wasn't going to give this wasp knucklehead the time to change his mind about being cooperative.

"On the floor, facedown. Cross your ankles."

Carefully, he relieved the wasp man of his weapon. It was not until he had taken the clip out of it that he noticed that the Brandenburg Concerto was still playing. For some minutes—could it have been only minutes?—he had been concentrating on the wasp man to the exclusion of all else. He cuffed him just as the old woman called out, "Is it okay now?"

"You were faking?" the wasp man said, incredulous.

"Shut up!" Frank told him, glad that she was all right but worried that she might be more difficult to control than the handcuffed man on the floor.

This concern seemed warranted when the woman stood and started to walk out from behind the counter.

"Stay back," Frank warned. "Don't come any closer. Just stay right there."

"For God's sake," she said to Frank, sounding more calm than he did. "Took you long enough. What was I going to have to do next? Strip naked to scare him out of here?"

"You knew I was in here?"

"Oh, yes, I saw you back by the roses a little earlier. Do you have a cold, dear?"

"No. You couldn't know that I wasn't with him," he said, indicating the wasp man. Although the man stayed perfectly still and did not seem inclined to cause trouble, Frank never took his eyes off him.

"Well, yes, I did know. I expected you."

"Expected me?"

"Yes, you personally. The man he's been asking about gave me your picture."

"What?"

"You're Mr. Lefebvre's other illegitimate brother, the policeman, right? Your brother—the living brother—told me you might see those flowers and use your police know-how to find out where they came from. And he said to tell you that there was no need to feel obligated to him or to me and that he'd already paid me in full. Which he did. Now, I must ask you—do you have a picture of your father? He must have been some man!"

Mercifully, the SWAT team arrived, sparing him from having to answer her.

33

He was tired, he was hungry, and it occurred to him that after talking to
Mrs. Garrity and dealing with all that had followed, he hadn't remembered
to buy flowers. The arrest had kept him at the station longer than it did the
wasp man, whose lawyers—Dane's lawyers—had him out of jail almost before he was booked, saying that he had done nothing more than try to help
an elderly woman whom he believed was suffering a heart attack.

Mrs. Garrity had readily identified the spray of flowers in Frank's photo,
but hadn't been able to provide many clues to the identity of the man who
bought them.

"He was wearing a disguise, of course," she said.

"You knew this at the time?" Frank asked. "And weren't suspicious?"

"Yes, but after all, a person doesn't want everyone on earth to know he
was born out of wedlock. So I understood perfectly. He was wearing sunglasses, and a hat, and a wig—not a very good one. No mustache."

"Well, that's something to go on!" Pete said.

"Sarcasm does not become you," she said.

"How tall was he?" Frank asked.

"Not as tall as you, not as diminutive as Detective Sass here. Did he pass
the height requirements for the department?"

"I used to," Pete answered, "but witnesses like you have worn me down."

She had not studied the man too closely, having been distracted by stories of legions of bastards roaming Las Piernas and by envisioning the all-

white arrangement of flowers. She had complimented Frank on his photography and asked if he would send a copy of the photo to her.

"I'm quite proud of that arrangement!" she said. "Now, if you don't mind, I need to go home and change my clothes."

As he came in the door, the dogs greeted him. Seth was not far behind, jumping up and down and shouting, "He's home! He's home!" as if a fanfare ought to be playing, a red carpet rolled out.

"Hello, Seth," he said, not feeling so tired after all.

"We've been watching about you on TV! Tell me about the bad guy in the flower shop."

He groaned. There must have been a TV news team among the helicopters.

Irene came hurrying toward him, face full of worry, and hugged him tightly. "Are you okay?"

"Fine, I'm fine."

"Your voice—"

"The smoke got it," Seth explained. "My mom broke our window, so we got air. But he was in the smoke."

Irene looked more worried than ever.

"Safe and sound," Frank said. "Both then and this evening. Sorry you even had to think about it—it wasn't a big deal."

"Did you shoot him?" Seth asked.

"No. Nobody shot anybody."

"Seth!" Elena's voice called. "Let Frank have a chance to come in the door."

Frank bent closer to Irene's ear and said softly, "I didn't mean to spring them on you like this . . ."

She laughed, but he didn't think there was a lot of humor in it.

"You missed it!" Seth said with relish.

"Seth!" Elena's voice warned.

He walked in to find Elena sitting on the couch. She was petting Cody, who had taken up residence on her lap. He still had an arm around Irene and felt the tension in her shoulders.

"Everything okay?" he asked warily.

"Fine," Irene said.

"They were going to kill each other!" Seth said.

"A misunderstanding," Irene said, blushing.

Elena looked embarrassed, too.

Frank felt a nearly overwhelming urge to go back to the office.

"It's okay now," Seth said. "I made them be friends. But they were fighting! And saying the S-word! And the B-word. And even . . ."

"Seth . . ." Elena warned.

". . . the F-word!"

"Seth Lefebvre!"

"*And*," he added in a lowered voice, "they fought naked!"

"I had a robe on!" Irene protested.

"Naked fighting . . ."

"And I had grabbed a towel by the time you came in, Mr. Tattletale," Elena said.

". . . swearing ladies!"

"Seth!" the women shouted in unison.

Seth gave Frank a look that asked *Who are you going to believe?*

"Well," said Frank, doing his damnedest not to laugh, "I'm glad you were able to make them be friends." He looked between the women and saw that he wasn't going to get any immediate answers. Certainly not about naked fighting swearing ladies. Not only was he not going to get answers, their faces said, he shouldn't dare to ask any questions. He was still tempted to try, but decided he'd had enough heroic action for one day, and accordingly changed the subject. "Have you eaten yet?" he asked Seth.

"I wanted to wait . . ." Seth began.

"He did," Irene said. "But I was hungry after all that swearing and nude boxing, so I went ahead and ordered pizza. Is that okay?"

"That's great," he said. "I get home late a lot, Seth—so you should eat when you're hungry."

"I want to eat with you."

The pizza arrived, and over dinner the mood seemed more relaxed, although Elena was quiet. Seth talked about going for a walk on the beach with Irene and the dogs. When Frank asked if Elena had joined them, he learned that she had stayed at home.

"I was admiring your garden," she said quickly. "One of the things I miss—we can't have a garden at the condo."

"I grew a potato in a jar," Seth reminded her.

"Yes, I'd forgotten that."

"Irene flew with my dad in his plane," Seth said to Frank.

Frank happened to be looking at Elena when Seth said it and saw her wince.

Seth was rambling on, talking a mile a minute about the dogs, the beach, his new pal Irene.

"So, Elena," Frank said when Seth paused for breath, "I haven't even asked you about where you work."

"I'm a PI now," she said. "I got my license not long after I left the department."

"Pete's wife is a PI. You should meet her. You'd get along great. Are you on your own or with a company?"

"On my own. I do a little insurance work, mostly workers' comp investigation, some heir hunting."

"So that gives you time to home-school Seth?"

"You told him about that, huh?" she asked Seth.

"Yes. My mom's a good teacher," he said to Irene, then frowned. "Mom, am I going to flunk now?"

"No, why should you?"

"I can't study. You know—the fire."

"We'll be able to get our things out soon. What we can't get out, the insurance company will help us replace."

"Gordie Howe?"

"He might be just fine. We don't know yet. What's important is you're safe, and I'm safe, and My Dog's safe."

"And Frank."

"Yes, and Frank."

"And I have my treasures."

"Yes, but if we're ever in a fire again—"

"I know."

"You scared me to death, Seth Lefebvre."

"I'm sorry." He turned away from her and back to Irene. "Stay here—I have something to show you." He stood up, seemed to remember something, turned back to Elena and said, "May I please be excused?"

"Yes, you may."

He hurried to the guest room, taking care to prevent Cody from following him in.

"He's great," Irene said. "You must be so proud of him."

"I am," Elena said. "I am."

Frank thought of the videotape Polly Logan had given him. "Elena—has he ever seen a videotape of Phil?"

"What? You have a tape of Phil?"

"Yes." He explained where he got it. "I brought it home."

Seth had overheard the last of this and said, "I have a tape of him too! Wanna hear?"

"Sure," Irene said, then glanced at Elena, who was pressing her fingertips to her lips. "But maybe we should save it for another time."

"No," Elena said. "No, it's fine."

He ran over to the stereo, treasure box in hand. "Hey, Frank! Can you show me how to work this thing?"

Frank obliged. They gathered in the living room. Frank noticed that Elena was focusing on the cat, not meeting anyone's eyes. What the hell was going to be on Seth's tape?

As soon as Irene came in, Seth said, "Ready?"

"Yes."

He opened the lid of his treasure box a narrow crack, slipped his hand in, and pulled out a cassette. Frank put it in the machine and pressed the play button. Seth reached into the box again and pulled out a black-and-white photo. A photo of Lefebvre as a young man, in a U.S. Air Force uniform, standing next to a plane. "That's him," he whispered to Frank as the tape went past the leader. Through the speakers, they heard a male voice say, "You've reached 429-5555. You know what to do." There was an electronic beep, the soft hiss of tape, then silence.

"Wow, that's so awesome!" Seth said. "I've never heard it on a big speaker before. Play it again!"

Elena's head was down, her hair hiding her face.

Frank rewound the tape and played it again. This time Seth said the words along with his father.

"It was on his answering machine," Seth explained to the silent adults. "We made a bunch of copies of it, because it was inside the machine and we were afraid the machine would break, right, Mom?"

"Right, Seth," she said softly. "A digital recording."

"The only one you have of him?" Frank asked.

"Mom has the other copies of it," Seth said. "But this is my own. That's why it's in my treasure box."

"Seth, I'm so glad you and your mom came to visit us," Frank said, "because I have something I think you are going to love."

For the next two hours, they watched Phil Lefebvre. At first, Irene and Elena fought back tears, but Seth was so totally captivated—and thrilled— his enthusiasm became contagious. "That's him! Mom, look! He was on TV! My dad was famous!" he kept saying. "Frank, those people at the church were right!"

He would listen carefully any time Lefebvre spoke. Frank turned up the volume and Seth thanked him.

In one interview, Polly Logan asked Lefebvre about being a pilot. For once, Lefebvre smiled when he answered.

"God, how he loved flying," Elena said. "He spoke about it in just that way to me on—when he took me out for dinner one night."

"He took Mom to the Prop Room," Seth said. "Tante Marie waited on them. Now she owns it." He studied Elena, then moved over to sit beside her. "Are you sad, Mom?"

"A little, but only because I miss him," she said.

Frank looked toward Irene, silently sending her another apology. She smiled, but he wasn't sure that meant the apology was accepted.

Frank noticed that Lefebvre typically minimized his own role in solving cases, always mentioning anyone in the department who had given him help. In one of the last short segments before the final press conference, the tail end of one of Polly Logan's questions could be heard: ". . . brilliant rescue of the boy?"

"There was nothing brilliant about it—I was at the marina by the purest chance and had the help of Detectives Elena Rosario and Robert Hitchcock," Lefebvre said, quite obviously trying to get away from Logan. "You should talk to Detective Rosario—she hasn't received the credit she deserves."

"But you must have suspected something to be at the marina at that time," Logan persisted.

"No. An anonymous tip on another case brought us there—a false lead. So you see, we were just lucky."

Frank was thinking about this set of coincidences when the segment with the final press conference began. It was rough footage, not edited as the others were—Frank noticed there was much more background noise in this one than in the others. As the camera roved over the small crowd in the hospital room, Frank was struck by the fact that the lists in Lefebvre's notebook could have been used as roll call sheets for the members of the PD who were there.

Seth was up on his feet again and gleefully pointed out Irene and his mother as they appeared on the screen. When Seth Randolph came on, he was momentarily solemn. "There's the boy I got my name from," he informed Frank. "He was in the newspaper, too. He fought bad guys, but he died. My dad loved him like he would have loved me if he knew about me, so my mom gave me his name." Although he was serious during this recital, he seemed to take all of this as simple fact and did not seem overly disturbed by it. He was too enthralled at seeing his father in something other than still photos to remain solemn for long. He showed an obvious dislike of Tory Randolph, making a "gag me" motion when she was speaking and once yawning loudly.

"Seth," Elena warned.

And then Frank heard it—softly but distinctly. Amid all the chatter and the sounds of movement on the audio track, he almost missed it. Most likely, if he hadn't already come across it in Lefebvre's notes, he would have never noticed the tones among all the other recorded noises.

Do-re-mi, do-re-mi . . .

They heard Lefebvre's voice saying, "Easy . . . Seth, it's all right."

"He said my name!" Seth shouted.

"Let's hear it again," Frank said, pausing and rewinding the tape back to the point just before he heard the electronic notes. This time he tried to watch reactions, to see if the camera caught anyone moving or responding to the sound, but the camera was focused on Tory Randolph, who seemed not to notice the sound at all.

But as he kept watching, it seemed clear to Frank that Seth Randolph had reacted to the sound. In early shots, the boy appeared uninterested—almost bored—by the press conference. After the sound was heard, he was pale, frightened, and holding on to Lefebvre.

Frank glanced at Elena, who appeared almost as shocked as Seth Randolph did on the tape.

On the tape, Lefebvre said, "A little too much excitement," in answer to Tory Randolph's anxious questions. "Perhaps it would be best if we let Seth rest."

The tape ended. He would watch it again later, Frank decided. For now, he focused on the boy who was bouncing around his living room, elated.

"I'll get a couple of copies of this made for you," Frank said.

"Really?"

"Really. One for your mom and one for your treasure box."

"Thank you!" Seth said. "Thank you *so* much!"

It was some time before he wound down enough to go to bed, but he didn't argue with Elena when she asked him to put on his pj's and brush his teeth. He hugged Irene, and then Frank, and then the dogs, and even Cody, who—to Frank's astonishment—put up with it. He came back to Frank and gave him a second one, then went off to bed with Elena.

Frank tried to think of all the things that might make the "do-re-mi" sounds like the ones on the tape. A pager, a cell phone—the alarm on a watch.

A watch.

"Would you mind playing the end of the tape again?" Irene asked. "There was something going on—I remember now that I wanted to stay and ask Phil about it."

"Yes, I think I know what it was, but I'm just not sure what it means." He told her his theory of the alarm on the watch. He had just finished when Elena came back into the room.

"I didn't want to get into this in front of Seth," she said, "but there's something important on that tape."

"The alarm on the watch?" Frank asked.

Startled, she said, "You already know about the watch?"

"Until now, guesswork. Why don't you tell me the rest of it?"

34

"A watch?" Chief Hale asked in disbelief. "You think he was killed over a watch? What was it, a solid gold Rolex?"

Until that moment Frank thought Hale had been softening a little. He had been unsettled by the story of the fire at Lefebvre's condo. He had listened almost patiently when Frank explained that the person who had stolen the florist's license plate had probably set the fires in the garage and on the staircase.

"No, sir. A model of a Time Masters watch called Time Master Three."

"A Time Master?" he scoffed.

"The watch in the evidence box for the Randolph case."

"You believe Lefebvre was killed over a watch like that? Before I was briefed about the one in the box, I'd never heard of them. How many of them can there be?"

"I spoke to the manufacturer today. The answer is, over a seven-year period, about sixty-five thousand, mostly in California. Not as big as Timex or Rolex, perhaps, but too many to track their owners down one by one. Although—"

"Why would I want to find any of them?" Hale interrupted.

"They can be programmed so that the alarm makes a particular sound— part of a musical scale. *Do-re-mi.*"

"Harriman—"

"Humor me, sir."

"What the hell have I been doing so far?" he groused, but waited.

"I want you to take a look at this." Frank plugged in the AV cart he had rolled into the chief's office—over an aide's objections concerning the potential ruin of Hale's carpet—then put the Logan tape into the VCR. To his relief, both the VCR and television worked—never a given with the aging department equipment. The tape was cued up to the moment just before the watch sounded. He explained to Hale where he had obtained the tape. "You'll hear the sound I've told you about. I want you to notice Seth Randolph's reaction to it."

Hale watched in brooding silence. Frank rewound the tape and played it again. Then he waited.

"Could be a coincidence," Hale said. "Something else in the room—or someone else—could have upset the boy."

"But not Lefebvre. You saw how the boy turned to him."

Hale frowned.

Frank told him about Lefebvre's notes and what Elena Rosario had said about Lefebvre's attempts to discover the identity of the owner of the watch.

"And the reason she didn't come forward? Or Matt Arden? For God's sake—if she didn't know any better, he did!"

"They didn't think they would be believed."

"Nonsense!"

Frank met his stare.

Hale lowered his eyes, frowning.

"The watch supposedly left in the evidence box by Lefebvre had signs of wear on it, but it had never been worn by Lefebvre. Lefebvre wore an old Omega inscribed to him from his sister. I know about that because Ben Sheridan took cadaver dog teams up to the mountains a couple of days ago and found Lefebvre's watch near the wreckage of his plane."

"Maybe he had two watches—"

"You don't believe that, do you? I checked on it anyway. Dale Britton did the original examination of the Time Masters watch. He was vague about the alarms—said the watch made 'various patterns of musical notes.' I suppose he was more interested in clues about the man who wore the watch—so he used the wear marks on the band to figure out where it had been fastened and took some measurements. That allowed him to estimate the size of the man's wrist. I'm sure the idea was that, if Lefebvre was caught, they could prove it fit him."

"Well? What of it?"

"It's too bad Lefebvre wasn't arrested before he reached Seth Randolph's room. Maybe he would have been shown to be innocent then and there, and lived. Ben gave the watch he found to the coroner, but being a forensic anthropologist, he couldn't let it go without making every possible observation about it that he could. I called him late last night and asked him to look at his notes on the watch—especially the size of the metal wristband."

"That wouldn't be accurate," Hale said. "A metal band can stretch." He pulled on the segments of his own watchband to illustrate his point.

"Yes, but it can't shrink down past a certain size. Take your watch off."

Hale did.

"You see? When the tension is off the segments, they close up to a fixed size. A person with a larger wrist than yours might be able to wear your watch. But if a person with a smaller wrist than yours put it on, it would slide around on him. The wear pattern on the Time Masters watch indicated a man with a smaller wrist."

"So it wasn't Lefebvre's watch in that evidence box. That doesn't mean he didn't put it there."

"I think that's unlikely. Lefebvre only saw that box once, very briefly, and not long before he was murdered."

"No—you've got that much wrong. His name was on the evidence log twice."

"His name, but not his signature. The first signature was forged. Ask Flynn if you don't want to buy that off me."

"Flynn? How the hell many members of this department have been hiding this for the last ten years?"

"Flynn just discovered the forgery on Monday. He got curious about people who had looked at that evidence box, because Bredloe had looked at it just before he went to the Sheffield Club. And Bredloe was asking Flynn questions—wanted to know who in the department knew what was in that box."

"Damned near everybody, unless I miss my guess."

"Flynn said as much to Captain Bredloe."

"So what are you going to do? Go around making everyone who was at that press conference try the watch on? It will probably work something more like O.J. and the glove than Cinderella and the slipper."

Frank shook his head. "Even if I had that original Time Masters watch, people gain and lose weight over ten years."

"What do you mean 'that original'?"

"Someone replaced that watch since Lefebvre disappeared. The one down in the box in Evidence Control isn't the one that Lefebvre saw that night."

"Replaced? Why?"

"I'm not sure. All I know is that the watch that was substituted for it is newer. From the looks of it, it hasn't ever been worn. And when I spoke to Time Masters this morning, I learned that this one was made seven years ago. They could tell by the serial number and by the 'China' stamp. They were making them in the U.S. until then."

Hale sat down heavily in his chair, his face set in stubborn lines. But he said nothing. As he watched the chief, Frank took hope from that silence. He knew that Hale was going over all that he had said, looking for holes, for weaknesses. Hale was the bishop in this little cathedral, and the man clearly didn't want to change religions at this point—for ten years, Hale had knelt at the altar of Lefebvre's guilt and preached it to not only his congregation, but city hall, the press, the public.

"Whatever else you want to believe about Lefebvre," Frank said, "you know he couldn't get up out of that wreckage to go buy a watch, then stick it into an evidence box before heading off for his final reward."

"Don't get cocky. It may have been impossible for Lefebvre, but it was nearly as impossible for anyone else to do so, with security cameras, and—"

"Seven years ago, sir."

"Oh, back to calling me 'sir,' are you?"

"Seven years ago."

Hale's face reddened. "Don't push me, Harriman."

"Seven years ago, sir, Flynn was not in charge of the property room. Five years ago an investigation into the theft of drugs and other materials from the—"

"Yes, yes, you've made your point. There were no cameras before Flynn, and we did have problems with evidence control."

Hale stood up and began pacing.

"Whom do you suspect?"

"No one in particular yet, sir."

"So you're telling me that you've spent your first week creating chaos."

"I wouldn't put it like that, sir."

Hale stopped pacing. "No. Neither would I." He paced again.

"I want to talk to a couple of commissioners today, sir."

"Police commissioners? About this? At this stage of your endeavors? Don't be an ass."

"No, sir, about Trent Randolph. I need to know who in this department identified him as an enemy."

"Maybe you're still looking at Dane, you know. Dane hated him, and while I will admit that there appears to be insider help here, we've always known that Dane must be getting at least some assistance from someone in this department."

Frank said nothing.

"You don't believe it."

"Why would Dane frame himself?"

"If he knew he would have insider help getting out of trouble, he might have found it all a pleasant game."

"He wasn't at the press conference."

Hale sighed. "I'm not happy, Harriman. I'm not happy at all."

"No, sir. But you'll do what's right."

Hale smiled a small, quick smile. "That sounded more like hope than certainty to me."

"If I doubted you, I'd be talking to the attorney general instead of you, sir." He kept to himself the fact that he had looked up the number this morning but hadn't called.

Hale gave a bark of laughter. "Laugh, Harriman, because that had better be a damned joke. I don't want you to talk to anyone. Not anyone. Not even Pete Baird."

"I'd rather you didn't ask that of me. Pete can be trusted to keep it to himself. As it is—I like working with Pete, sir. He knows about Elena Rosario and her son, and—"

"And your partnership is feeling the strain of this case," Hale said. "I'll think about it. With Rosario and her son under your roof, you've probably blabbed to your wife—did you swear her to secrecy?"

"She won't talk to the paper about it, if that's what you're asking—sir."

"Which commissioners do you want to talk to?"

"Soury and Pickens."

"Hmm. You'll get very different views of Randolph. Be sure to tell them this is in the strictest confidence."

"Yes, sir. If you'll excuse me, I'll be on my way—"

"Not so fast. One other thing you should know." He tapped the ends of his fingers together, looking suddenly ill at ease. He cleared his throat, then said, "When someone is appointed to a commission that will be reviewing highly sensitive materials such as those seen by the police commission, we very naturally do a background check on that person."

Frank waited. There was something slightly defensive in Hale's tone.

"A couple of years before he became a commissioner," Hale said, "Randolph had been involved with studies of the department and so on, so we were aware of him. He seemed to be a very straight arrow. He dumped his wife, but no one had ever been able to stand her, and he threw her over for a woman that had every man in the department green with envy. A real beauty—blond hair, blue eyes, gorgeous. But then, just after he was appointed, we learned that the woman he was dating was associated with Whitey Dane."

"Tessa Satel—the one he left his wife for?"

"Yes. We had never observed her anywhere near Dane. We might never have made the connection except for a lucky break. One of our surveillance teams had noticed that Dane visited this one house fairly often. Turns out it belongs to an aunt of his—his mother's sister. Good-looking woman. No criminal activity that we could discover—can't exactly arrest everyone whose nephew grows up to be a jerk. He was over there often, though, so we started to watch the place. Every day, she picks up a little girl after school, baby-sits her until the kid's mom comes by. Nobody stays around, nobody carries packages in and out of the house—nothing even remotely criminal.

"So we take the surveillance off. Dane visits his aunt—big deal. Some of these creeps, you know, they're saints in their own families. Guilty of murder, theft, drug dealing, every sort of crime you can think of—but he loves his dear old auntie—who isn't all that old. He's more of an auntie than she is, you ask me. Have you ever seen who works at that house? I guess you met one of his houseboys yesterday."

"About this relationship of Randolph's—" Frank said, refusing to be sidetracked.

"Oh, yes—well, I'm getting to that. One day, while I was at lunch with Trent, he told me that he felt sorry for Tessa, because she and her daughter were all alone in the world. According to him, she's a widowed orphan and has no family whatsoever—no brothers, no sisters, no nothing. And I had this funny feeling—you know, something bothered me about this for no apparent reason."

"Except that if a person wants to hide her past, she might give out a story like that."

"Exactly. So I decided to let someone outside of Narcotics take another look at her—"

"Why?"

"I wanted to know more—"

"No, I mean, why not someone in Narcotics?"

Hale shifted uncomfortably. "They hadn't done a very good job of checking her out. That's all."

"And you suspected someone in Narcotics of working for Dane."

Hale shrugged. "Such things are always a possibility. In any case, I asked Pete Baird to see what he could learn. On the first day he followed her, guess where she went after work?"

"Dane's aunt's house."

"Right. Because guess who did the child care for her while she played tickle the bird with Trent Randolph?"

"The aunt."

"Right. And the aunt isn't charging her a dime. Because Tessa is her daughter. Tessa is Dane's cousin."

"So you told Randolph about this?"

"Yes. That was very difficult. But in truth, I think he had tired of her. He broke up with her not long before he died."

"Which made you further suspect Whitey Dane of killing him."

"I didn't need that to suspect him! Whitey Dane had been seen by the only living witness!"

"Seth Randolph."

The chief nodded, then suddenly smiled. "So maybe you had better think of this possibility—maybe Dane put on a different watch on the night he killed Trent and Amanda. Maybe someone in our department was indeed wearing a similar watch—after all, you tell me there were thousands of these watches sold."

Frank didn't say anything.

"It's a possibility," Hale said defensively.

"Why wasn't the information about Trent Randolph's girlfriend in the file on his murder?"

Hale said nothing.

"It wasn't in there," Frank answered, "because you wouldn't let it be placed there."

"There was no need. He was on the police commission, for God's sake!"

"And if the public found out a pro-department commissioner might have been under the sway of a woman with close connections to a crime lord like Dane—when Dane was eluding the police, and suspicions about a leak in the department were rife—well, then, that would have made Trent Randolph's good friend, the chief of police, look bad indeed."

"Don't presume you can understand the various pressures on a man in my position!"

"No," Frank said, standing. "I'm sure I can't understand them."

"Am I supposed to be deaf to the insult in that reply?"

"I'm sure I can't, *sir*."

"Harriman—"

"I'm too unsophisticated," Frank said, pausing as he reached the door. "But maybe I could have understood something simpler. If you had told me, for example, that you believed Randolph was an honest man and you couldn't stand to see your friend's good name damaged after he was no longer around to defend himself—or that you couldn't bear to see young Seth Randolph shamed at a time when he had already been through so much—that sort of thing, I might have understood."

Hale lowered his gaze to the top of his desk. "You don't realize—" he began, but Frank Harriman was already gone.

35

Greenleaf's Café was within walking distance of the Las Piernas Police Department, and the Looking Glass Man was certain that it obtained most of its customers from members of the department. He patronized it not because of convenience, but because it was one of the cleanest eating establishments in the city.

He seldom ate food prepared by others. He mistrusted their commitment to personal hygiene, their willingness to adhere to safe food preparation practices. Even if he could force himself not to think of rampaging bacteria, he could not prevent himself from considering what vermin one might encounter in the cupboards, let alone the floors of such places—this was enough to make him choose fasting over dining out.

However, Greenleaf's was a notable exception. The counters were kept clean and sanitized, the floors scrubbed, the tables wiped down. The kitchen, entirely visible to the patrons, could have been cleaner only if it had been his own. Even the windows sparkled.

At this particular moment, he was sitting in the warmth of summer sunlight coming in through one of these windows. He was not warm.

He was nearly alone here. The breakfast crowd had left, the lunch crowd had not yet arrived. He could sit here, drinking his coffee, so excellently prepared and thoughtfully warmed up for him by Mrs. Greenleaf, for as long as he chose to do so.

Louise Oswald, adrift without her beloved Captain Bredloe, had stood

before his desk not long ago on the pretext of bringing some paperwork to
him. The moment he saw her, he realized she was big with news and invited her to make herself comfortable.

To obtain this news, he had to play the game her way, which was irritating but ultimately worthwhile. And so he agreed with her when she said
that no one could appreciate the burden the captain's absence had placed
on her, nodded mutely when she said that the chief's decision that she
should report to Lieutenant Carlson for the time being was a bad one,
agreed that Carlson, puffed up after this announcement, was an insuffer-
able horse's ass unfit to supervise anyone, and so on.

Carlson, generally the sort of political animal who knew better, had
been so stupid as to criticize her habit of making certain kinds of improvements in the memos he dictated to her, and would undoubtedly find it difficult to recover from this fall from grace. It was one thing to ride roughshod
over one's underlings. To mistreat the person who sat outside the boss's door
was downright dumb.

Finally, she began her confidences. ("Don't tell anyone," she said, invok-
ing the favorite phrase of those who tell everyone.) Her news was that the rebellion against Carlson—whom she had once supported, but against whom
she was now ready to don armor and do battle—was gaining ground. Her
two best indications of this were that yesterday afternoon the chief himself
had ordered Carlson to send Detective Baird on a particular assignment
and that Frank Harriman—who hadn't reported in to Carlson in *days*,
much to Carlson's wrath—was sitting in the chief's office that very moment.

"And I hope he is telling him that we in Homicide can't take much more
of Lieutenant Carlson. Carlson is worried sick, I'm happy to say. I was going
to tell you about Pete yesterday afternoon, but you weren't in," she said. He
disliked the speculative glance that accompanied this remark.

"Why is Frank Harriman talking to the chief?" he asked.

"It has something to do with the Randolph cases," she said. "And
watches."

"Watches?" he asked, unable to hide his surprise.

"Yes," she said, smiling knowingly. "I passed by his desk before he went
into his meeting with the chief, and he was asking someone when a watch
with a particular serial number was made."

"That might have been in connection with any of his cases," the Looking
Glass Man said, hoping she didn't detect his uneasiness.

"No, he had the Randolph files open. He locked those away, then gathered his notes and took them in with him when he went to see the chief."

• • •

He could not go near the chief's office without attracting unwanted attention. Unlike the relatively open area surrounding the office of the captain of the Homicide Division, the chief's office was in the center of a labyrinth filled with administrative creatures who jealously guarded his time and attention.

And Harriman was invited in. To talk about watches.

This was so much worse than he had suspected. Harriman must have seen the evidence. Harriman had handled the Randolph case evidence, but the Looking Glass Man had not received a message on his pager, as he had when Captain Bredloe had examined it. What had happened? Had his little property room computer hacking been discovered? Were they searching for him even now, as he sat here?

He remembered a moment from the day before, when he had looked in the mirror and thought himself invisible. Invisible! Far from it.

He gazed into the window next to him, not at the street beyond, but at the window itself. He could see his reflection. It was the reflection of a fearful man. He looked away.

He arranged the bottom of the folded paper napkin to the right of his coffee cup, moving one edge up a quarter of an inch or so, so that it was aligned parallel to the edge of the table. He then lifted the fork and placed it carefully on the napkin, so that the upper edges of the tines were parallel to the top of the napkin.

Pleased with the result, he felt calmer, and checking his reflection again, he saw that indeed, he appeared to be more himself now.

He began to think about this problem of Harriman.

Yesterday he had overreacted. He had laid himself open for premature discovery. He must approach this problem logically, or he would fail again.

He could not indulge in strange, frightening fantasies of Lefebvre being alive. Now—sitting in this clean booth, his hands on the hard, shiny table, fingers forming parallel lines—the panic that had come over him yesterday seemed alien, something that another man had experienced. Not him.

Today he could consider his position coolly.

The difficulty lay in not knowing how much Harriman knew or to whom he had spoken. That he did not know everything was certain. That his suspicions continued to lead him in dangerous directions was equally clear. So many people might now share these suspicions of Harriman's—the chief, Pete Baird, Irene Kelly, Elena Rosario, Matt Arden. Then again, Harriman had so alienated his fellow homicide detectives, it was entirely possible that no one had spoken with him. How could Harriman convince them of any theory he might be developing if they refused to do so much as give him the time of day?

He returned to considering plans for Harriman's demise. Any number of them could be set up within the next few hours. And in the meantime he would take steps to throw Harriman off his scent. He would then stay in Las Piernas only long enough to fulfill his most important obligations before making his escape.

Escape. Far from engendering visions of a carefree life, the word saddened him. Once the Looking Glass Man retired, who would see to it that justice was done? Who would be able to stop the next Judge Lewis Kerr?

The Looking Glass Man acknowledged to himself that it was all coming to an end. He had always known that it would have to, sooner or later. He was, of course, prepared for the possibility of discovery. As years of work for the Las Piernas Police Department had taught him, there was a vast difference between being discovered and being caught. He had no intention of being caught.

He had a great deal to do, then.

He would need to go to the several banks where he had stored cash and identification papers of one sort or another. Once he had gathered these, he would go to the airport and, staying below radar, fly his lovely Cessna to Mexico. He would not stay there, of course. Depending on the actions of law enforcement personnel, he had several alternatives available. At the moment, he was considering a cool climate.

He would have to part with the Cessna at some point, probably in Mexico. The loss would be painful to him. He had not owned a Cessna ten years ago. He had only rented planes. All the same, destroying Lefebvre's Cessna had bothered him almost as much as it had bothered him to kill Lefebvre. Now he would have to leave his own plane behind. Harriman deserved everything that was coming to him.

The Looking Glass Man had only two other remaining objectives: Whitey Dane and Judge Lewis Kerr.

Kerr was hardly a worry now. Everything was already in place. He consulted his watch. In a little more than twenty-four hours from now, Judge Lewis Kerr would no longer be able to lead justice astray.

Whitey Dane was proving to be a bigger challenge than the judge—the Looking Glass Man feared that he would have to wait even longer for his revenge against Dane. Years, perhaps, when it was safe to return to Las Piernas.

Dane's workers were a vigilant and suspicious lot, so one could not dress as a gardener or a florist or an alarm systems repairman and get past them. The Las Piernas Police Department's relentless pursuit of Dane had resulted in making him a less vulnerable target—Bredloe, a captain of detectives, had been easier to harm.

The Looking Glass Man had tried to needle Dane into exposing himself to danger—teasing him in ways that might tempt him to come out into the open. He had hoped for a more personal response to the flowers. Instead, he had almost caused that poor florist to lose her life.

Harriman had done what was expected of him, though. The Looking Glass Man smiled, picturing what Frank Harriman's face must have looked like when Mrs. Garrity called him the illegitimate brother of Lefebvre's!

"I'm glad to see you perk up a bit," a voice said beside him, causing him to jump.

He looked up to see Mrs. Greenleaf, exchanging his cold cup of coffee for a fresh, hot one.

"Oh, I'm sorry," she said. "I startled you."

"I was daydreaming, that's all," he said, and thanked her before she went back to the kitchen.

He glanced around. The café was still empty, but that would change soon. He had taken a few precautions at work, but needed to stop by a drugstore before going back there—there were a few inexpensive but necessary purchases to make. His other errands would need to wait until this afternoon. He was an efficient man and knew he could manage everything before him, but still . . . He looked across the street again at the police department. With so many errands, he wouldn't be able to spend as many hours inside that beloved building as he'd like. Very little time remained for him there.

He took out his wallet, in which all the bills were facing the same way, smallest denomination to largest, and left a large tip. Just before he refolded the wallet and put it away, he allowed himself a brief glance at the single photograph within it.

He felt the same surge of grief and hopeless longing that he felt every time he saw it.

Yes, he must do something about Mr. Dane.

The idea of killing Harriman troubled him less and less. Harriman deserved some sort of punishment for not listening to his superiors. Hadn't everyone in the department told him what must be done? But had he listened? No. Just like Lefebvre and Trent Randolph—if they had only left well enough alone! To have his work disrupted by meddlers who never would be able to grasp the importance of it—who would never see that the criminal justice system was damaged beyond repair, that he was fighting the evil that men like Judge Lewis Kerr set loose upon the innocent—no, that sort of interference was not to be borne!

As these thoughts occurred to him, he felt a little hum within his bones, a little heat within his blood. He looked at his reflection to see if he looked different to himself. He did—he really did! He knew what it was now, this heat and hum, and how to handle it. It was a mixture of fear and anger. Just a little of each. This time, he knew how to mix it up right. Yesterday he had let the fear dominate. Today it would be anger.

He put the wallet back in his pocket and stood. Although he knew the restroom in the Greenleaf Café was as clean as it was possible for a public restroom to be, he decided to wash his hands at work, where he could use the brand of soap he preferred, and his own towels and hand lotion.

36

Commissioner Michael Pickens agreed to talk to him, but warned that he could spare only a few minutes. Pickens owned a large chain of tire stores and managed them from a building not far from the department.

Frank rode the elevator up to a suite of plush executive offices. The door to Pickens's office was closed, but even through it, Frank could hear him haranguing someone. His secretary, who had timidly asked Frank to wait, cast a worried look at the door, then resolutely returned to her paperwork.

"One of his good days?" Frank asked.

She glanced up nervously.

"So they're all this good, right?" he said. "Or does he ever take a vacation?"

"Never," she said sadly.

"If you tell me he also enjoys perfect health, I'm going to really feel sorry for you."

"Never sick a day in his life," she said, but smiled.

"How inconsiderate can a man be?" he asked, and she laughed.

The door opened and a red-faced employee strode past them, eyes downcast.

Pickens stood in his office doorway, watching him go. He held a sheaf of papers in his hand.

"Mr. Pickens," the secretary began, "this is—"

"Betty, let me show you something," he said. The large man marched over to her desk and began berating her—he disliked the angle at which she had placed the staple in the corner of several reports. "That's not the way to do it!" he said again and again, not sparing her anything on account of an audience.

When he finally acknowledged Frank's presence, it was to say, "I suppose I'll have to talk to you now." He turned on his heel and marched toward his office. As Frank passed Betty's desk, he surprised her by picking up her staple remover. He rapidly worked it like a set of maniacal teeth, chasing after Pickens's back end.

Pickens turned at the sound, but Frank, looking all innocence, quickly palmed the device. He returned it to her desk only after Pickens resumed his angry strides toward his office. She smiled up at Frank as he left to follow her boss.

"So you're interested in Randolph," Pickens said, taking a chair behind an oversize desk. "A little late, aren't you?"

Realizing that waiting for an invitation would be futile, Frank found a chair and sat opposite him. "The case is old," Frank agreed, "but that doesn't mean we should forget about it."

"I have. Hardly remember the man."

"Word is, the two of you didn't get along very well."

"No, that's untrue. We disagreed over the matter of the lab, but that wasn't anything personal. He wasn't a man I admired. He didn't understand how to finesse things. Just rolled right over everybody. If he thought there was a problem with something, he'd write himself a report, issue it to half the planet. He rolled along through your department like a bazooka-proof tank division. He had something to say about everything, and nothing could stop him." He laughed, then added, "Well, now, I guess Whitey Dane stopped him."

When Frank didn't join in his laughter, Pickens fell silent.

"Why would Whitey Dane choose him for an enemy?"

"Randolph donated all kinds of money and equipment to the lab so that they could do fingerprint comparisons by computer, and some other load of gadgets so that they could do something else to do with chemical analysis. Randolph enjoyed that, too—playing Santa."

"And this upset Dane?"

"Sure. The chemical analysis goodie helped the department bust up one of his drug operations. And the fingerprint system allowed the department to find out the real names of some of his key people. Surprise, surprise— many of them had outstanding warrants. So that hurt. Whitey recovered from all of that, but he didn't like what it cost him."

"Do you have any of the reports Randolph made to the commission?"

"Reports by Randolph?" He looked away, then said, "Nope. Not a one. Now, if that's all . . . ?"

Frank tried asking him other questions—about Randolph's plans for that Catalina weekend and who might have known about them. He received vague answers. "So long ago," Pickens kept saying. Frank tried to get more specific information about possible enemies of Randolph's, with the same result. He decided to try his luck with Soury.

As he walked out, he noticed that Betty, Pickens's secretary, was away from her desk. Maybe she wised up and decided to resign, he thought. But then, as he walked out of the elevator into the lobby, he found her sitting on a bench nearby. She was holding a dusty box, but when she saw him, she stood and spilled its contents onto the marble floor in such a blatantly contrived manner, he hoped that if she did have plans to resign, she wasn't aiming for a career on the stage.

"Oh, how clumsy of me!" she said.

Grateful that he was the only audience for this performance, Frank bent to help her pick up the folders and steno pads that had fallen out.

"Thank you!" she said, then extended a spiral-bound phone message log toward him. "Would you mind holding this for a moment? If you'll do that, I can get the rest of these old files back into the box in order."

The message log was open, and he immediately saw a name that caught his attention: Trent Randolph. The message was dated Thursday, May 31. No year was shown. At eleven-fifteen that morning, Randolph had called to ask Pickens to join him at a meeting in Chief Hale's office at eight o'clock the next day. There was an additional note: "Soury, Larson, also to attend."

Frank turned the page and saw another message from later in the day— Chief Hale canceling the meeting, rescheduling it for the following Monday—by which time Trent Randolph and his daughter were dead.

"I overheard you in his office," Betty said. "I remembered that he was supposed to meet with Mr. Randolph that Monday, because he was extremely upset about it."

"Upset in what way?"

"Oh, not exactly grief-stricken over Randolph's death, although I think he was shocked—everyone was. But mainly he was convinced that someone might have it out for the members of the police commission. He was scared out of his wits. For weeks, we had guards around the place. Eventually, he calmed down."

Frank thanked her for her help, and after a moment's hesitation, handed back the message pad. If he managed to arrest someone in connection with these murders, he didn't want any courtroom problems to arise out of how he had obtained the evidence. He'd get a warrant. "You have a safe place to keep this?" he asked.

"Yes, absolutely. You'll have a warrant if you need it again?"

He smiled. "If you can think of anything else I'll need to name on it, let me know."

"Oh, I will. Not for nothing have I worked for a police commissioner— although some days, it feels that way."

He waited on the deck near the north end of the indoor Olympic-size pool. Rapidly coming toward him, in the lane reserved for fastest swimmers, was the man he hoped to speak to, but Commissioner Dan Soury finished the lap, completed his turn, and headed for the other end without seeing or hearing Frank.

Although he had been trying to capture Soury's attention for only a minute or two, it was too warm and humid to be standing around an indoor pool in a suit, breathing air saturated with the scent of pool chemicals. This meeting might turn out to be even less pleasant than the one he had just finished with Commissioner Pickens.

"Mr. Soury?" Frank called out. His voice was better today, but he still couldn't shout as loud as usual. The acoustics in the room must have helped, though, because Soury nodded. He was a slender man of medium height. There was a goodly amount of silver in his short dark hair and in his mustache. The mustache made Frank remember something—in the Randolph file, he had seen a group photograph of the commission members. Soury had worn a beard. He didn't fit the description of the man who attacked the Randolphs on the *Amanda*.

This thought, in turn, reminded him to pick up Seth Randolph's computer. There might be more information about the attacker on it.

Soury's workout had left him slightly out of breath; he swam back at an easier pace to where Frank waited.

Frank introduced himself and told Soury that he wanted to talk to him about Trent Randolph. "Your secretary told me I might find you here. I hope you don't mind—"

"Not at all, not at all. But you must be uncomfortable. If you'll wait for me in the club's lobby, I'll be out in fifteen minutes."

• • •

Frank used the time while he waited to call Mayumi. She put him in touch with a friend at the FAA, who promised to check a list of names for him. Whoever had sabotaged Lefebvre's plane knew something about aircraft. Frank wanted to know if any of the names on Lefebvre's lists were licensed pilots.

He didn't have time for any other calls—Soury had taken no longer than he said he would. Attired in a dark, elegantly tailored suit, he smiled as he approached Frank and apologized for keeping him waiting.

"Have you eaten?" he asked. "There's a pasta place next door."

They walked the short distance to the small restaurant.

It was soon clear that Soury was a regular and favorite customer. Although the restaurant was crowded, they were given a private booth near the back.

Soury made small talk until their beverages were brought and their orders taken. When the waiter walked away, he said, "So what can I do for you, Detective Harriman?"

"I'm trying to learn more about Trent Randolph. I'm especially interested in the last few weeks of his life, and I hope you can tell me about any projects he was working on just before his death."

"Projects in connection with the police department?"

"Yes."

Soury seemed amused. "Why? Is Whitey Dane no longer the department's favorite suspect for every crime in Las Piernas?"

"I'm just covering all the bases."

"It's about time someone did," he said. "I don't imagine Chief Hale is pleased with you for it, though."

Frank hesitated. "He knows I'm talking to you. He knows what some of my suspicions are. He didn't forbid me to ask any questions."

"I'm greatly relieved to hear that."

"Do you know if Randolph had any enemies within the department?"

"Enemies? A strong term. People who bore him some sort of grudge? You could find them quite easily—starting with his ex-wife, but by no means ending there."

"But within the department or on the commission?"

"Within both. Trent was subject to all the problems of those who are very bright. He didn't converse, he lectured. Few adults enjoy that. He also loved to solve problems and attacked them with enthusiasm—fine, but if he found a solution for a problem, he was impatient with any delay in implementing it. Very tough on bureaucracies such as the one you work in. He was sometimes a little quick to criticize. Not bound to win friends that way. And he was not easily fooled—at least not by men. Which was terribly difficult for those who tried to blow smoke at him."

"When you say 'at least not by men—'"

"Oh, the only woman in his life who was worth a damn was his daughter, Amanda. His ex-wife is a shrew. His girlfriend—Tessa? A lovely, doting nothing. Scratch the surface and you could see daylight out the other side. She's the only reason I've ever considered the possibility that Dane might have actually killed Trent."

"I don't understand," Frank said.

"Don't you? Trent told me that he broke up with her because she had lied about her past. When I questioned him a little further, he told me that he thought she had connections to the criminal world. In Las Piernas, that is spelled D-A-N-E. And Dane was not pleased at the progress Trent was making with the police lab, so perhaps he did have him killed."

"Do you remember the last conversation you had with Trent Randolph?"

"Yes," Soury said, suddenly solemn. "Yes, I do. He called me at my office the day before he left for Catalina, to ask if we could reschedule a meeting with Chief Hale. I'm not certain, but I think Pickens and Dr. Larson were supposed to be there, too. Trent wanted to talk at length, but I was in a hurry, so I . . . I interrupted him. Cut him off. Told him he could give me all the details on Monday. That's when we were to meet—first thing Monday morning. By which time, of course, Trent and Amanda had been murdered."

"What was the subject of the meeting?"

"I confess, I hadn't listened very carefully. He had been studying the property room and the lab and had already made some suggestions. But I think this had to do with narcotics and homicide investigations. I remember he used the phrase 'disturbing patterns.' Later, of course, we stumbled across what he had seen all along—the lack of security and proper handling of evidence in the property room. Too many people had access to too many areas. Unfortunately, the mismanagement and theft of evidence continued for some time before any of the rest of us saw those 'disturbing patterns.'"

He was interrupted by the sound of a man saying, "Dan! How are you?"

"Fine, Lew—Judge Lewis Kerr, do you know Frank Harriman? One of our detectives. Homicide Division."

Kerr smiled. "Yes, of course. You're Irene Kelly's husband, aren't you? Just saw her yesterday. Will you be joining us at the courthouse ceremonies tomorrow?"

"No, I'm sorry, I won't," Frank answered.

"How about you, Dan?"

"Wouldn't miss it. Saw you on the news, Lew—congratulations on the award."

They continued to chat for a moment. Kerr wasn't a favorite of Frank's— he thought the man was a better politician than judge. Around the department, he was often known as Judge Curse, not because he did, but because he was considered the kiss of death to any case that wasn't rock solid. Kerr was too inclined to make life easy for the defense, as far as Frank was concerned. Irene liked him, though—and once, when they had argued about Kerr, threatened to buy "Bill of Rights wallpaper" for the bedroom.

Seeing him hadn't made the day any more pleasant. Not long after Kerr went back to his table, Frank took his leave of Soury.

On the drive back to the department, Frank thought about the meeting Randolph had tried to schedule. He felt sure that Randolph wasn't setting it up because of the problems in the property room. According to Flynn, Randolph had already made recommendations for that area, even if the report was bureaucratically buried by those who were threatened by it.

But evidence didn't go to just the property room—it was also handled by detectives and the lab. He considered the fact that Al Larson was invited to Randolph's meeting. Randolph's strongest area of expertise in connection with the department was scientific—the lab. He might have seen some problem in the control of evidence going to and from the lab or ways in which a detective might compromise it before it got there. Perhaps he had even noticed patterns in connection with a particular detective's work.

Frank called Tory Randolph and made arrangements to pick up her son's computer.

"It isn't working, you know," she said. "They told me everything was erased off it. And the battery is dead. It's one big blank. Really outdated now. People probably have watches with more memory in them."

"I understand. But we might be able to find something on it anyway."

"I guess those lab types come up with new stuff all the time. That's why I married Dale. Never a dull day."

• • •

He pulled into the department garage, noticed how damned many white Chevy vans were parked in it, and found a space. He sat in his car for a moment, thinking about watches. Why would the killer go to the trouble of switching a new watch for an old one? Even for someone inside the department, and despite the lax property room procedures in effect until recently, it would have involved risk. Why?

The old watch could not have had any damning bits of evidence on it—bloodstains or the like—Britton's examination would have discovered them ten years ago.

What had happened seven years ago to trigger that change? Some event?

He got out of the car hastily, abrading his knuckle on the edge of the door as he did. He glanced at it. A little sting—it didn't even bleed, just scraped the skin up a little.

Skin. No blood.

Suddenly he recalled Tory's comments about labs coming up with new stuff all the time and saw what he had missed.

The sort of DNA evidence the Las Piernas Police Department lab could not have handled ten years ago, but could handle now. DNA testing that had evolved from the earliest versions—now capable of detecting DNA patterns from the skin cells that might have rubbed off the wearer of a watch and onto a watchband.

He hurried upstairs, not noticing the man who waited in the dark interior of one of the many white vans.

37

Robert Hitchcock left enough cash on the table to cover the bill and a fifteen percent tip. He dabbed his forehead with his cloth napkin, then added a few more dollars to bring the tip up to twenty percent. Hitch worried that in a swanky place like the Cliffside, fifteen percent wouldn't do. He didn't want to tip too little or too much. His concern had nothing to do with the excellent service he had received. Hitch didn't want to be remembered— not for generosity, not for stinginess.

He was distracted for a moment by the sight of the money on the mirror finish of the salver that had held the tab. He knew that there was at least a trace of cocaine on almost every piece of American currency. Cash and drug dealing. During Prohibition, he wondered, had every dollar reeked of gin?

At this thought, he held his hand up as if he were about to sneeze, in front of his nose and mouth. He exhaled softly through his mouth, then inhaled through his nose. No, he didn't reek of gin. At least he didn't think he did.

If someone had been watching him, they might have seen that he rose from the table a little carefully. He had enjoyed the martinis. The Cliffside was famous for serving a good martini. It also boasted one of the best restaurants in the city. Today, the first time he had dined here, he discovered that its good reputation was well deserved.

Hitch had been eating lunches in fine restaurants all week. The Cliffside hadn't been able to give him a reservation until today, and he was almost tempted to see if they could give him another reservation for next week. But what use would that be?

Harriman. That stubborn asshole.

Hitch had been around long enough to read a guy like Frank Harriman. They could fire Harriman and Harriman would work the case on his own. He had seen that on Sunday. Vince Adams was wasting his time trying to pressure Harriman. Why couldn't Vince see that?

Hitch left the restaurant, stood awhile in the hotel's grand lobby, then walked outside. It was terribly hot, he thought, and started to dab his forehead. To his horror, he realized he had taken the napkin with him. Jesus! Was the waiter on his way out now to accost him? He would be remembered. He would be the man who stole the napkin. The cop who stole the napkin. Quickly, he stuffed it into his pants pocket, which made the pocket bulge clownishly. It seemed as big as a damned tablecloth in there now, that napkin. He hurried toward his car. He unlocked it, tossed the napkin into the front seat, shut the door and locked it, locked it away from him.

He stepped back from the car, feeling a little dizzy, breathing heavily. He turned and stumbled toward the low wall that ran along the far side of the parking lot, at last leaning against the railing there, looking out over the cliff that gave the hotel its name. The wind was stronger here, blowing hard across the beach and up the face of the sheer rocky surface, on to his own heated face. He needed the cool ocean air to calm him, the sound of the sea to soothe him.

Hitch told himself that he had no reason to feel vulnerable. But that was bullshit, and he knew it. He had been vulnerable for ten years. Not long after Lefebvre disappeared, he had been terrified, certain he would be next. When Rosario left the force, he had gone down on his knees before God and begged for mercy.

He got a miracle. For ten years, nothing.

Now this. His miracle, it seemed, had an expiration date.

Maybe Dale Britton was wrong. Maybe it wasn't Elena Rosario he had seen at the funeral.

A voice behind him said, "Did you drop something?"

He turned to see Myles Volmer holding the napkin. He was smiling.

Hitch felt his spine turn to cold jelly.

"Wh-what are you d-doing here?" he stammered, noticing two other burly giants standing not far away.

"Isn't the question what are *you* doing here?" Myles asked.

Hitch glanced nervously toward the hotel, at the large, tinted windows that looked out toward the water.

"You're right," Myles said. "It isn't good for us to stand out here where we might be seen. Although I doubt many police officers lunch at the Cliffside. A bit above your touch, isn't it?"

"How did you know—"

"Hold your hands out to your sides," Myles said, suddenly stepping very close to him.

Hitch's legs felt wobbly. The bastard was going to take his weapon from him. He knew he shouldn't let him do it, but Hitch couldn't find it in himself to resist. He wanted to weep from the fear and shame he felt as Myles reached for the button of his suit coat and unfastened it. Myles smiled down at him again, a hard, icy smile. Myles's hand moved slowly inside the jacket—then he startled Hitch by plunging that hand into Hitch's pants pocket and pulling out his keys.

Myles stepped back, still smiling, and tossed them to one of the other men.

Hitch felt a rush of relief that Myles all too apparently observed, so that the relief was quickly followed by anger and a deeper sense of humiliation than he had felt when the other man was touching him.

"What?" Hitch said with false bravado. "All of a sudden you need keys to get into my car? Or were you just copping a feel?"

"Let's go," Myles said in a bored tone, then turned and started walking toward a white limo.

"Fuck, no!" Hitch said, knowing whose limo it must be. "You've probably just blown everything. What is it with you guys? You were fool enough to show up at that funeral, one of his other men causes a scene—at a flower shop, for God's sake—"

Myles kept walking.

"I'm telling you, the department is watching his every move!"

Myles stopped, turned, and said, "Do you want to see me in a mood as foul as your language?"

Hitch hurried after him.

Myles held a door to the limo open, making a mocking "after you" gesture.

As he bent to enter, Hitch hesitated. The interior of the limousine was warm and white and smelled of sex.

He saw the woman first—her white stiletto heels, her lacy underwear around her slender ankles, her white silk skirt pushed up almost to her hips, her nipples dark beneath her thin white blouse, her full red lips, her blue eyes, her long blond hair. He had seen her a few times before, of course, but never this close. She wasn't young, maybe in her thirties, but he had seen plenty of women in their twenties who didn't have half of what she had going for her. Even in his anxiety, he responded to her. She leaned back lazily, posing alluringly in the corner, her long legs falling slightly apart at the knees.

Hitch blushed. She smiled at him.

Then he saw Dane. If someone had dumped a bucket of ice water on his crotch, it could not have more effectively taken his mind off the woman.

He had known Dane would be in the car, of course. Dane wasn't looking at him, or at the woman, but he felt sure that Dane knew he had been staring at the woman's thighs, at the way her nipples showed through her blouse. Dane's own clothes were not in the least disarrayed.

"Get in," Myles said behind him, and Hitch climbed in, perching his large body on the edge of the long leather seat opposite Dane. Through the tinted rear window, he saw his own car pull up behind the limo.

Myles entered after Hitch, shutting the door. As soon as it closed, the limo began moving, pulling out of the parking lot. The driver of Hitch's car followed.

The woman leaned over to pull her panties up from around her ankles.

"No, Tessa," Dane said, not looking at her. Tessa sat back, seemingly untroubled by the idea of leaving the panties where they were.

Hitch averted his eyes, not looking at either of them for a time. But soon he found himself watching Dane, and only Dane.

Dane sat silently, looking out the window nearest him, his head turned so that Hitch saw only one side of his face—the left side, the side on which he wore the eye patch. Hitch was always uneasy when beholding that black wedge on Dane's pale face, and it now seemed more menacing than ever, as if that unseeing profile were all-seeing, as if his every thought had been scanned by that darkness, his fears absorbed through its cloth into Dane's awareness. It stared at him, and nothing could be hidden from it.

He remained silent, knowing that Dane would not take kindly to an initiation of conversation. He had learned this early on. He did not ask questions, although his head was full of them. Or at least one question.

It was not *Where is he taking me?*

It was *Is he going to kill me?*

Hitch felt his fine midday meal roiling in his stomach. The martinis threatened to rise with it into his throat. He looked for a switch to lower a window, but found none.

"An old friend of yours is in town," Myles said, startling him.

"Who?" Hitch asked, a little tremor in his voice making him sound, even to his own ears, like an ailing owl.

"Elena Rosario—but please, don't ask any other question to which you already know the answer."

Hitch looked over at Dane, who hadn't moved.

"Mr. Dane has questions for Ms. Rosario," Myles said.

"Look, I haven't seen her in ten years. She won't talk to me about anything, so I can't help you. I didn't even know she was back—someone told me she might have been the veiled woman at the funeral yesterday—"

But this protest was cut short when Myles, in a move Hitch never saw coming, jabbed him hard and fast in the ribs with an elbow that seemed to be made of steel. Hitch's breath expelled in a whoosh and he doubled over, eyes tearing as he held his side.

Hitch felt the gun at his hip, and for a brief second he thought of using it, of pulling it out and blowing a hole right through Myles's fucking head, and then through Dane's dead eye, but he looked up to see that Dane had turned his face toward him, and the impulse quickly faded.

"As much as I enjoyed that," Dane said, "he won't be able to play his part this evening if you injure him too badly, Myles."

"I'm sorry, sir."

"Oh, don't apologize. As I said, I quite enjoyed it. Perhaps now, Detective Hitchcock, you will be so good as to refrain from interrupting."

Hitch said nothing.

"Mr. Dane has questions for Ms. Rosario," Myles began again. "Mr. Dane will need your assistance in order to obtain her full cooperation."

Hitch opened his mouth and drew breath to speak. He felt the ache in his ribs and stayed silent.

"You know where Detective Frank Harriman lives, is that correct?" Myles asked.

Hitch nodded. "Went over there after a hockey tournament once."

Dane said, "Of course. You attended college on a hockey scholarship, as I recall. What a wreckage you've made of yourself since then. I confess I'm rather amazed that you can still manage to skate."

"I can skate."

Dane smiled at the hint of defiance in Hitch's voice.

"Tonight you will visit Detective Harriman's home," Myles said.

"I'll see him at the game tonight—my team plays his."

Myles looked over at Dane. Dane nodded. Myles slapped Hitch across the face, hard enough to make Hitch's head snap back against the seat.

"Are you paying attention now?" Myles asked.

Hitch rubbed the heated mark on his face, but nodded.

"Tonight you will visit the Harriman home before the game. Ms. Rosario is staying there."

Hitch grew wide-eyed.

Dane leaned forward. "Your reaction interests me, Detective Hitchcock. Is it one of surprise? Anticipation? Or fear?"

"Surprise. Like I said—"

"Yes, my hearing is fine, thank you." But he studied Hitch in a way that made the detective call upon whatever shreds of courage were left to him in order not to shrink back. After what seemed to Hitch an eternity, Dane smiled, released him from his gaze, and turned to Myles.

Myles immediately said, "I have further instructions, Detective Hitchcock. I will give them to you in a moment." He picked up a cell phone and handed it to Hitch. "First, call your bank."

"My bank?" Hitch said.

"Apparently his own hearing is suffering," Dane said.

Hitch cringed, expecting another blow. When it didn't come, he began dialing.

"No," Myles said. "The other bank. Where you keep the account the Internal Affairs Division will have difficulty tracing to you."

Hitch hung up, and—hands shaking—dialed again.

"Use the automated, self-service system to check your account balance."

Hitch froze. Myles took the phone from him and entered all the required information, including the account number and the phony Social Security number Hitch had used to establish the account.

Myles handed the phone back just in time for Hitch to hear the mechanical recorded voice say, "Your account balance is four dollars and fifty-two cents."

All color drained from Hitch's face.

"Shall we save some time?" Myles said. "Or would you like to hear what has become of your airline reservations?"

"Tsk, tsk," Dane said. "After all our years together? Not even a kiss good-bye? I feel so used, Detective Hitchcock!"

"Has Mr. Dane ever treated you unfairly?" Miles asked.

Hitch shook his head.

"No?"

"No."

"Has he ever required you to do anything that you could not easily do?"

"No."

"Has he ever failed to richly compensate you for the risks you took on his behalf?"

"No."

"Then you will not hesitate to be of service to him in this small matter, will you?"

"No," Hitch said miserably.

"Do you begin to see that if certain parties were made aware of the extent to which you have helped Mr. Dane and shown readily available documentation regarding the rewards you have received in his service, you would soon find yourself in prison?"

"Yes," Hitch whispered.

Myles paused, then said, "And do you see that it would be extremely unwise to fail him, or to return his generosity with double-dealing, or to in any way disappoint him?"

"Yes," Hitch said, tears rolling down his face.

"Then please pay the strictest attention to the instructions I am about to give you."

As Myles spoke, Dane reached over to Tessa, moving his long white fingers along the inside of her thigh. She sighed in pleasure and moved closer to him, reaching for his belt buckle.

Hitch noticed none of this, and later, when the sounds they were making intruded on his concentration, he forced himself to keep his eyes on Myles Volmer, so that when the limousine stopped and he was left standing at the side of the road, near the open door of his own car, he had an imperfect idea of what had taken place between Whitey Dane and Tessa Satel, but a perfectly clear understanding of what he must do that evening.

38

After talking to Soury, Frank had spent an hour or so looking over Lefeb-vre's notes. The Wheeze stopped by his desk and gave him a note saying that Larson wanted to talk to him, but when he called the lab, he just got Larson's voice mail.

He went downstairs to see if he could find him. He took a quick look around, but didn't see the lab director. He walked by Larson's office, but the door was closed. Frank knocked, but didn't get an answer. Frank wasn't sur-prised—he seldom saw Larson in his office. Larson spent most of his time at meetings or in the lab itself.

He decided to talk to Koza, the questioned documents examiner. Koza told him that the business card found on Lefebvre was Elena Rosario's, but that an address and phone number had been handwritten on the back. Frank had the Randolph case files with him and thumbed through one of the fold-ers until he found an old interview with Elena. Elena's old home address and number matched those on the business card. Another dead end.

He stopped by the lab director's office again.

"Looking for Dr. Larson?"

He turned to see the toxicologist standing at the end of the hall. She was fairly new here, had only worked for the lab for about six months. He couldn't recall her name, and he was too far away from her to read it off her ID badge.

"Sorry," she was saying, "Al went home sick. One too many mocha lattes, you ask me. Paul Haycroft asked me to send anyone who was looking for Al to talk to him."

Frank still wanted to take a more careful look through the folders Professor Wilkes had given him, and that would take plenty of time. But at the toxicologist's suggestion, he decided to talk to Haycroft again as long as he was down here—he had more questions about the *Amanda* lab work. The toxicologist told Frank he could find Haycroft working on a set of latents in the fingerprint-identification area.

"Frank!" Haycroft said when he looked up from the fingerprint computer system. Frank saw that he was using the lab's new digital imaging software to enhance an image of a partial fingerprint. "The big man himself was down here just before lunch, talking about you."

"Hale?"

"Yes. Asking about paper airplanes. Seems you gave him something to think about."

"Thinking about asking me to resign, you mean."

"No, I doubt that. Did you get Al's note?"

"Al's note?"

"He left early—some sort of digestive problem. But he said if you came by, to make sure you got the note he left for you on his desk. I guess he wanted to talk to you earlier, but the chief said you were visiting commissioners this afternoon."

Mentally cussing out the "big man himself" for blabbing that to Haycroft and Larson, Frank said, "I'm trying to talk to anyone who knew Trent Randolph. While I'm here with you—mind if I ask you about the Randolph cases?"

"Not at all."

He was distracted by watching Haycroft clean the screen on the computer monitor.

"No wonder you think Pete's a slob," Frank said.

"Helps to see the image better," he said, then smiled. "I'm not just being anal-retentive."

"Don't get me wrong—I'm not saying orderliness is a bad thing. I suppose it's especially important down here."

Haycroft shrugged. "I've seen cluttered crime labs. Larson wouldn't stand for it here, though, and I think he's right. Why give a defense attorney—or the D.A., for that matter—an opportunity to say you were careless or contaminated the evidence?"

"One of my questions is about that," Frank said, opening one of the file folders he had with him and turning to a page he had marked. "There was some problem with cat hair?"

"Let me try to remember. May I see that?"

Haycroft read the notes and said, "Oh, yes, now I remember. A few stray hairs inside the shoes we recovered. Unknown source. We thought Vince or Dale might have brought them to the scene when they were searching Dane's boat, but when we tested their cats' fur against a sample, it didn't seem to match in color." He frowned. "I recall talking about this to Lefebvre, showing it to him under the microscope. It bothered me, because Dane is highly allergic to cats. And also, Vince was so touchy about the whole business—his lieutenant had to pressure him into letting us comb his cat. Then Vince told me not to talk about it to anyone."

"But you have—and you wrote it up in the report."

"Vince isn't my supervisor." He suddenly seemed embarrassed and said, "I'm not as brave as I'm making it sound. I added the information to the formal report after talking to Lefebvre about it. Then he disappeared, and no one seemed to care about what I'd written. The cat hairs were gone with all the other evidence, so what did it matter?"

"You examined the watch that was left in the evidence box?"

"I didn't do more than take a look at it. Dale Britton did the real work on it."

"And it was definitely worn? I mean, not a new watch?"

"Not new, no. As I recall, Dale got a wrist measurement from it. I don't suppose your forensic anthropologist friend might be able to help us compare it with Lefebvre's?"

"I'll ask him," Frank said, deciding not to let Haycroft know that Ben had already discussed it with him. "Do you remember anyone else around here who had a watch like that?"

"Well, yes. We all did."

"What?"

"Everyone in the lab. One of the vendors gave Al a dozen of them when we bought some equipment. He gave one to me, one to Dale, one to each of the technicians, and then a few to detectives—Vince received one, I believe. Pete, too. Lefebvre must have been given one also." He hesitated, then said, "They weren't that expensive—not meant as a bribe or anything of that nature."

"Not asking about it because of that—listen, are you sure Dr. Larson gave them all away?"

"Well . . . I hate to say that any were stolen, but I think some people may have believed that if the watches were a giveaway, they were free—so why not take one without asking? Al was looking for one of them a few years later and couldn't find them in the place where he'd left them. Really became upset about it."

"Remember when that happened?"

"Oh, about six or seven years ago."

"What makes you think it was then?"

"Because that same vendor sold us the DNA equipment. I suppose that's what made Al think of the watches. That's seven years ago, I believe."

"Maybe Dr. Larson just misplaced them," Frank said, wishing the vendor had been less generous.

"Misplaced?" Haycroft said in disbelief, then laughed. "Have you ever been in Al Larson's office?"

"Not more than once or twice," Frank said. "Now that I think about it, I haven't ever been inside yours. Usually, when I've come down here, you've both been in the lab itself."

"Or we've come up to your desk in Homicide. If you'd like to take a look in my office, go right ahead. I'm in the middle of doing this comparison or I'd show it to you myself."

"I'll take a rain check."

"Yes, I imagine you have better things to do than look at my desk. Anyway, my point was that Al doesn't misplace things. When you pick up the note he left for you, take a look around his office and tell me if you think the man who occupies it ever had a disorganized moment in his life."

"Any idea what he wanted to talk to me about? I'm a little uncomfortable about going into his office if he's not in—"

"The door is never locked."

"Still—"

"You aren't going to tell me you've never been in an office without the owner's knowledge?"

"Never a colleague's office."

"No need to take offense," Haycroft said. "He left the note for you there, after all."

"I wonder why he didn't just send it up to my desk?"

"Well—he probably wasn't thinking straight. Not to get into embarrassing detail, but from what he told me, he seemed to have a case of food poisoning—stomach cramps and so on. He was distracted, as you might imagine, and left in something of a hurry."

"Oh."

"I'm sure he'll feel better by tomorrow. And I wouldn't tell you to go into his office if I thought you'd be violating his privacy or compromising cases. He's very security-conscious, Frank—his desk and file cabinets will be locked. You don't need to touch anything—just pick up the note. You'll see what I'm talking about."

"Okay, but one other question—back to the cat hair business. Actually, not the hairs, but the shoes you found them in—the shoes that were discovered aboard the *Cygnet*. You examined them, but there were no wear patterns noted."

"May I see the photos?"

Frank showed him the photos of the shoes and of the bloody footprints on the *Amanda*.

"Now I remember. The shoes were brand new. There was blood and little else on them. As far as we could tell, Trent had hosed down the decks of his yacht just before Dane arrived."

"Any attempt made to find out if Dane had bought the shoes around here recently?"

"Yes, but we weren't successful. That doesn't mean anything—he could have had closets full of shoes he had never worn, bought them months earlier."

Or, Frank thought, someone else bought a pair to match ones seen on Dane.

Frank again stood before the door of Larson's office, telling himself that he had no real reason to feel so uneasy. He reached for the doorknob and turned it. As Haycroft had predicted, it was unlocked.

Gone for the day—not feeling well after lunch, Haycroft had said. And Hale had been down here asking about paper airplanes and talking about commissioners just before lunch.

Frank pushed the door open and stepped into the room. In the darkness, he could smell a faint odor of glass cleaner and furniture polish. He reached for the light switch.

In the sudden illumination, Larson's desk, which was protected by a thick piece of glass, was the first thing to catch his eye. It held only two objects: a telephone and a framed photograph. The telephone was squared with the right-hand corner of the desk; the photograph, which was facing away from Frank, was at a forty-five-degree angle on the left. Although as an administrator Larson must have handled a tremendous amount of paper-work, there were no loose papers anywhere in the office. The wastebasket was empty.

Frank took another step inside.

The bookshelves were neat and dusted. Diplomas and other certificates hung perfectly aligned. Rolled up against another wall, a typewriter cart with wheels held a laptop computer. Frank could see that locks on the file drawers were pushed in, in the locked position.

Frank put his hands in his pockets, conscious of a desire not to leave any personal mark on this blank setting. He walked farther into the room, around the desk, so that he stood behind the large chair. He could see his own reflection in the desktop.

No note. Maybe Larson had sent it upstairs after all.

He was about to leave, but the photo on the desk caught his interest. A young boy, perhaps three years old, holding a tabby cat.

He hadn't known that Larson had a son. He was a little surprised that the boy was so young. He vaguely recalled hearing that the lab director had been divorced for a dozen years or so. Didn't he have a more current pho-tograph of his child? Frank picked up the photo and studied it. A boy with a cat. Had the cat in this picture lived with Al Larson ten years ago?

"You lost?"

He jumped guiltily at the sound of the voice. He looked up to see the toxicologist watching him speculatively.

"I was told Dr. Larson left a note for me."

She walked over to him, disbelief written all over her face. He saw her ID badge then—Mary Michaels. She held out her hand, palm up, and he real-ized he was still holding the photo. He handed it to her, then felt absurd for doing so.

She glanced around, and he thought she was looking to see if all the de-grees were still on the wall.

"Look, Paul Haycroft—"

"Oh, Paul Haycroft comes in here all the time when Dr. Larson isn't around. Just because he's been in here doesn't mean—"

"No, of course not," he said quickly. "I don't suppose that you'll believe me if I tell you that I objected when he suggested it?"

She softened a little. "I'm sure he couldn't resist having you see how neat and clean it is."

"Exactly. And like I said, there was this note . . ."

"They are the weirdest pair of guys, if you ask me," she said, interrupting. "And they have been working together *way* too long."

She was still holding the picture. Seeing the direction of his glance, she said, "I'll put it back for you—unless you'd like me to give you a tour of Haycroft's office while you're snooping around?"

"For God's sake, I was not snooping around." Not really, he added silently.

She clearly didn't buy it.

They heard another voice say, "Mary, surely you don't suspect Detective Harriman of burgling the office of the lab director in the middle of the day?"

To Frank's relief, Haycroft stood in the doorway.

The toxicologist shook her head, then said, "If you really don't think Dr. Larson would mind—you know him better than I do. I've got to get back to work." She started to walk out, realized she still held the photo, and quickly handed it to Haycroft as she left.

"Thanks for the rescue," Frank said.

"No problem," Haycroft said absently, studying the photo before placing it back on the desk.

"Have you met his boy?"

Haycroft looked up. "Don't you know? Kit's been dead for many years."

"Kit?"

"Christopher." He turned the photograph toward Frank. "Kit for short."

"I'm sorry, I didn't know."

"He was killed in a bank robbery."

"He worked in a bank?"

"Oh, no," he said sadly. "He was only four years old when he died. His mother, his stepfather, a stepsister, and Kit. A long time ago now, before you were in the department. A parent never gets over such a thing, of course—you've seen that in your own work, I'm sure."

"The cases involving children are always the hardest to take. And you're right, the parents never really get over it."

"This affected all of us. Still does. Because the case hit so close to home, that photo of Kit has become—oh, I guess you could say it reminds us that this isn't just lab work—reminds us that what we do is important to the families. Does that make sense to you?"

"Perfect sense. Listen—there was no note in here."

"I'll be darned. I wonder what the heck he did with it? I'm sorry, Frank, I could swear it was in here." Haycroft frowned, pulled the chair back, and looked beneath the desk. "Here it is. Must have fallen." He bent and picked up a white envelope. Frank's name was neatly printed on it.

Frank thanked him and pocketed the envelope without opening it.

• • •

On his way out of the lab, he saw Mary Michaels again. He had the feeling the toxicologist had been watching for him.

"Detective Harriman—"

"Frank."

"Look, I'm sorry about how I acted back there."

"Don't be. You had every right to ask me what I was doing."

She hesitated, then said, "He talked to you about Kit?"

"Yes."

"I haven't been with the department very long, so I don't know the whole story, but I guess it was big news around here ten or twelve years ago, because it had something to do with another cop or detective, too."

"Involved in the robbery?"

"No—maybe someone else was killed in the robbery? Some guy's wife?"

"I wasn't with the department then, either," he said, although now he had a feeling that he had heard something about this robbery, and not so very long ago. What was it?

He wondered, as he climbed the stairs toward the homicide room, if he was going to be able to manage finding Lefebvre's killer without a damned history book.

Unfortunately, except for a PR publication or two, there was no department history book for the LPPD, which was what he'd need. The local newspaper, whose reporters didn't always seem to grasp the full story, was as close as anyone could come.

The elusive memory suddenly returned to him. It wasn't something someone told him recently—it was something he had been thinking about himself, here on this stairway. He paused halfway up, then raced to his desk, hoping to catch Irene before she left the *Express* for the day.

He read Larson's note while he waited for Irene to call him back. After all he had been through to receive it, the note wasn't all that exciting. On a single sheet of his letterhead, in neat block letters, he had written:

IMPORTANT THAT I TALK TO YOU REGARDING THE RANDOLPH CASES. NOT FEELING WELL TODAY, BUT HOPE WE WILL BE ABLE TO MEET TOMORROW AFTERNOON.

The phone rang. Frank set the note aside and answered the call.

"Frank? It's Irene. I found something. I'll fax it over."

"Thanks—you're amazing. I know I didn't give you much to go on—"

"I'll figure out *some* way for you to repay me."

He smiled. "Can't wait."

He stood by the fax machine, retrieving each page as it emerged, anxiously reading over one as the next printed. It had taken Irene less time than he thought it would to locate the article. He had only been able to supply a vague description of what he needed. He had asked her to look for a story about the bank robbery in which Vince Adams's ex-wife had participated. He wasn't sure what name the ex-wife had used then—was she still calling herself Lisa Adams after they split up? He didn't know the date of the robbery, wasn't even positive about what year it took place. He thought it was about a dozen years ago, but that might be wrong.

There was also a possibility that Mary Michaels was talking about some other bank robbery. But the toxicologist had said the robbery was big news, and most weren't, especially not ten or so years ago. They were so frequent in the area then, at one point the L.A. office of the FBI had the slogan "Bank Robbery Capital of the United States" printed on its letterhead. Still, a robbery that ended in the killing of a family of four would make news. It would be even bigger news in the department if an officer's ex-wife was involved.

Now, as he read the newspaper story, he was certain it was the same robbery. The article mentioned that a young boy named Christopher had been killed, but his last name wasn't given as Larson in the story—all the last names were given as Dillon, the stepfather's name. The fifth victim was a security guard. The five photographs didn't reproduce very well over the fax, but he could see enough of the boy's photo to tell that it was the same child as the boy in the portrait on Larson's desk.

The article barely mentioned the victims, focusing instead on Lisa Adams—Vince's ex-wife—and Carl Sudas, the suspected robber, who escaped. Sudas had been recently out of prison after serving time on a felony assault charge. He was arrested not long after his release, this time on drug charges. Judge Lewis Kerr tossed that case out during the preliminary hearing. Kerr ruled that the arresting officer, narcotics detective Robert Hitchcock, had acted improperly when he searched Sudas's car and failed to show the probable cause necessary for a warrantless search of the vehicle.

Within six months of his release, Sudas met up with Lisa Adams and sought her help with the robbery.

Frank took the pages back to his desk. He reread the article more slowly now. The largest photo was of Lisa Adams, looking blankly at the camera. Even in this poor reproduction, she appeared to be in shock. He was studying the photo when suddenly the fax was snatched from his hands.

"You asshole," Vince said, tearing the pages in half and crumpling them into a ball. "You fucking asshole. You want to get back at me, you leave Lisa out of it!"

"This isn't about her, Vince. Or you. That's not why I was looking at that article."

"Bullshit! Reading that crap in the paper." He tightened his fists. "What'd you do? Get your wife to help you find something on me? Maybe I'll start dragging your wife's name through the mud. See how you like it."

Frank stood up. "I said, this isn't about your wife or you."

"I don't give a shit how big you are, Harriman," he said, leaning closer. "You damned liar."

"Get out of my face, Vince. Now."

"I can't believe you'd sink this low."

Reed and Pete walked in the room just then. "Vince!" Reed called. "What the hell has gotten into you?"

Vince threw the torn fax at him without saying anything. He reclenched his fists.

Reed uncrumpled the ball, saw what the fax was about, and said, "Frank?" in a tone full of disappointment.

"I told him," Frank said, "this isn't about his ex. I was checking out something else."

"Well, then," Reed said, relieved. "Nothing to be upset about, is there, Vince?"

Vince was silent.

"Pete, help me out here," Reed said. "Frank wouldn't lie to any of us, right, Pete?"

Pete said nothing. Outraged, Frank turned to look at him. Pete looked away—just as Vince threw a punch.

Frank had expected it, though, and easily dodged the blow. He grabbed Vince's wrist and pulled him halfway across the desk, then pinned him to it, holding him down with most of his weight. He pressed Vince's face into the desk and said, "The only person around here who has mentioned her name is you."

Vince struggled, but Frank was stronger. And nearly as angry.

"Frank . . ." Reed said.

"I'll let him go when my partner asks me to," Frank said. "Oh, wait—I can't. I don't have a partner."

He straightened and shoved Vince off the desk. Vince wasn't able to get his footing and landed hard on his ass.

Carlson came into the room just then.

"What's going on here?" he asked.

"Nothing," Vince said.

"Then why are you on the floor?"

"I slipped and fell."

Carlson looked at the other three. No one spoke. When the lieutenant turned toward Frank, Reed silently pocketed the fax.

"You," Carlson said, pointing at Frank. "You seem to be at the center of a number of disturbances in our office lately."

"It wasn't Frank," Pete said. "It was me. Just a joke I played on Vince that got a little out of hand, that's all."

"Read the department regulations!" Carlson said, rounding on him. "Horseplay is strictly forbidden!" He pointed a finger at Pete's chest. "Do you know what we can do to those who engage in horseplay?"

"Ask for a blindfold and a cigarette, Pete," Frank said. "They say it goes easier that way."

The others laughed, with the exception of Carlson. He marched off toward his office.

The moment he was gone, the sour mood descended on the others again. Vince regained his feet and left the office. Pete and Reed followed suit.

39

He placed his skates, helmet, and uniform in a large duffel bag—already occupied by shin guards, elbow pads, and other hockey gear—and hoisted it
onto his shoulder. He was choosing a pair of sticks when the dogs began
barking, and soon after, someone rang the doorbell.

He swore softly. Irene wasn't home—she had taken Seth to the skating
rink not long after dinner, to enjoy some of the public skating time before the
evening's hockey games started. Elena was depressed or pouting or both—he
couldn't tell which—and had stayed behind, shutting herself up in the guest
room. And now, just before he needed to leave, someone was at the door.

But by the time he was inside, the dogs had stopped barking and were
merely standing before the door, apparently listening to something on the
other side. He noticed the guest room door was open now.

"Elena?" he called as he set the equipment down.

No response.

He looked through the peephole and saw Bob Hitchcock standing on the
front lawn, talking to her. Hitch seemed to be pleading, Elena looked obsti-
nate. Hitch wore a dark golf shirt and slacks and was dabbing at his face
with a handkerchief.

What the hell was Hitch doing here? he wondered. He stepped outside.

"Frank!" Hitch said with a smile, but it wasn't a smile Frank liked much.
Although the evening air was cool, Hitch was sweating, and Frank could see
the pulse in his neck.

But Elena's reaction bothered him more. She wouldn't meet his eyes.

"What brings you to my door, Hitch?"

"I heard my old partner Rosario was staying with you, Frank."

"Heard it where?"

"Word gets around."

"Really? Who brought it around to you?"

"No, no—I'm not naming names. Besides, that's not important. I gotta talk to the two of you."

"About what?"

Hitch looked toward the ocean, as if he hadn't heard the question. "Jesus, this is a great setup you have here, Frank. This close to the water—I never could afford a piece of property like this."

Elena muttered something, and Hitch dabbed at his chin with the handkerchief. "I'm not implying anything," he said quickly. "Everybody in the department knows the old lady that lived next door rented it to him and then sold it to him on the cheap 'cause she liked him. Well, who could blame her? Say, how about we take a walk along the beach?"

Elena glanced at Frank then, but Frank let the silence stretch. Hitch shifted his weight from one foot to the other.

"Talk about what?" Frank asked again.

"Lefebvre. The Randolphs. There are things I should have spoken up about before now." He stared at Elena for a moment. "Jesus—and now I learn he had a kid with you, Rosario—God damn, that was a shock."

Frank thought it was the first time that evening Hitch had been completely truthful. "I'm curious, Hitch—why now? In the evening, at my home? Why not just talk to me at the game tonight?"

"Screw the game!" He tried another smile. It looked more forced than ever. "Well, take a gander at me, Frank. I'm a fucking wreck—I can't sleep, I'm on edge all the time—I can't live like this, Frank." He looked to see if he was having any effect. A little more desperately, he said, "Tonight I thought of being out on the ice with you, surrounded by everybody else on your team, knowing what I know—"

"Didn't bother you much a few days ago at breakfast. Surrounded by the same guys."

"Jesus Christ almighty, Frank, please don't start being stubborn about this!"

"Leave Frank out of it, Hitch," Elena said tonelessly. "This mess is between the two of us."

Frank turned to her in surprise, but she had already moved away, starting to walk quickly toward the beach. He hurried after her.

"What the hell is going on?" he asked when he reached her, but she said nothing and still wouldn't meet his eyes. "If you're in some kind of trouble, Elena, for God's sake tell me. You know I'll try to help you."

She halted for a moment, but in the next instant Hitch caught up to them, and she shook her head and kept walking.

Hitch was panting now, straining to match her pace. "Could we go just a little slower?"

She speeded up.

She reached the stairs, paused briefly, then resolutely made her way toward a group of three men on the beach.

Frank had no difficulty recognizing them. Whitey Dane, Myles Volmer, and the wasp man. He turned to Hitch and said, "You're on his fucking payroll, aren't you, you bastard?"

Hitch wheezed and held his hands up as if to ward off a blow.

Frank turned his attention to the others now, ready to do all he could to protect Elena. But he soon realized that she wasn't acting afraid.

Despite all the possibilities he considered in those few moments, he was still surprised to hear Dane call out, "If it isn't my dear old friend Elena."

40

"I'm not your friend, Dane," Elena said. "Not then, not now."

Dane placed a hand over his heart. "You wound me." As Frank approached, Dane extended a hand and said, "Detective Harriman! So good of you to join us."

Frank stood with his fists clenched.

"There is no need for hostility or violence, Detective Harriman, I assure you. I'm not wearing a gun, and neither are Myles and Derrick. Have you met Myles and Derrick?" He smiled. "You may have seen them around town, at funerals or florists."

Frank didn't trust Dane to be telling the truth about being unarmed. He thought of his gun, locked away out of concern for Seth's safety. He looked up and down the beach, but the nearest group of people were some way off, on the boardwalk near the pier.

"I would have preferred a comfortable little coze in your living room," Dane went on, "but I asked Detective Hitchcock to bring you to me here — you see, I understand you share your home with a rather large *Felis catus*. There is much I admire in cats," he said, taking a long and considering look at Elena. "However, ultimately, they may be the death of me." He smiled, then turned to Frank. "That is, I am severely allergic to them. And I must admit that I also sent the intrepid Detective Hitchcock to your door because I thought you might be a tad more willing to open it to a fellow detective than to me."

"'A tad,'" Elena said, mimicking his voice. "Whitey thinks that bullshit way of talking makes him sound elegant, but he still acts like the little pimp from Pittsburgh he's always been. That's a tad pathetic, isn't it?"

Derrick moved forward a little, but Dane checked him with a small gesture. "Still too impulsive for your own good, aren't you, Elena? I wonder—all those years ago, was it impulse that led you to betray me?"

"I don't know what the hell you're talking about."

"Such poise! When I compare your response to the rather anxious one of your former partner, I must say, I'm tempted to believe you." Dane studied her again, then glanced at Hitch, who was edging back. "Derrick, please make sure Detective Hitchcock remains with us."

"Mr. Dane, please—" Hitch began, but fell silent as Derrick put an arm around his shoulders—a friendly gesture belied by Hitch's wince—and moved him closer to Dane. Hitch's face was pale, but he said nothing.

"Let's not waste time," Dane said. "Let me tell you my concerns. It's just so—how shall I say it?—so *inconvenient* to be accused of murders one hasn't committed. And now, at a time when I am winning the trust of businessmen and civic leaders—"

"Buying votes and favors is more like it," Elena scoffed.

"Calling the kettle black, my dear? In return for a favor, I believe I once received certain assurances from you."

She flinched and glanced at Frank. In a low voice, she said, "I kept my word, Whitey, and until tonight you kept yours." She smiled coldly. "At this rate, I'm going to stop believing in the old adage about honor among thieves."

"How tragic that would be! Perhaps I have been misinformed." He turned toward Hitch, who appeared to be close to fainting, then back to Elena. "But you, my dear, seem so much more likely to have been an enemy posing as friend! Someone who had information about where I would be that evening. Someone who knew I would be among friends whose—shall we say, histories?—might be an obstacle for jurors asked to believe my alibi."

"I'm not the only one who knew where you'd be that night," Elena said. "And neither is Hitch, for that matter. You surround yourself with all these muscle-bound boy toys, they start to get jealous and spiteful."

He shook his head. "Elena, Elena. Do strive to be more original."

"What are you worried about, anyway?" Frank said. "The Randolph case never went to trial."

"Oh, that's another sore point. I've never been allowed to prove my innocence, have I? Indeed, I'd even settle for having all that phony evidence in my own hands. But someone else has it. Suppose it's suddenly rediscovered in the LPPD property room?"

Frank shrugged. "Then your lawyers say the department lost control of the evidence for ten years, and the D.A. says good-bye to the case."

"Detective Harriman, I have no doubt I would be able to extricate myself from any legal difficulties, but surely you understand how offended I am that someone attempted to set me up?"

"Get over it," Elena said.

"No, I'm afraid I'm the type who isn't forgiving. I keep thinking of all the elements that had to be in place, and I cannot help but see that I was betrayed by someone who knew me." He began counting off points on his long, milky fingers. "Someone who knew that I favored deck shoes of a particular type, who knew that I would not be out on the *Cygnet* myself that night, who knew how to steal a boat—and let's face it, who learns more about tricks of the criminal trade than police officers?—someone who made sure Lefebvre, the department's star homicide detective, was at the marina and made certain that he discovered the *Amanda*."

"Phil made that discovery on his own."

"Did he? Or were you there to make sure he lingered near it? You see, I've heard a recent rumor that my old friend Elena Rosario—"

"I have never been your friend!"

"—Elena Rosario was being naughty with Lefebvre. You can hardly deny that rumor, my dear."

"I'm proud of every moment I spent with Phil."

"But when it comes to me—"

"I can't think of anything I'm more ashamed of."

Dane laughed. "Derrick?"

Frank stepped forward to protect her, but he had misjudged the target—the wasp man moved like lightning and planted a hard right in Hitch's gut. Hitch doubled over and went to his knees, retching on the sand.

"On the other hand, Detective Hitchcock, I'm afraid, has no shame," Dane said. "That's what leads me to believe he lied to me a few years ago when he told me you tipped off Lefebvre."

Elena stared at Hitch in disbelief. Hitch was weeping.

"Yes," Dane said, looking between them, "I do believe I have my answer now. To one question at least. Myles? Derrick? Detective Hitchcock seems to be in need of medical attention. Let's remove him to a place where he will get the level of care he deserves, shall we?"

"Frank, Elena!" Hitch pleaded. "I'm begging you, please! Don't let him take me!"

"What happened to 'no violence'?" Elena said to Dane.

"Oh, dear. I'm afraid I meant to you or Detective Harriman."

Myles hoisted Hitch to his feet and held on to him, keeping Hitch's arms pulled back.

Frank stepped a little closer to Derrick, who in turn moved back slightly, staying out of range. Frank wondered at this—he didn't believe for a moment that Derrick was afraid of him. He glanced at Elena. She met his eyes now, and although she did not betray it by any signal to him, he knew she was calm—and ready. Again watching Derrick, he said to Dane, "Let Hitch go."

"You would speak up on behalf of this piece of offal?" Dane said. "Well, then—perhaps I should hear what Detective Hitchcock has to say for himself."

Derrick moved closer to Hitch, his right side toward Frank. Frank shifted his own stance.

"Mr. Dane," Hitch began, "you've got to believe me—I didn't know what he planned."

"Of whom are you speaking?"

"I don't know! The guy called me—that's all it was, a phone call. Disguised his voice. I swear it. I swear it!"

Dane waited.

"I told him where you'd be, that's all. Nothing more than that—nothing! He—he paid me. He left a little cash for me, but I swear to you, I didn't know he was gonna try to stick you with a murder rap! You've got to believe me, Mr. Dane!"

Dane sighed. "A false assumption. Derrick?"

Just as Derrick's fist connected with Hitch's face, Frank moved, landing a hard kick to the outside of the wasp man's right knee. Frank heard a muffled cracking noise—Derrick gave a shout of pain and lost his balance as the knee gave. He rolled to the right. Elena grabbed his left wrist as he fell, yanked his arm out straight, and kneed him hard in the face. He dropped like a stone.

"Enough," Dane said.

Myles dropped Hitch, whose bloodied nose sent a crimson flow over the front of his shirt. He held his hands open, out at his sides, a gesture of half-surrender.

"Now look what a mess you've made!" Dane scolded. "None of this was necessary."

"You thought I'd stand here and watch you beat the crap out of Hitch?" Frank asked.

"He can't be very precious to you. You've just halted the only punishment he's likely to receive."

"You've learned what you wanted to know. Besides, if you think he arranged the killings on the *Amanda*, you're a hell of a lot dumber than I think you are."

"Detective Harriman! I'm so pleased. Now we come to my interest in your investigations. I believe you can see why I'm determined to bring Trent Randolph's killer to justice."

Derrick rolled to his side and groaned.

"It had better wait, unless you want to watch your lapdog suffer."

"Arrest him," Elena said, and Frank could see the misery in her—that she knew what that would mean to her. "Arrest all of them."

"I don't think he will," Dane said. "You see, I believe Detective Harriman is better at thinking ahead than you are, my impulsive—oh, don't scowl—all right, you aren't my friend."

Frank bent to help Hitch to his feet.

"Take Detective Hitchcock, for example. Detective Harriman realizes that he has no real proof of anything other than Detective Hitchcock's confession of conspiring to convict me of murder."

"He just saw two of your men assault an officer, on your orders."

"And he knows that poor Derrick never attempted to defend himself from either of you. Besides, I promise you, your name will not be left out of any statements I make to the police."

She hesitated, then said, "Don't let that stop you, Frank. This is your chance."

Frank pulled Hitch's arm over his shoulders. He knew an impulse of his own, to reach down and grab a handful of sand and throw it into Dane's good eye. Childish, he told himself. "Help me with Hitch," he said to her.

Elena moved to Hitch's right side, but as they lifted him, she reached across Hitch's shoulders to place her hand on Frank's arm. "Frank—"

"What would happen to Seth then, Elena?"

"Maybe he'd be better off with—"

"Fuck you and your self-pity," he said. "Think of Seth."

She lowered her hand to Hitch's waist, so that she was no longer touching Frank.

Dane came closer and patted Hitch's cheek. "You do know I hate unfinished business, don't you, Robert? I know you lied to me to protect your own hide, but why did you choose Elena for your scapegoat? Revenge because she let Lefebvre get into her pants?" He laughed.

Frank suddenly felt Hitch's full weight—Elena had let go of him.

Her punch came from Dane's left—hard and fast across the bridge of his nose, catching him in the right eye. Dane howled and grabbed at her.

Frank dropped Hitch and stepped between them, shoving Dane aside. Myles tried to come to Dane's aid and soon demanded all of Frank's attention. He landed a dizzying blow above Frank's eye, splitting his brow. Frank brought his own left up hard under Myles's jaw and followed it with a quick right to his gut. Myles's head snapped back, and the air left his lungs in a whoosh. Frank deflected a wild punch and hit him again in the face, throwing everything he had into it. Myles fell on his ass with a thud. He stayed there.

"Myles, Myles, Myles," Dane said. "What were my orders?"

Myles lowered his head as if in shame.

Frank tried to wipe the blood from his right eye and saw that Dane had Elena pinned beneath him. He stumbled toward them. Dane tilted his head, trying to see around the swelling in his own right eye. Seeing Frank's injury, he laughed.

"Shall we leave it at an eye for an eye, Detective Harriman?"

Frank nodded.

"Elena?"

"Yes, damn you."

Dane released her and said, "Myles, help Derrick."

Elena came toward Frank, but he turned away. He pulled his T-shirt off, which required a set of motions that made his head swim. He held it to his brow to stanch the bleeding.

"Get up," he heard Elena say to Hitch. "You've had enough time to get your wind back."

Hitch shakily came to his feet.

"Another time, Detective Harriman," Whitey Dane said as they slowly walked away. "Another time."

41

"You need your sleep, too," Irene whispered as she came into the guest bedroom.

"Can't," he said. "Careful—don't trip over the dogs."

"Your head still bothering you?"

"I'll be all right. It's a good thing I was awake, anyway—he just had a nightmare about the fire. I think all of this is tougher on him than he lets on."

Seth and Irene had returned from the rink, worried when Frank hadn't shown up for his game, pulling into the driveway just after Hitch drove off.

Irene had rolled down a window, said, "Get him into the backseat" to Elena, but Frank went inside long enough to wash his hands and face, get another shirt on, and lock up. In the car, Seth had been frightened and wouldn't let him out of his sight. Frank thought of lying to him and telling him he had tripped over something in the garage, but decided against it. He wasn't going to lie to Seth if he could help it.

"I had a fight with a bad guy," he said.

Seth's eyes widened.

"He kicked the bad guy's ass," Elena said.

"Cool! Is the bad guy dead?"

"What a bloodthirsty kid you are," she said, making him laugh. "No, he isn't dead, but he knows better than to mess with Frank."

"Did you help Frank fight him?"

She glanced nervously at Frank. "No, Frank didn't need any help from me."

Irene must have heard Elena's slight hesitation, though, because she looked into the rearview mirror at them.

"Tell me about skating," Frank said.

While he was waiting to get stitched up, and out of Seth's and Elena's hearing, he told Irene the full story.

Now she sat beside him on the edge of Seth's bed. He put an arm around her, but left his other hand in Seth's grasp.

"You're disappointed in Elena, aren't you?" she whispered.

"Yes," Frank said. "I am."

"What about Hitch?"

"So far he's leaving Elena's name out of it." Hale himself had called to give Frank the news that Hitch had walked into headquarters with his lawyer in tow.

"Do you think he could cause her trouble?"

"Maybe. At some point she knew Hitch was on Dane's payroll. I don't think she was on it herself or Dane wouldn't have let her walk away from her job with the narcotics squad—she would have been too great an asset to him. And he would have kept better tabs on her after she left."

Irene nodded. "She couldn't have had much dirt on either of them, or they would have seen her as a big threat."

"If he had ever really believed that, Dane would have had her killed. He came here tonight because he had questions. I don't know if he believes Hitch about the anonymous call, but I do. Lefebvre wrote notes about getting an anonymous tip on the night the *Amanda* was attacked."

They sat in silence for a time, listening to the steady rhythm of Seth's breathing. The dogs awakened and moved out of the room. Frank could hear their nails clicking on the floor as they moved toward the front door.

Irene said, "So if Hitch had come forward earlier about the anonymous call—"

"Then maybe the department wouldn't have stayed so obsessed with the idea that Dane was the killer. And who knows? Maybe Seth Randolph and Phil Lefebvre would be alive today. Instead, an asshole like Hitch is crying for mercy, and four good people are cold in their graves. You can play the 'if' game another way—if Elena had told what she knew about Hitch, maybe he would have caved in ten years ago and Lefebvre would be alive."

Suddenly, the dogs began barking wildly—startling both of them.

Seth awakened and sat up, wide-eyed with fear.

"Just the dogs," Frank said, but Seth held his hand more tightly.

They waited, expecting the dogs to quickly settle down. Instead, the barking increased in intensity.

"What the hell has gotten into them?" Irene said, and started to get up.

"For God's sake, stay here," Frank said, pulling her back. "I'll check it out."

The dogs were growling now, focusing on something beyond the front door. They began barking again.

Seth held tightly to him. "It's the bad guy. He's come back."

"You didn't believe your mom when she told you I kicked his ass?" Frank said lightly. "Stay here with Irene, okay? I'll ask your mom to come in here, too. I'm going to take a look outside. The dogs are probably just after a skunk or something, but let's play it safe."

"Okay," Seth said, but he still looked scared.

As Frank stepped out into the hall, he saw that the dogs had awakened Elena. "What's wrong?" she asked.

"I'll handle it," he said curtly. "Your son needs you."

She looked away from him, but didn't argue.

Frank took his gun from its locked compartment, loaded it, and moved to the front of the house. He looked through the door's peephole and noticed it was dark out on the porch. He glanced at the switch—it was on. The bulb was new; he had just changed it about a week ago.

His head started throbbing again.

There weren't many windows on this side of the house—no way to get a clear view of what was out there. He moved to the back of the house instead, and after taking a moment to look around, opened the door to the patio. The dogs liked the plan, too, and raced out ahead of him, rounding the corner of the house. Dunk, the German shepherd, was pawing furiously at the back gate in a "let me at 'em" style. Frank used their noise to cover his own movements and reached the back gate just as he heard an engine start up. He let them out, and they sprinted toward a white van—Deke, the black Labrador, giving chase even after it pulled away. Dunk, meanwhile, concentrated on Frank's car, sniffing all around it, especially curious about the driver's side.

Frank started toward it, then came to a halt.

Watch your back, Detective Harriman.

The thought made him look over his shoulder. His next-door neighbor's lights were on. Jack was a night owl—and a good friend.

He called the dogs back. Deke had joined Dunk now, and they were reluctant to leave the driver's side of the car. Frank called to them again, more sharply.

He hurried them inside the house. "Grab some clothes and the animals," he said to the others, "and let's go over to Jack's."

Once there, he made a series of calls.

Not long after they reached Jack's, the bomb squad arrived. The explosives experts only looked at the car for a few moments before rapping on the door of Jack's house and asking for Frank.

"You were right to call us—there's at least one device on the car. Why don't you take everybody down to the beach? We're going to evacuate the neighborhood."

There was some grumbling among his neighbors, but most were more anxious than angry. Jack had the foresight to bring some wood, and they built a fire. Cody yowled pitifully from inside his cat carrier, and Seth had to be convinced again and again that only the cat's dignity was wounded and that it would not be a good idea to let him out. Elena sat slightly apart from all of them, looking out at the water and not conversing with the others.

Seth asked Frank where the bad guy lived, and seeing that he was feeling afraid, Frank tried to distract him. The water was relatively calm, and so he showed Seth how to find a good skipping stone and how to throw it. Seth took to it quickly and was soon challenging Jack to try to beat his record.

Frank had wondered if Jack's biker appearance—his tattoos, shaved head, and scarred face—would make Seth feel uneasy, but the two of them hit it off immediately. Seth listened with rapt attention while Jack began regaling him with stories from his days on the road.

"You've heard them all before," Irene whispered to Frank. "Catch a few z's. Seth will be safe." At her urging, he pillowed his head on her lap, and as she softly stroked his hair, allowed himself to fall asleep.

She roused him some time later, when they were told they could return to their homes. The sun was up, but it was still cool along the beach. He shook off his sleepiness and stretched, then did his best to get past the aches from the fight with Myles as they made their way back. Seth took his hand, but talked of nothing but Jack. Frank almost wished he hadn't seen Irene's look of sympathy.

Seth's new hero had fallen back to the rear of the group, to talk to Elena. Frank told himself that being angry with her accomplished nothing. But he would think of the man in the wreckage of the Cessna, and this boy without a father, and he could not bring himself to forgive her for her silence.

His aging Volvo was, he was relieved to see, still in one piece.

"Two devices," one of the bomb squad members told him. "And for working so quickly, he worked neatly. One was on your ignition. Actually, that was the backup device, in case the first one failed—a pressure device."

"Where was that one?"

"Under the driver's-side seat. When you told me the dogs had been interested in that side of the car, I made sure we checked it out. The device was rigged so that if you sat down on the seat, your weight would trigger an explosion. If something went wrong with that, when you started the car, you would have triggered a second device, under the hood."

Frank's mouth went dry, but he managed to ask, "Any clues to the identity of the bomber?"

"When we study the devices, we'll probably know more about him than he'd ever guess we could know. They weren't unique in construction, per se, but—strange thing is, they are built almost exactly like the ones a guy named Wendell Leroy Wallace built seven or eight years ago—same materials, same design, everything—and the really weird thing is, his initials were on this one—W.L.W."

"I remember those cases," Frank said. "Series of car bombs. He had some grudge against the company he worked for."

"Right, that's the one. But Wendell's been dead for years. He went the way of a lot of the guys who take up this bomb-making work—the on-the-job training is murder. I'll bet there are still little pieces of him embedded in the oak tree near what was left of his garage."

Frank thought for a moment, then said, "Who did the lab work on those cases, county or city?"

"County, mostly. We've got the bomb squad. But of course, there was cooperation between your lab and ours. On that case, we were going all-out, so I'm sure the information was shared."

"You've been in this business awhile?" Frank asked.

"Yes, and I've still got all my fingers, although my hearing's going."

"How long?"

"About eighteen years. Why?"

"What's your guess about this guy—the one who placed these bombs?"

"An off-the-record guess? Whoever made them hasn't done this sort of thing around here lately, because I would have recognized anything done in Wendell's style. So it's someone who has read about Wendell, or studied him somehow, because I don't believe that Wendell's come back from the dead. I almost would believe that, because like Wendell, this guy is as anal as all get-out."

"What do you mean?"

"A neat little set of packages, all lined up just so, everything clean, ends of the wires carefully clipped and attached, and so on. I'd like to see him caught, because I don't need any careful bombers—especially any who can install quickly—working in my neck of the woods." He looked at the stitches in Frank's eyebrow, the black eye and other bruises, and said, "I suppose it's foolish to ask if you have any enemies?"

"A few."

"Well, in your line of work, I guess that's a given." He started to walk off, then paused and turned back. "Hey, you think you could show me how to fold a paper airplane the way you do?"

"What?"

"We found this one under the passenger seat, figured it must be yours. I've never seen one folded so elaborately."

"I have," Frank said as the man showed him the plane. "Once before." And he suddenly remembered the form in one of Professor Wilkes's folders—the contest entry that had been filled out so neatly by W. L. Wallace.

42

"Myles, why these lucubrations?" Dane said, entering Myles's small study. "Are you feeling guilty about striking Detective Harriman?"

Myles looked up from his desk to see Mr. Dane smiling at him. Mr. Dane was clad in a blue silk dressing gown into which a pattern of swans had been embroidered. Only the slight swelling and darkening of the area around his right eye marred his beauty.

"I do regret that deeply, Mr. Dane, but only because it went against your wishes."

"Naturally you felt compelled to defend me, Myles. Please don't lose another moment's sleep over it."

"Yes, sir. But I should point out that I've stayed up late going over these papers because I believe I've found the pattern we were looking for, sir. I wanted to be certain I was on the right track."

"What track is that?"

"I've found something in common in many of the eleven cases you asked me to look into—something other than the fact that the defendants either died unexpectedly or were later convicted of crimes of which you believed them to be innocent."

"Yes?"

"Judge Lewis Kerr, sir."

"Kerr? Are you certain?"

"Yes, sir."

"I'm afraid I don't follow you, Myles."

"Of the eleven, nine of them had been tried before Judge Kerr on other charges."

"And found guilty?"

"No, sir. The judge dismissed their cases. On what some would call technicalities."

"Yes, but we all know what that means. When the police fail to obey the law, that law is suddenly reduced to a technicality."

"Yes, sir."

"And the remaining two cases?"

"I believe we are looking at random chance there, sir."

"You interest me, Myles. Tell me more about the other nine."

And so Myles spent an hour reviewing cases with Mr. Dane. At the end of that time, Mr. Dane said, "I would like to have a conversation with Judge Kerr. I don't think he is our enemy, but he has met our enemy."

"'The enemy of my enemy is my friend'?"

"Something like that, yes."

Myles glanced at the clock. "Later today Judge Kerr will dedicate the new courthouse building—the new annex, I should say."

Dane smiled. "My dear Myles, what would I ever do without you?"

43

The Looking Glass Man sat in the cockpit of the Cessna, engine running, cleared for takeoff. He had completed his final preflight checks and taxied to the assigned runway, but now he hesitated.

He had laid his trap for Harriman. Harriman would be dead before he could back out of his driveway.

He knew Harriman had seen his van—damn those dogs! Still, he doubted Harriman suspected more than a little late-night snooping. At most, he might check to see if an arsonist had placed gasoline-soaked rags on his front porch. That was the behavior Harriman would expect of a man in a white van.

The Looking Glass Man had taken care of the porch light first. He had simply used a stream of ice water from a spray bottle to accomplish that. Then he had broken into the car and put the pressure bomb in place without incident. It was only when he lifted the hood that the dogs gave the alarm—the ignition device, probably an entirely unnecessary precaution, was the one that had nearly got him caught. But nearly getting caught was not what made him hesitate now.

It was Hitchcock, of course.

He had failed to see how deeply involved the man was with Dane. That was irritating. Years ago, when he made his plans to kill Trent Randolph, he had used Hitchcock—chosen him, because of all the members of the task force that was after Dane, he seemed the most vulnerable. Hitch often complained of being in debt. But like others in the department, he seemed completely devoted to putting Dane away.

To think he had been fooled! Fooled by that doughnut-eating dumpling Hitchcock!

It took so much of the pleasure out of Dane's defeat. Why hadn't he seen that if he could bribe Hitchcock, so could Dane?

The tower called, asking if there was a problem.

He replied that he wasn't sure, that he was going to return to the hangar.

He had time to spare. One should never fly an airplane while distracted. If he had lived, Phil Lefebvre could have given lectures about that.

He made up a story for the mechanic about the engine not running smoothly. The mechanic, who had long shown his resentment of the Looking Glass Man's desire for perfection, agreed to take a look at it.

The Looking Glass Man removed the smallest of the canvas bags from among his luggage, went into the restroom, and, after unfolding the plastic trash bag he carried in his pocket and laying it out on the floor, set the canvas bag on top of it. He took out a second, smaller bag and placed it on the edge of the sink. On this he neatly aligned the disinfectant spray, paper towels, glass cleaner, and good plain soap that he always carried with him, making sure all the labels pointed the same way.

His complaints to the owners of this property had ensured that this restroom was cleaner than many public restrooms, but that was not saying much at all.

He sprayed the disinfectant first, not because he would ever use the toilet in a place like this or even because he thought the spray was effective.

He liked the smell of it.

His mother had believed in the powers of this particular brand and had sprayed it rather liberally about their house. For the Looking Glass Man, this scent was as homey as that of baking cookies or hot mulled cider to others.

Next, he cleaned off the mirror.

He studied himself.

The man in the mirror seemed a trifle sad.

I know just the thing to cheer you up, he told the man in the mirror.

The man in the mirror appeared bashful.

Yes, I thought so. You should have just spoken up, you know. There's really no reason to deny yourself the treat, is there?

The reflected face showed its complete agreement.

It's settled, then. You've worked hard all these years. That was the trouble, wasn't it? You can't walk away—or fly away—now. Not when all you've dedicated yourself to is about to reach its conclusion. Well, you shall have your treat! A few minutes of watching the dust settle over Judge Kerr's tomb won't bring you to harm.

He looked away from the mirror and began to wash his hands. He didn't use antibacterial soaps, because he believed that overexposure to antibiotics was bad policy. Warm water and soap would do the job. No use overdoing it.

When he was finished, he would don gloves and put everything away, carefully bagging the trash in the large plastic bag without touching the filthy bag itself. For now, he enjoyed the almost scalding water on his hands.

He heard a sound, an unfamiliar sound, that stopped almost as soon as he became aware of it. He smiled a little nervously as recognition came to him. He had been humming.

He never hummed.

Maybe he was happy.

He looked in the mirror and thought perhaps he was.

But still, he couldn't be sure.

44

Although the bomb squad had assured him that the car was free of explosives now, it had been hard for him to get in the driver's seat and turn the key. He started to park in the department garage, decided he didn't want to make it easy for the bomber to take another shot at it, and left the car a couple of blocks away.

There were three calls on his voice mail, two that had come in after he had left the office on Thursday. The first was from the FAA. Vince Adams, Michael Pickens, Paul Haycroft, and Dr. Al Larson had pilot's licenses. No one else on Lefebvre's list of suspects was on the FAA's list.

The second was from Blake Halloran, the arson investigator, asking Frank to give him a call back. Frank called, but got Halloran's voice mail. Phone tag.

The third was from Chief Hale's secretary. The chief wanted Frank to meet with him at a quarter to nine.

He took the paper airplane from his pocket and studied it, then looked over at Vince's desk.

The surface was dusty. Papers were piled up loosely in the in box. The phone sat in the middle of the blotter, where Vince had left it after his last call. Vince was only slightly less sloppy than Pete. Not the man he was after. Had he ever believed in the possibility? Vince? He felt a wave of shame. Yes, he had.

Then he told himself that he should have felt shame only if he *hadn't* considered Vince as a suspect. He had to consider everyone, no matter how close they were to him. That was the problem with these cases all along—no one had looked at any member of the department other than Lefebvre.

Commissioner Pickens would not have had access to the property room. Which left Haycroft and Larson. Something Dane had said came back to him: "*Who learns more about tricks of the criminal trade than police officers?*"

A crime lab worker—especially one with years of experience. He wouldn't just see it all, he would study it in detail. There was incredible range in these cases, the sort of range a criminalist would see, especially in a lab the size of the LPPD's. Arson, explosives, booby traps, forgery. Murder.

He felt his stomach tighten. The implications of having a murderer working in the crime lab went far beyond the Randolph cases or Lefebvre's death—what else had been tampered with? And how could such an expert be caught?

The lab wasn't just a place to learn how crimes were committed, he realized. A criminalist would also know how to avoid getting caught—how to avoid leaving evidence—or how to leave just enough false evidence to point an investigation in a particular direction. He'd have easy access to the property room. Frank, working in an elite detective group like Homicide, didn't have as much access to evidence.

While a detective handling evidence from a case to which he wasn't assigned would risk discovery, lab workers handled evidence from many cases. A criminalist knew which investigators were working which cases—so that he would have known how to devise an anonymous tip that might interest Lefebvre or anyone else.

And somewhere along the way a forensic scientist might easily have learned how a man like Wendell Leroy Wallace devised a signature bomb to be placed under a car seat.

He felt his mouth go dry.

The bomb squad expert had said the maker of the bomb was neat and tidy—anal.

Al Larson's pristine office came to mind. Even other workers in the lab thought he went too far in his demands for neatness. He would have the most access to the highest number of cases. He could walk into any crime scene and never be suspected of doing anything other than being a hands-on supervisor. He was probably the department liaison to the county investigation of the Wendell Leroy Wallace car-bombing cases. He had not only worn the type of watch the *Amanda*'s attacker wore, he had had a supply of them so that he could replace the DNA-laden watchband when new testing capabilities made that necessary.

He had means. He had opportunity. And he had motives in every case.

Randolph had been a man of science, someone who could have noticed irregularities in the lab. He had supported improvement of the lab, but he had also been critical of it. He was murdered the night before he was due to meet with the chief and other commissioners about problems in the lab. Larson had known about the meeting.

What if Larson suspected that Randolph's report would lead to his being fired or worse?

Or worse. Frank frowned. What could have been worse for Larson?

Being discredited, unable to work in the field or to testify? Having previous cases overturned because of incompetence? Or corruption. Cases fixed against people like Whitey Dane. Tainting of evidence.

What if Trent Randolph was about to reveal something that might eventually lead to criminal prosecution of Larson? Frank thought of the lax property room procedures that had been in effect before Flynn stepped in. He thought of the watch in the evidence box.

Ten years ago, and Larson had been on the job at least fifteen—more than long enough to have learned all about Wendell Leroy Wallace. Jesus—how many cases might be affected?

Randolph had urgently wanted to meet with Hale, Pickens, Soury, and Larson. How desperate might Larson have been to prevent that meeting? There would have been a reprieve of sorts when the chief delayed the meeting until Monday morning. Time had been running out, though. Larson could have easily learned that Trent Randolph was going to take his new yacht to Catalina that weekend. He could have laid his plans and seen an opportunity to get a measure of revenge on an old enemy—Whitey Dane.

Larson had an excellent motive to seek revenge against Dane. One of Dane's minions had murdered Larson's only son.

Trent Randolph had to be stopped before he had a chance to meet with Hale and the others. The marina presented an opportunity to lay the blame on Dane.

Frank wondered if Amanda and Seth Randolph would have been spared if they had remained belowdecks. Amanda had gone up the companionway because she heard her father arguing with someone. Had she been killed because she heard Randolph say something that might identify his attacker? Perhaps Larson had planned to kill them—he could control physical evidence more easily than he could control witnesses.

Ironically, until the moment at the press conference when he reacted to hearing the watch, Seth was useful in pointing the blame toward Dane. Likewise, Phil Lefebvre became dangerous once it was clear he doubted that Dane was the killer.

Great, Frank thought. Now all he had to do was prove that any of it was true.

He called Hale's office to say he'd be there at nine. Last night he had given the bomb squad expert the paper airplane contest entry form, on the remote chance that the sheriff's department lab could learn something from it. He trusted Koza, his own department's questioned documents man, but he found himself wanting to keep the evidence for these cases out of the reach of the LPPD.

Suddenly he remembered the neatly printed note from Larson, the one saying he had gone home sick, but wanted to meet about the Randolph cases. What had he done with it? He had read it and set it aside on his desk. He looked through his in box and all the desk drawers. Nothing. He told himself that it was one of hundreds of pieces of paper that crossed his path in a week, that he wasn't clairvoyant and that yesterday he had no reason to think the note might become a piece of evidence. Still, he cussed himself out for not locking it up.

He decided to work with what he did have. He was going over Lefebvre's notes again, looking at them to see if anything excluded Larson as a suspect, when Pete came in, sat down at his desk, and said, "Wish you would have let me know you didn't plan to show up at the game last night. But maybe Vince is right—you don't give a shit about anybody but yourself."

Frank looked up.

Pete's jaw dropped. "Jesus, Mary, and Joseph—what the fuck happened to you?"

"I kicked a bad guy's ass."

"What?"

"Nothing. Just a run-in with an asshole on the beach. I meet assholes everywhere these days."

Pete frowned and looked as if he had more to say, but the phone on his desk rang. "Baird," he answered.

Frank went back to Lefebvre's notes, but he became aware, from Pete's side of the conversation, that the grapevine was humming. "Hitch" and "Dane" and "confession" and "bomb squad" were said frequently. Without ever looking over at him, Frank knew Pete well enough to tell from his voice that he was shocked. The long silence that followed his hanging up the phone was as big an indicator as any. Frank timed it at a full five minutes before Pete said, "So . . ."

Frank waited.

"So . . . I hear you had a little trouble out at the house."

Frank gave a short laugh.

"You doing all right?"

His head felt as if a team of mules was trying to buck its way out of his skull, he hadn't had a full night's sleep in a week, and the simple act of starting his car this morning had nearly required more courage than he thought he could come up with. "I'm fine," he said.

Vince came in, followed by Reed. They looked at him uneasily. So they knew, too.

"Everybody okay at your place?" Vince asked.

"Just dandy."

He saw the others exchange glances.

"All this must be hard on the kid," Pete said. "I like the little guy. He's a tough little kid."

"Lefebvre," Frank said angrily. "The kid's name is Seth Lefebvre. I know you don't like the name much."

"Oh, no," Pete said. "I love the name Lefebvre. I can't get tired of saying it. I've got the zeal of a convert now. Build a statue to the guy. Call the town the City of Lefebvre. I mean it. I can admit when I'm wrong."

"Very big of you, Pete—but you're wasting it on me. In another ten years, ask Seth to accept your apologies."

"Frank—"

"Tell him you're sorry you all had your minds made up about his dad, because his dad didn't know how to be one of the boys. That you're sorry you put your faith in a guy like Hitch instead of Lefebvre, because Hitch showed up for hockey games. Tell him that because of bullshit like that, you're sorry his dad never had a chance to see what a 'tough little kid' he is."

Vince and Pete looked away. Reed said quietly, "You're right."

"That's no comfort to the *kid*, is it? Two nights ago he brings out one of his big treasures to show me. You know what it was, Vince? An answering machine tape. A goddamned answering machine tape. That's the only way he could hear his own father's voice. He's nine, and he's played it over and over—less than a dozen words. That's what you left for the son of Phil Lefebvre."

The room was silent.

"You give Lefebvre the cold shoulder, like the one I've been getting around here lately? What did he do to get cut out of the herd?"

"Look, I apologize for that, too," Pete said. "But Phil—Frank, he was always a loner."

"From birth? You never did anything to make the guy feel isolated, is that it?"

Pete opened his mouth to protest, closed it, and looked away.

"Yes, I read the files," Frank said. "And you wonder why the guy didn't trust you? Any of you?"

Pete turned red.

"Frank," Vince said, "can't we just put this all behind us?"

"What, Vince? Get together for breakfast, like old times?"

Frank strode out of the room.

Without conscious thought, really, of where he was going, he ended up at the lab. Once there, he decided to look for Haycroft. As the assistant director of the lab, Haycroft might have an idea as to Larson's expertise and recent movements. The door to Haycroft's office was closed, and Frank received no response when he knocked. He thought of the reprimand he had received from the toxicologist on the previous day, then tried the doorknob anyway. It was locked. Maybe the toxicologist had told everyone that he was going around stealing personal effects, such as photographs.

He looked through other areas of the lab, but didn't see Haycroft. He noticed Larson's door was open and peered in. There was a neat stack of papers in the center of the desk. The photograph was gone.

"Frank! What brings you here this morning?"

He turned to see Al Larson walking toward him. Smiling, although it faltered slightly at the sight of his black eye.

Frank forced a smile of his own and said, "What a surprise, right?"

Larson looked at him uncertainly. "What can I do for you?"

He was tempted to say, "You haven't seen that note you left for me yesterday, by any chance, have you?" But he could see he had already made Larson wary—which wouldn't help him build a solid case against the man. Or stay alive. "Actually," he said, "I wanted to talk to Paul Haycroft."

"Oh, I'm sorry, Paul's taking some time off. He won't be in for a week."

"Really? He didn't mention anything about that when I saw him yesterday."

"No, probably not. A death in the family. He called me at home late last night—he so seldom misses work, I couldn't think of denying his request. Will this cause difficulties with any of your cases in progress? I'd be happy to give my personal attention to anything you need."

I'm sure you would. "Thanks, but I'll just wait until he returns."

"Fine, then. Let me know if you change your mind."

He had almost reached the door of the lab when Mary Michaels, the toxicologist, saw him. She winced at the bruises on his face.

He held up his hands and said, "I'm not taking anything with me this time, I promise."

"Hmm," she said, eyeing him. "Maybe I ought to pat you down, just to make sure."

He looked away, embarrassed by the comment.

"Hell, no," another voice said. "If you're going to make offers like that, tell him you'll strip-search him."

He turned to see Vince.

"Jesus, Harriman," Vince said, laughing. "You're blushing."

"Well," she said to Vince, "nobody's going to offer to strip-search *you.* You've already let every woman in the department see that you aren't carrying a thing."

"That's not true," Vince said. "I've never been naked with Louise Oswald."

She made a face and walked away.

"We used to date," he explained to Frank.

"Ah. That accounts for the rapport."

Vince shrugged. "Yeah, that's me. Mr. Smooth. You got a minute?"

Frank almost said no—it would have been easy to make up an excuse. He felt awkward, and angry still, and wished that Vince would have given him a little more time to cool off. But he wasn't proud of losing his temper, and he didn't want the tension between them to get worse. So he said, "Sure. Let's move out of the doorway."

A small table and two chairs were nearby. They moved a few steps closer, but neither man sat down.

"Upstairs," Vince began, "you said something that's been eating at me. About Phil. You really think he didn't trust us? I mean—the guy seldom worked with partners, but I just figured he always thought he was better than us. Shit, he *was* better—at the job, anyway. But that's different from thinking that the people you're working with are crooked. And that's what you meant, right?"

Frank hesitated, then said, "I don't think it was a personal thing, Vince."

"What the hell are you talking about? How can that *not* be personal?"

"I'm saying he didn't know who in the department could be trusted, who couldn't. It wasn't a matter of mistrusting any one individual."

Vince was clearly unsatisfied with this answer, but seemed unwilling to start a new argument with Frank. He indicated the lab door and asked, "You coming or going?"

"Going. I was trying to see Haycroft, but he's on funeral leave."

"Jesus, I'm sorry to hear that. That poor guy can't have much family left."

"What do you mean?"

Vince looked extremely uncomfortable. "You know—you read about the robbery." Seeing Frank's blank look, he added in a low voice, "The fax Irene sent you from the newspaper."

"That was Larson's son," Frank said, bewildered.

"The hell it was. You think I don't know who died in that robbery?" He sighed and shook his head. "Let me tell you something, Frank. Not a day goes by I don't think about that family—every single one of those five people who were killed—and wonder if somehow—maybe if I'd been more patient with Lisa or forced her to get help . . ." He swallowed hard. "But I gave up on her, and look what happened. I let her go her own way after the divorce, and she gets mixed up with one of Dane's bunch, and that prick Sudas kills the security guard, Haycroft's ex-wife, Haycroft's son, the ex's new husband—Dillon—and Dillon's little girl from his first marriage. And Lisa—I know Lisa, and I know she didn't know what was going to happen, not really—and God knows fucking Sudas might as well have shot her, too, because in her head, that's the last day that ever was. I know that as sure as I'm sitting here. I haven't been able to look Haycroft in the eye ever since. He's never said a word to me about it or blamed me in any way, but I sure as hell know that boy was his."

Frank sat down. "My God."

"Hey," Vince said, "you feeling okay? You look a little pale."

Frank leaned his elbows on the table and cradled his forehead in his palms. "My God . . ."

"Frank? Maybe you should have taken the day off. You're looking like hell."

"No—no, it's not that, it's just that—Haycroft—Jesus, Kit was Haycroft's boy?"

"How many times I gotta tell you? Yes. Kit Haycroft. That's why I feel sorry for the guy now—"

"Don't. Don't feel sorry for him," Frank said. "When I think of those photographs of Amanda Randolph . . . and all the others! Christ, what a bastard!"

Vince narrowed his eyes. "You aren't making a hell of a lot of sense."

"Listen, you were asking about Lefebvre not trusting anyone. He was trying to figure something out—a day or so before he was murdered—"

"*Murdered?*"

It hit him, then. Just like Lefebvre, he had been working alone, not trusting anyone. He didn't really blame Lefebvre—things had happened too quickly for him to figure out whom he could trust. Lefebvre didn't have much more than a day to work out what might be going on with the case.

And now, ten years later, things were happening quickly again. If Haycroft's arson attempt had succeeded in destroying the condo and everyone in it, who would have known where to look for Frank's own killer? Or if one of the car bombs had done its work? In either case, Dane would have doubtless been blamed.

Over the past few days, Hale had heard Frank's theories, but Hale was an administrator. He'd never get involved in a case the way these guys would. At the end of the day, Hale was what any other chief of police was—a politician. A politician who would always be thinking about the department's image.

Frank looked at Vince, who was waiting for him to explain. He decided he wasn't going to play it Lefebvre's way.

"I'm talking about the fact that Phil Lefebvre was killed by someone in this department."

Vince looked at him in utter bewilderment, as if Frank had suddenly spoken in a foreign language. "What?"

Frank looked over his shoulder—this part of the lab was still empty, but he felt ill at ease being anywhere near Haycroft's territory. "Let's go upstairs. I need to talk to you and Reed and Pete about this."

Looking at their faces, seeing the mixture of disbelief and confusion and anger there, Frank thought that if he had taken the bombs that were in his car a few hours earlier and set them off in the middle of the squad room, the effect wouldn't have been any less devastating.

They listened patiently while he outlined what he had learned as well as his theories. They had questions, but he could see that as each minute passed, they became more convinced. If he had given them the same information the day before, they would have accused him of going to wild lengths to clear Lefebvre's name. But the events of the night before had changed everything.

At one point the Wheeze came by, and Frank asked her who had told her Larson wanted to speak to him the previous day.

"Paul Haycroft," she said. "I'm sorry, I guess Dr. Larson had gone home by the time I gave you the message."

"Haycroft must have put his son's picture on Larson's desk," Frank said when she had left. "And then he made sure I went into Larson's office when Larson wasn't there. I walked into a staged scene."

"Must have also made sure Larson went home sick," Reed said.

"Mary did mention something about mocha lattes—"

"Oldest trick in the book," Vince said. "Wonder if Haycroft bought any chocolate-flavored laxatives somewhere yesterday?"

"Why did he leave the photo?" Pete asked. "That was a big risk on his part."

"Yes, but maybe not much of one. How likely was it that I would know whose child that was? He wanted me to walk away with a particular set of ideas about his boss." Frank shook his head. "And I fell for it. I have to admit, the photo was the part of that whole scene that ultimately convinced me."

"You didn't have time to ask a lot about it, right?"

"I was in there late in the day," Frank agreed.

"It's like what you said about Lefebvre," Vince said. "Haycroft did the same thing to you—he put pressure on you. You can be damned sure he knew what was safe for him to do and what wasn't. You're married to a reporter who's lived here most of her life, so he probably figured you'd ask her if she remembered the story. He knew what was in the newspaper about his boy. If it was your kid, you would have had that article memorized, too."

"The toxicologist almost blew it for him," Reed said. "He had to be the one to tell you the story that went with that photo."

"But if I had asked you, Vince—"

"He knew what the situation was in here—everybody in the department knows you've been getting the silent treatment."

"Haycroft only needed to throw you off his scent for a few hours," Pete said grimly.

"Right," Reed said. "Just so he could have time to rig a couple of bombs and put them in your car. As of this morning, you weren't supposed to be a problem."

They again fell silent, looking at Frank in a way that made him say, "Cremation. And don't let Pete give the eulogy—nobody wants to sit in a pew that long."

"That's not even funny," Pete said. "You've come too damned close to being cremated already. That fire at Rosario's place . . ." He shook his head.

"Pete's right," Reed said. "Think of what Haycroft knows about crime and killing people."

"And here we were, being such fucking assholes—"

"I'm not ready to walk through the exit door yet," Frank said, but he wondered what Haycroft's next plan of attack might be. Once Haycroft realized that Frank was still alive, would he give up—leave the area? Or would he make some other attempt?

"So you think Randolph might have been on to something oddball going on in the lab?" Pete asked.

"Yes. I think that's why it was important that he not be allowed to hold that meeting with the chief and the other commissioners. Until I talked to Vince about Haycroft's boy, I thought the problem had been with Larson. Now I think Trent Randolph was probably going to ask Larson to get rid of Haycroft."

"Or to charge him with a felony," Vince said.

"Let's talk to Larson," Pete said.

Frank looked at his watch. "I've got to get over to Hale's office. And I want to talk to Irene—since I don't know what Haycroft might try next."

"I'll call downstairs and see if we can get a unit out to watch your place," Vince said. "Between the car bombs and that business with Dane last night, no one should question it."

"What are your plans for the day?" Frank asked, trying to keep his voice casual.

"What's wrong?" Irene said. "Has something else happened?"

He briefly told her about Haycroft. "You remember what he looks like?"

"I think so. Brown hair, medium build?"

"Yes. Keep an eye out for him, but stay the hell away from him."

"Sure. Okay to tell Seth and Elena about this?"

"Yes, absolutely—now tell me your plans."

"Seth is coming to work with me this morning—he's excited about seeing the newspaper. Elena has an appointment with her attorney."

"She can afford one?"

Irene hesitated, then said, "None of our business, is it?"

"You talked Brennan into helping her out." Brennan was one of Las Piernas's top attorneys. Irene—who had needed his help more than once—was a personal favorite of his.

"She's going to do some investigative work for him to repay him."

He felt his anger toward Elena return, but decided that he had bigger worries for the moment. "So you'll be in the office all day?"

"No—later on we'll be going over to the dedication of the new wing of the courthouse. Judge Kerr is going to give us front-row seats and a personal tour. But don't worry—there won't be more law enforcement types in any one place than the courthouse today."

"That's true," he said. "But take the cell phone with you today—all right? I'd just feel better."

When he went back to the others, he found them huddled in intense discussion.

"Mind if I take a casual stroll down to the lab to try to get some hint about where the bereaved Mr. Haycroft might be?" Pete asked him. "I'd feel better about riding in your car if we could keep an eye on him."

"Yeah," Vince said. "I'll go with you—I want to ask Mary Michaels about how Haycroft has been spending his time lately—see if he was out of the lab when those fires were started."

"I think I'll have a long talk with Flynn down in the property room," Reed said. "Maybe we can let that guy who works with Tom Cassidy—"

"Hank Freeman," Frank said.

"The computer geek?" Pete said.

"The computer *expert*," Reed corrected, and Pete shrugged.

"I've already got him looking at Seth Randolph's computer," Frank said.

"I thought maybe he should take a look at Flynn's machine, too—see if there's any reason Haycroft knows who checks out the evidence from the Randolph case."

"If all that's okay with you, Frank?" Vince asked uneasily. "It's your case."

"I think I'll talk to the chief about changing that," Frank said.

"You want off the case?" Pete asked.

"No. I want to stop working solo."

45

The plan was in motion. Everyone knew their role, their place in the activity that centered on Paul Haycroft's home. Convincing Chief Hale that a killer worked in his lab hadn't been easy, but once convinced, Hale had the zeal of a convert. He offered personnel and resources—and made sure that the search warrant, faxed over while they were setting up the operation, was worded so that they were given plenty of latitude.

The entire block was cordoned off and evacuated. There were patrol cars everywhere—as well as vehicles belonging to the bomb squad, the SWAT team, and a medical emergency team. The SWAT team, dressed in full tactical gear, carrying Heckler & Koch assault rifles, had taken up their initial positions. This was their part of the show—and as calm as most of them appeared, Frank knew their adrenaline was pumping.

His own was, even as he stood next to Pete, studying the house while they waited for it to be cleared.

"Big attic area," he said to Pete.

"I noticed that, too. It's too big, don't you think?"

A group from the SWAT team cautiously approached the house carrying an "Arizona toothpick"—a four-foot-long metal device, about two inches in diameter, with a claw on one end and a narrow point at the other. Avoiding the doormat—which might have been a pressure-sensitive trigger for a booby-trapped door—they knocked and shouted their warning.

They did not wait long for a reply. The toothpick made short work of the door and they were in, quickly sweeping through the house. The bomb squad was on their heels, dogs in harness. Within minutes, the leader of the SWAT unit came back out to talk to Frank.

"There's no one in there, but we've found an entrance into the attic that looks as suspicious as hell. It's not your usual crawl-space access. It's some kind of specially built door, and it's got an alarm on it. I'm going to order a portable X-ray so that we can take a look through the roof before we go in that way."

"How about the vent?"

"Sure," he said with a smile. "Crude but effective."

They brought a ladder up to the side of the house, attached one end of a chain to the vent, and hooked the other end to the rear bumper of a patrol car. "Stand back!" a SWAT officer warned, removing the ladder and making sure no one was beneath the vent. He then signaled the driver of the car.

"Wagons ho!" Pete said as the car moved forward and the vent came out of the wall with a bang, bringing stucco, the heavy chain, and a cloud of debris with it—and leaving a rough-edged observation port below the roofline.

The ladder was repositioned. Another SWAT team member climbed it, took a cautious look through the hole, then radioed that the attic was a finished room—it appeared to be an office with a workbench of some kind. Someone brought a fire ax to him and he quickly enlarged the hole.

"Our dogs aren't hitting on anything on the first floor," a member of the bomb squad said. "We'll check out the attic next."

"Can your dogs climb a ladder?" Frank asked a member of the bomb squad.

"Oh, yeah. Part of their training. Mine doesn't like it much, but he can do it."

Frank's cell phone rang. "I'll get things started on the ground floor," Pete said.

Frank nodded to him as he answered the call.

"Frank—it's Reed. Thought I'd let you know what we have so far. Haycroft was seen at the airport this morning. Got there really early, then aborted a flight. Apparently he drove off after he decided not to fly. He's got a little Cessna. The chief got a search warrant for it, and Vince is going over it now. Vince says it has some kind of special storage lockers on it."

"Any news on where Haycroft went after that?"

"No, but we think we know which plates he has on the van this morning—he's actually using the ones registered to the vehicle. The parking garage at the airport videotapes a vehicle's license plates as they enter, and the tapes are date and time stamped—it's a way of preventing people from parking for a week, then claiming they were there for a day and lost their ticket. Vince checked the ones from this morning—a late-model white Chevy van went in at about the time Haycroft was seen there, and sure enough, it was his."

"That's a break, anyway. With luck, he won't believe he needs to change them."

"There's more—and, man, I'm glad you're the one who will have to tell this to the chief, because it's all going to hit the fan when you do."

"Tell him what?"

"Freeman says that there are over forty files monitored by the program."

"Jesus H. Christ."

"They go back twelve years."

"Twelve? How can that be? That computer isn't that old."

"Haycroft was on the committee that chose the computer hardware and software for the property room. We think he must have kept track of the older cases some other way before the new computers were installed. Maybe he had a program on the old computer, too. However he did it, he had his list of cases, and the property room computer called his whenever anyone looked at the evidence for them."

"Wouldn't the evidence control software indicate tampering with the files? Otherwise, we're way too vulnerable."

"Apparently there are plenty of safeguards to keep anyone from getting into the evidence control program and making entries or changing anything. But Haycroft never changed any of that data, so no alarms went off. He just rigged a little extra 'notification program' that would get word to his computer."

"If he could get into the property room computer, why didn't he zap the special program and list of files before he left?"

"That's the best part—and it's gonna make you look good with Hale. Flynn said that he took that computer off-line after you were in here on Wednesday night. Guess you had a conversation about it that made him take precautions. By the way, he says to tell you to keep watching out for those ancient Egyptians, whatever that means."

"So Haycroft was forced to leave his watchdog program behind. What about these files—anything in common?"

"We haven't gotten very far yet, but after you call Hale, we'll probably get lots of assistance. I've looked at two. That's not enough to make a study."

"But you found something."

"Maybe. They were cases where an anonymous phone call led to discovery of evidence—and then to an arrest."

"Shit."

"I had the same reaction."

"Haycroft was the caller."

"In the two cases I looked at, the men who were arrested had each previously been in custody on other cases—suspected but ultimately released. This time, they proclaimed their innocence, but the evidence was against them."

"Lack of evidence on the previous?"

"Sort of. Enough for us, enough for the D.A., but not enough for Judge Curse. Like I said, only two cases, so who knows what I'll find with the others."

"Things are hopping here, but as soon as I get a minute, I'll call Hale."

"Good luck. I also talked to the bomb squad administrative offices. They looked up the records. You were right—Haycroft was the liaison on the Wendell Leroy Wallace cases. I asked them to put me in touch with the guys who had been on those cases."

Frank walked along the sidewalk in front of the house as Reed told him about his conversations with four members of the squad who each remembered Haycroft for his avid interest in the cases he worked on.

"He even asked them to let him photocopy Wallace's notebooks," Reed said.

"Which I'm sure they took to be a healthy scientific interest," Frank said, looking up at the high-pitched roof of the house. "Remind me about the other Wallace cases."

"He blew up three cars, but the bomb squad defused two others—everybody in this company he had a grudge against started taking taxis and riding buses. He also bombed a building—placed explosives in an empty office below the victim's. He made studies of other kinds of explosives, too. I've got the details when you need them."

"Larson have any further ideas?"

"The guy is useless. He's seriously pissing me off—he just won't face it. We still can't get him to believe this is possible. Even with Chief Hale riding his ass, all he can say is that he trusted Haycroft completely."

"That may be the problem Randolph saw all those years ago. Or maybe he noticed the anonymous-tip pattern."

"I'll bet Haycroft will know."

"I can't wait to ask him," Frank said.

"We did get one other break—the toxicologist says that the Wheeze has been having breakfast with Haycroft at Greenleaf's and slipping down to the lab for all kinds of other little meetings."

Frank was speechless.

"No one thinks it's romantic," Reed said, "but maybe that's just because no one other than Vince can think of the Wheeze in the nude."

"Have you talked to her?"

"No, I'm on the outs with her. Since you're her golden boy of the moment, why don't you see what you can learn from her?"

Frank sighed. "Okay, but it will have to wait. Gotta go, Reed. If you have trouble getting through to me, it's this house of Haycroft's. I'm looking at the roof and I'd swear he's done something to try to make it tough for infrared. Who knows what it will do to phone signals?"

The SWAT team leader approached him. "The bomb squad tells me we're clear up in the attic—but they got an iffy sort of alert from the dogs—mild reaction from one of them around this one area near the workbench. They think material may have been stored up here at some time—probably the stuff he used to make the devices for your car. They want you to test the top of that table for residue."

"Okay, I'll make sure it comes with us when we leave."

"You want to come up the ladder and take a look at the rest of what's up there?"

"Sure."

The phone rang again before he reached the ladder.

"Frank! It's Blake Halloran. I think we have your fire starter on videotape. From a gas station not far from the police department. Not a very good image—but it's something. A gardener in a white van filling a can with gasoline—only he handles everything the way you do when you don't want to leave prints."

"Great," Frank said. "I think we've identified the arsonist." He told him about Haycroft and made arrangements to have someone pick up a copy of the tape. "Do me a favor and ask your other arson investigators if any of them have ever worked with him, okay?"

The evidence against Haycroft was falling into place. He felt certain they were going to be able to nail him. He started up the ladder.

46

Paul Haycroft placed a white kitchen garbage bag on the bench before he sat on it. He intensely disliked sitting on such benches, but this one was across from the county courthouse. There were big doings at the courthouse today. The temporary stage was in place, and chairs were already in rows across the plaza. This wasn't a gathering that would draw much of a crowd from the general public, but there would be plenty of politicians, lawyers, judges, and law enforcement types. A few civic groups, of course. A local high school marching band. Lots of press. The courthouse was not far from the water, but even so, under the July sun, the spectators would be miserable on their plastic folding chairs.

Not so the dignitaries on the stage. He watched as workers raised a white canvas cover over the stage itself. Those on the stage would enjoy its shade. They could drone on and on while their audience broiled.

The sound system, bunting, a podium—gradually, the plaza was being converted into a theater. The audience would enter expecting a dull play. Haycroft smiled. He would prevent everyone from being bored.

He studied the new wing from this safe distance. This was not the first day anyone would enter the building, after all. He had been there on a number of occasions, sometimes openly. He knew that Kerr had been inside the building almost every day for the past few weeks, making sure all would be in order for this day. Desks and bookcases had been moved in, phones were installed, lights were working, security systems were at the ready. So much could be done, though, before security systems were truly at the ready.

Today the building would be officially dedicated, and tomorrow—according to the county's plans—Judge Lewis Kerr would preside over the first case to be heard there.

At this moment, Kerr would be in his new office on the seventh floor. Haycroft focused his attention on the window of that office and pictured Kerr as clearly as if he had telescopic vision. Kerr on the phone, Kerr rehearsing his speech, Kerr using the final hours of his life to deal with trivialities. His staff busy with last-minute details before the event. He had studied Kerr's behavior over the years and knew that Kerr would be one of the last people out of the building before the ceremonies.

Kerr, he thought with a smirk, was a theatrical man. He belonged in costume, not judge's robes. He loved nothing so much as an entrance. Every time Haycroft had observed him in public—at every political dinner, every civic function—Kerr had swept in as the last of the polite arrivals—never precisely late, never taking too much advantage of his host's or hostess's tolerance, but always looked for, always anticipated.

Haycroft knew Kerr's habits and timing as well as if they were doing a trapeze act together. Thirty minutes or so before the beginning of the event, when the organizers would have been gratified and relieved to see the judge, Kerr would send his minions ahead to assure everyone that His Honor was on his way. Kerr would next send Maggie, his clerk, last of all. And with less than five minutes to spare, when the audience was already accustomed to the presence of all the other dignitaries, Kerr would come shining into their midst. He would allow enough time to be shown to his place on the dais and little more. Just in time to cause a little stir.

Yes, Kerr would stay in his office, far above it all, judging nothing so well as his moment.

Haycroft knew exactly where Kerr's desk was positioned. Perhaps even now Kerr was looking down on the plaza from behind his mirrored window. Or slightly beyond the plaza, to a man sitting on a bench, looking up at him.

Sadly, at this distance Haycroft could not see the reflection of his own face in Kerr's window. Although he had no difficulty imagining Kerr and his office, he could never imagine his own likeness. That had to be seen for itself.

"Dr. Haycroft?"

He gave a small start and turned to see one of the guards from the old courthouse.

"Hello, Denise," he said, smiling. He didn't bother correcting the "doctor." He had a master's degree and much more experience than Dr. Larson. If this kind woman wanted to confer a doctorate on him, so be it. She had seen him many times in the older court building. He always made a point of getting to know such persons in any setting. After all, a janitor usually had more keys to city hall than the mayor.

"Whatcha doing out here all by yourself so early? The big to-do won't start until noon."

"I'll be gone then, I'm afraid."

"Oh, now that's a shame. They work you too hard in that lab."

"Actually, I'm on leave and about to go out of town." He added the lie he'd told Larson. "There's been a death in my family—an aunt of mine."

"I'm so sorry!"

Her look of genuine sympathy touched him. "Thank you. It's made life rather chaotic, I'm afraid. Are you on your morning break?"

"Yes, just on my way to that coffee place across the way. I'm gonna get me a real cup of coffee. You ever drink the awful stuff they serve in the courthouse?"

"No," he said, horrified.

She laughed.

"Will you be watching the ceremony, Denise?"

"No, you and me, we'll be the only ones to miss it. I'll be working."

"Where?" he asked sharply.

She laughed. "Where? Where do I always work? Somebody has to guard the entrance to the old building—even on a day like today."

He relaxed and smiled. "Maybe that won't be such a bad place to be after all."

She shaded her eyes and looked up at the cloudless sky. "Yes, you may be right. Maybe I'll make that an iced coffee. You take care, Dr. Haycroft."

He watched her enter the coffee shop, then stood up and, making sure he did not touch any part of the bag that had touched the bench, threw the bag away. He felt uneasy. He would have preferred not to have been seen here by anyone he knew, but there was no reason to panic. Still, he should be more careful.

He could go back to the van for a time, listen to the radio—any moment now he should be able to hear the reports of the death of Detective Frank Harriman of the Las Piernas Police Department. He looked at his watch and released a breath he did not even realize he had been holding. He had time.

He had a little moment of mistrust in himself. Had he done everything properly? Did he follow Wendell Leroy Wallace's instructions as he should have?

Of course he had! Was anyone more conscientious than he was? No. The device would go off at the appointed hour. There was nothing to worry about. The great day was here. Kerr, that most unjust of judges, would be gone, as would his monument to his own ego!

Although he was eager to hear about the results of his work at Harriman's home, he wasn't sure he could pull himself away from looking at the new courthouse annex. After all, Harriman was undoubtedly already dead. Haycroft could stay here and watch the destruction of the courthouse—see the grand results for himself—all the while knowing that Kerr would be entombed in its rubble.

He debated over this for some time, but decided he would make one last trip to the van now, so that he could satisfy his curiosity about the outcry that would be attached to Harriman's death. If he waited much longer to do so, he might not ever hear about Harriman, because that rather minor news item would be bumped right off the air by the courthouse debacle.

He must hurry. The first of the little events he had planned for the courthouse was not far away.

47

"Ms. Kelly and Mr. Lefebvre," the guard said, smiling at Seth as they passed through the metal detectors. She handed Irene's purse back to her as it came through the X-ray machine, then gave them each a visitor's tag. "If you'll have a seat right over there, Judge Kerr's clerk will be down in just a moment to escort you up to his office."

"Thank you," Seth said.

As they took their seats, Irene thought Seth seemed restless.

"Would you like me to call Jack?" she asked. "You don't have to be here with me, you know."

"No, I have to see the judge."

She raised her brows. "You do?"

"Yes. About a please bargain."

"A please bargain?" she asked in a strained voice.

"You know, you ask, 'Pretty please, Judge, will you let me go?' and you do something nice for him, and it's a bargain."

She looked away for just a moment, then said, "Do you think maybe you mean a plea bargain?"

He shrugged.

"Is this about your mom?"

"Yes. I don't want her to go to jail."

Irene put an arm around his shoulders. "You know, Seth, she may not be in any trouble at all. And she has a good lawyer—he's a friend of mine. He's kept me out of jail a couple of times."

His eyes widened. "You were arrested?"

"No, thanks to my lawyer. Your mom isn't under arrest, either. But this is one of those times when you just have to let other people help her."

He thought about this for a moment, then said, "May I please call her?"

It was not the first time today that he had checked on Elena, and Irene saw this as a sign that he had been more frightened by recent events than he was letting on. "Sure." She handed him her phone.

He turned it on, pressed the redial button, but it beeped twice without making the call.

"It's not working," he said, then read the screen. "It says 'No Signal.'"

"We'll try again when we're outside. Sometimes my phone doesn't work so well inside buildings."

Maggie Koopman, the judge's clerk, arrived and took them up in the new elevator, fawning over Seth in much the same way he had been fawned over all morning but talking to him as if he were a not-too-bright two-year-old. The irritation Irene felt over this distracted her from the mild claustrophobia she felt in any elevator. But when Maggie stepped out of the elevator ahead of them to lead the way, she was allowed some comic relief—Seth turned to her, rolled his eyes, and pantomimed "gag me." She wondered what Maggie would say if she told her that only Tory Randolph had previously earned this rating.

"Irene, welcome!" Judge Kerr said as they entered the office. "The rest of my staff is already downstairs, but Maggie here stayed behind so that I could take a few minutes to show you around before the ceremonies." He offered a hand to Seth. "And you must be Seth Lefebvre. I'm Judge Kerr, and I'm glad you were able to come to the party today."

Like Maggie, Judge Kerr was all smiles, but he seemed to have a better sense of the dignity due a boy of nine. If Kerr wasn't thrilled about having a kid hanging around at a time like this, he was too smart to show it. He undoubtedly wanted her to write a flattering article about the building and the ceremony—and himself—and probably would have let her bring just about anything short of a wild boar along with her if she had asked.

Seth had immediately gone to the big window. Irene quickly joined him there—she needed to counteract the effects of the elevator. Seth began asking Kerr about the arrangements for the ceremony and the new building. She hoped that the impish streak she had noticed in Seth would not resurface over the next few minutes. They were doing fine until Seth—perhaps building up to his "please bargain"—decided to pay Kerr a compliment.

"That's a nice dress you have on," he said.

To her relief, Kerr laughed and thanked him.

Maggie knocked softly on the open door. "Excuse me, Judge Kerr, but the telephones just went dead! Shall I go downstairs to see what the problem is?"

"Of all the confounded nuisances!" the judge said. "Yes, thank you, Maggie."

"Perhaps we should all go downstairs," Irene said. "We can always get the tour later."

"Oh, no," Maggie said. "You two just got here. Relax—I'll be right back."

48

"You are certain we will be able to reach his offices from this building?" Dane asked.

"Yes, sir. The older building and the new one are connected by a stair-well."

"And why did you choose this route?"

"Because we have influence over persons in this building, sir. We haven't yet made arrangements with anyone in the new annex."

"Perhaps we should have anticipated that need?" Dane suggested.

"I urged Derrick to do so, sir."

Dane smiled to himself but said nothing.

In that silence, they heard the first sound, a muffled bang.

"Gunfire?" Dane asked.

"No, sir, at least I don't think so. It didn't quite have that sound."

"Do you have your weapons handy?"

"Yes, sir. That's another reason why we must take the stairs."

"Because our friends who are guards don't work near the damned eleva-tors. Yes, I understand. Lead on, Myles."

49

Frank looked through the opening made by the ax. Except for the mess caused by the removal of the vent, the room before him was clean and orderly. File cabinets lined one wall. A workbench was along another. There was nothing on it.

He put on gloves, then stepped inside. Pete came up the ladder after him.

"So far, nothing downstairs—place hardly looks lived in," Pete said. "To the point of being strange. And two other things—mirrors in every room, and it smells weird—like bathroom spray." He stepped through the opening in the attic wall. "Will you look at this? I kept thinking all that spray meant there was a body rotting up here for sure. And it's nothing but an office. All I smell now is a lawsuit."

"I wouldn't be too sure it's only an office," Frank said. "Not with that alarm system and steel access door." He moved closer to the file cabinets. "The dates go back twelve years."

"That's about when his son died," Pete said.

"Got your lock picks?"

"I'm better at it than he is," Pete told the SWAT officer. "My first wife proposed to me after she saw me pick a lock."

"On what, her chastity belt?" he asked.

But Pete was focusing on his work. Within seconds, he popped the lock on the first cabinet. He opened a drawer—it was filled with carefully labeled folders filed by date.

Frank pulled a few of them out. "Court cases. Transcripts. A few newspaper clippings." He quickly looked through four of them. The charges varied in each case, from drug dealing to assault, from kidnapping to murder. They all had two things in common—the defense prevailed and Judge Lewis Kerr presided. All the budding confidence of a few moments ago left him, replaced by a sense of dread.

You've only looked at a few. Don't jump to conclusions.

He absently reached to rub his forehead, felt the surface of the glove, and stopped.

"What was the name of the shooter at the bank?" Frank asked.

"What bank?" Pete was concentrating on the other file cabinets. But now he looked up and said, "Oh, you mean the one Lisa got involved with?"

"Right," Frank said, feeling his hands dampen inside the gloves. "Christ, it's hot in here."

The SWAT officer and Pete exchanged a look.

"Carl Sudas," Pete said. "Prime asshole." He finished the file cabinet locks and moved on to the desk, which took even less time. "Empty," he said. "Except for a book. *Winging It.*"

"By Bray and Killeen," Frank said. "Look on page ninety-eight. You'll find Dinterman's Stunt Flyer."

"That's your plane, all right. You can even see where he traced the lines on the plans."

"Not much by itself, but maybe it will help. Take it as evidence."

"Paper airplanes?" the SWAT officer asked. "The guy builds a damned fortress for files and a paper airplane factory?"

Frank studied the access door. Haycroft's ceiling had larger than usual joists—two-by-twelves. There was a gap of about eleven inches between the floor of the attic and the ceiling below it. "Maybe he's swept it all under the rug. Let's start over by that workbench."

Frank lifted a corner of the carpet. "Not tacked down."

"Bingo," Pete said as Frank slid a long section of the plywood beneath it away.

Tucked in the spaces between joists were numerous small containers.

Frank gently lifted one. "Look at this. He's sorted all the nuts and bolts by size, marked the containers."

"Those are spools of fuse material," the SWAT officer said, pointing to another section.

"Better let those bomb squad folks take a look at this stuff. They might be able to match up some of the hardware to the devices they defused last night."

The SWAT officer used his radio to put in a request for a bomb tech.

Frank forced himself to go back to the files. He pulled a few more out and found that these, too, were defense wins in Kerr's court. He moved to the end cabinet. More of the same.

"Jesus," Frank said, feeling his stomach knot. "Kerr was the one who cut Sudas loose, right?"

"Yeah, but Hitch blew that case and everyone in Detectives knew it. The department doesn't like to paint it that way, but that's the truth."

But Frank was thinking of Irene, at the courthouse with Seth, visiting the man who was so clearly the object of Haycroft's obsession—Haycroft loose, nowhere to be found.

"I've got to go."

"What?"

"Call Kerr—tell him he's Haycroft's next target."

"Hoo, baby," Pete said. "Hold on a minute. A judge? You're going to tell Judge Curse we've got a nut from the lab on a twelve-year-old revenge trip—a guy who's also been fucking with evidence all that time? Think twice about that one. Besides, I thought Carlson was supposed to handle all the release of information to media and other agencies."

"Haycroft's obviously focusing on Kerr. The man's life might be in danger—and Seth and my wife are with him."

"What?"

"Irene is interviewing him today. She's got Seth with her. Never mind—I'll call."

"Look, there are guards and metal detectors at the new courthouse, and twice as much law enforcement there today as on any other. Besides, Irene will be watching for him," Pete said. "If I were you, I'd take a minute to run it past Hale."

Frank decided that might not be a bad idea—but not because he was seeking Hale's permission. Hale could mobilize all kinds of personnel. Frank walked to the opening in the wall, where the signal was stronger. But when he made the call, the chief's secretary said, "He's not in, Detective Harriman. Shall I take a message?"

"Page him. Tell him it's extremely urgent—an emergency involving a judge's life."

He disconnected and called Irene. To hell with the department. He got her voice mail. "Irene, if you can get out of this appointment with Kerr, please do so. If you're already with him, warn him—I think Haycroft's going to try to kill him today—maybe at the ceremony."

He had no sooner disconnected than the phone rang.

"They found his van," Reed said. "We're closing in on the bastard!"

"Where?"

"In an alley near Third and Magnolia."

"Downtown?" He swallowed hard. "Any sign of him?"

"No, not yet. I'm on my way over there. They told me they took a quick look at the van, but only found a canvas bag with some soap and towels and plastic bags in it. It's near a church and the library parking lot. The chief's down there, and they told him about finding it before I got the call. He's already sent a dozen guys in to search the library."

"The chief—oh, Christ—"

"Yes, he's in some kind of ceremony—"

"Reed, listen to me—we've got to get through to Hale immediately. And to Judge Kerr—especially Kerr! They've got to clear the plaza. They've got to get everybody out of there. Get the bomb squad down there. Now!"

"Frank—"

"Haycroft's a one-man judge and jury, right? Jesus, Reed—think of who'll be there! Every attorney, every supervisor, every judge. But especially Kerr. I'm sitting here looking at a shitload of stuff on Kerr. Everything in Haycroft's files is about him—I think it goes back to the Sudas case, Haycroft's son's death."

"Jesus—I think those files Freeman found on the computer—I think they all had Kerr connected to them, too."

"Fuck all that, Reed—listen to me—Irene's at the courthouse interviewing him. She's there with Seth. Call Kerr and call Hale—and get that plaza cleared!"

Pete came to his feet, anxious now.

Frank hung up, dialed Irene's cell phone number again. "Come on, Irene, come on, come on, answer it!"

He got her voice mail again. "God damn it!"

The tone sounded. "Irene, please, this is urgent—if you and Seth are at the courthouse, get out now! Get everybody the hell away from there as fast as you can. Get as far away as you can."

"Go on, go!" Pete shouted to him, tossing him the keys to his car. "I'll stay here and deal with the search. Get your ass over there."

"I've got to call Kerr's office—" he said frantically.

"I'll do that, too," Pete said in a voice that made him take a deep breath, calm himself a little. "Now go."

Frank went down the ladder at a speed that had the crew on the ground shouting at him, then ran to the Chevy. He put the light on the roof and peeled out.

50

Haycroft knew he needed to appear calm.

He was shaking. He was perspiring. He could actually smell his own body odor. He had been jostled and touched again and again by others. The thought nauseated him.

From the sidewalk where he had temporarily stationed himself, he glanced in the window of the sandwich shop behind him. He did not appear calm.

Police had surrounded the van.

It was inconceivable to him. He had nearly been caught then and there. Strolling along, ready to listen to the story of Harriman's demise. And there was his van, surrounded by black-and-white patrol cars.

How could this be? Had the late Harriman talked more than anticipated?

He stood staring for a moment, then tried not to attract attention as he walked away. He felt as if every eye were watching him, laughing secretly as he headed straight into a trap.

Somehow, he managed to return to the plaza without being seen by the police. And now this, this further ruin.

They streamed around him, hurriedly but calmly leaving. Like cattle drovers trying hard not to stampede their herd, the uniformed officers of the LPPD and the fire department urged the audience to leave. Announce-

ments were being made. He was making himself obvious, he suddenly realized. Standing like a rock in the plaza as the greater and greater rush of hoi
polloi flowed past him.

Then came the little thunderclap. The first charge, in the telephone
equipment room, had been too small to be heard by anyone who was not
near it. This second one, a small charge going off in an elevator shaft, was
surprisingly loud. It was just a little device, designed like one he had studied
in Wallace's notes. It had relied on a timer. He was pleased that something
was going right.

It freed him to move again, to join the throng that was now panicking,
rushing into the street, bringing traffic to a halt. He allowed himself to be
carried along by this swell of frightened lawyers and politicians and civil servants, to be deposited by it on the street's opposite shore. He escaped it by
hurrying up into the shelter of the shops that formed the lower floor of the
high-rise directly across from the courthouse.

Only a few minutes now.

He would need to steal a car. This was not among his many areas of expertise. He was good with mechanical devices, though, and he understood
the principles involved. He had once stolen a boat—could stealing a car be
much different? Perhaps he would try it. What other choices did he have? A
taxi? The driver would report him. Public transportation? Hah! Might as
well shoot himself. They weren't buses, they were vermin-mobiles.

He walked back to the sidewalk, watching the building, waiting. The police were watching it, too. No one was going in. Better yet, no one was coming out.

He was only seconds away from achieving his dream.

A horn honked. Startled, he looked down to see an old Plymouth sedan
pull up alongside the curb. He was about to run when he recognized the
driver. The guard from the old courthouse.

"Get in, Dr. Haycroft," Denise said. "There's some crazy bomber on the
loose around here!"

51

He tried to concentrate on his driving while listening to the reports. There had just been a small explosion in the new wing of the courthouse. No one was believed hurt. The police had started clearing the plaza moments before. There had been some panic at the sound of the blast, but for the most part, dispersal was orderly. Officials were still in the process of securing the area. Haycroft had not returned to his van. Both the fire department and the bomb squad had arrived and a command center had been set up—they were getting ready to go about the long process of clearing the building.

But he wouldn't feel relieved until he talked to Irene.

His cell phone rang.

He answered it and nearly lost control of the car. "Irene?"

"No, Vince—listen, I got those locked compartments open on Haycroft's Cessna. You would not believe what I found in them. This guy kept these lab notebooks. Experiments. Only the experiments are on people. Or, I should say, how to kill them or set them up for a conviction. The asshole rates himself based on how well he did. Guess who's in here?"

"The Randolphs."

"Yes, and Lefebvre. And Bredloe. And you. Second to last."

"Is the courthouse dedication the last entry?"

"The courthouse? No—but good thinking on that one, Harriman—I hear they managed to clear just about everybody from the plaza before the one in the building went off. I think our boy hit another dud thanks to you."

"Who's the last entry?"

"Judge Lewis Kerr."

"Has he been accounted for?"

"Not yet, but you know, a lot of folks just hightailed it out of there, so—"

"So we don't know. Watch that plane, Vince—Haycroft may be coming back to it."

"I'm praying he does," Vince said.

Frank called the paper and asked for Irene's boss, John Walters.

"John—has Irene reported in yet from the courthouse?"

"No, not yet. If you hear from her—"

"Was she in the audience?"

"Probably had a front-row seat. She and Seth were the guests of Judge Kerr. I'd give you the number, but the phones are out in Kerr's office."

His hand tightened on the steering wheel. "Oh, God . . ."

"Frank? You there?"

"I'll call you back, John."

He reached Ocean Boulevard and Magnolia Avenue in spite of a heavy exodus of cars and pedestrians, but at Ocean, traffic came to a halt. The sidewalk on the plaza side of the street was nearly empty. Ahead, he could see fire engines, emergency vehicles, the fire department command center. He drove Pete's car over the curb, parking it on the sidewalk. He pocketed the phone and began running toward the new building.

He saw a man with a briefcase running in the opposite direction. Frank stepped in front of him. "Judge Kerr's office—where is it?"

"Get out of my way!"

Frank grabbed him by the lapels. "Where's Kerr's office?"

The man paled. Then he saw Frank's badge and shoulder holster. "You're a cop. You're not allowed to do this."

"You don't read the newspapers, do you?"

He pointed a shaking finger. "Seventh floor, corner office."

Frank let him go and ran faster.

He dodged more and more members of his own department. As he got closer to the building, the majority of them were wearing protective gear. They yelled at him to get back, then relented as he held up his ID. A more persistent officer stepped aside when Frank yelled, "Chief's office."

The members of the bomb squad weren't impressed with the "chief" routine and began shouting to the others to stop him.

Halfway across the open space, weaving through the abandoned folding chairs, he looked up at Kerr's office. All his concentration was centered on it, on the people he knew were within it.

Be safe, Irene, he thought. Be safe, Seth. Please be safe. I'm almost there.

He heard the shouting of the others mixing with the pleading in his mind, both more frantic as he moved forward, the distance between him and the corner office seeming to double with every step, as if each passing second robbed him of progress.

The blast struck like a thunderclap that could take the world apart—all the shouts and pleas lost in the deafening roar of an explosion that shook the ground beneath his feet and thrummed in the marrow of his bones.

In helpless horror he watched as Kerr's window and a hundred windows near it blasted out and the upper floors of the building crumpled in on one another.

He screamed her name, but even he could not hear it among the other screams, the answering rattle from every building around the plaza, the hard rain of glass and debris that pelted down on them, as if falling from the thick clouds of smoke billowing from the building. Walls and ceilings and floors collapsed, banging down on one another, then lay askew like drunks who had caused one another to stumble. As they fell, bits of concrete shot from them as if from cannons, arcing down into the courtyard with murderous force.

In an instant, he saw the world go out of order, no longer operating as it should, and some part of his mind resisted all the uproar of his senses—the vision of destruction, the ringing in his ears, the choking dust. In defiance of this chaos, his thoughts sought possibilities.

Maybe she got his phone message and never got here.

Maybe they're already safe, in another part of the city.

Maybe she heard the message and was already making her way back to him.

These thoughts circled through his mind like a toy train on its track, no sooner gone than they returned, while some other, darker knowledge moved him forward, toward a goal that was no longer where he had last seen it, toward a location that had vanished—the knowledge that he must lay aside this resistance, because the very place he could not bear to be was exactly the place he must seek.

52

The first hour passed in a warped version of time. What he waited and hoped for made the minutes seem too long, what he feared made them pass too quickly.

He knew the statistics. About ninety percent of survivors would be rescued in the first forty-five minutes. He watched in silence, anxiously studying every dazed creature who emerged from the ruins of the building and then every stretcher, and finally, every body bag. These were the "surface victims"—those able to walk out on their own and the ones who could be easily seen by rescuers. The next group must be found by a careful search of the rubble of the building. With luck, survivors would be discovered in the void spaces—pockets formed by the angles of collapse and by objects and materials in the building—a row of filing cabinets might prop up a portion of a fallen ceiling, the area under a sturdy desk might shelter someone from crushing debris.

At one point he became aware that his muscles ached from nothing more than tension, from the strain of keeping his emotions in check—knowing that any loss of control would mean the loss of this horrible privilege of nearness to the scene. At first, rescue workers had tried to force him away and he had missed seeing a few of the injured. But the director of the bomb squad activities was the man who had been at his home just that morning—that long-ago morning—and he took pity on Frank and allowed him to stand near where the first of the injured and the dead were brought out.

He also told the others that Frank had made the warning call, and some thanked him then—because even with such little warning they had gained a few advantages. Before the blast, they had been able to evacuate the courtyard and most of the building, so that relatively few people were in it when the largest device detonated. A fire department battalion chief was on-site, and a command center had already been set up to coordinate the activities of the bomb squad, paramedics, police, firefighters, and the technical rescue team. The first responding unit had been able to shut off the utilities so that the fire damage had been minimal.

The building, they told him, was made of reinforced concrete—if the older building had been bombed, the damage would have been more severe.

Again and again, they told him how much worse it might have been.

He tried to find comfort in that, and couldn't.

A few of the rescuers and firefighters talked to him briefly as they passed by or while they waited for clearance to enter the building. They tried to give him a word of encouragement, to tell him more about what was going on.

Once the fire was out, the bomb squad went in first. Often bombers left secondary devices—insidiously designed to injure rescue personnel or to slow the rescue process and thereby raise the number of deaths the bomber had "scored."

While the bomb squad looked for these devices, the Urban Search and Rescue teams—the USAR teams—prepared to enter the building as soon as possible. These technical rescue squads were elite teams of firefighters, as specialized in their work as SWAT teams were in the police department.

Still others interviewed survivors, asking, "Who was in there with you? Was anyone else in the office? Where did you last see this person?" and so on. Some survivors were unable to do more than gaze blankly at their rescuers, while others were frenzied in their desire to be farther away from the place, but most tried to concentrate, to recall the moment before the blast—doing their best to remain calm, to be precise—all while managing their own lingering terror and sudden exhaustion, the high-octane rush of relief and burden of guilt that often came to the rescued. Some were reunited with family members or with coworkers they had thought lost—some who had been little more than acquaintances now weepingly embraced.

Although the fire had been quickly extinguished, a few of the injured and many of the dead were terribly burned. Others had been crushed. Some were unrecognizable—the worst, hardly recognizable as human.

Of each of these, Frank made himself ask the questions:

Could this be Irene? Could this be Seth?

And always answered no, hoping he had not lied to himself.

He continued to watch the stretchers—the noisy, bustling activities of rescue around him going on as if at a great distance—all his awareness focused on this macabre parade, so that he stood like a man waiting at the end of a jetway for a loved one to disembark from some ruinous flight. But the number rapidly dwindled, for the ones the workers could quickly and safely reach had been brought out, and he realized that Irene and Seth would not be among them.

From his own department's training, Frank knew the basic procedures for "major incidents"—a phrase that seemed so inadequate now—and he forced himself to think through what he had learned in those training sessions. Again and again he tried to think of what he could do, what he must do.

Kerr's office was on the seventh floor. There was no way to get up to what was left of it except by helicopter or fire truck ladder. He knew a couple of helicopter pilots, and for a time he wondered what they would say if he asked them to risk losing their licenses for interference in this type of crisis situation. But the first numbness was wearing off, and he knew he could not value his own misery above that of others who stood beyond the police barrier tape—moaning and crying, or simply staring up at the ruin with anguished faces—waiting for word of missing friends and family.

Still, there must be something he could do. When he could not think of what that might be, a kind of hollowness carved itself into his chest.

The body of a security guard was found. She had apparently gone to investigate the sound made by the first and smallest explosion, the one that took out the telephones, and had been killed by the second one, the one in the elevator shaft. The rescuers, although taking no joy in her death, could not help but feel excitement—for near her body, and quite undamaged, was a clipboard. The clipboard held a sign-in sheet. From it, they gained a better sense of who, in addition to workers, was in the building when the bombs went off.

For Frank, though, the discovery only confirmed that Seth and Irene had indeed signed in, had been escorted to Kerr's office on the seventh floor, and had not come out—it denied him his denials, that persistent hope that she had never made it here after all, that she was somewhere else, repairing a flat tire on the Jeep or stuck in line at a bank.

No, they were here. He had known it, of course.

He tried to study the building. He thought of what the various rescue personnel had told him. The east stairwell, the one nearest Kerr's office, had collapsed completely. The top two floors of the west stairwell had also sustained severe damage, but where the old and new courthouse buildings were attached to each other on the lower five floors, there had been less destruction. From that point downward, the west stairwell was, in fact, two adjoining stairwells, with connecting doors between each flight of the old and new. Each had collapsed in a different way. Portions of the stairways for the second, third, fourth, and fifth floors were inaccessible, but they were not reduced to dust.

The bomb squad suspected that additional charges had been placed near the stairwells to close off escape routes to survivors. Or at least, Frank thought bitterly, to survivors on the seventh floor. The more damaged east stairwell had been the one they thought Judge Kerr would have most likely used.

Another five minutes and he would have been inside. Once inside, it would have been hard to stop him from—from what? he asked himself. From dying in the blast? From being buried in the rubble? If Irene and Seth were trapped in there, what help could he offer, even now?

Word came to him that the bomb squad had cleared the building. The technical rescue operation went into full swing—core teams of four to six members with highly specialized training, each supported by eight to twelve others. Using jacks and lifts and other equipment, they would shore up the collapsed structure, level by level—all the while trying to locate trapped victims, knowing every minute might be one a victim spent bleeding or crushed, suffocating or in pain, the likelihood of survival decreasing.

He should just get the hell out of the way, he told himself. But he couldn't make himself leave. Not when they were so close. Irene was a survivor. She had proven it again and again. Frank had to wait. He had to be sure.

He thought of how much she hated enclosed spaces. Of all that Seth had already been through. *Please, God, don't let them be terrified. Don't let them be hurt. Don't let them be suffering. Don't let them be* . . .

No, he wouldn't even think it.

After a time, he wasn't waiting alone. He wasn't entirely sure when it had come about, but Reed and Pete found him. Hale, too. Vince was still keeping an eye on the airport, they said, and would have been here if he didn't want to capture Haycroft so badly. Frank didn't want to capture him. He wanted to kill him. He would have gladly killed him for what he had seen in the last twenty minutes alone.

Somehow Hale had made it possible for them to remain within this highly restricted area. They did not try to cheer Frank up with talk of miracles or try to buoy him up with false hope. For that, he was grateful. The waiting changed—his tension eased slightly in their presence, although they said little.

Utter helplessness should not be discussed, he thought, even among friends.

No, he told himself. There is something you can do. What?

He closed his eyes and forced himself to think of the scene here an hour or so ago. In a second call to Irene's boss, he had learned that she had had an appointment to meet with Kerr just before the ceremonies. Kerr was going to show off the new office for a few minutes, then walk down to the dais with them. She would have been there when the first small blast had taken out the telephones, though she might not have heard it, up on the seventh floor. She would have heard the second one—the one that had taken out the elevators.

He was picturing the big window, Seth and Irene looking down at the plaza, seeing everyone seated in anticipation of the ceremony—but no, that's not what she would have seen. She would have seen people being evacuated.

"Frank?"

He gave a start, then turned to see Reed Collins. Next to Reed, seeking support on his arm, was a weeping woman in her fifties. She was wearing business attire. There was something in Reed's manner, in his reddened eyes, that made Frank want to stop time. He wanted Reed to stop walking forward with this woman.

He knew what this primly dressed woman was. She was a harbinger.

And he knew what was weighing Reed down. Sympathy.

"No," he said aloud, but he didn't move.

"This is Maggie . . ."

"Maggie Koopman," she supplied.

"Kerr's clerk," Reed said.

"I'm so sorry," Maggie said. "It's all my fault!"

Frank looked at Reed.

"She says Irene and Seth were with the judge when the phones got knocked out. She said she told them that they should stay—" Reed stopped, then rephrased it. "She offered to go downstairs to check on the problem, which she was convinced was a new-building glitch."

"A glitch," Frank repeated dully, looking at the ruins.

"There was no way of knowing it was anything else," Reed said. "So she left."

"And the others stayed." All these words were turning him to stone. He could feel it happening, from the inside out.

"Yes. She's sure of it. As it was, she went down to the first floor and then, of course, she wasn't allowed to remain in the building."

"I told them!" she said miserably. "I told them, 'I have to go back! Judge Kerr and a reporter and a little boy are still inside!'"

Frank felt Reed's hand tighten on his shoulder, and he realized he had swayed on his feet. He tried to steady himself, but found he couldn't, and reached out for Reed's shoulder with his own hand, bracing himself.

"I told them, 'You've got to let me go back and get them!'" Maggie Koopman was saying. "They told me officers were going through the building floor by floor, evacuating it, and that they'd make sure the judge and the others were brought out safely. But they didn't!"

"The guy they sent up to get them was on the east stairwell when the next blast hit," Reed said.

Frank looked at the ruins of the stairwell.

"No," he said. "No."

Pete stayed next to him. Talkative Pete, not saying a word. Reed took Maggie Koopman, mourning a man she had worked with for twenty years — whose death she was convinced she had caused — to where her daughter waited to take her home. Pete still hadn't said a word by the time Reed came back.

"We've left a message on your home phone for Elena," Reed said. "Unless she's been near a radio or TV, she probably doesn't even know this has happened."

Was it a good thing or a bad thing, not to know? he wondered.

Too damn bad, he told himself. You know. So think!

He closed his eyes and thought of Irene looking down on the plaza, seeing the evacuation. He felt sure that she had done so. She looked out windows, and not only because she was claustrophobic. She was an astute observer. They both worked in professions where one survived by observing others.

So Irene looks out on the plaza and sees the evacuation. A clerk tells her to stay where she is. And Irene — Irene stays put?

"She didn't stay in that office," he said aloud.

Reed and Pete exchanged a look.

I know Irene, he thought. What did she do next?

His thoughts were interrupted by the barking of a dog—a German shepherd wearing an orange vest bounded over to greet him.

"Hello, Bingle," he said. "Am I ever glad to see you."

"He's glad to see you, too," Ben Sheridan said as he caught up with his dog. He was wearing orange coveralls with "SAR" printed on the back. "Bingle wouldn't forgive me if I didn't let him say hello before we got started."

"Anna here, too?" Frank asked. Ben's girlfriend was also a dog handler.

"Our whole search-and-rescue dog team is here." He paused, then said, "They've just briefed us."

Frank looked up but didn't see the look of sympathy that Pete and Reed wore now. Did Ben know?

"Yes, I know," Ben said. "Actually, this little greeting ceremony has another purpose." He smiled. "I told the team that you and Bingle are old friends. I stretched the truth a bit and said that you had already worked with Bingle on a search and that I wanted you to search with us again."

Frank felt a rush of gratitude so overwhelming, he couldn't speak for a moment. He finally managed, "Thanks, Ben."

"Before you thank me, make sure you want to do it. Aside from the fact that it's dangerous to be crawling around in a structurally damaged building, this work can be grim—even for a homicide detective. We aren't expecting many victims, thanks to the evacuation. But many is not zero, and we may not make any live finds. And a person found alive may not make it—it takes time to get them out and the injuries tend to be severe."

Frank nodded.

"Allow me to be ruthless, Frank. Whether the people they find are dead, alive, crushed, or mutilated, these dogs do this work because it's a game to them—so I'll have to respond to Bingle's finds in a positive way, praising him, playing with him—and you have to get the hell away from him if you think you might start to give him any other kind of response. I don't want you to deck me if I'm playing Frisbee with my dog a few feet away from your wife's body. That's one reason we don't usually bring relatives along for these searches—it's asking a lot of you."

"I understand."

"Then understand this, too—you can't just focus on three people. That might be the hardest part."

"Let me help. Let me do something besides . . . imagining."

"All right. We'll have to hurry—we're expecting the bomb squad to let us get to work any time now. I've brought equipment for you—hard hat, goggles, radio set, work gloves, that kind of thing. Let me see if I can get you a set of coveralls. Nothing we can do about the shoes, I'm afraid."

"I'll go barefoot, if that's what it takes," Frank said.

Anna, Ben's girlfriend, was an easygoing, athletic blonde. Still, for all her affability, she had a mind of her own, and Frank wondered if she would be angry when he showed up posing as a SAR dog handler. Like all of the handlers in Ben's group, she took her work with the dogs seriously. But when he approached the group, she completely backed up Ben's story. At one point she glanced at him, looking worried, and he realized that he had not factored in her fondness for Irene.

Bingle knew his job so well, Frank had little doubt that his biggest task would be staying out of the dog's way. Not so long ago, Ben and Bingle had lived with Frank and Irene—in the first months after Ben's leg was amputated, he had stayed with them. Even after he moved out, they had seen Ben and Bingle often, so Frank's familiarity with the dog now allowed him to fake his way along to some extent. The dog responded to commands in Spanish, a language Frank spoke fluently. Still, he was glad Ben would be nearby to "read" the dog—to pick up on all the subtleties of the dog's behavior that were part and parcel of dog and handler communication.

Some members of the SAR team were going through the remains of the new wing of the courthouse, but Ben and Anna and Frank were focusing on the stairwell between the old and new courthouses. Each person had been assigned a specific area to search. Other means of locating the missing would be used as well—but the dogs on this team had a high rate of success, so Frank felt the burden of doing his best to help Bingle.

When Ben told him where they would be working, he had not been able to hide his own anticipation.

"Yes," Ben said. "If she was up on the seventh floor and is alive now, she's on that stairway. But remember—"

"There's a big range covered in 'alive,'" Frank said, thinking of some of the victims he had already seen.

"Right."

• • •

They entered the darkened older courthouse through a doorway near an undamaged stairwell. This stairwell was some distance from the one they would be searching. They parted from Anna at the first floor. "You and Ben will start on the second floor," she explained. "I'll radio you if I need a confirmation."

Ben explained to him that if a dog alerted—indicated a find—another dog and handler would be brought in to confirm the alert before the next expert team of rescuers was called in. "It's dangerous and difficult to do the excavation work," Ben said. "So we want to be fairly sure we've got a real find before they start all the work that goes into trying to move slabs of concrete."

Ben reminded Frank of the basic commands and hand signals and of Bingle's alerts. "He'll bark on a live find. Otherwise he'll howl."

Frank remembered to speak to Bingle in excited tones, to ask him in Spanish, "¿Estás listo?"—"Are you ready?" The dog looked at him and cocked his head to the side, as if not quite convinced Frank knew what he was doing. Frank remembered the proverb that it is impossible to lie to a dog. But after a moment Bingle seemed to accept that commands were going to come from Frank.

During most of their walk through the empty building, they didn't need to use flashlights or the lights on their safety helmets and could rely on the light coming in through the windows at the ends of the halls. There was no obvious damage in this part of the older courthouse, but the building would be thoroughly inspected before anyone was allowed to return to offices, chambers, and courtrooms. As they entered the corridor leading to the west stairwell, they were in darkness and turned their flashlights on.

The air here had an odd musty smell to it, and Ben explained that when older buildings suffered damage, this was not unusual. "I've heard it's caused by all the accumulated dust up in ceilings and on pipes and on any other surface that hasn't been mopped or vacuumed for fifty years."

Bingle did not seem to be bothered by the dust or the darkness, but they hadn't gone far down the corridor before Frank sensed a change in the dog. Bingle's ears were up and pitched forward, he carried his tail erect and walked high on his toes. He seemed to be both focused on something and excited.

Suddenly he looked intently at first Frank, then Ben. Rascal, the dog Ben was handling—one of Anna's Labradors—was reacting to something, too.

"He's alerting, isn't he?" Frank said. "¡Búscalos! Find 'em, Bingle!"

Bingle strained on the lead, now in the spirit of things. They reached the edge of a pile of rubble, and Bingle pushed his nose into a crevice between two pieces of concrete, then lifted his head back.

"Frank," Ben said suddenly, but he was too late.

Bingle began to howl.

53

It could be anyone, he told himself.

He braced himself as he took a closer look, while Ben called Bingle aside and praised the dog lavishly. He was grateful to Ben for taking over that responsibility for him.

Impossible to lie to a dog.

In among the jagged pieces of gray concrete that spilled down the older portion of the stairs, he saw a woman's black dress shoe. He closed his eyes for a moment, then forced himself to keep looking, letting the light seek the owner of the shoe. It suddenly illuminated a length of dark hair, which he then saw was attached to a loose piece of scalp, which was lying a few inches from a crushed skull and a remarkably pale but unscathed hand.

He fought a wave of nausea. He heard a screaming inside his head and wondered for a brief moment if he had screamed aloud.

Ben was playing with Bingle but watching Frank. Frank heard Ben's voice catch, even as he kept telling the dog he was handsome and smart. The shepherd paraded past Frank with a floppy toss-toy, then came back and nudged him with it.

"He's just . . . he's only trying to engage you in his game."

Engage. Frank looked up at Ben suddenly and then forced himself to look again into the crevice. He saw that the hand was a well-manicured left hand with no rings on it. Irene had short nails and was never without her wedding and engagement rings.

"It's not her," he choked out. "It's not Irene."

They radioed in what little description of the dead woman they could provide and set a marker. Removing the dead was, necessarily, a lower priority than looking for survivors. Anna hadn't found anyone on the first floor and had already moved up to the third. Once Ben was satisfied there were no other victims on this level, they retraced their way to the intact stairwell and were almost up to the fourth floor when Anna radioed that she needed a confirmation. She could see one male victim, but she was not sure if there was a second—in another area, she was getting a vague alert from Devil, the dog she was handling.

When they arrived, she said, "Shouldn't be hard to ID the one male. He's wearing an eye patch."

"Whitey Dane," Frank said even before he managed to get a look at him. Dane's chest had been crushed by a section of wall that had fallen in on him. "What the hell was he doing here?" He looked up at Anna. "Myles Volmer or one of his other bodyguards can't be too far away."

Frank saw that on this floor, unlike the one below, the connecting door to the newer stairwell was open, although several chunks of concrete lying across it now made it half its normal size. Bingle seemed interested in this space. So while Ben and Anna worked with Devil and Rascal, Frank cautiously crawled into the remaining opening and flashed his light around. He was relieved not to find a long drop on the other side. He was looking at the landing of the newer stairwell now and saw that it had less debris on it than its counterpart in the older building. It formed a cavern of sorts—the stairs above and below appeared to be impassable, but this space was relatively open, making it the largest "void space" he had seen along the stairwell.

He moved through the opening to the landing on the other side of the door, then helped Bingle scramble through. Bingle was no sooner on the landing than he cocked his head back and forth, as if listening to something. He immediately tried to make it up the stairs, whining when he could not get through, then barking sharply. It echoed loudly in the enclosed space.

"Bingle—¡Quieto!"

The dog looked back at him, then up at the stairs, whining.

Ben's face appeared at the opening. "What's going on?"

"I think there's someone alive on the next floor up," Frank said, feeling hope rise. "Bingle hears something up there."

Ben helped Frank lift the dog back through, and soon they were on their way up to the next floor. Ben radioed the USAR team, asking them to meet them at the stairwell of the fourth floor.

They were moving fast now, hurrying down the last corridor. Bingle suddenly halted, though, and cocked his head again. Rascal did the same, then looked back at Ben. Bingle wagged his tail and made a wavering, high-pitched howling sound.

"No . . ."

"I don't think he's howling," Ben said quickly. "That's his singing voice."

Frank had heard Bingle's famous crooning—the inspiration for the dog's name—and didn't think this had been much like it. He wondered if Ben was merely trying to soften a blow.

Bingle and Rascal moved off again, pulling hard at their leads.

"Anna?" Ben said into the radio. "Hurry."

Hurry, Frank thought. That isn't what you say if the victim is dead.

"What kind of alert is singing?" he asked, quickening his pace to keep up with Bingle's.

"It's not an alert. It's just one of his tricks. But sometimes he does it when he hears someone else singing."

As they neared the entrance to the stairwell, Bingle made the sound again, then looked back at Frank. Frank followed him over the debris in the older stairwell. Here the metal door leading to the newer stairs was closed and blocked, but the dog scratched furiously at it. Barking at the door, and then Frank, and then turning back to Ben to bark at him.

Telling the dog he was marvelous and intelligent, Ben called him back to his side. He commanded him to stop barking, but took out the toss-toy and played quietly with him.

At the stairwell door, Frank immediately heard a distinct, rhythmic tapping sound.

"Hello? Can you hear me?" Frank shouted.

There was no answer, but the tapping continued in the same rhythm. Ben was talking into the radio now, telling the USAR team that they had definitely found a live victim and describing the location.

Frank used the end of his flashlight to tap against the door three times.

This time there was a pause in the tapping, and then three taps came back.

Frank tapped again.

A small segment of Morse code came back—three dots, three dashes, three dots—SOS.

Frank tried tapping back in the same code: Are you hurt?

There was a long pause and then the SOS was repeated.

Frank relayed this information to Ben, who passed it along by radio.

Frank continued to tap and repeat patterns of tapping, hoping to reassure the trapped person.

Soon the technical rescue team arrived—it had taken them less than four minutes despite the fact that they were also carrying equipment—an exothermic cutting torch, a concrete saw, lift pillows, breathing canisters, first aid supplies, a microphone that could be threaded through small openings, and cribbing wood.

"On to the next floor," Ben said as the team went to work on cutting the door. "Unless you want to stay here?"

"No, I'll come along. But—"

"I've already asked them to contact you when they learn who it is."

On the fifth floor, instead of darkness near the stairwell, they found daylight.

The west stairwell bomb had gone off on the seventh floor of the new stairwell, blowing out chunks of concrete that then fell through the roof of the older stairwell—which started at the fifth floor. In addition to forming a crude skylight, the debris completely blocked access between the two stairwells. Dust and dirt from the roof lay everywhere.

But on this floor the dogs had their strongest response yet. Taken near the stairwell separately, all three alerted. Bingle didn't sing this time, but his interest in getting closer to the new stairwell was plain. Ben frowned, studying the obstacles before them, then said, "Bingle's the best climber of these three. Let's see what he wants to show us, Frank. Anna, hold on to Rascal for me, will you? I'll follow along, Frank, just in case you need help with him."

As Bingle led them over boulder-sized pieces of concrete and fallen beams, he became more and more excited. Finally he stopped and cocked his head. He stood in the sun near a small opening formed by two large pieces of concrete that had fallen against each other in a tent shape.

For a moment, Frank was afraid the dog was going to try to burrow into the space, but as he came closer, he saw that it was too small even for Bingle to squeeze through. Bingle stuck most of his snout into the opening, snuffling loudly, and began wagging his tail. Abruptly, he pulled his nose out and raised his head up high. Frank braced himself to hear howling, but instead the dog sneezed—then began barking.

Ben had come closer then, too, and once again managed to both praise and reward Bingle while getting him to be quiet. Suddenly, Frank realized why the dogs had been so sure this time—through the opening he could hear the faint sound of a voice.

A familiar voice calling, "Hello! Hello! We're down here!"

"Irene!" Frank began shouting. "Irene!"

"Frank? In here!" came the faint but clear response. "Oh, Frank! I'm here! Seth and Judge Kerr, too."

"Irene—" he said, and for a moment couldn't say anything more. He felt tears on his face and let them fall.

"I'm okay, Frank—Seth, too."

He heard Ben calling on the radio, asking for more help. He didn't sound much steadier.

"Are any of you hurt?" Frank asked.

"The judge is hurt the worst. Seth is with him—they ended up a little farther down, but Seth and I can hear each other. Seth says Kerr is breathing, but he's unconscious."

"And you?"

"A little bumped around, that's all. Were you the one who was tapping?"

"Yes. Ben and Bingle and Anna and her dogs are here. Bingle is the star of the day. Are you sure you're okay?"

"From the moment Seth told me someone was answering his taps, I've been doing better and better."

He continued to talk to her until the second technical team arrived. He moved back into the corridor then, watching as they used inflatable lift pillows to widen the opening and began the work of shoring up the space they'd use to free her.

Ben put a hand on his shoulder. Frank turned to see Anna waiting down the corridor with the dogs. "We've got to move along," Ben said.

Frank glanced back at the rescue team, which was hammering cribbing in place.

"Sure," he said.

"Oh, no, you stay here. I think we can dispense with your help."

"I meant what I said—"

"I know you did. But if you haven't figured out that I risked being kicked off the SAR team just because I couldn't stand to think of you sitting out in the plaza while I looked for your trouble-prone wife—"

"I was going crazy down there, Ben. I—I don't know how to thank you—"

"I owe the two of you too much for thanks to be due. Besides, this was good for me—it will help me with the rest of the day."

He watched them take the dogs down the hall, Ben talking to Bingle in Spanish, Anna to Rascal and Devil in English, working up their enthusiasm, telling them to "find 'em," knowing that the outcome would seldom be the one that others hoped and waited for.

Frank moved back toward the stairwell, as close as the workers would allow him to come.

For now, he would wait. And silently offer thanks.

54

The doctors said they expected Judge Kerr to make a full recovery, but he would be hospitalized for a while. As the blast hit, he had tried to shield Seth from falling objects but was himself struck on the head by a small piece of concrete. He had lost consciousness and fallen down the stairs, taking Seth with him. A rain of debris had separated them from Irene.

Seth, who had been the first to be rescued, had a few scrapes and bruises. Frank had gone down to the fourth floor again when they brought him out. He held tightly to Frank from the moment he was freed until Elena met them at the hospital.

Irene was scraped and bruised, too, and more extensively. He had winced at all the abrasions on her face and arms and legs, and especially at a swollen spot just above her left eyebrow. "I'm so disappointed. I was trying to get mine in the same place as yours," she said, tracing a finger lightly along his stitches. "Do you mind if I tell people this happened when I kicked a bad guy's ass?"

"With this much damage, you'd better say it was a dozen bad guys."

He had held her gently when she was freed—neither of them able to say a word. She had been terrified, he could tell, although she had put up a brave front for Seth's sake—talking with him, singing songs with him—Bingle had been singing in response to one of these. They got away from the building as soon as possible, and he was relieved to see the fear gradually recede as she spent time in the open air.

Frank decided to visit Bredloe while Seth and Irene talked with Elena. Although it was hard for him to let either Irene or Seth out of his sight, he was still not comfortable with Elena. He was overdue for a visit to Bredloe in any case.

Bredloe recognized him and said a slow, slurred version of his name. And something that sounded like the word "sorry."

"No need to be, sir."

Frank couldn't make out the next phrase, but Miriam translated. "Yes, there is."

Miriam told Frank that while her husband was doing much better, the long-term effects of his injuries were still uncertain.

"Hard for you to be patient with it, I know," Frank said to him.

"Yes. Sometimes almost as frustrating as policework."

Miriam started to translate, but Frank smiled and said, "I understood that perfectly."

Because the captain tired quickly, and because he was anxious to return to Irene, Frank kept the visit short.

When he returned to the lobby, Irene was sitting alone. "Where are Seth and Elena?" he asked.

"Waiting outside. I asked them to give us a few minutes. I think they needed a little time to themselves, too." She tugged him toward a small office. "I asked one of the nurses if we could come in here to talk. She said it would be okay."

He pulled her gently into his arms, being careful of her bruises, and didn't let her say a word for a while. "This time," he said, "this time you really scared the hell out of me."

"Is that some freaked-out macho-man way of telling me you love me?"

He laughed, then kissed her again. "I've got all kinds of ways to do that."

His cell phone rang. He started to ignore it, but she said, "No rush—answer it."

It was Vince.

"You want to be in for the kill?" he said. "Haycroft is here."

"Have you arrested him?"

"Not yet. He's holding a hostage."

"Shit," he said.

"A lady from the courthouse. A guard. Nice woman. Anyway, get on over here, because my money is on the SWAT boys."

He hung up and explained the situation to Irene.

"Go on," she said. "I'm fine. A little tired, but fine."

"I'm not. Not after this afternoon."

"Do you want me to go with you?"

He shook his head, then looked into those blue eyes of hers. "Tonight."

"Maybe."

He laughed. "You know, I nearly forgot to tell you how glad I am that you almost never obey orders."

She looked at him for a long moment and said, "Come home as soon as you can."

55

He was inside the Cessna. Denise, bound and gagged, was whimpering in the seat next to his. Good God, didn't the woman understand what a privilege he had conferred on her? No one was allowed to fly with him!

He must end this standoff, if for no other reason than to be rid of her.

He started the engine, SWAT team or no. Actually, because of them. He let them know that he had set up a sort of reverse "dead-man's switch." If he were to be shot and killed, the plane would not shut off—it would, in fact, be uncontrolled, whether taxiing on land or flying in the air. He would smash Ms. Denise here into the side of the hangar, and she and anyone nearby would become crispy critters.

He was tired of listening to the hostage negotiator, Tom Cassidy. He knew all the tricks of Cassidy's trade, and he wasn't even interested in tormenting the fellow, as he well could have. As he had been tormented himself. Oh, yes, tormented.

The first thing Cassidy told him was that Harriman wasn't dead. Cassidy announced this as if it were a good thing, as if there were any doubt he'd be charged with murder anyway. His rage over Harriman's survival was nearly boundless.

Next he had learned that thanks to Harriman, Judge Lewis Kerr wasn't dead, either. When he had heard this news, he began to feel a little afraid of Harriman. He could almost believe that Lefebvre had come back to haunt him.

He despised Cassidy for ruining his day in this way. And so he had struck back and lied—told Cassidy that perhaps a person who would do something so heinous as planting bombs in a courthouse wouldn't stop at destroying just one government building. "If I were you," he told the big Texan, "I'd wonder if such a criminal had bombs all over town."

That one had been worth the price of admission!

Now the game grew tiresome, though. It was time he got away, created a new and better life, a whole new identity. He had no difficulty believing he'd get away once he was airborne. Denise would be released only after he had completed his disappearance.

And who was she, really? A little nobody.

But he knew they would allow him to escape—all in order to protect a woman who didn't know how to put a proper English sentence together. They would never want to be accused of causing her death. That's what he loved most about their rules. They had to play by them.

Their rules were what kept them from succeeding against crime in the spectacular way he had succeeded. If he were in Tom Cassidy's position, he would order the snipers to take him out immediately. To hell with anyone killed on the ground as a result.

There was some sort of commotion, and he realized that he had a new guest at his little bon voyage party. Frank Harriman.

When Frank met Vince outside the hangar, he handed him a brown bag. "This is all you need," he said.

"For what?"

"To catch Haycroft. I'm starting to get to know this son of a bitch." He told him his strategy.

"Cassidy will never go for it," Vince said.

"He will. It's all in the presentation. You ready to put on a show?"

Vince smiled. "Not much of a part, but yeah, sure."

"Frank Harriman," Cassidy drawled. "You amaze me. You have a couple of crazy-ass days—fifteen minutes of which would have been enough to get most of us served up on a marble slab—and instead you walk up to me looking ornery."

"Have a favor to ask, Tom."

"Yeah?"

"Let him go."

Cassidy laughed. He ran a hand over his short hair, which—although he was not much older than Frank—was mostly gray. "Oh, brother. You were out in the sun way too long today."

"Let Haycroft take off with the woman. Just let me say something to him as he taxis to the runway. I think he'll come back with her."

"'Think' is not good enough. But tell me what you have in mind."

"You're about to let him go anyway, aren't you, Tom?"

"We'll be following him."

Frank rolled his eyes.

"He says he's got more bombs planted around town," Cassidy said.

"Do you believe him?"

"To be honest, no, I don't."

"Your instincts are still good then, Tom, because it doesn't fit with his obsession with Kerr. And that's what this guy is all about—that, and protecting his own ass."

Cassidy calmly studied him for a moment. "So what's your idea?"

Haycroft watched as the discussion between Cassidy and Harriman became more and more acrimonious. In the end, Cassidy looked utterly defeated.

"Mr. Haycroft?"

God, how he hated that damned drawl!

"Detective Harriman has just informed me that you may have your wish. He claims the district attorney refuses to file against you—I guess the D.A. is saying our department has no real physical evidence against you. Can that possibly be true?"

Haycroft hesitated. This could only mean they hadn't found anything at the house and had not discovered the problem with the computer program in the property room. Managing a hostage meant that he had not had time to check on his diaries, and with all of the department watching him now, he was not about to reveal where he had hidden them on the plane.

Did they know about the diaries?

No, if they did, he was convinced, Cassidy would have gloated about it, as he had about the survival of Harriman and Kerr.

"If what he says is true," Haycroft said slowly, "why were you waiting for me here? What led Detective Harriman to me in the first place?"

"Well, Detective Harriman claims it started with you telling him some fib about your son's photograph, which made him suspicious, and he ultimately realized you had a darned good reason to dislike Judge Kerr. But even though he may be convinced you're guilty as sin, the irony is this—if the D.A. doesn't have more to go on than that, some dumb judge like Kerr will toss the case out on its rear end. Isn't that right?"

"Why, yes, it's true. But you see, there is this little problem of my having taken a hostage now."

"Well, this is awfully embarrassing to the department, of course. I'm sure Denise there would be happy to say it was all a joke that she went along with just in order to help you out. You release her, and all is fair and square."

He looked at Denise, who was nodding furiously.

"I think not. I feel safer with her here, you might say. And I am concerned that Vince Adams must have had a little look-see through my plane while he waited for me, so I don't really believe I can rely on your story. I will be leaving now."

He began to taxi out of the hangar. "Haycroft!" a new voice said.

"Detective Harriman, forgive me, but I must be on my way."

"That's fine with me, but I just wondered if you really believe your papers are the only thing Vince and I might have messed with on that Cessna today."

He stopped taxiing, then smiled to himself. "Nice try. It's running perfectly well."

"To tell you the truth, I hope you think so."

"You wouldn't be trying to tell me that you in some way disabled a plane carrying a hostage?"

"How was I to know there would be one? Besides, sometimes lambs must be sacrificed."

"But you, dear Frank, are no killer of lambs."

"Things happen to change a man. You weren't either, before Kit."

Haycroft was silent. He allowed the plane to move a little farther forward.

"You should know better than anyone, Haycroft, that, sometimes, the legal ways are not the effective ways. I've learned that from you. I applied it to your case, too. You just couldn't be caught by normal means. So I had to come up with something special."

"You don't know the first thing about airplanes," Haycroft sneered. The plane nosed out of the hangar.

"Vince has a pilot's license. And I don't need to tell you that a person can learn a lot when he's investigating a homicide. For example, the NTSB showed me how little it might take to sabotage a plane."

"I still don't believe you."

"Okay, my conscience is clear. Have a *sweet* plane ride, just like Lefebvre did all those years ago. And don't forget to wave to Vince on your way out. He's just to your left."

As Haycroft passed, Vince smiled and waved. He was holding an opened five-pound bag of sugar.

"This is nonsense," Haycroft said, as much to himself as to Frank.

But he thought of Lefebvre's fall from the sky.

He taxied to the runaway that had been assigned to him that morning.

"Nice try, Frank," Cassidy whispered to Frank.

"I'll bet you've wondered what it was like for Lefebvre, that last flight," Frank said, not giving up.

Haycroft was silent.

"I'll bet you've asked yourself, 'Was he calm when he heard the engine cough and then go silent? Did he panic and scream?' Now you can find out what you'll do in that situation. Personally, I've got you pegged as a screamer."

Haycroft let the plane drift a few feet forward.

"Maybe you think you're such a hot pilot, you'll be able to land it without power."

Haycroft increased power so that the engine droned louder.

"But then your emergency locator transmitter won't work any better than his did."

The plane did not move farther.

"And you never know what you'll be flying over when you start to hear that first little sputter. Water, trees, rocky ground. I guess it won't matter. It will all feel like a brick wall once you actually hit it."

The plane turned and continued turning. As everyone in the hangar held their breath, Haycroft taxied back. He shut down the plane and climbed out, leaving his hostage within. His hands were over his head. Within seconds, the SWAT team had him down on the floor and Denise was free.

56

He watched for a moment before going down the steps to the beach.

Seth and Irene and Jack were playing Frisbee, with Deke and Dunk doing their best to add a little chaos to the game. After a second interception, Jack put Seth on his shoulders. Seth giggled wildly.

Elena sat on a blanket, watching them. He continued down to the beach.

"Mind if I sit here?" he asked Elena.

She looked up at him, shielding her eyes from the sun. "I don't if you don't."

They sat in silence for a time, then he said, "Hitch did a little more talking."

She kept watching her son.

"He said that Dane deposited money in your account by forging your endorsement on a check and threatened to say you had extorted it from him. And Hitch threatened to back him up. That you refused to keep the money, but were afraid no one would believe you."

"I like your friend Jack," she said. "He's good with Seth."

He looked out at the water. "Jack's a good man," he said quietly. "My best friend, really."

She looked at him in surprise, but didn't say anything.

"I should have started out by saying I'm sorry," he said.

"You have nothing to apologize for. I wasn't much of a cop."

"There's more to life than being a cop. You were surprised when I said Jack was my best friend. You thought, 'Why didn't he say Pete?'"

"Okay, I admit it, I did."

"But even though I love Pete like a brother—it often *is* as if he's a brother. An annoying one. He's uneasy around me now, because I got pissed off with him about Lefebvre. But for Pete, being partners means we'll have to work all that through. For him, just about all of life is about being a cop. I'm not like that, I guess."

"Why not? You grew up in a cop family, right?"

He nodded. "My dad was more like Pete—true-blue. But I guess I don't have their zeal. Sometimes, I take a step back, I don't know that I really do any good."

"Are you crazy?" she said.

"Take this week. What the hell did I accomplish? Lefebvre is no more alive than he was ten years ago. Whitey Dane is dead—but not because of anything the police did to stop him."

"I hear Myles Volmer survived."

"Yes—word is, just before the bomb went off, he stepped out into one of the hallways of the new building to see if he could sneak Dane in to see Kerr. Even if he had been killed, Derrick or some other asshole would take over Dane's kingdom from here—and I doubt Hitch's testimony is going to be able to deliver anything to change that."

"That doesn't mean that what you did this week is unimportant."

"Worse than unimportant. Carlson hates me more than ever, Bredloe's hardly able to speak, and the Wheeze is fawning over me—which is unbearable. We'll probably lose the lab. The taxpayers just had a new building blown to hell. And as Internal Affairs learns more about Haycroft's 'experiment books,' more lawsuits will be filed and violent offenders released. You ask me, I did more for the forces of evil than good this week."

"You saved my son's life in that fire."

"You would have saved him—you would have gotten out without me. At best, I saved a guinea pig. And maybe if I had just played it the way the department asked me to, there never would have been a fire in your home. You'd have been living there in peace."

She shook her head. "Whatever else you can say about my existence before that fire, I was not at peace. And I only recently realized how much that was costing Seth. You want to know what good you did this week? Look at my son. Right now. Look at him."

Seth was searching through the sand. He picked up a flat rock and smiled at Jack. "Have you found one yet?"

"Okay," Jack said. "I'm ready."

"You first."

Jack grinned and skipped his rock.

"Three!" Seth announced. "Now it's my turn." His face was a picture of concentration. He threw the rock exactly as Frank had shown him. "Four!"

Before Frank could say anything, they heard a voice call, "Hey, it's Nereault!"

A group of four boys who appeared to be brothers came running over. Deke and Dunk positioned themselves at Seth's side.

"They live in our condo complex," Elena said. "The middle two are twins who are his age."

They were peppering him with questions about the dogs, the fire at the condo, and asking if My Dog had survived.

"Yes," Seth said, pointing to Frank, "my friend saved him. But my name isn't Nereault anymore. It's Lefebvre."

"Is that true?" one asked Elena.

"Yes, it has always been true. Lefebvre was Seth's father's name."

"My father was a hero. I'll show you a videotape one day."

"Say that name again," the youngest pleaded.

"Lefebvre," Seth said slowly. "Lefebvre. Lefebvre."

"You haven't done shit this week, have you?" Elena whispered to Frank.

"I forgot to tell you something," Frank said. "I talked to Joe Koza, our questioned documents examiner, the other day. I asked him about a business card I had bagged at the scene of the crash. Turns out it was yours, with a handwritten number on the back."

She looked up at him, searching his face.

"Lefebvre had it in his shirt pocket." He put his hand over his heart. "He carried it right here."

"Thanks," she said, and quickly walked away.

Irene came up to him then, saying, "The kids want to watch the video, so I told their mom they could all come up to our place. Is that okay?"

"Sure," he said, still watching Elena.

Irene followed his gaze and said, "Did you make her cry?"

"No, another cop did," he said, then smiled as Jack began to follow her.

They led the boys up the stairs. Behind him, he heard a chant, a boy saying "Lefebvre" perfectly, four others getting better at it as they repeated, "Lefebvre, Lefebvre, Lefebvre, Lefebvre . . ."

The Looking Glass Man stood very still near the center of the cell. He did not want to touch any surface. The cell was filthy. No amount of complaining would improve conditions in this hellhole.

There was one small victory this evening. He had stolen a spoon during dinner. He took it out now and polished it with his shirttail. He polished it, whispering to himself as he did. Then he paused and looked at his reflected image—first convex, then concave.

Not very satisfactory.

Nothing was anymore.

He took hold of the shirttail again. As he polished and polished the spoon, more vigorously this time, he whispered a little louder:

"Lefebvre, Lefebvre, Lefebvre, Lefebvre . . ."

ACKNOWLEDGMENTS

The research for this book required the help of a number of experts whose kindness in offering it should not result in their being blamed for any of my mistakes. I'm especially grateful to fellow author Detective Paul Bishop, Los Angeles Police Department; Officer John Pearsley, Jr., El Cajon Police Department; and Detective Bill Valles of the Long Beach Police Department. My special thanks to Detective Sergeant Ed Cavanaugh, Evidence Control, Long Beach Police Department, for his time and willingness to answer my many questions, and for all he does to keep the LBPD Evidence Control area free of the problems the fictional Sergeant Flynn faces.

Barry A. J. Fisher, author of *Techniques of Crime Scene Investigation*, director of the Los Angeles County Sheriff's Department Crime Laboratory, and former president of the American Academy of Forensic Sciences, is an inspiring teacher who's generous with his time to writers and former students.

For the sections concerning Lefebvre's plane, I am indebted to Jeff Rich, Senior Safety Investigator, National Transportation Safety Board, Southwest Regional Office, and to Manny Raefsky, who spent a career investigating aviation disasters.

SAR and cadaver dog trainer Beth Barkely provided help with passages concerning Bingle (but please don't assume she'd break the rules Ben Sheridan breaks!) and also with the collapsed building scenes. I also had help regarding Ben and Bingle's mountain searches—especially the wood rat's nest—from the members of the Internet Listserv SAR-DOGS, and I thank Leo Delany, Travis County SAR; Fleta Kirk, MARK-9 SAR, Dallas; Bev Peabody, Placer County Sheriff's SAR K9 Team; and Laura Rathe, California Rescue Dog Association for their assistance.

The technical rescue scenes and information about collapsed buildings grew out of conversations with Mark Ghilarducci, Federal Coordinating Officer for the Federal Emergency Management Agency and a specialist in urban search and rescue; with Bob Caldon, Public Information Officer for the Long Beach Fire Department; and most especially with the help of Captain Jeff Reeb, Long Beach Fire Department.

I appreciate the time and effort given by forensic anthropologists Madeleine Hinkes—who allowed me to picture the crash site much more clearly—Paul Sledzik, Diane France, and Marilyn London; Sandra Cvar for guinea pig sound effects and for helping me catch errors in the manuscript; John G. Fischer for fight scenes; Jonathan Beggs for help with constructing the attic; Melodie Johnson Howe for reconstruction and encouragement. Timbrely Pearsley provided computer information, and Tonya Pearsley gave feedback on early drafts.

Shortly after I named a character Lefebvre, I began to hear five or six different pronunciations of his Quebecois name. Thanks are due to the members of DorothyL, an Internet Listserv dedicated to mystery fiction, who kindly answered my plea for help with this matter, especially Nicole Leclerc, C. Tessier, Carole Epstein, Catherine, Gail, Marlyn, Nina, and Mary Jane. As Phil Lefebvre explains, there are several ways the owners of the name may say it, and I hope my readers in Quebec will find the one I chose to be believable for his background.

In addition to surviving jobs in television news, the real Marcia Wolfe-Gruber is a dear friend, Video Vixen, and kick in the pants—her husband, Dr. James Gruber, also my friend, and inventor of the Grubescope, answered medical questions.

One evening at the Mystery Lovers Bookshop in Oakmont, Pennsylvania, I was introduced to Erin Declan Philbin, a speech and language pathologist who specializes in alternative augmentation communication—and soon enlisted her aid in understanding how Seth Randolph would communicate after his injuries. My thanks to Erin and the MLB.

Thanks also to Scott Carrier of the Los Angeles County Department of the Coroner for his assistance.

Marysue Rucci is an extraordinary editor whose commitment to this book and influence in helping it to outgrow an awkward adolescence have earned her my deepest gratitude and respect.

Tim Burke, you're still the one.

ABOUT THE AUTHOR

Jan Burke is the recipient of the Edgar Award for Best Novel of 1999 (*Bones*), the Macavity Award, the Ellery Queen Mystery Magazine Readers Award, and the Romantic Times's Career Achievement Award for Contemporary Suspense. She lives in Southern California with her husband, Tim, and her dogs, Cappy and Britches. She is currently at work on her next novel. Her Web site is at www.janburke.com.